Moonstone Dreams

S.C. Miotto

Dedicated to all my loves.
Especially my wonderful husband, with whom I am
living my very own moonstone dream.

MOONSTONE DREAMS

It is said that if you give your lover a moonstone,
it means that you will love them forever...

CHAPTER 1

It was by far the darkest moment of my life, on a hot summer evening in Alpine, NJ. I lay there with no escape, my bedroom becoming an inferno as flames danced from the floor to the ceiling. My clothes stuck to me like a second skin, soaked from blood loss. I could not focus as my head spun and everything appeared to be in another dimension. The walls that used to be a soft, comforting auburn were now black. Charred and singed, synonymous to everything else in my life. The blaze quickly spread from the wall to the curtains and dresser. I was motionless in the middle of the floor, with one hand in a cast, and the other one dripping red and stinging. I watched while the room slowly reduced to ashes, becoming nothing more than the fire's supper.

The sounds around me were muffled, my state of mind compromised. Dizziness, nausea, and fatigue alternately waved through me. The screaming and banging on the other side of the door sounded far away as if it were happening in another time. The sirens that were once distant to my ears seemed to be blaring outside my home. It was nothing but commotion. Commotion and blood. Blood everywhere. It was something out of the goriest horror movie, except it was real. Was I ready to die at thirty-two? The last tiny bit of fight I had left should be used to push that dresser away from the door and let them save me. However, I couldn't do it. Not this time. I was no longer myself. My mind was as possessed as my body was wounded and my heart was far beyond broken.

The thick black air began to engulf the space. I had two choices: get out or die. Visions of my sweet children surfaced, providing the impetus for me to drag myself across the floor.
I crawled over the remains of broken picture frames, thrown liquor bottles, and the smashed TV. Using my cast to keep glass out of my palms, I struggled to maneuver my body into the bathroom while everything continued to burn around me.

A puddle of blood continued to spread, as the floor stained in front of the Jacuzzi tub. Scattered crimson streaks and handprints smeared across our tub and white floor tiles. Shards of broken glass covered the floor from the mirror, shattered earlier in the evening. It seems as if I was right back where the intense argument began.

With a trembling, bloody hand, I picked up a piece of the mirror from the floor. I couldn't recognize the puffy brown-eyed, bruised woman on the other side. My usually bouncy beautiful long hair looked like a mangled birds nest. The dark bronze strands were clumped together and mangy looking. My own reflection had become a stranger and I no longer pitied her. I never thought I was capable of what I'd done.

The air grew thicker, and the smell of burning wood and fabric was overwhelming. I coughed violently as the smoke started to fill my lungs.

My eyes began to water from the pain. Maybe also from the memory of how many other times I'd spent crippled on that very bathroom floor, bloody and beaten. Resting my head on the cold tiles, I paused, surrendering to mental and physical exhaustion. Disoriented and psychologically drained, I felt certain death awaited me as I listened to the pounding of firefighters attempting to force their way inside.

Coldness consumed my body despite the fire that still roared around me. Everything felt surreal, and I wasn't sure if I was awake anymore. The images went through my mind quickly. It felt like there was a mini projection screen in my thoughts as if my life seemed to play back to me.

My loving mother's face smiling down on me when I was a baby, my beautiful sister Brooke hugging me, and my children laughing, all momentarily filled my heart with joy. Then, the image of the most amazing man I ever met, whom I loved so intensely, with every single centimeter of my soul. What I felt when I saw him was a love embedded deeper than any scar ever could. I was willing to let go knowing that I was one of the lucky few in the world to experience that kind of true love. A bright light drew me in like a magnet, as it got closer and closer. Brighter and brighter.

Suddenly, what sounded like a stampede storming up my stairs followed by four or five loud bangs jolted my body awake. An ax shattered through the wood of the door. With some effort, they pushed the dresser aside. Black and yellow coats and hats rushed in and scattered throughout my bedroom with fire extinguishers. I didn't look up at the faces clambering over to me before scooping me from the floor. A long, high-pitched scream was the last sound I heard before I lost consciousness.

10

I woke up tied to a bed in a white room with no windows. *Where am I?* Wondering if it was a dream, or nightmare, I began to look around. A nurse with a light caramel complexion and long flaxen hair, stood over me holding a clear clipboard, and was proceeding to take my blood pressure. Her hazel eyes widened when she noticed I was awake. She looked shocked and relieved at the same time before she dashed to the door and called out to someone in the hallway.

"Dr. Bailey! She's awake!"

Waking up in that strange place, both wrists bound at my sides and held secured by restraints, sent my heart beating like an erratic drum. Through hazy eyes, I saw a black strap taut around my waist, and my feet tightly bound to the bed as well. I couldn't hear anything over the thumping in my ears. Breathing wasn't an easy task either, my chest was burning and it tasted and felt like I had swallowed charcoal. The fire didn't feel like it really happened. It seemed like a bad dream. I was still trying to decide; *was it all a dream? I* glanced down at my hands and noticed some remnant of dried blood on them. No. It wasn't a dream.

"Hello?" My attempt to call for someone failed and triggered an episode of violent coughing.

The hazel-eyed nurse hurried back to my side.

"I'm sorry," she said looking down at me with a warm smile. "I needed to alert the doctor. We were all very worried about you."

I couldn't speak, but I did manage a half-hearted smile in return.

The young woman, dressed in mint green scrubs, didn't look a day over twenty-five. She unraveled the blood pressure cuff and placed the Velcro strap around my arm. As she studied the results, I once again attempted to speak.

"Where am I? Why am I strapped down?" I asked in a low detached voice with unsuccessful attempts to pull my limbs free.

Calmly she touched my shoulder and said, "Please try to relax. My name is Myra Vasquez, I'm a resident doctor. You're in Bergen Valley Hospital; you were admitted here two nights ago."

"I can't remember anything. Just. The fire," I replied, my

voice scratchy and my mind unable to quickly process my surroundings.

"It's okay. You can talk to Dr. Bailey or me about it. One step at a time." Now turning her head to look at her watch, she squeezed the ball several times. The cuff gradually tightened around my bicep, causing me to grimace at the discomfort.

"Let me know if anything hurts," she said as she glanced up at me.

"Everything hurts. And I'm lightheaded." I was trying to figure out what happened. I must have passed out. Being confined was crippling my ability to think straight.

"This is very uncomfortable. Please untie my arms," I pleaded, as I tugged at my arm restraints.

She backed away from the bed. "You lost a lot of blood, Mrs. Carlisle. You may feel lightheaded for a little while. We had to restrain you for your safety. You can talk to Dr. Bailey about taking them off."

I was starting to feel claustrophobic. The thought of being held down for another second was agitating me.

"This is bull shit!" I screamed out and used all my might—which wasn't much—and every last effort to break free until I felt like I was going to pass out. "Let me out of here!" My legs kicked and I yanked my wrists ferociously in protest.

"Mrs. Carlisle, please!" Myra pushed my arms down and turned toward the door asking for help before she brought her attention back to me. "You need to calm down if you want them to release you." She kept her voice low. "You're going to tear your stitches if you keep pulling like that. If you can control yourself, I'll help you, okay?"

Myra was calm and sincere, which helped me try to calm down. I wanted to trust her, and for me trust did not come easy. However, her gentle sincerity reminded me of Brooke, which was an added bonus. At that moment, I missed my sister so much.

I took a deep breath and nodded. Two nurses, one man and one woman, both wearing white scrubs, came rushing in.

"Is everything okay?" the male nurse asked.

"Could you please let Doctor Bailey know that Mrs. Carlisle is experiencing extreme discomfort and is requesting that we remove the restraints," Myra instructed them.

"I … I don't think …" the female nurse began to protest.

"I wasn't asking." Myra had a tough side. Both of the

nurses froze, staring at her.

"Now! Please!" she ordered and they scurried out.

"Thank you," I whispered.

"You're welcome. I can't imagine how uncomfortable you must be."

"Why did they ..." I stopped because I wasn't sure if I wanted the answer. What could possibly have happened that they felt the need to strap me down? "Did they feel as though I were a threat?"

"You were ..." Myra looked away searching for the right words. Continuing she said, "...Not in the right frame of mind." When she looked at me, she must have known how confused and humiliated I felt.

"Which is understandable, given your situation," she added, as she softly touched my hand.

My situation. Wish I knew what that was.

"Do you know what happened?" My eyes begged for some clarity.

She opened her mouth to answer, but her words cut short as the doctor walked in. He was a tall, pleasant looking man in his late forties. His chestnut eyes matched his smooth mahogany complexion.

"Hello Victoria, my name is William Bailey." His voice was as rich and welcoming as his appearance. "I am the psychiatrist here at Bergen Valley. I am going to ask you a few questions, if that's okay." He stood over me and was sporting a clipboard as well as a beige medical file folder.

"Okay. But I'm sorry, I can't remember much," I said feeling as if I woke up in another time zone, or decade.

"We know. You told us that already yesterday. It's to be expected. You're suffering from amnesia due to what is known as Post Traumatic Stress Disorder. It's a result of enduring traumatic or life-threatening events. Every person copes with the trauma differently. Some will have flashes of their experience, while those who have been through repeated trauma have been known to have no recollection of the event at all."

"Oh," I said, dumbfounded. I glanced at Myra who was jotting notes down in a little notepad. Dr. Bailey was attentively awaiting my response. "So, when do you think I'll have my memory back?"

"That depends. It could be days, months, years,

sometimes if you keep them shut out, they never do return."

"I'll try."

The two nurses from earlier re-entered, summonsing Dr. Bailey and Myra. They all stepped halfway into the hallway where they began debating and all still within earshot. I overheard a few words here and there and knew they were talking about me. Myra said, "She seems safe now," and another nurse let them know "I'll be right down the hall if she gets out of hand again."

Myra and Dr. Bailey came back into the room with three other nurses who started to remove the restraints from my wrists.

"Victoria, the nurses are releasing the restraints. You will need to cooperate with our staff and remain calm or we will be forced to restrain you again."

"Of course," I nodded eager to be somewhat free. My body was cramping up and I wanted to walk around. I turned to Myra and whispered, "What the hell happened?"

Finally, my hands were freed somewhat of a bittersweet victory as now everything hurt when I rotated my wrists. Slowly stretching my arms, I noticed how many bandages were wrapped around them. I must have been badly burned.

"I need you to tell me what you remember," Dr. Bailey said again, holding his clipboard and pen as if information was ready and waiting to flow from my mouth and flood those waiting pages. Boy, was he going to be disappointed.

"I ... I really don't know." I struggled to remember any detail beyond that fire.

"Mrs. Carlisle, we want to help you, but all I have are the police reports. I need your side of the story," he said. "Close your eyes and try to reconnect with some of the events that might have led up to that night."

I complied. Thinking was actually causing me physical pain. I saw my bedroom and bright orange flames. I could feel the burning heat again. Wedding photos on fire. And the blood. All that damn blood. The shattered bathroom mirror—I abruptly opened my eyes.

"I can't." I shook my head.

"Try, Victoria," Myra encouraged with a nod.

I took a deep breath and closed my eyes again, but this time tuned out the pain. And tuned out the hung-over, groggy, dizzy feeling. Every effort to connect to my emotions was present. Then it crept up on me as if I had just been

14

hypnotized. My chest filled with the overwhelming feeling of recent anguishing memories.

"Breathe," Myra reminded me.

Jeez, I wasn't even breathing. I then knew why I suppressed the feelings.

"I'm not sure what happened the other night. But it was something really terrible. Wasn't it? More than just a fire ..." Tears stung my eyes like the memories that were stabbing at me. "I think I know why I did it now."

Myra handed me a tissue. I took a moment before continuing.

"I loved him so much that I just couldn't handle it ... when I found out." The words took my breath away as I was barely able to whisper them.

"Who are you talking about, Mrs. Carlisle? Your husband?" Dr. Bailey asked, but I dismissed his question. I was so engrossed in the deep reverie, I could feel it. I could feel the heartache again.

"When you're so deeply in love that it consumes your every thought, you breathe love. You feel it. And live it. That person becomes your *everything*. And when you lose it, you lose everything. It dies, and you die. That feeling is something I'll never forget. No matter how hard I try." I patted more tears that streamed down my cheeks.

Myra was staring at me, baffled and interested. She looked over at Dr. Bailey who was sitting with one long leg draped over the other, his index finger resting over his upper lip. Every so often, he scribbled something down before looking up at me again.

"Well, it's a start," he said. "You're in tune with your emotions, which are good. Now, can you tell us about this man whom you say you loved?"

"I am still very much in love with him," I said, correcting the doctor. "And to answer your question ... no, I can't talk about him yet. But maybe I can go a little further back and tell you about my husband instead."

Dr. Bailey and Myra looked at each other before getting comfortable and giving me their undivided attention. They knew they were going to be in that room for a while as I reminisced aloud, allowing them into the calamitous abyss that was my life.

"So this man ... wasn't your husband?" Myra asked

"I know how it sounds. Please hear me out, and you'll understand. It's not how I planned things. There was a time when my husband, Frank, had my unconditional love. It was a long time ago. Before he ever hurt me. He was perfect in my mind. I was a naive child. It was about eighteen years ago, and I remember it as if it were yesterday."

CHAPTER 2

It was the middle of December 1993, and looked like we would be getting a white Christmas in New Jersey that year. Little flurries began to dust the ground as I waited, tapping my fingers on the green park bench before I stood up, paced around, glanced at my watch, then repeated the process. *Where is he?* I muttered to myself. The gray mist of every breath I exhaled evaporated in the frosty air. As I rubbed my hands together, I regretted not bringing my favorite blue snowflake printed mittens with me.

I sat down again and placed my forehead in my palms. What was I going to do? I was so damned stupid. *What are we going to do? How is he going to react? If he's not here in the next two minutes I'm going to move into panic mode and start freaking out.* Taking a deep breath, I hoped to slow the pace of my racing mind. *Breathe. Everything is going to be okay.*

As I sat there, I struggled to keep warm. My feet were snug and cozy in my comfortable brown boots, filled with fuzzy wool on the inside. Unfortunately, the entire rest of my body fell victim to the brisk air. Even the bench was cold against my jeans. At that moment, nothing seemed a greater luxury than having a car. I still wouldn't have been able to drive it since I couldn't get my driver's license until I turned sixteen, which wasn't for another two years.

Aside from my stomach feeling as if it might turn into an icicle, it began to growl ravenously. It starts now, I thought sighing. The hunger pains were hard to ignore. "Where's my peanut butter cup?" I trembled while rummaging through my purse, hoping to find it. Through my mittens, I touched a tube of pink lip-gloss, a few pens, random papers, my wallet, and other items before a wrapper crinkled under my fingers. Victory! As I unwrapped the piece of candy, I silently wished it were a bowl of green olives instead. Random as it was, I blamed my strange craving on my newly discovered delicate condition.

I wouldn't have to worry about craving pickles, ice cream, or anything else for too much longer. After attending my appointment, I had spent all day considering my options. I was confident, but sad, about the decision I made.

Frank and I really needed to focus on ourselves before we

could take on such a huge responsibility. He needed to grow up. We both did. However, sitting alone on that thirty-four degree Tuesday in December was my proof that he wasn't reliable or responsible enough yet.

"God, how is he going to react?" I wondered aloud before gobbling my candy in two bites. As the last taste of chocolate left my mouth, so did its temporary soothing. I placed my forehead back into my palms, agonizing over what his reaction might be. My legs were shaking. Was it the cold or my nerves? A bicyclist rode by and I glanced up hoping it was Frank, but my wonderful boyfriend had yet to appear.

The pond, not yet frozen, had tiny ripples reeling across. A blanket of crisp brown leaves spread across the dried grass.

I knew I was going to have to walk the mile and a half, and hoped it wouldn't be alone. I stood up and started to walk slowly since I was already late. My pager went off for the third time as my poor grandmother attempted to reach me. I could just imagine her face, full of concern, but not angry. Never angry. Her eyes, brown like mine and my mother's, were soft and held years of wisdom and secrets that I'll never know.

My grandmother had every right to worry about me. Losing both parents on the same day, one at the hands of the grim reaper and the other one to the New Jersey State Penitentiary, devastated my sister and me. Our bond kept us moving forward. Brooke was strong. She distracted herself with music, sports, friends, and TV. She was only eight, so the pain she was feeling was blurred by confusion, anger, and denial.

My pain, confusion, anger, and denial were fueled by the devastating truths I knew that Brooke was unaware of. Becoming an orphan over night was rough. Suddenly the cute boy, who gave me his number at the football game weeks before, who also had no parents, was the only person who I felt could relate to me. Six months later, I had fallen deeply in love with Frank. Or so thought my young, naive self.

Down the bicycle path the naked trees stood as still as the cold air. I waited by the duck pond, near the swings in our usual spot. No ducks, no birds, no squirrels, and no sign of life anywhere near. Cars zoomed in the background. Finally, I squinted and spotted Frank from afar.

"Hey, sorry I'm late," he said with a guilty expression. He gave me an unrequited hug and I continued to walk, faster, my hands buried as far into my jacket as they could go.

"How do you feel?" he asked.

My eyes pierced into him.

"Cold," I said and continued trotting.

"C'mon babe. I said I was sorry." He jogged to catch up to me and grabbed my arm stopping me in my tracks.

I turned to him and shot him an annoyed look. "Why are you late anyway?" I wanted to talk to him, but had so many emotions to process, even more than when I got to the park almost two hours ago. I wondered if he was home debating whether to meet with me or not—which wouldn't surprise me, given the situation.

"Mrs. Jenn stopped me on my way out."

"For what?"

"Remember how I cut class last week? Yeah, I got the whole lecture as usual."

"Can't blame her," I said quietly. I couldn't imagine what Jennifer Cavallari, or Mrs. Jenn, had to deal with. She opened her home to three kids that other foster parents couldn't handle anymore — Frank being one of them. He had been living with her for the past three years, ever since he was fourteen. We were only together for six months, and I was already tired of his mischief. Mrs. Jenn tolerated a fair share of his waywardness.

"Yeah. I guess so." He shrugged. His brown eyes gleamed as he stared out distantly, his expression incomprehensible. He always had that look when we touched on any subject that reminded him of his birth mother.

"You went to your appointment?" he asked suddenly remembering.

I looked at him and sighed. "Yeah."

"Oh. Sorry babe, I wish I could have gone with you."

I didn't answer him. He should have known I needed his support. It was equally one of the most terrifying and embarrassing doctor appointments I'd ever had to go through.

"You know I can't miss any more classes, I'll get suspended again," he said, his tone apologetic.

"Of course you will," I said rolling my eyes.

"Why are you so mad?" he asked.

"You mean besides the fact that I can't feel my fingers?" I stopped myself, taking a deep breath. I didn't want to argue. I found the closest bench and tried to calm my nerves. Frank sat next to me.

"Was it what you thought?" His voice was unsteady and I

knew he was hoping that I was wrong.

I nodded.

"Damn. Really?" Now he was the one sitting with his palms pressed against his forehead, stressed, the way I was earlier that evening. He looked up at me. "Are you serious? You'd better not be joking."

"I wouldn't joke about something this serious."

His expression changed completely as his face took on a pallid complexion. I was surprised he didn't pass out.

"She said I'm seven weeks," I added hoping he would be willing to talk more about it.

"So, what does that mean?"

"Honestly, I have no idea." I was as confused as he was. "I guess I'm almost two months. Even though it happened one month ago. I don't get how this stuff works."

He sighed and didn't say anything else for a while. I didn't know what to say either, and sat quietly next to him wondering what was going on in his head. However, I didn't dare ask. I wasn't sure if it was fueled by fear or hormones but I began to cry uncontrollably.

"Don't cry. We'll figure this out," he said as he hugged me close to him.

"Figure … it … out?" I asked, stuttering in between sobs. "We're n-not ready for this."

"I know," he said warming my arms with his hands.

"What should we do?" I asked looking up at him. "I can't have a baby. Where would we stay? My grandma can hardly handle Brooke and me. We definitely can't stay at Mrs. Jenn's."

"I'll get a job. Get us a place." His attempt to convince me wasn't working. I knew we couldn't handle the responsibilities that come with having a baby.

"How? Can't rent an apartment 'till you're eighteen," I pointed out.

"Jeez, Victoria. I'm trying here. And you keep shutting me down."

"I'm sorry. But we have another option, you know."

"Like what?" he asked.

"Find a family that could take care of it."

He looked at me with the grimmest expression I've ever seen. Eyes dark. Lips straight. His comforting touches ceased as he narrowed his eyes in complete outrage.

"No. I would never let some stranger have my kid. Why

would you even… " He paused then exhaled, exasperated. "You already know what I've been through. Why would you even say that?"

"I'm really scared. Sorry. I don't know what else to do," I said, my voice small. "I don't know if I can be a mother yet. Not now."

I was looking forward to finishing high school. Nothing was more important to me than maintaining my honor roll status. I expected to have full scholarship offers to several of the best schools in the area by junior year. I wanted to graduate, and do normal teenage stuff. How was I supposed to do that with a baby?

"You would be an amazing mom. You're smart. Sweet. And I see how you are with Brooke."

"Frank. I'm fourteen. Remember? I'm a baby myself. Brooke is amazing. She's easy. That doesn't count. I'm only doing what my mother would want."

My internal conflict was at an all-time high. Part of me wanted to go with my gut feeling. I really wasn't ready to take care of, or raise, another person. My hands were already full helping my grandmother. The other half, the one that my heart ruled, wanted to give Frank and me the opportunity to strengthen our relationship.

"Why don't you want to keep it? I'm scared too, but you know I'll be there for you." He took his coat off and draped it over me like a blanket. "Here, you two need to stay warm."

"If we do this, you have to promise … No more getting suspended and no cutting classes …"

"I know. I know," he said cutting me off.

"Oh and please stop trying to fight every guy that tries to talk to me. I can't do this if you're locked up again."

"I only did that once."

"Seriously? You've gotten into like three fights since we've been together."

"Look, tomorrow I'll see my guidance counselor and get working papers. I know you don't think I can do it, but I'll take care of our family. I swear. Just give me a chance."

"Okay. Let me know tomorrow. I'll think about what I want to do."

"Vicky, I'll go crazy. You have to decide now, please. I love you. You know that, right?"

It was the first time he told me that he loved me and my

whole body tingled when he said it. "I love you, too." I felt like doing back flips. I finally had someone who cared about me. And a baby who would love me unconditionally might actually be an added bonus.

"We both don't have a real family. This is our chance to make our own," he added not giving me the time to process everything that was just thrown at me.

"Okay." My answer was impulsive and my confidence was absent. "I think we can do this." I tried to hide the skepticism in my voice. And just like that I agreed to become a teen mom.

Frank walked me home and left to return to Mrs. Jenn's. As I walked into my house, I wondered how I was supposed to tell Nana.

Brooke ran over and hugged me as soon when I stepped through the door. Her bright blue eyes twinkled as she looked up at me, a smile spread across her face. She was holding Molly, her favorite doll that our mother gave to her.

"Hey missy shouldn't you be sleeping?" I said pulling her into a tight hug.

"We," she said referring to her and Molly, "were waiting for you to get home!"

"I missed you too." I gave her another squeeze. "Where's Nana? I have to talk to her."

"She's sleeping already."

It was after nine. The talk would have to wait. I spent an hour with Brooke before tucking her into bed, and then Frank called. That night I fell asleep with the phone still under my ear and doubt in my heart.

Despite my fears, Frank proved me wrong when he was hired at a local restaurant and waited tables after school every day, saving for our own place. Our baby boy was due in July, and Frank would be eighteen by then, the legal age to rent an apartment.

Eight months pregnant and through perseverance, I barely managed to finish my sophomore year of high school. When the summer came around Frank had exactly eight hundred and fifty-four dollars saved in a shoebox under his bed. To rent a decent apartment in Westwood, we would need a minimum of three thousand bucks. And that would only pay the first month's rent and security deposit. I didn't want to move out of town because I wanted to graduate from the same high school I was already attending.

Against my initial hesitation, I agreed to an idea Frank suggested during the winter. We were desperate. To help us bring in an extra income, Frank partnered up with Juan Carlos Sanchez, a school acquaintance who was heavy into drug dealing. It was a temporary solution, just until we got our finances together. Within weeks, we saw hundreds easily turn into thousands.

Given the time sensitive situation, we settled for a tiny one-bedroom apartment for Frank, our unborn baby, and I. I'll never forget the look on Brooke's little face when I told her we were moving.

She and I sat curled up in the living room on the old green and yellow flower printed sofa. Nana was baking a chocolate cake for us.

"You're leaving me," she said clinging to Molly, tears falling all over the ragged doll.

"It's only a few blocks away. I'll visit you all the time."

"No you won't. Mommy and daddy left and never came back."

My heart broke. She didn't understand yet, why they couldn't come back. I don't know why we thought it would work out. Brooke and I never spent more than a day apart since she was born. She cried that day and every day after that for two weeks straight. Despite the responsibilities that were ahead of me, leaving Brooke behind wasn't an option. Finally, after I spoke to her, our grandmother reluctantly agreed to let Brooke live with Frank and me under two conditions. Brooke's school couldn't find out, and we had to get married. Frank and I were married in a courthouse on July 5, 1994.

It was a mild, warm, morning when Thomas Matthew Carlisle arrived three weeks later, July 29, 1994. He was the most beautiful thing I'd ever seen, even if he looked like a little wrinkled old man with a sunburn. He had his father's gleaming chestnut eyes and my thick brown straight hair. I wasn't expecting to fall in love with him as soon as he was handed to me in the hospital, but I did. I fell in love with him as well as the idea to have my dream life.

CHAPTER 3

I finished my junior year; taking care of a baby, sister, apartment and all. We were finally getting on our feet, and then shortly after Tommy's first birthday we encountered another unplanned pregnancy. My reaction was different the second time. Being a teenage mother wasn't at all what I expected. Thomas was a perfect baby. He never cried, he slept through the night, and kept me company while Frank worked and Brooke was in school. We had our place to live and I knew that our finances would improve soon since Frank applied to several different restaurants and stores.

Therefore, despite our young ages, only one year later, we were more than happy to welcome our second brunette baby, Ashley Rose into the world. I always wanted a happy family and holding my daughter for the first time made me believe that my dream was coming true. Every time I looked at Thomas and Ashley, I felt blessed. Whenever Frank came home with flowers, the hopeless romantic inside me did cartwheels. We weren't rich financially and that didn't matter to me because I knew everything could only get better.

By age seventeen, I had the most unconventional life. Two kids and a husband. And a little sister for whom I took full responsibility. What others thought of me didn't matter because I was happy. As far as I was concerned, my life was almost perfect. The only thing causing that "almost" was the drug dealing. I asked Frank to end the side work, and despite a lot of disagreement about it, he agreed.

Life was good for a while. However, there was a darkness lurking that I was unaware of. Frank started distancing himself from me and was drinking almost every night. He was getting home progressively later and blamed it on his job. Something wasn't adding up; he was working more and making less.

Before I knew it, we were behind on our rent, electricity, and car insurance. Even the simplicities, like buying groceries, started to seem like a luxury.

Months after waiting for everything to improve, I finally decided to talk to Frank one night after work. It seemed to be the only time we ever had together anymore.

"I know it's late, but I really want to go over these with

you." I said, holding a small pile of envelopes and statements, most of them stamped with red letters reading "past due" and "urgent."

"Okay. What about them?" Frank asked as he threw his sweater, which reeked of smoke and alcohol, onto the bed.

"I'm a little worried." I casually picked up his sweater and threw it into the hamper. "PSE and G are going to shut the lights off on Friday if we don't send them something."

"And what do you want me to do?"

"What do you mean? I just told you they're going to shut off our power. I haven't seen any money in a while."

"You know I get paid on Saturday."

"What about tips?" I asked. I was trying so hard not to be nagging, but the situation was pressing, and he just wasn't taking it seriously.

He let out an exaggerated sigh and pulled a few dollar bills from his jeans. "Here!" He practically shoved the money into my hand, dropping half of it.

I looked at him, exasperated, but exhaled patiently before picking up a few ones and fives from the carpet.

"This is forty dollars. The bill is ninety five … and that doesn't even count rent."

He ignored me as he took off his gold chain and rings and placed them on the dresser. I put my hands on my hips waiting for a response.

"If you're going to complain every second of every God damn day, why don't you work and I'll sit on my ass instead."

I was taken aback before I could react.

"What the hell is your problem?" I finally said. My heart sank. We had never spoken so disrespectfully to each other.

"You're acting like this is my fault."

"It kind of is."

"Why would you say that? I know you work a lot and we're so grateful," I said wrapping my arms around him. "You know if I could work I would, but with what we would pay for day care …"

"That's not it," he snapped, freeing from my embrace. "You already know where the money we had was coming from. It sure as hell wasn't from tips or my two-dollar-an-hour paychecks. You're the one who asked me to stop. Therefore, I stopped. And look at us now."

"Is that why you're mad? Because I didn't want to survive

on drug money?"

"You really have no idea what Juan Carlos is getting into right now, do you? He just hooked up with these dudes from the city. Tripled his clientele. While you're complaining about my forty dollars a day, I could have been making forty thousand."

My eyes widened. "You could make that much selling weed?"

"No, Victoria." He sat and rubbed his temples as if I'd just given him a migraine.

"So fucking stupid," he muttered the words under his breath, but they hurt nonetheless.

"You don't tell me anything. How am I supposed to know?"

I didn't think he could possibly let out another annoyed sigh, but I was wrong.

"We don't sell weed … Look, I'm not going to sit here and explain every single thing I do to you. Any way it doesn't matter because you'd rather eat Ramen noodles every night than *live like criminals* or whatever the fuck it was that you said," he said sardonically.

I had a lot of patience, but I couldn't stand to look at his face anymore. "Frank, do whatever you think is best for our family." I walked out of the room and shut the door behind me.

I went to check on Brooke. She looked so peaceful, sound asleep in her bed. Her blonde hair, which unfortunately resembled that of our father's, fell over her face and across her pillow. I curled into the bed next to her and brushed the hair out of her face.

What is wrong with Frank? We never argue. Are we going to end up starving with no electricity? With stresses heavy on my mind, I ended up sleeping in Brooke's bed that night.

My relationship with Frank didn't improve, and I struggled with two toddlers all day until Brooke came home from school and helped me. It was a disappointment that my eleven-year-old sister was there for me more than Frank was. One day I was feeling sick and asked Brooke to stay home from school.

I was laying on the armrest of our worn out olive green sofa that my grandmother had given us. It was the only piece of furniture we had aside from our beds and kitchen table, the television sat on the floor.

"Thank you so much for this. I owe you," I said to Brooke as she gave Ashley a bottle.

"You don't owe me anything. They're my niece and nephew. How do you feel? You look a little better."

"I was throwing up all morning. I'm so tired. I think I got that stomach virus that's going around."

"Are you sure?" She raised her eyebrows at me.

"I think so. Why?"

"Remember? You were like this with Ashley," she said with a hinting undertone.

I thought for a second.

"I'm not pregnant. You can't get pregnant when you're breastfeeding," I said trying to convince myself.

"That's not what I learned in health class," she said.

"Okay smarty pants," I said trying to be silly with her, but on the inside my stomach churned with nausea at the thought. *I was extremely tired lately.* But pregnant … again? We would have been the most irresponsible couple ever.

"Well, I wouldn't keep it," I finally said after some consideration.

"Victoria, don't say that."

"I'm not saying it to be mean. I just can't. I'm not going to be nineteen with three kids. That's ridiculous."

"Actually, you would be twenty."

I shot Brooke an annoyed look. "That doesn't help. It's already too much as it is. Frank doesn't know anything. He's been acting so strange lately, I'm not sure another baby is what we need. I'll go to the doctor tomorrow."

"First of all you have to tell Frank, it wouldn't be right if you didn't. Second, how would you get there? And what money would you use? Abortions aren't free, you know."

"Okay, Brooke, end of discussion. I'm probably not pregnant any way. I shouldn't be talking about this with you. I forget how young you are sometimes."

"I'm not a baby, Vick."

"You'll still be telling me that thirty years from now you know."

She smiled at me and rolled around on the floor with Ashley, playing with the Molly doll that she had given to her niece. Then the lights, TV, and computer turned off simultaneously, and we both looked up.

"Must be a power outage," I lied, knowing exactly what it

was.

"Are you sure? Isn't the bill overdue? Do I need to get a job?"

"You don't worry about any of that. Okay? Everything will be fine." I made a promise that I hoped I could keep to my baby sister who was being forced to grow up excessively fast.

That day and night dragged as I waited for Frank to come home. Several hours after Thomas and Ashley fell asleep; Brooke and I played Uno until she finally fell asleep too. With candles lit and a book in my lap, I sat in the living room waiting for Frank to come home.

Hours later I was startled awake by the sound of the front door slamming shut when Frank walked in.

"Hey." I cleared my throat as I stood up from the sofa and stretched. "Is everything okay?"

"Yeah, I went out after work."

"Went out?"

"Yup."

"Great. Therefore, while I'm sitting here in the dark with your children you're out having the time of your life! Where did you go? Who are you hanging out with all the damn time?"

He exhaled, annoyed.

"What?" I demanded.

"Is this interrogation shit going to be an everyday thing?"

"Interrogation?"

"Yeah. Like a fucking cop."

"I have a right to know what you're doing, especially when you're coming home at three and four in the morning and your family is here with no electricity!"

"I don't have time for this." He turned around and walked toward the bedroom.

"Don't walk away from me! This discussion isn't over," I yelled, charging after him.

He spun around locking his focus on me, an ominous look loomed in his eyes; one I've never seen before. He said nothing and instead he lunged at me slamming me into the wall, my entire throat encased in his hands.

"Never raise your voice at me again, do you understand?" He spoke slowly and clearly in a low, threatening tone that raised every hair on my body.

I nodded, terrified, tears in my eyes, barely able to breathe.

"This discussion *is* over." His words pierced through my

heart as I struggled to find my own voice.

He released his grip and I gasped for air, looking at him in a way I've also never looked at him. Eerily quiet, Frank said nothing else to me before disappearing into the room.

I'll never forget the fear I felt, the dark look that possessed him. I was destroyed by the overwhelming sense that our relationship was shattering. I couldn't sleep all night as the violent event, dark eyes, and threatening words replayed and haunted me. I stayed awake for hours and spent another night curled up with my sister while wondering: what did I get myself into?

CHAPTER 4

Frank and I attempted to rebuild a broken relationship, but failed miserably and somewhere along the line I think we gave up. I did everything I thought a wife was supposed to do. What example did I have to follow? We were just there; bound by the commitment we had to our family. Nothing more.

Frank started working with Juan Carlos again. Not only were we able to pay the bills that were behind, within three years we had enough money to put down on a mansion in Alpine, New Jersey. Frank's attitude started to change and the love that was once there suffered due to the time we spent apart and his drug and alcohol use.

We rode a bumpy path to get to where we were, and I believed that we could redeem our relationship until the most horrific moment of my life. It was when the marriage ended and was replaced with something dark and evil. The chance of love, which was never there to begin with, was gone forever.

"Ashley is crying," I mumbled to Frank, but it may as well have been to myself. Never in my life did I experience what tired felt like until I tried to put three children to bed by myself, as well as tend to my younger sister.

Thomas and Ashley were usually easy. I wasn't so lucky with 2-year-old Nicholas, who never wanted to leave my bed. He was always coloring on walls, running into streets, and breaking things. Everything. He threw tantrums that made me want to curl up into a ball and cry with him. And sometimes I did.

Frank disappeared into the bathroom and I heard the shower water turn on.

"I really have to shower now, got to be up early tomorrow," he called from inside the bathroom.

I let out an annoyed sigh but otherwise kept the complaining to myself.

"Look, leave Nick in our bed, he falls asleep there easier anyway," he said.

"I know he will. I've been trying to get them used to their own beds though."

"What's one more night?"

Shrugging off his lazy suggestion was my best answer. I

didn't want to do anything to give myself more work at that point. I switched on the television for our drowsy 2-year-old and went into Ashley's room. I didn't have any work to do there as my wonderful sister had already gotten her to fall back asleep.

Finally, everyone was sleeping. It was taking all of us time to adjust to our brand new house. For the first time we had our own rooms, and it was amazing. The master bedroom was modern and elegant, with white marble floors and a skylight. Attached was a private master bathroom complete with twin sinks and a Jacuzzi tub.

I exhaled; it was shortly after midnight and at that moment, nothing looked better than my bed. Climbing in, I grabbed a little black remote from the night table. One button dimmed the lights and the other turned on the fireplace. I stared at the crown moldings on the ceiling and the chandelier and still couldn't believe that it was our home. Feeling nothing but contentment I snuggled under the fluffy black and gold duvet, which matched the thick velvet curtains.

Curling up, with a now sleeping Nick, my leg brushed against something fuzzy. I reached down and fished for the fabric object, assuming it would be a baby t-shirt or a sock, I pulled it out from under the covers, and in disbelief was suddenly holding and staring at a pink leopard thong. I definitely didn't own a pink leopard thong. I gasped as my stomach dropped and the most uneasy mix of denial and sadness flushed through my veins.

I shot up from the bed feeling sick. I couldn't breathe as my brain desperately fished for any logical explanation for the foreign undergarment. No matter how many directions I went with it the same exact conclusion was the most logical. I dreaded the truth, but knew that with time I spent out of the house from noon to dinner every day it wasn't impossible. A well-oiled daily schedule from Ashley's pre-k pick-up and dance class, Tommy's karate class, Nick's swim lessons, and running errands kept me out of the house for the biggest portion of the afternoon.

My husband happened to be getting out of the shower and walked into the bedroom with a white towel wrapped around his waist. Standing there in shock as he rummaged through his dressers I froze and felt dread course through my body. My eyes began to sting and water up as I stared at him.

"What?" he asked me while I still tried to find my voice.

"Is there something … you need to tell me?" The words staggered out over my every effort to choke back tears.

"No," he answered, not looking at me. When I didn't respond he looked at me.

"Why? Should I?" he asked dryly.

"No? Are you sure about that?"

"Victoria, I don't have time for games if you have something to say just say it."

"Games? I'm the one playing games? Well then, why don't you tell me what the hell this is?" I asked, throwing the thong at him, waiting for his explanation.

"How the hell am I supposed to know? They're not yours?"

"Are you kidding? How stupid do you think I am?"

He continued about his routine, returning to his dresser, as if I didn't just find pink leopard underwear in our bed. Even with physical evidence that he was cheating on me, he didn't feel the need to explain himself.

"How could you do this to me? You brought some whore into *our bed*?"

Raising my voice, I accidentally woke up Nick. He started crying and I went over to try to soothe him until he fell asleep again all the while Frank was doing everything but giving me a reason to be furious.

"Aren't you going to say something?" I crossed my arms demanding the explanation I had yet to receive.

"What the fuck do you want me to say?" he lashed out.

"God damn it Victoria! You're always on my shit about something. What did I tell you about this?"

"Excuse me?" I looked at him astonished. I realized that he was nothing more than a stranger screaming at me. The man I met, who would do anything for me, wasn't there anymore. He hadn't been for a while.

"Frank why are you being like this? I'm your *wife*! I deserve respect," I protested.

"So, sometimes you decide to be my wife and I'm not supposed to explore my options?" he snapped as he brushed past me heading back into the bathroom.

"What the hell is that supposed to mean?"

"Don't act stupid. You know what it means."

His words were like daggers that I couldn't dodge and I didn't even know how to respond. When he walked out of the

32

bathroom, again I stood in his way, blocking him, so that he would be forced to acknowledge me.

"Please get out of my face."

"Are you serious? You have nothing else to say?" I waited for seconds, minutes, who knows, hoping for an apology, or some sign of remorse, but when he just shrugged I could feel my face burning red with anger.

"Say something. Who the hell is this whore?"

"She's nothing. Some bitch I've been fucking. Is that what you want to hear?"

"You're an asshole. I hate you!" I threw myself at him, hitting him in an uncontrollable fit.

"How could you do this to me?" I yelled as my little fists propelled blows on his chest and arms. "I swear this is it! It's over." Despite all my efforts, I never caused him one ounce of pain. I knew I couldn't actually physically hurt him, which just enraged me more.

He grabbed my wrists tight, stopping my hits.

"What did you just say?" he asked through clenched teeth.

"It's over! I'm leaving you!" My every effort to wrestle my wrists free from his grip was unsuccessful. I struggled with him pulling my body weight away from him in a tug of war battle.

"Let go of me."

He released my arms and I rushed to the closet grabbing a suitcase throwing anything I could into it.

"You're leaving me? Yeah? Where are you gonna go?" he asked, as he laughed, testing me.

"I don't know, but I can't do this," I said as I shook my head and tears of anger fell from my eyes. I grabbed the duffle bag and figured I could stay with the kids in a hotel for the night. Cool off, think about things. How could I sleep in that bed as if nothing ever happened?

He stood in front of the door blocking me.

"Please move," I said, my voice low.

"Don't do this. Look she doesn't mean anything. I still love you very much, Babe."

"I'm sorry Frank but I need a little space." I reached around him for the doorknob pulled the door open and he pushed it closed.

"Please get out of my way."

"No."

"Frank ... move. I'm serious."

"You're not going anywhere."

I exhaled annoyed. "Get out of my way!"

With one quick motion the back of his hand met with my face. I was thrown to the floor from the blunt force and lifting my hand to my stinging cheek, stared at him in shock. I was not his wife at that moment.

"What did I tell you about that shit?" He threw himself at me, punching me twice in the face. I screamed out in pain waking our son again. Nick cried as he watched his father repeatedly hit his mother.

My face was throbbing and my lip was bleeding. Blood spattered around the marble floor as he mercilessly continued to assault me. I managed to start crawling away until he grabbed me and dragged me like a rag doll across the floor. "You ungrateful little bitch. I work my ass off, get you this house, this is the thanks I get." Another punch lashed directly across my cheekbone. I cried out again.

I wanted to fight back but I couldn't. My body was in defense mode and I tried to curl up into a ball to shield myself from his unrelenting fists.

Desperate, I begged him to stop as Nick cried in the background. I was more concerned about traumatizing our son than I was about myself. Every part of my body burned and throbbed. All of his weight beat repeatedly against my 125-pound body. He was cursing at me and insulting me, but the exact words never registered as I withdrew myself completely, hoping it wasn't real. *This has to be a nightmare. This isn't really happening.* I recite this repeatedly to myself, still curled in a ball with my arms shielding my head.

He pulled my hair, lifting my head, forcing me to look at him. My eyes meet with his cold stare. The smell of whiskey on his breath was strong and overbearing.

"What are you gonna do now? Leave me?"

"No," I whispered, my voice small and shaking.

"I can't fucking hear you!" he screamed yanking my hair harder.

"No!" I yelled, as I broke down and cried.

"Good girl. That's what I thought," he said petting my head with his other hand. "I will do whatever the fuck I want, do you understand?"

I nodded, sobbing. My neck twisted, as my hair balled up in his hands.

I looked around the room trying to find anything that I could bludgeon him with. Anything that could help me, but I found nothing. All I saw was that empty whisky bottle on the night table, which I considered trying to grab, until I realized I was too scared to move.

Tears streamed down my face. *I'm such a good wife. I'm a good mother to his three children. Why is he doing this?* I was in a daze and couldn't attempt to fight back any more. My body just lay there limp.

Lowering his lips to my ear he whispered, "Don't be jealous baby. She's nothing like you." Then he kissed my neck and I felt his hands slide under my nightgown.

My entire body was shaking, petrified, pressed against the cold hard marble. "Please Frank. Why are you doing this?" I asked, whimpering; weak, hurt, and humiliated.

"Shh … be a good wife," he ordered leaning closer to me and again, a whiff of whiskey on his breath gagged me. My futile pleading couldn't stop him from pulling off my panties.

"Stop!" I said more firmly this time but it didn't matter.

He slapped me again.

"Damn it! What did I just say? That's not being a good girl," he warned with a devious smile under his words. Now it was like a game to him.

I did as I was told, terrified of being hit and terrified for my life and of the monstrous demon that possessed my husband. Still paralyzed, my body aching and pinned under him. I lay as still as possible.

He grabbed my face hard, "If you ever try to leave me I'll kill you. You hear me? You're mine." His menacing threat shook every nerve in my body. If I ever thought I felt fear before, I was wrong.

I was still crying when he kissed me. I was actually crying the entire time, which didn't remotely affect him. It hurt me that our child was watching everything, yet Frank was unaffected by that as well.

I don't know how long the ordeal lasted, but hours after Frank passed out on his bed I was still in the same damned spot on the floor; crying, traumatized, and afraid to look myself in the mirror.

My head was spinning and every part of my body hurt. I just wanted to throw up. Actually … I needed to. I turned to my side and got sick onto the floor. I couldn't stand for a while and when I did eventually peel myself up I staggered into the bathroom and ran the warm water. I got into the shower and curled into a ball in the tub while the water hit me. My body was still shaking and my tears that never stopped flowing. The same carousel of thoughts circled my mind. *How could he do this to me? Why? How can I stay with him after this?* The physical evidence of that beating was the least of the pain I experienced. I was emotionally scarred after that night.

I was never able to look at my husband the same way. A demon was unleashed in him that night that appeared again every time he drank. It killed me inside knowing that I had nowhere else to go, and even if I did, fear condemned me to staying with him. Defeated, torn, and scared. There was no way out.

CHAPTER 5

For years, life was thoroughly routine; waking up, going to bed and, in the intervening period, the constant effort to keep moving forward. It wasn't always bad. And it wasn't always good. After I first caught Frank cheating on me, I couldn't stand being in that house. After the violent attack, it opened the door for the abuse to start. I detached myself as much as possible from my life at home. I opened my own business, Little Treasures. We sold collectibles, rare items, gently used and new items, it was similar to some of the other auction sites that were out there, but without the big business label. I was only able to do this because Frank didn't take it seriously. He saw it as a hobby. The business was a chance to work, a distraction — or yes, a hobby, perhaps. Whatever it was, it got me out of the house and placed me at the head of something much more manageable than a dysfunctional home.

The office on this Monday morning was surprisingly quiet and peaceful. Maybe Michelle was still hung over from the party I overheard her talking about on Friday night.

"Good morning, Mrs. Carlisle." She made every effort to smile as I passed by her desk.

"Michelle," I said cordially and kept walking.

Michelle Swanson, who nailed her interview in the first three minutes, worked for me for three years. I hired her in the recognition that I wasn't computer savvy enough to perform the, for me, tedious technology-related duties of running a business. Michelle was the reason we had a website at all. She kept us actively linked to all the popular social networking sites as well.

The cubicles were light gray and white, large floor-to-ceiling windows stretched across one entire wall and small areas of the adjacent wall were painted lime green. All of our printers and copy machines were directly in the center, against the wall of the average sized office.

My private office was a separate room in the back of the main room. When I started the business I knew I would need an area for myself; a space where stress, drama, fighting, and problems didn't exist. The many advantages to being at work included being in a positive environment where I was respected and well liked. And, of course, being away from my husband.

Sue was a sweet, gray-haired older woman who helped me with simple tasks like, bubble wrapping fragile items and matching invoices to their receipts. She was like a second mother to Brooke and I, giving us advice and looking out for us in ways our mother would have if she were around.

The reception desk was a large maple wood and chrome semi-circle with a glass top. It matched our modern decor, even though we were actually old-fashioned and out dated. I liked it that way. Using paper-based systems and limited technology kept us grounded and simple. It helped us build a personal connection with our customers.

"Hey!" I smiled as I approached Brooke, giving her a warm hug.

"Hey. I missed you this weekend," she said squeezing me back.

I hired Brooke as the receptionist while she was trying to pay for college, but it was mostly so I could keep an eye on her. She took orders over the phone, received deliveries, handled any appointments, performed appraisals, and was my right hand, as she always was throughout our whole lives.

"I know. Sorry, we went to Hershey Park early on Friday and stayed until Sunday instead of Saturday. I tried to call you, though," I said leaning against the desk.

"I've been dying to talk to you though. I had a very good weekend," she said with a secretive smile.

"Oh?"

"I went on an amazing date," she said with a huge grin planted on her glowing face.

"Really?" I pulled a chair next to her intrigued.

For some young women this was ordinary news, but Brooke was extremely fussy, and any man worth her time was a big deal. She wasn't the type to randomly date, and it wasn't hard for her to find a suitor. She was beautiful, with 1995 Nicole Kidman blonde locks and gray-blue eyes. Hands always manicured impeccably, eyebrows always done. She was a catch but was still available, because she focused on other things. Everything else, in fact.

"You? Brooke Angela Soto actually went on a date worthy enough to dub as *incredible?*"

"Could you believe it?" she asked.

"No, I can't. With who? The cute doctor again?" Jake, the

almost too friendly medical student, was Brooke's most recent interest. She initially ignored Jake for the entire 2010 winter semester. He finally won her over when he gave her a ride home when she had a flat tire. He was finishing his Bachelor's degree program in a little over two years. He had properly introduced himself to me before taking her out, and I approved of him for her.

"Who Jake? Ew, no," she said with a disgusted look on her face. She turned on the computer and keyed in her user name and password to log into the company network.

"Only you would find something wrong with a doctor," I said.

"He is not a doctor, just a student. And he's super creepy."

"Why? What did this one do?" I asked.

"No seriously, I think you'll agree with me this time. He called me like fifteen times on Friday night after work. I didn't feel like hanging out, so I didn't answer."

"Okay," I said waiting for her to go on.

"Then my phone died for few hours and the second I turned it back on he was calling literally that exact second."

"That's it?" I asked and laughed.

"No. But didn't he have anything better to do? Was he just sitting there calling and calling until I turned it back on? And what freaked me even out more ... when I got home on Saturday night he was in front of my house waiting for me."

"Oh. So he's a stalker."

"Yeah, exactly. A stalker, so he's done," she said and laughed. Continuing, her voice turned back to excitement, "Anyway, I finally went out with Collin."

"Who?"

"You *did not* just say that. You know!" She sounded outraged as if she were speaking about some celebrity.

I shrugged. It was too early in the morning to think.

"Oh my God. He does like all our deliveries and you don't even know his name."

"Sean?"

"No. The cute one. Collin Turner."

"Oh." I scowled at her revelation.

"What?"

"Not sure how I feel about that," I said dryly.

"Why?" she asked.

Of our two alternating regular delivery guys, this was the first time Brooke fell for looks over personality. Sean, like every other young man in Bergen County, was interested in Brooke, but she wouldn't give him the time of day either. Collin, on the other hand, had Brooke's eye for the last few months, but I never thought it would amount to anything beyond that. He didn't seem interested in her. In fact, he never really said much to either of us. And that kid was in desperate need of a haircut. That was all I knew about him.

"Just a vibe I get. Seems like a player."

"I don't think so. He's amazing! And really sweet. On Friday we finally exchanged numbers and talked for a few hours."

"Great. I blame myself. Remind me to never take off on Friday again."

"Would you let me tell you what happened," she asked as she hit my arm.

"You ignored the stalker's calls to talk to the mysterious delivery boy?"

She smiled, but otherwise didn't respond to my sarcastic banter. That's just how we were with each other.

"Anyway. We went to the South Street Seaport on Saturday. We ate at this super nice restaurant on the dock. It had a breathtaking view of Jersey. Then we went on the Circle Line cruise around the city which stopped at Ellis Island so we also visited the Statue of Liberty."

"Cute, sounds like one of Ashley's field trips," I said with a fake smile plastered on my face.

"Shut up. It was very romantic."

"I bet it was. And what else do you know about him?"

"He has his own place in downtown Manhattan, he used to model, he's in his second year of college."

I sighed unimpressed. "What else?"

She shrugged. "Well, have you seen him? It's hard to care about the details."

I rolled my eyes.

"He's gorgeous!" she said in a dreamy teenage girl with a crush voice. Then she turned pinker than the blush she was wearing.

"Just don't get too caught up," I warned. "Looks only go so far." After the way my mother and I were treated by the men in our lives, I learned to be very wary of the ones that Brooke

40

dated. I already made the mistake of being fooled. Frank was handsome and charming, with the plus of the sexy bad boy exterior, and that proved to be a failure.

"At least give him a chance," she pleaded seeking my approval.

"We'll see."

Brooke and I continued to chat and filled a few orders that came in. The day flew by and it seemed that as fast as we clocked in eight hours earlier, we all started to clock out. Sadly, this was the part of the day that I dreaded the most.

I tried to kill some time after leaving the office, running as many errands as I could. Tasks that would have kept other "normal" moms busy eluded me. We used a cleaning service that took care of the house and an au pair who helped with the kids. It was times like this that I had really begun to resent the luxuries my family had been afforded. Being broke and eating ramen noodles in the dark didn't always seem so bad anymore. At least we were happier then.

I pulled up to my house and turned off the engine, but couldn't bring myself to leave the car. Frank's car, the black Range Rover, was there. He was hardly ever home before midnight and at that moment I would have preferred to be somewhere -- anywhere else, but day to day my kids were the only motivation I had to not disappear and never come back home.

Okay. It's Monday night. Our favorite shows are on tonight, I think. Or more like his favorite shows that I forced myself to get into. Maybe it might actually be a good night. Every time I walked into my house I didn't know what to expect, and hoped to leave the next morning in one piece.

On the outside my life was everything many others would kill for yet, I was still sitting in my car after 15 minutes, scared to return to that envied life. I sent text messages to Brooke and checked my emails from my phone. After my now 20 minutes stalling, and a short pep talk to myself, I stepped out of my car and took a deep breath then walked up to the door. I paused again before I turned the key and braced myself, entering my home.

Quietly shutting the door behind me, I noticed the usual black and purple skull printed loafers; hot pink sandals, navy blue flip-flops, and black alligator skin shoes were lined up neatly to the left of the door on the tan mat that covered the white Dal-Tile granite floor. Galina must still be here, I thought. I kicked off my beige pumps and added them to the organized collection.

The foyer, which the upstairs loft overlooked, was met by ornate marble stairs and was filled with a delicious tomato and basil aroma. Kiwi, our Yorkie, who always appeared to have just eaten a bag of coffee, which I wouldn't put past her, happily bounced at my feet.

In the background, a chorus of "Hi mom" greeted me from the kitchen. Ashley was setting the table while Galina put the final changes on what looked like filet mignon with potatoes and green beans. Galina was our Russian Au Pair, whom I hired, despite the objections I received from the children. I felt more comfortable knowing someone was home with them after school when Thomas graduated and enrolled in the Air Force.

"How was your day"? Galina asked me as I picked at a green bean from the pan.

"Good, thank you. Everything ok around here?"

"Yes, of course. Homework done. Garbage out. I run dishwasher after dinner," she said, each word rolled up in her thick accent.

"Thank you again. Don't worry about the dishes. You can head out whenever you're ready."

Nick sat at the table, all kinds of shooting and exploding sounds coming from his phone as he tapped away at the keys.

"Killing stuff again?" I asked as I kissed him on his head. I tussled his hair which looked like it travelled through a rainbow every week. This particular week his blonde strands were highlighted blue. It didn't bother me as much as his spiky accessories and piercings did.

"No games at the table," I reminded him.

"Ugh. Okay mom," he grumbled.

"How was school?"

The only response I received was an annoyed "fine," but after raising Thomas, I learned that 13-years-old boys had their moments. It bothered me that we didn't have the best relationship. Nick could never open up to us. The only person who could get through to Nick was his aunt Debra.

Debra Carlisle was married to Frank's older brother Paul. They re-connected when Paul found us in the yellow pages 12 years prior.

Paul was a maître d at one of the most upscale banquet

halls in Bergen County. He worked long hours to provide for his family. They lived in Lodi, a blue-collar town, with their two sons Charlie who was 17 and Matthew who was 13, like Nick. The kids got along great and spent a lot of time at Paul and Debra's house. I couldn't help but to find myself envy them. We had the six-figure income, lived in a rich neighborhood with the mansion to match. Sent our children to private schools. Yet I envied them and their four-bedroom $350,000 house, Honda and Nissan cars and television-like lifestyle. It took me too long to realize that material possessions meant nothing. Yet I always found myself having a hard time imagining living without all of it. However, either way Debra and Paul were a genuinely happy couple who thrived on love and worked together toward their goals.

Being so young and inexperienced when I had all of my children, and no model to follow, every day was a learning experience for me. Ashley grew, so did I. Debra was 41-years-old and had more patience than anyone I've ever known. She was established financially, emotionally, and in every way, a person can be. Debra was better than I was. Although, I would never give her the satisfaction to hear me utter those words aloud.

"How's studying for your finals going, Ashley?"

"Good, we had a practice test in English and I scored in the top five of the class," she said proudly. I was surprised but grateful that she never gave us the issues that teenage girls were known to give their parents.

"I'm so proud of you, Ashley," I said as I pulled a bag of lettuce, a cucumber, and a tomato out of the refrigerator and handed them to her because she always made the salad.

"Before I forget, can Morgan stay over this Friday night after the movies?" she asked while placing the tomato onto a cutting board and slicing it.

"Sure," I said as I shrugged my shoulders. "Is it okay with Wendy?"

"Yes. She doesn't really care what Morgan does anyway, Mom, you know that."

"I'm just making sure. By the way did Tommy call today"?

"Yes, he called when we got here from school."

"And he's okay?"

"Yes, they're fine."

Galina was loading the dishwasher.

"Where's Frank?" I asked her.

"He went upstairs. Went to nap when he got home."

I simply nodded, as my emotions toward Frank were usually indifferent.

"Don't you have class?" I asked Galina.

"Summer session starts in one week," she said and nodded.

That night ended up being a good night. We sat around and enjoyed our family dinner. Some nights were better than others. The ones when Frank was home early meant he most likely wasn't drinking, and I most likely was safe. Not every night was a good night and things were about to get even more complicated.

CHAPTER 6

Waking to an empty bedroom was my norm. I went into the bathroom and pulled out the usual three bottles from the medicine cabinet. Taking two of each kept me functioning for the day without having any nervous breakdowns or dramatic mood changes. There was no enthusiasm toward taking them, but the psychiatrists that I started seeing 13 years earlier insisted that anti-depressants would improve my mood. A few months later, they added mood stabilizers to treat the depression associated with my self-injury, which was only half-true. It all sounded contradictory to me and when they added anti-psychotics to help with anxiety and Ambien to cure the insomnia, which was a side effect to the anti-psychotics, there was nothing left to do but throw my hands up and accepted it.

After taking a shower, my regimen for the day began. My long hair was wrapped up in a towel while choosing an outfit. The white blazer with a tan shirt underneath paired nicely with a black skirt that fit snug against my hips and cut off above the knees. Afterwards, my hair was freshly blow-dried, flat ironed, curled at the ends. Dark brown mascara accentuated my already long lashes and matched my natural hair color. Brown eyeliner, foundation, and blush were applied to my eyes, cheeks, and face. With my favorite black pumps completing the outfit, I headed downstairs.

Galina was turning over a few pieces of turkey bacon and scrambling eggs. Buttered toast, orange juice, and milk in a glass carafe were already on the table.

"Good morning," I said to Galina with a smile. Oh, what would I do without her?

"Morning," she said setting a plate on the table for me. Then she placed a mug of vanilla chai tea next to it.

"Thank you," I said. After eating and drinking my tea, I cleared the plate and headed out. The drive to Ridgewood was about a half hour from home. There wasn't much traffic yet. Never was, since I always left before rush hour.

Unlike that quiet Monday a few weeks prior, the office was extremely busy with orders, mostly for last-minute graduation gifts, and I was trying to keep everything organized.

The phones were ringing non-stop, Michelle was typing a mile a minute, Sue was quickly scribbling some labels, and yes everyone was busy, everyone except Brooke.

Princess Brooke was at her desk pushing buttons on the phone to place incoming calls on hold or send them to Michelle. For whatever reason, she felt that flirting took a priority over our customers. This had been going on for the last few weeks, and I was starting to lose my patience.

I rolled my eyes at the display. Brooke was trying to act cute with Collin. *Trying.* He leaned against her desk smiling at her, and whispered something into her ear. She giggled and batted her eyes. Yuck. It was as if the two of them were engrossed in some hilarious inside joke. *Come on Brooke, show some class!*

Michelle glanced at me and must have seen the agitated look on my face. "It's cool, Mrs. Carlisle, don't worry. I can handle all the calls," she said, defending Brooke.

"No, it's not. I'm tired of this. She's been doing this for two weeks straight now," I said walking over to the two of them. I dropped a stack of copy paper onto her desk, the loud slam seeming to cause the room to pause.

"Sorry to interrupt, but whenever you have a minute there are about two hundred receipts that need to be printed by tomorrow morning. Then those orders need to be filled and some of them shipped by Friday. Not to mention the calls you keep ignoring."

"Alright. I get it. Give me a sec," she snapped as she shot me an impatient glare, which was returned with an evenly annoyed expression. She casually returned her focus back to him.

"Wait, so where did you want to go on Friday?" she asked Collin disregarding me altogether.

"We could talk about it later," Collin said to her, catching my harsh scowl as he glanced at me.

"Oh, don't mind my sister," she said flipping her hair in my direction. "She gets like this sometimes."

"You've got some nerve ..." I started to say to Brooke.

"I'm just gonna go..." Collin interjected, obviously uncomfortable with our bickering.

Brooke turned to me, eyes piercing. "Why do you have to get all bitchy for no reason and take it out on everyone all the time?"

"Brooke, don't blame this on me," I said calmly. "I understand that this is new for you, but you're on the clock and it's super busy..."

She glanced at him again, placing her hand up, indicating to him to wait for her then she took a few steps closer to me.

"You don't have to be so rude though. The first time I actually really like someone and this is how you act," she said to me in a low voice so that he couldn't hear her.

"This isn't the time or place for this conversation," I said.

"Whatever."

I could hear her frustration, but there was no way I was going to let her off that easy. She was blindly falling into a bear trap of lust and physical attraction, nothing more. Her work ethic was compromised, her attitude was nasty, and something had to give.

"Just because you're in a shitty relationship doesn't mean you have to make everyone else's miserable," she said as she gathered her beige and tawny coach purse and light pink cardigan from her desk.

"Where are you going?" I demanded.

"I'm taking a sick day. Suddenly I don't feel so good," she said before spinning around.

"Come on," she said to Collin who looked detached from the situation. He looked back at me before reluctantly following her out.

I stood staring at the closed door, my chin almost touching the floor. She never raised her voice at me, walked out during work, or disrespected me in front of everyone. We were not the type to have petty fights. And the whole ordeal was so unprofessional.

I had 115 more orders to deal with, and I knew it was impossible to be out of there by five, so with the new goal of seven I quietly sat at Brooke's desk and took on both jobs. Several hours later, my hands were cramped up and full of paper cuts, and I was barely half way done. It was already 4:55. So much for finishing by seven.

As she always did, Michelle punched out her time card at five on the dot.

"Do you need me to stay late?" Sue asked, noticing how much paperwork remained. She looked like she was almost ready for bed. I had no intention of making her work any more than she needed to and I didn't generally make a habit of keeping them after five anyway.

"No, I'm okay. Thank you, though," I said volunteering to endure the burden of the workload alone.

"Well, don't stay too late. Big storm coming," she warned in the motherly way that she did.

"Don't worry, I won't," I said. "Just to make sure these last-minute orders are done by Friday."

"Okay. See you tomorrow," she said with a warm smile.

"See you tomorrow. Get home safe," I said as she left me to be alone in the office with one hand on a paper pile and the other on the computer keyboard.

It was a bit creepy in the office all alone, as dusk and a summer storm slowly crept in. The wind slammed against the windows as it swooshed and whistled by.

I jumped as the buzz of my phone broke my concentration. The little envelope icon on the screen indicated that I had received a text message. It was from Ashley.

Ashley: Hi Mom. Just finished helping Galina with dinner. Where are you?

Me: Thank you honey! I Love you! I'm still at the office.

I sent the message and realized that my phone was dying and I didn't have my charger.

Ashley: Love you too! Could you please bring home colored ink?

Me: I Can't. Working late tonight. Ask your father. He's been getting home early on Mondays.

Ashley: He was home but just left. Forgot to ask him. His phone is off.

Of course it was. I sighed as my phone beeped again warning that the battery life was low. My daughter was so independent and helpful, which made it easy for me to forget that she was only a teenager. She couldn't do everything by herself. Monday and Thursday nights Galina attended classes at Fairleigh Dickinson University, so I assumed she had already left for the evening. I had to help her even if it meant going to the 24-hour Wal-Mart after working a busy ten hour day.

After a few minutes passed and she still hadn't received a response from me as I contemplated leaving the office at that moment, another message came through.

Ashley: I need it for a school assignment due tomorrow.

Me: Ok. No problem. I'll bring it. Leave the assignment open and I'll print it for you.

She thanked me and I placed my phone down which then played a little wind chime-like melody indicating that it was completely drained and shutting down. I thought for a second and remembered that I may have ordered a bunch of ink cartridges wholesale a few months back. How lucky would I be to find one compatible with the printer we had at home? The walk through the quiet office all the way to the back and into my private office room seemed long. I felt silly for being scared as I quickly rummaged through the supply cabinet. My wild imagination came from seeing too many '80s horror flicks with Brooke.

It saddened me as Brooke crossed my mind. She didn't call or message me after the argument earlier in the day. I knew there was something I didn't like about her new obsession the minute she told me she was interested in him. She was a completely different Brooke because of him. Maybe I also didn't like Collin because, in some weird way, he reminded me of Frank when we first started dating.

In the tall metal supply closet there were endless stacks of paper, more paperclips than any office ever really used, staples, which we really did use and then a small victory of the day. *Found the cartridge!* Also stumbled across an old bottle of red wine that was given to me last Christmas from Sue. Well, I could use this. Shrugging I took it from the shelf and hurried back to the reception desk; where I decided was the least creepy area to finish the orders.

I stared wide-eyed at the stack of papers on the desk. *Was there this much before I walked back there?* First, pulling a plastic cup from the water cooler then filling it with the wine, I sat down and committed to the work.

As the evening grew on thunder began rumbling outside as the office windows shook a little with each occurrence. Lately, storm season was in full effect.

Several cups, and a small dent in the pile later, I was deeply engrossed in my work with Adele serenading me via my MP3 player. I entered a nice zone of peaceful concentration. My problems eluded me as the contents of the bottle began to disappear. Then I remembered why I didn't drink anymore. At one point in my life I found myself too often turning to it, because it was an easy escape. Suddenly my peaceful zone disintegrated as I was startled by a knock at the door.

I stood up realizing that I was a little tipsy. It was 6:45, who could be knocking this late? A part of me hoped it was Brooke. My hopes were shattered when I opened the door and unexpectedly found myself alone in the office with the object of my sister's affection instead. *What is he doing here this late?*

Collin looked at me with his deep brown eyes that drew me in for a split second. His hair fell across his forehead like some Hollywood actor. It actually didn't look bad on him. With an unshaven somewhat scruffy five o'clock shadow, he was boyishly cute. *Wait no he's not. He's the enemy, remember? Damn that wine.* I blinked back into focus.

"She's not here," I said after recovering from my initial shock of his presence.

"I know," he said closing the door behind him.

"Sorry to bother you. Do you have a minute?" he asked.

I have many minutes. For you? No.

"What are you doing here?" I asked while spinning a quick 180 to return to the desk.

"Um ... Brooke just dropped me off. She saw that your car was still here. Anyway, I figured maybe we could talk?"

"Well, you're wasting your time." I didn't have time to stop to chit chat with the pretty boy who was causing friction between my sister and me. I wanted to finish my work. "We have nothing to talk about."

"Listen. I feel bad about earlier."

"It's between me and my sister."

"I know..."

"Did Brooke send you up here?" I asked cutting him off

again.

"No," he said.

"So then don't worry about it."

"But ... I know it's somewhat because of me."

I laughed. "So sure of yourself, huh?"

"I just don't want to cause any problems."

"What you saw earlier," I said, "Brooke and I aren't like that. We don't fight. Ever."

"She told me the same thing which is why ..."

"Look, ever since you two started, whatever this is. She acts different. With me. With work," I said firmly. "I don't like it."

"I'll talk to her," he said.

"I don't need you to talk to her for me," I said heading over to the door, opening it. "Now, if you don't mind, I have a lot of work to do."

"You know what ..." he said, "Just forget it." He sighed, shook his head and added as he walked out frustrated, "Brooke was right. You're impossible to talk to."

I hesitated to respond and actually felt a little guilty. *She said that?* Maybe I was a little hard on her sometimes but *impossible?* And no, I wasn't his biggest fan but maybe I was being unnecessarily hard on him. I wasn't used to someone taking so much of Brooke's attention from the family. And I couldn't shake the gut feeling that there wasn't any real chemistry between them, and that she was going to end up getting hurt.

"Collin, it's nothing personal. I'm only... looking out for my sister. That's all."

"It's fine. I get it," he said. "Have a good night."

"Yeah. You too," I said closing the door behind him.

Thank God he left. That was weird. I shook my head as if to clear my thoughts. *Back to work woman that's what you're here for!* I still had more orders finished than could be done in one night.

Back down at my computer, but my concentration was absent. Different thoughts clouded my mind. Maybe I was jealous of their closeness. He was a cute kid. I admitted to myself shrugging. And he seemed harmless, I guess. I closed my eyes and rubbed my temples. *Why are you still thinking about him!* While trying to regain my focus again, suddenly the wind grew stronger and the lights dimmed, threatening to turn off. *Come on.* The only other source of light was in my phone, which was dead. The last thing I needed was to sit in an almost dark office, alone. Unfortunately, for me my internal plea wasn't heard as the computer screen faded off along with all the lights. *Damn!*

CHAPTER 7

"Great," I muttered under my breath to a vacant room. I waited a few seconds and realized that the power wasn't going to be restored. Brooke's desk drawer didn't have a flashlight. I couldn't think of anywhere else where there might be an extra one. Thankfully, the office wasn't completely dark yet, since the summer's stormy cobalt sky provided some dim illumination. It may have been another hour before the sun set completely, but the clouds were taking over. *Great, I knew I should have gotten that generator that was on sale a few weeks ago.* The only reason I didn't buy it was because once it was in my car there was no one to carry it upstairs for us.

Startled *again* by another knock at the door. *Who is it this time?* I was ready to throw the pile on my desk into the storm at this point. Annoyed, I opened the door only to see that Collin had come back. *Yes, this is exactly what I need, another distraction.*

"Oh. You're back?" My tone sounded crass, but it wasn't intentionally. Why couldn't I be nice to Collin? Then those therapy sessions resurfaced where I was told I needed to let go of my anger toward my father and husband or it would compromise both my professional and personal relationships. Okay, maybe that's why. My anger toward my father and husband transferred to all men in general. I just couldn't help it. I was just so hard.

"Hey. Are you alright?" Collin asked me. "I heard on the radio that the roads to the tunnel are bad. So I was waiting in my car … the whole block just lost power."

"You were waiting in your car? Here?"

"I left with Brooke earlier. She dropped me off here. I came up to talk to you. Well, then you threw me out," he said, taking a few steps inside.

Checking on me? Then I can run back and tell Brooke. Gets him a few points. Makes sense.

"Look, I just came up to see if you're okay, that's all. You're obviously here by yourself," he added noticing my unwelcoming energy.

"Yes, I'm fine. It's just a little power outage."

"Do you want me to wait with you, until it's restored?"

"Why would I need you to stay with me?"

"You know what?" Collin's tone started to grow harsh. "I was just trying to be nice. Maybe I'm better off out there anyway. I don't even know why I bothered."

"Wait!" I sighed. "My phone died and I can't do much in this dark so…" I couldn't believe I was saying it; I was actually being vulnerable and asking for help.

"I suppose you could stay for a little while," I added, sighing apathetically.

"Well, thank you for the generous offer," Collin replied, sarcastically.

I ignored him. "Can you help me find some candles? I'm sure we have some. I have a lot of work to do, and I don't feel like being here all night."

"Okay."

Using the flashlight on his phone Collin helped me rummage around trying to find the candles in the office.

"So how long have you guys been here?" he asked, trying to make pleasant small talk.

"What? The business?" I asked, sounding irked, I'm sure.

"Yeah."

Okay, so he didn't notice my tone.

"Eleven years," I answered him dryly.

"That's good. Did you take any business classes?" He continued to converse casually.

"No." Another curt answer, by me. *Did he not notice I was in no mood for mindless chitchat?*

"Oh, so you probably just did some research? Read a few books on it?"

"Something like that."

"It must be nice. Not working under anyone…"

"Ah! Here are two!" I exclaimed, cutting him off as I found two candles.

"And here's two more!" he said, pleasingly.

So, together, we managed to find four candles. Two of them were placed on the reception desk and two on the filing cabinet behind it. My excitement didn't last long as I realized I didn't have anything to light them with – no matches, no lighter sticks, no lighter.

However, lo and behold, Collin pulled a lighter from his pocket and lit all four candles. The room took on a navy blue inconsistent, bouncy glow. The thunder rumbled as the rain began to sound like an Amazon waterfall. One of the candles was scented, a sweet girly fragrance with a baby powder undertone.

"I'll be there someday," Collin said, still rambling on about independent businesses. "Get to make your own schedule. And call the shots. You know you seem like the type who would have a business ..."

"Can we *please* just sit here quietly?" I sharply interrupted. *When did he become so talkative?*

"I'm going to finish these orders, and you do... um... whatever it is that you do." I continued, briefly lifting a handful of pages. "We don't have to talk. We really don't have to be friends. It's fine."

"Okay then," he said.

I sighed and resumed my place at the reception desk, wondering how much actually would get accomplished in the dark, with Mr. Talkative there.

"Just sit wherever," I said. "Make yourself comfortable," I added, making substantial effort toward being as cordial as possible.

Since the entire office was empty, every single desk and chair was available. There was Sue's desk, which was neat and would have been far enough to give each of us enough space. Or Michelle's desk, even though it wasn't as organized, it was close enough to the reception desk to receive ample lighting from the candles. But no, instead he decided to pull a chair up *directly next to me*, sit comfortably as if he were in his living room turning it around and facing me. He leaned his chest against the back of the chair.

I rolled my eyes and exhaled impatiently. "Look, I have ..."

"A lot of work. I know. You said it like ten times."

"So... "

"Do you need help?"

How thick can this person be?

"No. I'm okay," I muttered, trying to remain cordial.

"Alright." He shrugged and pulled out his phone. Then, all in one smooth move, he stood up, spun the chair around, sat back down, now facing away from me, and put his feet up on the desk. Headphones appeared from I don't know where and his music was blaring through the ear buds. He started clicking away at his blackberry. I wondered if he was texting with

Brooke, or some other girlfriend. It was hard to concentrate on the workload and even though I should have ignored him and continued working, it was difficult. It was as if he was doing it purposely to get under my skin.

"Ahem!" I said, clearing my throat exaggeratedly. I leaned over and tapped his arm. He took *one* earphone out.

"First of all. Please take your feet off my desk," I said through a fake smile.

"But didn't you tell me to get comfortable?"

His annoying question was answered with an impatient glare. He then complied removing his feet and replacing his headphone and continued to text on his blackberry.

The rain slammed sideways against the windows. Thunder shook the office and it felt like we were right there in the clouds. I was secretly a little happy that he was there. *Just a little.* But, I wouldn't let him know that. I couldn't believe I was starting to miss his idiotic small talk.

As branches from a nearby tree tapped, the windows hard it made me wish I had put tape on them. Nevertheless, back to work. Resume to the pile. It didn't seem to be getting any smaller any more.

Although I'm *finally* engrossed in my papers, my concentration is broken several times. Collin is drumming and humming to some rock song. To make matters worse his stupid phone seemed to keep going off every 15 seconds. My patience wears thin as I spin my chair around tapping him again.

"Is there any reason you're doing that?" I snapped.

"What am I doing?" he asked innocently.

"You know... I *am* trying to work."

"Oh, you should have told me that earlier."

I rolled my eyes and rubbed my temples. *It's seriously time to tune him out.*

"This entire office and you choose to sit right here," I muttered.

"I didn't know there was assigned seating," he said.

"You know what I mean."

"No. I don't. Why don't you explain it to me?" he asked nonchalantly.

"If you must know, I like my space."

"Actually, I disagree," he countered.

"It wasn't meant for you to agree or not. Not everything is all about you, you know."

56

"Definitely not about me," he said. "I was talking about *you*!"

"What the hell does that mean?" I asked.

"I could tell you," he said. "But I know you have a lot of work to do."

He had me there! I had nothing to say so I just sighed again. *Okay, if I don't ignore him completely, he is going to be nothing but an absolute distraction. A cute distraction. Wait, no, did I just think that? Make that, just a distraction. Yes, an annoying one.*

"So how many of those do you have to do?" he asked.

"About eighty."

"How many have you done?"

"Before you got here? Twenty. After? Maybe three."

"Oh. Well maybe you should try to focus more on your work and less on talking to me," he said. It was then beyond obvious that he was messing with me.

"Are you kidding me? Between the drumming and music and treating the desk like a foot stool ..."

He cut me off saying, "I'm flattered that I could be a distraction to someone like you."

"Flattered? Someone like me? You're talking in young people guy codes or something," I huffed, exasperated. "I really don't understand you."

He laughed. "You know how many times a day you probably throw some poor guy off. Make him forget what he's about to say, cause a car accident, bump into a pole ..."

"What do you mean? Wait ... uh ... are you hitting on me?"

"I can't pay you a simple compliment?"

"I guess," I said through a smile that I glad could be hidden in the darkness. "Thank you?"

He replaced his headphones and I rotated toward the papers again. I adjusted myself back in place at the desk where little was accomplished and took a sip of the wine that I forgot was there. Suddenly I find comfort in the plastic cup. *Maybe this will save me.*

Two more minutes of the rain pitter-pattering against the windows, the faint blare of his music, text message dings, and the otherwise quiet, dark office was driving me to insanity.

I glanced over at Collin and he was absorbed into something on his phone. The candle light gave his already appealing features a soft golden glow. He had beautiful eyes, highlighted by long eyelashes. I never noticed before, but I guess I wouldn't have. *He's going to look up and catch me starting at him, I just know it.* But, I suddenly couldn't help it.

I stood up abruptly.

"You want a drink?" I asked him, taking a deep breath as I blindly made my way to the water cooler, grabbing another plastic cup to fill with wine.

He paused the music again. "Did you say something?"

"I asked you if you wanted a drink. Here, it's two-thousand-eight Spottswoode Cabernet Sauvignon." I extended the cup to him.

"Thanks," he said taking the small peace offering from my hand. He then shook his head at me. "You're too funny." He laughed to himself.

"Me? I don't think I'm that funny."

"Trust me, you are," he said still amused.

"Okay. Whatever."

We were only quiet for five minutes, which seemed to be a record before he broke the silence again.

"So, Victoria," he said, as we walked back to the desk together, "I have to know. What was so important that you had to be here, this late at night, by yourself, during a storm?"

"I already told you," I said simply.

"No. Seriously. You don't think this could have waited until tomorrow?"

"Maybe," I said, and even though I knew nothing about him, I felt a sudden relief to talk to somebody. "Probably could have done them in the morning. You're right."

"But you chose to be here instead?"

"Maybe I'm just avoiding being home ..." I caught myself, mid-sentence, realizing I was exposing my vulnerability – to Brooke's boyfriend.

"Why?" he asked and actually sounded interested.

"Let me not bore you with the details."

"I don't think anything you could say would bore me," he said. Was he doing it again? Those strange compliments that needed decoding. At this point it was unclear if he was coming on to me or trying to be nice for the sake of my sister.

"What are you listening to?" I asked, changing the subject.

"Do you really want to know or is this a trick question?"

I rolled my eyes and exhaled. "I can be nice too."

"I listen to everything."

"What's *everything?*"

"Here," he said, hanging me his phone which was where he had his play list saved.

I scrolled through the diversity of his play list which included songs by Savage Garden, Nirvana, Coldplay, Linkin Park, Lifehouse, Usher, Swedish House Mafia, Daft Punk ... the list was endless.

"You have very interesting selections," I said as I unplugged the headphones so the songs could play aloud.
We needed some music to break through the quiet room. I played short excerpts of different songs, some I'd never heard of and some that I had. It was surprising how many of my favorite songs were in his play list.

"I love this song," I whispered almost to myself, surprised, as Seal's "Crazy" started to play.

I pressed the "skip" button and the next song to come on was Brian McKnight's "Anytime."

"Next," he said, leaning over me pressing the "fast forward" arrow icon.

"Oh. Okay ..." Maybe that song reminded him of someone.

"Jackson Five? That has to be before you were born," I said, teasingly.

"Well, I was born in nineteen eighty-seven. Still like them though."

"Eighty-seven? So you're twenty four?" I couldn't hide the shock in my tone especially considering that he was only several years older than Thomas.

"Yes, ma'am."

"Wow. You're younger than Brooke."

"Yeah, I know."
Suddenly the music that was once alternative and oldies is now playing a song in Spanish.

"Another one I love," I said.

"Son by Four," he said agreeably.

"Even though I have no idea what they're saying," I added.
"Really? I thought you would."

I shook my head.

"Well it's your regular break up song. He's calls his ex and tells her that he's sorry for calling but that he needed to hear her voice one more time. He says that ever since they broke up he feels empty and wants to see her. And he tried to live without her but feels like he's dying, like he has no air. And at night is when it's the most painful."

"Wow. You really understood all that?"

"Yeah. That's pretty much the whole song just in different verses."

"That's beautiful. But really… sad," I said as we quietly listened to the rest of the song.

"So, can you relate to this?" I asked noticing a sudden quiet transformation in him.

"Calling an ex in the middle of the night after a break up? Not exactly," he said shaking his head. "But the way the singer describes his feelings, yes."

This conversation was deep and at a whole other level of personal and uncomfortable. Should I dare dig deeper? I was too curious not to.

"Who is she?" I asked.

"No one important," he said but seemed nostalgically sad. I suddenly missed his annoying and sarcastic side.

I skip through a cluster of slower songs looking for something upbeat until I came across a salsa song. Although I didn't understand the lyrics the song was so popular that I felt like I knew it anyway.

"So how do you know Spanish?"

"Studied a little in school. But mostly from being around my ex and her family."

"Oh," I said and suddenly he started to seem like a mystery that I wanted to solve. "Is this the same unimportant ex we weren't talking about before?"

"Uh. Yup, same one," he said. "Anyway," he continued, changing the subject, "do you know how to dance to this?"

"No. I wish," I said.

He laughed. Then stood up, extending his hand.

"No. No. I don't think …" I objected.

"Come on, I'll show you. I think you need to have some fun," he said and began blowing out the candles.

"Seriously?" I asked as pitch darkness took over with exception to the backlight of his phone.

"It's not like you're really working anyway." Collin smiled as he started moving his shoulders in time with the music.

I laughed knowing the truth behind his words. He softly took my hands in his, gently trying to pull me from my seat to get me moving.

"Yes, but," I said, not budging, "I'm terrible!"

"It's easy," he insisted. Noticing I was still hesitant, he persuaded me with a new offer. "I'll help you with every single one of those orders you have if you forget about work for a few minutes."

Why not? I had nothing to lose. Just because I never had much fun didn't mean I couldn't treat myself for a change.

"Fine!" I gave in and stood up, my hands still in his. "I can't see anything though."

"Hold on," he said and walked over to Michelle's cubicle. "I have an idea." He opened the flashlight in his phone again. Then he placed it on her desk. Suddenly the backlight began blinking: blue, green, red, and yellow alternately strobe from his phone brightening the room each respective color. A different song began playing which was simultaneously blinking the colored lights.

"That works," I said, shrugging.

As the music played through the dim room and he led me to the largest area, which would serve as our dance floor. He stood directly in front of me taking my left hand and placing it around his neck. *Whoa. Didn't know this was going to be such a personal lesson.* My breathing hitched for a moment before I casually regained my composure. He was comfortingly warm and smelled so good. His right hand sat firmly on my waist and he took my free hand with his.

He seemed unaffected by the fact that we were about six inches apart as he began explaining the steps to me: where to start, when to step, the counts with the beat, and to follow him.

"Step with this foot when I step with this one." He tried to patiently demonstrate realizing that I had two left feet.

"You're supposed to be following me," he said as I went in some other direction.

"I'm trying," I said sheepishly. Listening for the beat was something that should have been natural to me, given that it was in my blood. However, over the years of getting used to a lifestyle of not dancing I never bothered to practice.

"Sorry," I said after stepping on his foot. I felt so clumsy which is far from any word I ever wanted associated with myself. I was not clumsy. I also was not some silly young girl to dance salsa with a stranger in the night. He was completely changing the game.

"Okay, wait," he said bringing me back to point A.

"What? I'm un-teachable right?"

"No. But," he said taking a step back, looking at me as if to figure out what to do to fix me. "Take your shoes off."

"That's not happening," I objected.

"Well those are what, like five inches?"

"Three. And, no, seriously. I'm fine."

"If you say so." He shrugged and we resumed to our starting position as he took my left hand again.

I wasn't fine. Still a little tipsy, maybe. And after about 20 more apologies for stepping on his feet I finally took his advice, ditching my heels and dancing, or trying to, in bare feet. I couldn't believe it. Were we randomly dancing together? Sort of.

I must have had too much to drink, especially since it was carefree dancing, forgetting about the stresses of the world. We were in our own realm of international music, rainbow darkness, silly laughter and letting go. The colored lights continued pulsating around us as we swung and dipped and whatever twirling motions I was trying to pull off. Finally, several salsa and Bachata songs later I took over his phone to play something I actually knew how to dance to.

Michael Jackson's "Billie Jean" was a fun icebreaker as we laughed and sang along horribly using pens for microphones. We both had terrible moonwalk impressions. If he was trying to win me over, he managed to succeed. We let two more songs play through before going back into work mode. Returning to my desk a happier feeling came over me. It felt like I found a part of me that existed buried deep below anger, stress, and resentment. In just one hour, Collin was able to show me something I hadn't seen inside myself in years. Something carefree.

Whether he knew it or not, Collin ignited an enticing spark between us. And, intentional or not, there was nowhere for either of us to run from it.

CHAPTER 8

Collin and I sat at the desk hand writing package labels and filling boxes using the candles and his phone for light. I glanced over at him, still slightly able to see him as the room kept its dim navy blue glow. I was consciously trying to hide my sudden strange fondness of him and his company.

The muscles in my eyes were beginning to hurt from the strain of reading in the dark for so long. I complained under my breath, squinting, while trying to read each detail of a poorly printed order receipt, as the sun completely descended for the night. Collin walked over to me and stood behind my chair. Before I could ask him what he was doing, he leaned over me and held his phone out using the backlight to illuminate the small area where I was writing. My breathing tethered again as I felt his bodies warmth over me. He smelled very clean and masculine, like faded cologne and some fresh mountain scented laundry detergent.

"Better?" he asked in a low voice.

"Thank you." My heart was thumping in my chest. We were so inappropriately close but I said nothing. He made me feel just awkward enough for it to be intriguing. The feeling was similar to the thrill before riding a roller coaster. I hadn't felt that jolt in the pit of my stomach in years.

I stood up abruptly, again, trying to find my grounds. I needed a refill. Blindly walking over to the filing cabinet behind me where I left the bottle. I poured two new cups handing him one.

"Can I ask you something?" I asked sitting next to him.

"Sure."

"Why are you being so nice to me?"

He shrugged. "Why not?"

"Because I was ... kind of a bitch."

"Kind of?" he asked, obviously trying not to smile. But, he couldn't hide it. Something genuine was going on. It was undeniable.

Regardless, I shot him a look to let him know whose boss.

"I'm kidding," he said. "You're not as bad as you think. You could say that I'm used to it."

Interesting, I thought to myself.

We sat, makeshift wine cups in hands, and the wind began to blow so hard that large branches flew and hit the window. It looked like trees were going to come crashing through. Several transformers began exploding giving off little firework-like shows each occurrence. When the winds picked up beyond a safe force, we decided to take refuge under the desk.

Collin and I actually ended up having a decent conversation. He was in his third year at NYU with a major in film studies with hopes toward working on a movie set someday. He went to school at night in addition to doing deliveries full time.

In such a short time, I completely changed my mind about him and understood why Brooke found him so fascinating. And he was, as she said, "sweet."

We finished the bottle and it showed as we carried on and laughed about the silliest things. It turned out that we also had a lot in common, from our favorite movies to eclectic tastes in music. Songs and artists most people never heard of were on both of our mp3 players. We shared our theories about the zombie apocalypse and vampires and exchanged stories of our own supernatural experiences. It was as if there was no age difference between us at all. And these were things I could never talk about with Frank. We also discussed politics, how we felt about the war, and conspiracy theories.

I didn't have many friends and it was a good feeling that for once in my life I actually felt like myself around somebody. Not giving orders, worrying about being judged, or feeling as if what I said didn't matter. We talked and he listened, and made me laugh. At this point, the only reason I really was still in that office was to have more time with him.

It was almost hard to ignore the romantic ambiance the candles were setting, as the rain slowed down. The flickering glow of the little Glade candle illuminated his face. He had a soft, amused expression fixed on me as I laughed about some funny story he told me.

"What?" I asked when he continued to stare.

"You have a great laugh," he said, smiling at me.

I looked away feeling my face flush.

He leaned closer to me and gently took my chin between his thumb and index finger, turning my head to face him.

"And a beautiful smile," he whispered, his face only inches

from mine. I never noticed how gorgeous he was. Maybe a little earlier that night, but at that moment we were up close and personal. He was virtually flawless when it came to looks. Deep almond shaped eyes gave him an exotic look. His hair looked bouncy and soft and I was tempted to run my fingers through it, the same way he had been running his fingers through his own hair all night. And that smile. It sent chills through me.

An undeniable magnetic feeling grew inside me. My lips were tempted to tread untamed waters. Tingling and wanting to know how his would feel against mine, I was fighting it with every bone in my body. He leaned in a little more and his soft lips brushed slightly against mine. It was torture, I wanted to know more than anything and I couldn't. I quickly withdrew from him.

"Wait. This is crazy. We can't. You and Brooke," I said as I looked away from him.

"I know. You're right." He sat back and exhaled running his hand through that damn soft looking hair again. I remembered that at some point earlier in the day it sat tamed with gel. Now it was a tussled mess and it drove me wild. I took another deep breath and had to look away again because my willpower was slowly diminishing as the alcohol increased in my blood.

Then there was an awkward silence. Not awkward because of the fact that he was dating Brooke and I was married and that we almost kissed, but awkward because we both still wanted to.

"Sorry if I gave you the wrong idea," I said. "You know, huddled under the desk with candles and wine and all." I shrugged innocently. We both laughed.

He sighed then said, "Figures. I meet the perfect woman, and she's my girl's married sister."

Perfect? Well, that's a first despite being with someone who allegedly loved me for 18 years. Perfect was never a word in Frank's vocabulary when it came to describing me, our marriage, or anything else at that.

"Don't worry. I'm not so perfect. Plus I'm old," I said.

"No, you're not," he said objectively. "You're beautiful."

I looked down at my wedding band and twirled around the diamond-studded shackle that represented all the imperfections and baggage that came with my life. Insults and cold lonely nights swirled through my mind. What would it be like to share a passionate kiss and feel desired again? I looked up at Collin again and that tempting feeling that never subsided was even stronger now. It may have been that tiny ounce of human connection I felt for the first time in years that fueled my actions. It didn't even feel like I was controlling anything, more like watching a movie of it all happening.

Almost as if in slow motion, I crawled over to him and in a moment, my body was all over his with both my hands on the floor on either side of him. My chest pressed against his. I could feel his heartbeat beating against mine, both drumming rapidly. I leaned in closer, our foreheads lightly touched. A slow, shaky breath escaped me. I closed my eyes, licked my lips, and lingered for a minute, both of us hanging in an enthralling anticipation.

"Should we be doing this?" he whispered.

"Probably not." The words barely escaped my lips before I lightly pressed them against his. His lips were so sweet and molded perfectly against mine. I think he was in shock and didn't know what to do at first, but when he kissed me back, my insides collapsed. The thunder, the lightning, the darkness, everything around me was insignificant as we floated away into some far away, distant, magical dimension where only the two of us existed. I curled my arms around his neck bringing him closer to me, bringing myself closer to him. Electric waves surged through my entire body. I pulled back, suddenly breaking the current.

"Sorry," I whispered, then bit my bottom lip as my nerves started to take over. "I just couldn't resist."

I stared into his eyes and saw and felt something deep. It was as if our souls were being reunited after lifetimes apart. The taste of wine and need and want lingered on our lips. He gently placed his hands on either side of my face and kissed me again, but this time deeper, more sensually. I closed my eyes and wrapped my arms around him again, and for that moment I felt so amazingly close to him.

Then, we were no longer in slow motion. It was happening in real time - whatever *it* was. An unfamiliar feeling of want overcame me as my blood warmed inside my veins, rushing through every part of my body. Every kiss was so sexy, so exaggerated. Our tongues passionately met as his hands tangled through my hair and mine through his. Finally! I entwined my fingers through his beautiful, soft strands. My heart raced. Breathing increased. *What is this kid doing to me?*

And with that last thought, like a bad omen, or a warning from a higher power, the entire room was bright again. As if a hypnotist suddenly snapped his fingers, both Collin and I were released from the trance. Our spark extinguished as we both suddenly looked around, startled, blinking from the shock of the lights. We awkwardly scrambled out from under my desk and couldn't even look at each other.

"Um... wow... okay..." He searched for the same words I also struggled to find.

"What are we doing? What am *I* doing?" I ironed my hair and clothes with my hands feeling like a frazzled mess. "You should go," I said. Trying to steady my breathing was difficult as if I ran a mile or two.

He turned toward the door but hesitated for a moment then quickly swung back around facing me.

"Wait. Should we talk about this?" He asked, moving closer to me.

"No. You need to leave," I said, taking a step back still avoiding his eyes that I now believed held some kind of mystical powers. It was confusing and I needed to be alone.

He hesitated again. It was obvious that he wanted to say more.

"Are you okay getting home?"

"Yes. Just go." The words came out quickly because I wanted him to leave. "Please."

Defeated, he opened the door and stepped into the hallway. I think he was waiting for me to stop him, but I kept my eyes firmly planted on the desk.

"Okay... well... Goodnight. Be careful on the roads," he said quietly as he walked out.

Collin disappeared down the hall. I shut the door and exhaled. *Oh my God. How did that happen? What just happened? Call Brooke!* Wait, I can't call Brooke. Shit, did I kiss my sister's boyfriend? I paced back and forth through the office. I've never cheated on my husband. I never even came close. Never. He couldn't find out!

A million thoughts raced through my mind as I began to clear the evidence of my unintentionally romantic night. I felt so guilty. Of all the men for me to kiss why did it have to be him? In a situation like this Brooke would be the first person I would have run to for advice, and now I didn't know what to do. I felt like a fool. How could I let pure lust overrule common sense?

Damn! I'm so pissed at myself!

Did Collin just take advantage of the situation? No, he was too sweet. He wanted to talk about what happened. This was something real. Or the start of something real. No! This was not a start. It was a mistake. A huge mistake!

I'll just go back to my life and act as if this never happened.

I looked over my entire office and decided to take one step at a time to straighten up. I threw away the cups, put all the chairs back into their original places, threw the wine bottle into the recycling bin, and started to lock up. Then I realized I had Collin's awesome smell all over me. What was I to do now? Well, knowing that Frank he wouldn't even notice, but just in case, I went to the bathroom and quickly patted myself down with soap and water. Remembering I kept a toothbrush in my desk, I decided to brush my teeth too. I didn't want to take a chance that Frank may smell the wine on my breath.

How did I get into this mess! Before taking another step, I did another once-over to make sure everything looked normal. I took out the little garbage in the office knowing that the women wouldn't miss the wine contents in the bin. Then I had to sit and catch my breath. Once I finally had my bearings together, I finally locked up, and walked to my car.

As I sat in the car, the thought I was avoiding for the last 20 minutes crept back up on me. That kiss. That incredible close feeling that I never experienced with anyone, not even with Frank. As much as I tried to pull my thoughts back to reality, what happened *was* reality. It wasn't fake at all. It was something deep and scary. It didn't make sense. The drive home didn't help give me enough time to stop freaking out internally. Thank goodness, the black Range Rover wasn't there. I let out a huge sigh of relief.

At my house everyone was asleep, even Kiwi. I replaced the ink to the printer and printed Ashley's assignment for her. Galina left two plates of food with a cover on each one. Unable to eat, I put the chicken and rice into a Tupperware and stuck it in the refrigerator to save for lunch.

My bedroom was the same way I left it in the morning. The teal and plum duvet still tucked in place with all seven pillows assembled neatly on top. It was 11:30, yet it was no surprise that Frank wasn't home. I placed my phone on the nightstand to charge. He never even responded to my text. I did see where Brooke tried to get in touch with me and a wave of guilt encompassed me. *What did I just do – to my own sister?*

While undressing, I noticed a subtle hint of clean cologne that lingered on my shirt. *Damn*, I thought I washed all the evidence out in the bathroom at the office. Guess not! However, guilty as I felt, instead of my shirt being tossed into the laundry basket, it found a home in my dresser drawer. I climbed into my empty bed and snuggled with my pillow, hoping to maybe dream of untamed hair, mystical eyes and passionate kisses.

CHAPTER 9

The day after the blackout avoiding Brooke was my best solution while trying to sort out several confusing emotions that swam through my mind. It may have not been the best one, but what was I supposed to do? She falls for a guy who I lecture her about for weeks, because of my own negativity toward men in general. Then I kiss him and want nothing more than to do it again and again.

She finally stopped me before lunch, confronting me about avoiding her. She apologized again about the drama show she put on. Little did she know; I should be apologizing to her as well.

Of course, I would never intentionally have gone after someone that she was interested in. And there she was, in her ignorant bliss, excited about her next date with Collin. It hurt me that I couldn't tell her. What would her reaction be? This could possibly break her heart to pieces.

Considering that Frank couldn't find out, hoarding the secret was the best temporary solution, at least until I figured out what to do.

The paper pile that always seemed to grow was still staring at me yet another reminder of the blackout and all of the random, unspoken, experiences between Collin and me. After a few more hours of work, the pile gradually shrunk and finally, down to 11 more orders, even though it felt like 1100.

Every time I started to read addresses and item descriptions my mind drifted into a place, a place that brought sweet, comforting darkness back into the office and I could feel his mesmerizing presence and his warm, delicate touch. That electric feeling that ignited deep inside me when our lips met was impossible to forget. The butterflies came back to life, just thinking about it. I closed my eyes and inhaled a slow, deep breath. As I exhaled, I promised myself that with it to also exhale the memory of his touch, the electric feeling, and the naughty fantasy that kept replaying in my mind about what would have happened if the power hadn't come back on. *Okay,* I sighed to myself. Now, 10more orders to finish.

The day didn't get easier. All day and night on Thursday, thoughts of Collin constantly popped into my head: his captivating smile, his delicious clean smell, his soft lips … The constant absence of my children, husband, and sister left me way too much time for my mind to wander.

By Friday, I somehow managed to distract my thoughts only to be reminded of him again by Brooke. She was meeting with him after work. I tried to bury the little tinge of jealousy that was growing inside.

What a horrible sister I was. I couldn't help the way I felt about Collin after that one random night. Even though I knew the answer, I once again asked myself if it was real. Was he thinking about me too? After clocking out, I quickly escaped the office without giving Brooke the opportunity to boast, even though it would have been unintentional. *She still thinks I hate him.* Boy, things change so fast. First, I was avoiding her because of my guilt. Then I was avoiding her because I was jealous. *This is pure insanity. Why did I ever get involved? This is just so difficult on so many levels!*

The weekend dragged, most of it spent alone in my "home." Galina had the weekends off and utilized her time running her personal errands. Nick and Ashley were staying at Debra's for the weekend. She was having a campout in the backyard with the children, as they did. That was Aunt Debra: soccer mom, class mom, white picket fence, camp in the back yard, Debra. I rolled my eyes knowing how far from that I was.

Every sound in the house seemed to echo as I sorted through the assortment of mail that accumulated from the week. Kiwi chased her tail in the dining room, stopped, attacked a squeaky toy, and then repeated the process. I called her over, but the rubber burger was winning her attention. So much for companionship.

I sighed, clicking my pen. The numbers on the statements didn't interest me. Balances due, paid, current, I wasn't the least bit worried about how the bills were getting paid. Our checking account and CDs were worth well over $500,000. Those who envied my life, how little they knew. I was genuinely bored and all alone. Frank was somewhere, either at work or some other nightclub. A strip club maybe? I lost track of his whereabouts years prior.

The funny thing was that we had enough money for me to disappear and start a new life somewhere else; a peaceful place where Frank couldn't hurt me; where I didn't expose my children to a dysfunctional relationship. I would no longer live in fear that my daughter would follow in my footsteps, since it seemed to be a vicious cycle, starting with my mother. Or that my son would become just another chauvinistic abuser. I've created my utopian life in my mind several times. The weather was always warm, sky always blue, surrounded by only those who I truly loved.

Upset, and brought back to the real world, the thought of Collin and Brooke re-entered my mind. I wondered how their date went. *Lucky Brooke.* I may have been getting on her case over the last few weeks, but in the end, they were the ones whom I envied. He was so passionate. Then again, how could he look her in the eyes after what happened between us? Maybe the connection that I thought we had was just a figment of my bored and overactive imagination.

Despite my growing curiosity, I chose not to bother Brooke all weekend and she didn't get in touch with me at all either. Thank goodness, Monday rolled in when it did and anticipation freed me from its grip. Damn, they must have spent the entire weekend together. The thought was unnerving. I didn't know why it affected me so much, but I was truly bothered by it.

Again, as usual on Monday mornings, Michelle was quiet, Sue hummed old melodies to herself, and Brooke started up the computers, settling into her desk. I circled around pretending to have something better to do before going all Diane Sawyer on Brooke. Walking up to her expecting to see a Cheshire cat grin on her face I was surprised to find quite the opposite.

"How was your weekend?" I asked her casually, unsure if I should sit as her body language suggested otherwise. "I thought you would call me."

"It was okay," Brooke said simply. She placed her purse down and started checking the phones and computer. We didn't exchange any eye contact.

"Just okay?" A few weeks ago, he was the most amazing bachelor ever, a possible candidate to be her first serious boyfriend since high school. I spent the past 72 hours stressed over a weekend that was summarized as "okay."

"It's sort of complicated," she said, now fiddling with her cell phone.

Should I dare to ask her the specifics? What could be so "complicating" about a date?

Then my face got all flushed and my heart began racing.

Oh no! It dawned on me. She knew! She knew about what happened between Collin and me! No, he wouldn't tell her. Would he?

I tried so hard to play it cool. "Well … what about your date?"

"Eh," she said, frowning. "Yeah, that was a disaster." She grumbled. "Turns out, he's not really my type after all."

He's not her type or she's not his?

"Oh," I said, desperately trying to keep the pep in my tone to a minimum. "I'm surprised. You were so excited about him."

"What do you care?" she asked angrily, adding, "You were right. I'm sure that's what you want to hear." She started fiddling with anything else she could on her desk.

"No, I didn't mean it like that," I said, trying to sound concerned. I put my hand on her shoulder and asked, "Did something happen?"

"Yes," she said, pulling away from me and parking herself in front of the computer screen. "But I don't want to talk about it."

"Okay." Not wanting to beleaguer the situation, I walked away.

Her sudden change of heart was unexpected. I had to bury the little bit of me that was doing cartwheels inside about their unexpected breakup. It was so selfish and made me feel terrible for rejoicing in her heartache. Although, over the next few days she didn't really seem heartbroken. Brooke was quiet, mostly around me. However, it wasn't a sad kind of quiet, more mysterious than anything. She was hiding something from me. Did she know and not know how to confront me? Or was she choosing to silently resent me? Of course, there was only one other person who could confirm my suspicions and I hadn't seen him. Not once since that night.

Keeping an eye out for deliveries became an arduous task. Every day only Sean would show up. Knowing that Sean and Collin usually alternated, I couldn't help but wonder why Collin was avoiding us. The mystery of what happened between him and Brooke ate at me when I went home, still wondering and thinking about him.

* * * *

The house was busy that evening and more than just the

usual four pairs of shoes were scattered by the door. A pair of strappy fire engine red sandals and gray Converses was also strewn about. Quickly I reviewed through my mental calendar knowing there were no birthdays or special occasions that I'd forgotten about.

A collection of teenagers invaded my kitchen. "Hi mom!" Ashley greeted me happily. Her two favorite people, Terrance her boyfriend, and Morgan, were over for dinner and greeted me in unison. Frank was sitting with Nick in the living room watching a UFC fight. Galina made cooking for seven look like second nature.

"Thank you so much," I said to Galina putting my hand on her shoulder. "Do you need help?"

"No problem at all. Everything's ready," she said placing the wooden spoon onto the stainless steel spoon rest. Sauce from the fettuccine Alfredo dripped off the edge onto the chrome stovetop. She quickly whisked it away with a rag and brought the pot to the table. I followed her with a pan of sautéed mushrooms and onions and placed it onto a ceramic trivet that was already set on the dining room table.

"Everything good with the kids?" I asked.

"Hmm … yes..." She stretched out the "yes" and I knew it actually meant "no."

"Oh no. What happened now?"

"Nicholas has Saturday detention," she said with a scowl.

I shook my head. "What has gotten into this kid?" I walked into the living room where both Frank and Nick greeted me dryly without their eyes leaving the TV screen. I crossed my arms and cleared my throat barely stirring a reaction from either one.

"Nick, what's this I hear about detention?"

"Mom, it's nothing," he replied, frustrated. "Dad already talked to me."

My eyes darted to Frank and he glanced at me for a second. "Yeah, yeah, we went over this already."

"It's cool, Mom."

"No... it's not *cool* Nicholas." I sighed.

"Damn, Victoria!" Frank yelled at me. "Leave the kid alone. I discussed this with him already." Always making me the bad guy, always pitting my child against me, Frank was really making this kid turn out to be a monster.

I decided to stand my ground and said to Nick, "We will

talk about this later."

We didn't end up eating together as everyone scattered out. Morgan joined the guys in the living room, while Ashley and Terrance took Kiwi out for a walk. Maybe Morgan had a crush on Nick. That poor kid didn't know what she was in for if that's the case. I can't imagine Nick treating a girl right. No way. He's on the same path as his dad, unfortunately, a misogynist in the making. Or maybe she just didn't want to be a third wheel, I figured — and hoped, for her sake.

*   *   *   *

So now, it was a full three weeks after *that* night – the night that continued to invade my thoughts –and Collin seemed to have disappeared. He didn't come around to make any deliveries. Not to share inside jokes with Princess Brooke. And definitely not to flatter and amuse me.

"Hello?" Brooke was waving her hand in front of my face, breaking my momentary zone out as I leaned by the Xerox machine waiting for copies.
"Welcome back. You alright?" she asked.

No, I'm not! What happened? How could you be head over heels one second, then just stop talking and never mention him again?! I wanted to scream this out, but I suppressed it.

I blinked my eyes a few times and took a sip of my coffee hoping I'd find the answer to all my problems in the caffeine. I'd been feeling so off lately. If I were looking to feel normal again, I would need a triple shot espresso.
"Yes, sorry, I have lot on my mind," I answered.
If she only knew. For three weeks now so many questions filled my head. Why had Collin disappeared from the face of the earth? Did Brooke know what really happened? And if not, how and why did their relationship end? And, most of all, why did he continue to consume my thoughts? What did this young man do to my head?

"Oh. Well, I was asking you if you would be able to sit in front for me so I could go with Michelle to Panera."

"Sure," I said gathering a folder to stick the papers into. I followed behind her to the entrance of the office where I made myself comfortable at her desk. The reception desk. Great. For the next hour, I'll be sitting up here waiting for the phone to ring as thoughts of Collin invaded my head, once again. Those memories. How could he have had such an impact on me in that short time? We didn't even spend three hours together, and yet I couldn't shake the thought of him. That spell Brooke was under at one point was now apparent to me, and it was contagious, too.

I planned to ask Brooke to pick up lunch for me but, before I had the chance to speak, she disappeared with Michelle. I slumped into the chair. I guess the chips from the vending machine down the hall would have to be a sufficient substitute to a decent lunch.

She didn't even invite me, I thought, sulking a little. It was so unusual for Brooke to leave me out of her lunch plans. Was it because…? No. I had to stop obsessing over it. I could just ask her when she returned. Then again, what if she didn't know? I'd be giving her a reason to be angry with me. It was a lose/lose situation.

My thoughts were interrupted by someone walking into the office. All I saw were three brown packages and I immediately sat up straight, my heart in my throat, I quickly started to fix my hair. My optimism quickly morphed into disappointment when Sean's smile greeted me instead of *his*.

"Good afternoon," he said, placing each package to the side of the desk, then handing me the clipboard. "Just three today."

I took the packages from him still recovering from the letdown.

"Hi, Sean. How's your day going?" Despite my hopefulness to see our other delivery person, it was nice to encounter super-friendly, easy going Sean. At least he didn't make me feel frazzled.

"Can't complain. Day's half over. I'm headed to lunch from here," he said glancing around. "Hey where's your sis?"

"She actually just went to lunch," I said signing the electronic tab on the clipboard.

"Oh. What about you?" he asked casually.

"Got my lunch right here," I said holding up a bag of pretzels.

"That's not lunch! You should come with me to get pizza, I'm headed there now."

Not him too. *Did I have delivery boy bait stamped across my forehead?*

"Thanks, but I'm okay. You go ahead."

76

"Aw just come. This might be the last time you ever see me."

He had my attention. "Wait, why?"

"I graduated last week. I'm off to California next Tuesday. I start interning for Blue-jay Productions in Los Angeles."

"Wow, congratulations!" I said, going around the desk to give him a hug.

He turned around to walk out and a thought crossed my mind. If I wanted to talk to Collin again, Sean would be an easy way to connect back to him. It wasn't like I could get to him through Brooke. I decided that I was officially slightly delusional, but putting that aside, I grabbed my purse and called out to him.

"Wait. I changed my mind! I can peel out for a few. It's not too busy today."

I asked Sue to operate the phones while I was gone. Sean and I went to Renato's Pizzeria, which was around the corner from the office. Sitting in a booth, I felt like a high school student going out to lunch again. Ever since Frank started working all the time, we never got to enjoy simple things, like going out to eat at a pizzeria. Renato's was cute. Dark wooden tables were covered with picnic patterned red and white plaid tablecloths. The staff was friendly and it smelled amazing in there, like fresh tomato sauce and basil.

Sean devoured two not too greasy pepperoni slices as he told me about the school he planned to attend in California. I rolled little cherry tomatoes across a bed of lettuce. *Don't play with your food*, I could hear myself telling my children years ago. I couldn't help it, I was so distracted plotting how to bring Collin into the conversation without seeming obvious. The two work together, so Sean must know something.

Sean talked about college, until he paused to finish his food, and I found my opportunity to fulfill my hidden agenda. *Think fast*, I thought to myself. I need to speak up now because other than confronting Brooke there's no one else I knew who knew Collin. It would just tear me apart if I never saw him again. I needed answers and I was desperate.

"It's nice to see you pursing your dreams," I said, casually, as we continued to eat. "So, will Collin be taking over your route now?"

"Probably not," he said shrugging.

"Oh. Well I haven't seen him around. He did mention that

he goes to NYU. My daughter is interested in going there and it would be nice to get some information about campus life, tuition, things like that, you know?" That was the most believable lie I could fester.

"I'm sure Collin could give you some first-hand information!"

"You think so?" I played dumb and tried to hold out in asking for his number until Sean offered first, hoping he didn't already know my little secret.

"Of course he'll help you," said Sean. "He's really cool." Sean put down his fountain soda and pulled out his phone. "Let me get his number for you." Ah, bingo! It was a big relief to realize Sean was so clueless. I reached into my purse but realized that I left my phone on Brooke's desk next to my laptop. *Good job, Victoria.*

"Left my phone at the office."

"Oh. Okay. Well I'll text him now for you." He started clicking onto his keypad. What was he saying? I shifted around nervously. Twenty seconds after he stopped typing, his phone made a ding-like sound. Oh wow, he was talking to him *right now, about me.* What did he say? I felt the same fluttering in my stomach that I felt the night of the black out. A few more dings came through. Sitting in suspense. *Aren't I too old to be feeling like this?* I wondered to myself.

Sean looked up at me. "You want me to give him your number instead?"

"Oh. Um," I said caught off guard. I couldn't give him my number, not while being married to a modern day Henry Hill.

"Well... it's a new number. I don't remember it." I lied.

"Here, why don't you talk to him," Sean said handing me his phone. Me talk to him? The thought sent my heart working double-time.

"I'm getting another slice. Do you want anything else?" he offered. I shook my head and he made his way back to the counter leaving me there with his phone in my hand. Collin on the other end of the conversation. It was the closet I'd been to him since the kiss that haunted me.

All that time I spent thinking about him and suddenly I had no clue as to what to say. I started to type into Sean's phone. Hello? No. Delete. How are you? No. Delete. What do the young people say? Sup? Hell no. Quickly delete. Finally, I went with something simple.

78

Me: Hi.

A response came through after a few seconds.

Collin: Hey how r u?

Me: Fine. You?

Collin: I'm good.

Seriously? We're engaging in small talk? After going to this ridiculous extent to talk to him. I decided to take it up a notch.

Me: You've been avoiding us?

Collin: A little

Me: Is it because of me? Or Brooke?

Collin: Honestly?

Me: Please.

Collin: You

Me: Why?

He didn't respond right away. Was he thinking or busy? Or did he just decide to stop writing back? I put the phone down and returned to my salad. Another ding sound came through.

Collin: I think you already know why.

No, I don't know! That was the whole point. He hated me because I ruined his relationship with Brooke? Hopefully not. Or because he felt the same connection that I did and also couldn't understand it.

Me: Can we talk in person?

Collin: Yeah, can you meet me tonight?

Tonight? I should check my busy schedule first, of doing nothing and watching my dog run around in circles. Stare at all the wonderful money in our checking account that Frank was spending on mistresses.

Me: Sure. Where?

Collin: I have class till 7... could we meet after? 246 West 65th St.

Me: New York?

Collin: Yeah, or lemme know if you wanna meet in Jersey

Me: No. It's fine.

As I typed the last message, I rolled my eyes. His text grammar, or lack thereof, irked me. I memorized the address, deleted the conversation and returned Sean's phone to him. I started to feel my lips turn upward into a smile, thinking about how silly all this was, but quickly hid it behind my hand and casually coughed. Sean gave me a suspicious look, but shrugged it off.

"How was the pizza?" I asked in attempts to divert his attention from the situation.

"Great," he said nodding his head in approval. I know he considered it for a moment, but didn't dare ask what kind of weird exchange was going on between me and his co-worker.

Several minutes later, I thanked Sean for joining me for lunch and headed back to the office. While sitting at my desk I recited the address Collin gave me wondering if I should discard it into my mental trash can. Who was I kidding? All of those memories and daydreams — I had to see him. We definitely needed to talk. No, the memories and daydreams should not be the reason for this meeting! The motivation for meeting Collin will be strictly to talk. And not about me, not about us, but about Brooke. To make sure he didn't break up with her because of what happened with me. Even more important, that he didn't break up with her to be with me! Yes, he's many years younger than me, but we are both adults. We should have known better. Now, we are being adult about the whole situation and talking about it. After tonight, this whole Collin *thing* will be finished!

CHAPTER 10

That evening my house was quiet. Ashley and Morgan sat at the kitchen counter on the laptop looking through their social networking sites. My 16-year-old daughter convinced me, after several attempts, to join the social networking website, Facebook. It seemed so juvenile, but it was a good way for me to keep track of what she was doing. And stalk the rest of the world whenever there was nothing better to do.

I left the girls to their browsing and went upstairs —I had browsing of my own to do. In my closet. So. Many. Clothes. What to wear? What does one wear when she is meeting to talk with her sister's ex-boyfriend, to whom she is undeniably attracted? I didn't want him to get the wrong idea. Again. Still, my intentions were nothing more than to talk and get to the bottom of what happened with Brooke.

Finally, after rejecting every dress because they were inappropriate, every suit because they were too professional, and every pair of shorts because they were too laid back, I decided on a peach colored V-neck shirt with white jeans. My favorite gold sandals won the battle of the many shoes to pair with my outfit. I grabbed my denim jacket and looked in the mirror. Nice. Too nice? I shrugged and went downstairs. Both girls complimented my outfit, impressed. I lied to them about where I was going. Kiwi was happy when I threw her a treat before leaving.

I entered the address Collin gave me into my GPS. It took almost an hour to get through the Lincoln tunnel and into Manhattan. That hour was spent honking at crazy yellow taxicabs and singing aloud to Aerosmith. When I wasn't singing I was arguing with the nonexistent woman whose voice in my dashboard would occasionally tell me to "turn left" at the last minute. Finally, at my destination, I found myself in front of a stunning high-rise apartment building in midtown Manhattan, near Central Park West. This is where he lives?

I parked my car in a nearby lot on 66th street and walked to the building. A tornado of emotions overwhelmed me at the thought of seeing him again. When I approached the front, I stood under the maroon awning that extended across the sidewalk from the glass double doors to the street. I hesitated, feeling unsure, and lingered for a moment alongside some ornately sculptured bushes, then I entered the lobby and tried to brush away the negative feelings.

Gorgeous beige and black tiled floors sparkled in the well-lit space that smelled of a clean lemon scented floor wash. Red and cream leather sofas and chairs were carefully placed throughout the waiting area. Modern ivory and brown painted walls and panels, and round lights scattered across the ceiling. It looked like some five star hotel. Every detail was impeccable. There wasn't an ounce of dust or dirt in sight.

"Can I help you?" A friendly man, about 50-years-old, with a welcoming disposition was smiling at me and suddenly either the room was getting bigger or I was shrinking. It felt like a spotlight was shining on me on a stage on opening night. My face felt warm as I looked down at my wedding ring wondering if the man, whose bronze plated name-tag read Ian Johnson, would think it suspicious if I told him that I was there to see the newly single young male model in apartment 23J.

"Good evening," I said smiling at him as well. "Yes, I'm just visiting... uh... a friend." *Please don't ask me details. Just give me a visiting pass and I'll be on my way.*

"Sure. What apartment?"

Great. I reluctantly told him. He ran his finger along a list stopping at the number I had just given him then picked up a black old-fashioned telephone. He glanced up at me. "Your name, Miss?"

I froze. I had to give my name? I didn't want any record of me being there. I wanted to be invisible.

He noticed my hesitation. "I have to announce all guests." The opportunity of anonymity was lost. He was calling *him*.

"Victoria Carlisle," I said looking away, my voice small. He called up to the apartment before buzzing me through another glass door, which led to a hallway. To the left were two sets of elevators. I pressed 23 and waited as each floor number lit as the elevator ascended. I tried to remember exactly what I wanted to say but it all started to slip my mind as the shiny chrome doors parted open to a silver 23 placard on the wall. The hallway stretched to both the left and right of the elevators.

I hesitated at first not sure which way to go. The sign on the wall had two arrows indicating the correct direction for each apartment. A through M was to the left, N through Z to the right. I turned left and walked down the hallway reading the apartment letters on each door. G, H, I ... J. There was a little doorbell that I rang and waited a few moments until the door opened.

And there he was. A more beautiful site than what I remembered. Collin stood in the doorway, coolly, in dark denim ripped jeans and a charcoal gray t-shirt. He managed to make casual look super sexy. If I wanted to successfully have a conversation with him maybe, I should have brought a blindfold.

"Hi, Collin." It took every effort to keep a calm, collected exterior. On the inside? The complete opposite.

"Please, come in," he said backing into the door so I could pass him and enter. He shut the door behind him. A short hallway led to a large living room. A round glass table sat in what appeared to be an eating area that was on the opposite side of the kitchen. A breakfast bar divided the cooking and eating areas. I strolled slowly through his apartment and he cruised behind me.

One entire wall was made up of five floor to ceiling windows, a breathtaking view of lively New York City panned across the living room. A sliding glass door led to a large terrace. I ran my hands along the long door handle tempted to get a better view.

"Go 'head. Its open," he said, encouragingly.

"No. It's okay," I said, shaking my head. As much as I wanted to my fear of heights wouldn't allow it.

"So what's up?" he asked. So cool, and calm. He walked over to a set up bar area. "Can I get you a drink?"

"Some water. Thanks."

He looked over at me. "That's it?"

I nodded. Alcohol, him, and I didn't mix. Not again. I swallowed hard remembering that night.

"We should talk," I said over my shoulder as I continued scrutinizing his entire apartment.

"I think that was the plan," he said somewhat mocking me. I shot him a warning look. He was still cool and collected and now smiling at me as he leaned slightly against the counter. He was so nonchalant while I was over there fighting the fluttering from funneling in my belly.

The chic off-white leather sofa, which was adjacent to a grey leather chaise, complimented a white area rug. Meticulously

84

chosen wall art, which included large canvas oil paintings of abstract contemporary shapes, Michelangelo's The Creation of Adam, Van Gogh's Cypresses and Night Cafe, a poster of Salvador Dali's Melting Clocks, and random professional photographs of New York landmarks made me wonder who decorated his place. Maybe he's an interior designer on top of being a bilingual delivery driver, male model, film student, and apparently now possible bank robber, because how else could he afford an apartment in this neighborhood?

"So ... what are we talking about?" he asked gliding smoothly toward me.

"A few things," I said taking a sip of water, waiting for him to make one of his slick comments. He caught me off guard at the office, but this time I was guarded and ready.
"First of all," I continued, "what happened that night ..."

"You look beautiful by the way," he interrupted and was suddenly at my side. He carefully brushed aside the hair that fell over my shoulders running his fingers across the back of my neck.

I cautiously took a few steps away from him. I knew where this was going. "Thank you. But like I was saying..."
I paused ... *What was I saying?* He was doing it again. My mouth was dry. I took another sip of water and then it came back to me. "That... that kiss... or whatever it was."

"We don't have to talk about it," he said still inching closer to me and now I could smell his clean cologne scent. "I was there too. Remember?"

"Yes, but. It ... it shouldn't have happened. And, well... it is or was ... um it ..." I rambled, struggling to make sense and horribly failing. Pausing again to collect my thoughts before I made myself sound like a complete idiot if it wasn't already too late for that.

I finally blurted out, "So, what happened? Was there ... no chemistry?" Great, that didn't even make sense. I just couldn't talk to him.

"Huh?" he asked trying to figure out what I was talking about. "I think there was."

"Then ... she ended it?" I asked.

"Wait. Who?"

"Brooke."

"Brooke?" He stopped and stepped away from me a little. He looked surprised that I brought her up.

"No," he said, sounding confused.

"So, then *you* ended it?"

"Yeah. I guess." He shrugged. "Why are we talking about your sister?" He stopped for a moment looking down before his eyes met with mine again. "Is that why you're here? To talk about what happened between me and Brooke?" His eyes were soft and his full focus on me.

"Yes. Why what were you talking about?"

"Us."

"Us?" I asked stunned.

"That's what I said." As he said this, I looked at him and then it happened again. The rushing urges filled my veins. He moved in closer to me and there was nowhere to run. Backed against the wall trapped as his prey. And it didn't bother me one bit.

"So, I'll ask you again," he said. His forehead was lightly touching mine, every part of his body pinning me against the wall. "Are you sure that's why you came here?"

"Yes," I said softly, not able to believe my own lie as it came out.

"I thought you like your space," he said, challenging me.

"I lied," I whispered, wanting nothing more than his lips against mine.

His beautiful eyes were now dark and mesmerizing as they drew me in deeper. He ran his hand along the side of my face and gently raised my chin, intensely staring at me before leaning in to kiss me. He moved cautiously and confidently at the same time as if he was expecting me to push him away not realizing what I'd been fantasizing about every day for the last three weeks.

My knees wobbled … my body like gelatin as he embraced me. Our bodies pressed close together and I could feel his pulse rapidly increasing. I brought my lips to meet his as he gently took my face with both hands kissing me softly. Kissing him back, we were lost in a fiery explosion of intense desire.

He lowered his lips to my neck and shoulders, and his hands ran over my breasts then down slowly over the curves of my waist. Again, he locked his lips into mine. I couldn't stop him. I could no longer try to deny or understand the burning attraction I felt for him. Kissing him felt amazing. And the other amazing feeling; being wanted. Every single touch electrified me. Deep down I'd been yearning for the attention

86

that I got from him. It was just like the night at the office, except this time there were no boundaries.

We were enthralled in one passionate kiss after another. He ran his hands slowly up and down my sides. It felt like static electricity as he caressed my thighs. He kissed my cheek and neck and then moved his lips down to my chest, paying careful attention to every single detail of my body.

I pulled off his shirt, threw it on the floor, and ran my hands over his firm chest. I practically dissolved to nothing at the sight. Of course, he would have a perfect body. Amazing toned arms, chiseled abs, and to my surprise a few unexpected tattoos across his chest, biceps, and forearms. I ran my fingers over them, down to his abs and it just made me want him more.

I ran my hands up and down his back scraping slightly with my fingernails and kissing his neck. Who was I kidding? I couldn't resist him. I surrendered to my temptations.

I gasped with surprise when he picked me up, wrapping my legs around him. Pinning me harder against the wall. The room suddenly felt like an inferno and I desperately wanted to melt all over him. With my arms around his neck he carried me to the sofa and we both collapsed together never detaching from one another.

Damn, he's a really good kisser. He took his time and the way he touched me was perfect. I could hardly breathe. I closed my eyes and absorbed every single sensation that he sent through me. Every inch of my body was tingling with intense desire for more. He slowly unbuttoned my jeans and artfully worked them down my legs. This suddenly triggered a nervous, uneasy feeling. I was married and I'd never been with another man. *What if I regret it after? What if someone finds out? What if he just wanted to add me to his little black book of dozens of others? And what about Brooke?*

I was cursed with a mind that never settled, and I wanted to shut it off for a second and enjoy the gorgeous piece of work that was admiring me back. I finally had him, he was right there, and I couldn't enjoy it because it hit me like a bus. *I can't sleep with someone else.* It wasn't me. The vows I made 18 years before had to stand for something. Didn't they? It never seemed to stop Frank. *However, I'm better than him. I think.*

I placed an unsteady hand over his, breaking the spell.

"I'm sorry... I can't do this," I said, rolling to my side away from him. I stood up quickly pulling my jeans up.

"What's wrong?" he asked blinking at me, confused. There I was for the second time, showing interest in him then pushing him away. He must think I'm nuts.

"Everything," I said, buttoning my jeans. "This isn't me."

A shelf of picture frames caught my attention. A few group photos, maybe family photos, and some with him with young groups of friends were displayed. I didn't know who anyone was, where he was from, about his family life.

"I don't know you," I added as I glanced at the pictures.

He stood up behind me and wrapped his arms around me kissing my neck again. "So then... what do you want to know?"

I picked up a glass frame with a picture of an attractive couple toasting at a wedding or fancy dinner. They looked happy. The woman appeared to be 40, maybe younger. She had a short brown bob with bangs, very natural make up, and was glowing next to her husband, which was obvious that he was. I never took a picture with Frank and looked like that.

"That's my mom and dad," he said from behind me.

"Are they still together?"

"Yup. Almost thirty years."

I smiled and put the frame down. She couldn't be 40 then. Her youthful look must come from happiness then.

"They live here? In the city?" I asked. I started to fasten the straps to my shoes and grabbed my denim jacket.

He shook his head. "Newport Beach."

"Newport Beach," I said, thinking for a moment. "California?"

"That's the one."

"Is that where you're from?"

He stepped back and gave me the cutest look with a sexy half smile and the tips of his hair almost falling into his eyes. California and *him* would make sense. Young men from New York didn't act like that. He was mature and down to earth, despite his occasional harmless silliness. "You ask a lot of questions."

I looked up at him. "But didn't you just say..."

"No, I don't mind," he said smiling, gently taking my arm as I attempted to put my jacket on. "I mean, why don't you stay? We could talk. Get to know each other. I'll make us some drinks."

"No." I cut him off. Must remember the new rule. No alcohol. I wished he would put his shirt back on so the temptation I was feeling might be subdued. That six-pack. Those biceps…

"I have to go, it's late," I said quickly, grabbing my purse. I resisted fanning myself.

"Ok. I'll walk you out," he said and finally put his shirt back on. He opened the door for me and we strolled, mute, to the elevators.

He pressed the call button and we waited for the elevator that couldn't come any slower. I was waiting for a little cartoon character to pop out from around the corner and say *Awkward* in a drawn out way.

"So…" he said breaking the silence, "I have an early night on Thursday, no class, no work, and no internship. We could do dinner." It was half question half suggestion, so I guess the ball was in my court.

I thought for a minute and couldn't deny for a second that I wanted to see him again but I didn't know how to deal with the situation.

"What's in it for you?" I asked.

"Seeing you."

"That's it?"

"Yeah," he said caressing my cheek. "I think I'm a little addicted to you."

How does he do that? His words made me smile like a child on a snow day. I loved the attention. However, the reality was that fantasizing about having an affair was one thing; actually going ahead with it was another. I didn't know if I had it in me to continue sneaking around and lying especially without getting caught. It was so dangerous, which strangely gave the temptation an edge in his favor.

"You're a nice distraction, Collin, but I have to think about my family." What I really wanted to say was locked in a box in the back of my mind.

"I respect that," he said as usual combing his hand through his hair. "I'm not trying to steal you away or anything. It's just dinner."

"I'll think about it," I said as the elevator bell chimed and the door slid opened. I stepped inside. "I'm okay from here." I smiled politely at him. I didn't let him follow me in because I was paranoid of us being seen together by anyone, and maybe at the thought of the two of us inside an elevator together. "Good night," I added.

"Okay," he said. I expected him to turn around and disappear down the hall, back to his apartment. Instead, he pressed his palm against the closing door, leaned in and folded the other hand behind my back, pulling me to him. His lips molded perfectly into mine, it was a kiss that made the stability of my universe tremble. He literally swept me off my feet. He released me and I struggled not to let my knees give way.

"Good night," he said with that half smile. I was rendered speechless and could only stare at him with a blank expression as the chrome doors slid together.

I exhaled, falling into the elevator wall. My body tingled. Was my attraction to him entirely physical? No, it felt deeper. I placed my hand over my heart where it thudded erratically. When the doors opened onto the first floor it still felt like the ground was moving under my feet. Ian Johnson sent me off with a courteous nod and, "Have a wonderful evening." *Already did.*

I left quickly and wanted to run into my car as fast as possible. It left me wondering how I was going to go back home to the passionless man that was supposed to be my husband. Pandora kept me company playing as the "Three Doors Down" station played on my way home.

That entire drive a new set of questions plagued me as the realization set in that I didn't accomplish anything. Still not knowing the real reason why Brooke and Collin broke up was becoming the ultimate mystery. That was why I went there. Wasn't it? Maybe I subconsciously had an ulterior motive all along. What if he wasn't what he seemed to be? Brooke wouldn't have broken up with to him unless something happened. Actually, she would have. Nevertheless, what if he was another abusive guy with a fake charming exterior? Frank was sweet with me in the beginning. Serial killers were charming too. Collin intrigued me. We connected, I think. Unsure if I was willing to let go of the connection, I tried to figure out what to do.

CHAPTER 11

I spent two days tipping the scale in both directions. Eventually it annoyed me trying to make the decision. Should I show up to this possible date, casual hang out, or whatever it was? Should I meet with my sister's beautiful ex-boyfriend? She had no idea he and I ever exchanged more than two words to each other?.What would happen if Frank found out? *I think I know the answer to that.* Should I ditch him? Would it be wrong to cheat on my husband regardless to how he treated me? The questions went on and on.

Checking the calendar, Thursday night otherwise promised to be another night by myself at home. Ashley was going with Terrance and his family to Mountain Creek until Sunday night. Frank would never be home early Thursday through Sunday nights. He claimed they were the busiest nights at the club, but I knew there were other reasons too.

In the end, the decision wasn't entirely hard. And, regardless as to what was right or wrong, I already knew what I wanted.

This is the longest day ever, I remember thinking as I watched the clock on Thursday, though I wasn't sure why I was so eager for the day to end, not knowing exactly what was going to come of this time spent with Collin. I was too excited to see him that evening, like some teenage girl going to prom. It was a nice change to exist in someone's eyes again.

When the eternity of the workday finally concluded I went home to find Ashley sitting in the kitchen. Morgan, who I figured would start moving her things in any day, sat beside her with her laptop.

I went upstairs to prepare for my night. I finished getting dressed at around 6:30. I threw on a teal dress, figured I would get some use out of it before it was too cold for dresses, then slipped on my peep toe, champagne colored heels. I even took the time to paint my toenails a pretty rose. I felt sexy, yet subtle. I was several years older than Collin, but age had given me an edge – a sense of confidence, a sense of power. Because of the way Frank knocked me down all these years, my self-esteem took a major nose-dive. But something about the way Collin looked at me – I felt good. *I look just as good*, I thought, as I finished elegantly styling my hair in an up-do. I kept my make-up natural, but finished off with a touch of red lipstick, which I saved for those special occasions when I wanted to feel just a little sexier. I took one last glimpse in the mirror. *Yes, I do look good!* I thought to myself as I grabbed my matching champagne colored purse, ready to head out.

I headed back downstairs, all ready to go. *Wait a minute, one last thing.* It's been a really rough day, a quick cup of black tea to take with me on the road would give me just the additional pick me up my body could use.

I could make my tea while I say good-bye to the girls.

I got to the bottom of the stairs and then I stopped dead in my tracks. *Oh, shit. Juan Carlos, sitting at the table talking to my daughter.* Just great, the one man I held responsible for dragging Frank deeper into selling after he initially stopped. He was always around when we were younger. His influence was directly responsible for all of Frank's bad habits. Now they were both in so deep, using the club as a cover, that Juan Carlos wasn't going anywhere.

Not to mention his leering. There was nothing good about that man. Nothing like a little rain on my parade. *Could anything ever be easy? Maybe I should go upstairs and change? No. I already let Frank control my life, I'm not about to let his friend do the same thing.*

"Where's Morgan?" I asked Ashley, more than a little pissed off that she was alone with this creep. After a lewd comment he made about her when she was 13, I didn't want him anywhere near her. Of course when I mentioned this to Frank, he just laughed, saying it was "nothing." I can't believe the nerve of these men. They are all in cahoots with each other. One lies, the other will swear to it.

"Dad is dropping her off home. He didn't want me driving in the rain," she said.

"Finish your homework upstairs, please," I said to her firmly.

"Okay," she said, quietly gathering her notebook and vanished from sight. *At least someone in this house respects me.*

The energy in the air was grim. *Why is he in my house?* My chest tightened and I started grinding my teeth. My heart began to race too. The nerves were kicking in tremendously.

Juan Carlos wore an expensive button down and black

slacks. His dark hair was set in greasy tight curls. And there it was -- that leering stare again —his lips slightly parted with that insinuating half-smile of his. The strains of his day weighed heavily on his face, especially around his light eyes. He could have been an attractive man. However, like Frank, his dark persona masked what would have otherwise been handsome features.

"Hey, long time no see," he said acting like he didn't know that I despised him.

I ignored the bastard and just concentrated on what I came downstairs for, to make myself a quick cup of tea. I walked right past him, toward the stove.

"So, you jus' gonna pretend I'm not here?" he asked with his usual condescending tone.

I rolled my eyes.

"Juan Carlos," I said with a sigh. "What do you want?"

"Oh, Victoria, you're always so welcoming. It's nice to see you too."

"And you expected what? A warm welcome? You know how I feel about you talking to my daughter."

"Relax, I was just being friendly."

"You do know that she's *only* sixteen … right?"

"Yeah. Don't worry. That's not my thing. Frankie's maybe."

"What?" I asked, shooting him a look, daring him to elaborate on what he was obviously suggesting.

"Nothing," he said. "So how are you? Are you … happy?"

"Don't start." I warned him firmly, pointing my finger at him to show I wasn't afraid of him.

"With what? Just want to make sure all my hard work isn't for nothing."

"*Your* hard work? You seem to forget my husband's part in what you guys do."

"Please," he said dismissing my comment. "You already know the *real* reason he is where he is. You think I really need the help?" Juan Carlos paused, and chuckled. "Sure, maybe it's not a one man job. But Frank? He's hasty and inexperienced. His hot head has gotten us into so much shit before. And the shit he does behind your back … such a fine thing like you putting up with that crap …" he said inching closer to me.

I rolled my eyes at him then turned my back to him,. I ignored his taunts because I knew that he was trying to get a rise from me. He was the last person I needed to hear it from. As if this was news to me. At that point, his two minutes of my tolerance level for him was up.

As usual, not taking the hint, the asshole kept talking.

"But that's not my business, is it? As long as you're taken care of, I guess that was the deal. I see this big house and your family so ..." he said sarcastically and shrugged his shoulders.

"Thank you for summing that up for me," I said, equally as sarcastic. "Now please ..." I try to squeeze past him to get the teapot over to the sink to fill it up with water, but he blocked me with his body.

"I mean, you really wanna live like a white girl? Guess that's your thing. Sometimes I think you forget where you're from."

"Juan Carlos, you're so ignorant. Stop acting like you know me."

"I do know you. We go way back, don't we?" He loved to hold that over my head. Frank didn't know it, but before we were an item I actually went on a few dates with Juan Carlos in junior high school. Back then he wasn't creepy at all. And I, then a naïve 12-year-old, was apparently a terrible judge of character. I was the only reason Juan Carlos ever considered letting Frank get in on 'the business'.

"You know ... you could probably do your own thing ... while your man is doin' the same," he said suggestively.

"Me?" I asked, and laughed nervously because I knew where he was going with this. He didn't know my intentions for the night -- did he? How would he? "I don't cheat. Two wrongs don't make a right, or so I've heard."

"You been working out lately?" he asked, circling me as if I were a fresh steak and he, the hungry wolf. "When you gonna finally let me see what you got under that dress?"

"Back off," I said rolling my eyes. He could make passes at me all he wanted. It was always a nuisance, but that was *all* it was, he would never try anything else.

"So you tellin' me I don't have a chance anymore?" he asked smugly.

"Ugh. I don't have time for this," I said, and again tried to get to the sink, but he continued to block me.

"I know you lyin' ... I see the way you look at me! You still into me... aren't 'cha?" he asked. Then he caught me off guard and grabbed my face with his hand and pulled it toward him. "Come on baby, just one kiss for old time's sake!"

"UGH!" I pulled away and pushed his hand away, using both of my hands, which made me drop the teapot. I hoped the loud noise of it clanging against the floor didn't draw any attention from my daughter. "Don't you ever touch me again!" I tried to be firm, yet speak low enough so she wouldn't hear what was going on. "I'll tell Frank! See what happens!"

"He don't care, you're just his little house whore, nothing more." Juan Carlos was always like this, hitting on me then insulting me when he couldn't get what he wanted. He continued to block the sink, smirking at me, and exaggeratedly licking his lips, knowing he was getting to me.

I just stared at him. I gave him my nastiest glare, hoping he would break down. He continued to smirk and finally broke the silence by saying, "Just one little kiss. Frank will never know." Then he grabbed my hand pulling me toward him again.

"No!" I gasped.

I struggled so hard to get free, which made Juan Carlos hold on even tighter.

"Let me go, you piece of shit!" I demanded as I held back tears.

Then he grabbed my arm and twisted it up pinning it against my back. With all his strength he pushed me forward face first into the counter all his weight against my back and he whispered into my ear, "Someone needs to teach you a little respect."

"Go to hell," I said through clenched teeth. I was a bit shaken now at how ballsy and aggressive he was being.

His entire body draped over mine. He brought his nose to my hair and inhaled deeply.

"Mmm … you always smell so good," he said running his hand down my side. "Do you know how long I've wanted to do this?"

"Let go of me," I half ordered half begged. "Don't freaking touch me! I swear if you try anything…"

"You'll do nothing," he said, "Because if you do or say anything then I *will* make sure to develop an interest in a sexy little sixteen year old that I know." As his words registered, my heart seized.

"If you ever go near Ashley I'll kill you myself," I said with no fear in my voice, again trying to fight him off.

"Yeah, I'll fix that smart mouth on you," he said ignoring

my threat. "I'll bet you like it rough!" He bore his weight against my back with one arm and with the free arm, ran his hand up my dress. Then he suddenly paused, obviously distracted.

"What the hell was that?" he asked arching his neck up as if he were listening for something.

"Oh my God," I whispered to myself. "I think Frank is home." What a relief it was when I heard keys jingling to open the door. *Is that really Frank? I didn't even hear his car pull up in the driveway.*

It *was* Frank! One of the few times, I was actually relieved by the sound of my husband's heavy steps walking through the front door. My eyes lit up.

Juan Carlos smoothly backed away from me, releasing me from his restraint and then said, "I guess we'll finish this some other time." I regained my composure and shot him the dirtiest look as I smoothened out my dress then quickly picked up the teapot from the floor. *One day this asshole will get his! If not from Frank, it would be from me personally. But, for now, I'll bury it.*

I had my back to Frank when he got into the kitchen.

"Going somewhere?" Frank asked when he spotted me, all dressed up.

I turned to look at him.

"Um ... Just to dinner... with Brooke," I told my lie trying not to stutter as my nerves were still on edge.

"Oh," Frank said, hardly giving it any thought. It wasn't because he was gullible—it was because he was indifferent to whatever I did. Not that he trusted me, but he knew I wouldn't be so stupid to do anything remotely close to cheating.

"What time you goin'?" he asked.

Before I could answer, Juan Carlos decided to step in.

"You gon' let her go out at this time? And dressed like *that?*" he directed the question to Frank but his eyes stayed on me. I returned his stare and if looks could kill. I wished they could.

"You mind your damn business!" I snapped, my voice wavering as I was still shaken by the whole encounter. Immediately, I regretted my outburst as Frank, without hesitation, grabbed my arm and pulled me into the hallway.

"Who the hell do you think you're getting loud with?"

"I can't stand him!" I said, sternly, yet still under my breath, so Ashley wouldn't hear any arguing. "And I told you that I don't want him alone in the house making passes at me and your daughter."

"Making passes at you? Please. After being knocked up three times you think anyone would be hitting on you?" Then he added, in a deeper, lower voice, "And I told you that you don't disrespect him, or anyone I work with. *Ever.* Do you understand?"

"Him?" I laughed, nervously, tears stinging behind my lids.

"Okay Frank. Whatever," I said shaking my head, trying not to show my fear, yet needing desperately to defend my undesirable situation and myself. "Pick work over family, as usual."

"Victoria, don't start this shit again," he said putting his hand up as if he's heard enough.

"Fine. I have to go anyway."

"No," he said firmly as if he were talking to one of our children, "you'll go upstairs. And let Brooke know you can't make it."

"Wait, what? No..."

"No?" he asked, his eyes hardening.

"I'm sorry," I said quickly catching a mistake that I already knew the consequence for.

"Go. Upstairs," he said again, this time his tone was non-suggestive and harsh.

"I'll be up in a few. I need to talk to you," he added.

With my jaw clenched and eyes stinging, I turn away from him and make my way up the stairs.

CHAPTER 12

I shut the door to my bedroom, infuriated, as a determined tear escaped. A 31-year-old inmate in this jail of a life. The cute outfit returned to its position in my closet, where I'd found it, and I put my sweat pants back on. Now what? What did Frank want to talk about?

Pulling my phone from my purse, I contemplate texting Collin. Would he even care that I'm not coming? Probably not. Who was I kidding? *Me -- have an affair? Sure.* Shit! Did I really just defy Frank so I could see Collin? If he only knew what happened whenever I talked back to my husband. This would be a good time to end something that shouldn't have started in the first place. It was getting me into trouble already.

The phone went into the drawer in my nightstand along with that book I never get around to, and the silver 9mm that Frank left in there as protection when he isn't around, even though I had no idea how to use it. That may have been the nicest thing he's ever done for me.

It took longer than usual to remove the little bit of extra make up I used. I cared more about my appearance than I had in years. What a waste of time, being that only one who noticed was sleazy Juan Carlos. Once my face was mascara and eyeliner free I pulled my facial cleanser from the medicine cabinet. And there they were again. Those many, many prescription bottles, the reminders of my real problems. I slammed the cabinet shut dismissing the thought. Not tonight. Breaking one of the doctors, many rules I randomly started to skip the medications that I never thought were necessary to begin with.

After brushing my teeth, I tossed my toothbrush into the porcelain holder. Stepping into my bedroom, I found that Frank had returned from his 'important business meeting.' I looked over at him then moved my eyes to the floor, awaiting my fate.

"You're not going to like this," Frank said abruptly. Then he began his end of the day routine, removing white gold rings and chains, placing them on his dresser. He placed his phone into a small black box that was on top of his dresser, which I would never touch. Its contents were always a mystery to me. A collection of pink leopard printed thongs? Fingers that were cut from the hands of other men? Blood money?

Cringing at the thought, I returned my focus to my half of the room. He continued about as if he didn't just tell me to go upstairs and then give me a warning, purposely letting me sweat in anticipatory dread.

"You wanted to talk about something?" I swallow hard and tried hiding my nervous tone. *Please don't let it be about my talking back to him.* Those "conversations" ended up in black eyes and bruises of the worse kind.

"Yes. Just found out that I need to be outta town on and off for the next few weeks. Closing on some big deals," he said. He made drug-dealing sound so professional and important, as if they were selling houses to the Pope or something.

"Let me know if you need one of the guys to stay around," he added.

One of the guys? Sleeping in my house with my teenage daughter and me? All of them just like Juan Carlos. I'll pass.

"No. We'll manage," I said. We always do. "With Galina here, I should be fine."

"Alright," he said, simply, no argument there.

That's all? Phew. Frank always seemed to be paranoid, as if someone was going to come after us while he was gone, someone vigorously against him. Maybe he cares a little bit? I shrug at the thought as he settled into his side of the bed and I climbed into mine. I reached up and turn the night table lamp off.

"Can I ask you something?" I asked, my words breaking the silence of the night.

"What?" His response dry, and cold, like a robot, except a robot might have been more affectionate.

"Do you still love me?" I asked.

"Victoria, why are you asking me this?" his tone was slightly annoyed.

"I don't know," I said quietly. Why was there this little piece of me still hanging on to him? Was it because we had three kids together? "Just forget it." I was unable to answer the question myself.

"I'm still here. Right? What else do you want?"

"You really can't just say it?" I asked, hoping.

"I'm too tired to get into this with you now. You're so damn insecure sometimes."

I exhaled and decided to hold my tongue. *No, Frank, I don't have a reason to be insecure at all!* Then again, he would never admit that he was doing anything wrong. As long as we had food in the fridge and money in the bank, his job was done.

He said nothing else. I said nothing else. We recommitted to the previously broken silence. And that was as good as it was going to get. It was actually quite simple, what I wanted. Why I bothered asking in the first place was beyond me.

I closed my eyes, but couldn't sleep. The bed felt like a brick whether I was on my back, side, or stomach. *No sleep to be found tonight.* Onto my side again. Glancing over at the night table, the alarm clock read 12:48. Lonely, next to the robot, in a cold, hard bed, with a case of insomnia. *Never skip the little blue pills again.*

Turning again with all the space in the world to stir freely about the king size bed, the thought of those sweet hypnotic eyes emerged from where I had it buried. *He's* definitely the cuddling type. Maybe? No, he probably skips out in the middle of the night off to the next victim's house. I spent a few minute amusing myself, trying to figure Collin out. Maybe he's awake too? The little voice in the back of my mind was back. The same one that encouraged me to kiss him that first night, defraud Sean during our pizza date, and drive through crazy traffic to see him. It was talking to me again. *Text him. Call him. Email him.* The temptation was fierce as my hand slowly reached into my night table as if it had a mind of its own.

I glanced over at my husband who was in a deep slumber. I quietly escaped from the bed, cell phone in hand, and tiptoed into the hallway. Thank goodness for the marble floors that don't creak. Nick's light was visible from under his room door and the familiar sounds of him shooting at enemies escaped through. He was talking in a low voice, probably though his headset, to someone who was playing the same game with him from some far away location. *Because he really needed to play Call of Duty with a kid who lived in Australia at one in the morning. Teenagers.* I shook my head and descended the stairs.

The kitchen was dark except for the one little light over the stove that we always left on during the night. The tiny fluttering in my stomach while I held my phone made me wonder what was coming over me. I couldn't help it, finally deciding to send a quick text message. A simple hello. That's all, then I'll go to bed. Wow. I couldn't even go one whole day?

There! Sent!

I put the phone down but he responded within a few seconds. He's awake. Yay. I could feel the excitement build as I picked up my phone to read his response. His sweetness or even his playfulness would be uplifting after the two jerks that I had to encounter that day.

Collin: Hey, who's this?

Well that's disappointing. I was expecting something cute. *Oh, that's right. He doesn't have my number yet.*

Me: It's Victoria. I'm really sorry that I couldn't make it tonight. Hope it wasn't too much of an inconvenience.

Collin: Hi. Thought I wouldn't hear from you. Everything okay?

Me: Yes. Hope I'm not bothering you, this late.

No response.

Me: Are you mad?

Still nothing. *Okay, then.* The phone sat patiently on the counter while I pulled a pint of strawberries from the refrigerator. Cut the leaves off, washed them, sliced them into quarters, and sprinkled a little sugar onto them as I always did.

I sat down and stared at the phone that was still faceplate down. Why did I care that he wasn't writing back? Fine. *I don't care then.*

The text alert sound came through again. Without hesitation, I pick it up and turned it over.

Collin: How could I be mad at you? ☺

I crumbled a little. Wow, he even knew how to have me smiling childishly from miles away. Even after such a horrific night. I began typing back.

Me: Had to think about it?

Collin: No. Sorry, sweetie, I was on the phone.

On the phone? At one-thirty in the morning? With who? I could feel my lungs tighten a little. I simply replied.

Me: It's ok

Collin: So what are you doing up so late?

Thinking about you. I can't say that, though. Was lying in bed wondering if you're the cuddling type, secretly wishing I could find out.

Me: Can't sleep. You?

Aside from talking to God knows whom at one-thirty in the morning!

Collin: Writing an essay

An essay? Oh. That's right. *He's a college kid.* Rolling my eyes at the thought, it made me feel silly for a moment remembering how ridiculous this whole thing was. How young he was.

Me: At almost 2am? Really dedicated, I see.

Collin: Yep! Anyway, when can I see you again?

Frank said he'd be away again. But maybe I should tell him that we can't meet. And that I'm married. And not feed into these strange feelings that I didn't seem to have control over.

Me: I don't know.

Collin: Ok

Okay? What? No! That wasn't the response I was expecting. Oh, childish game playing. And he knew it too. Great, now I'll have to think of something clever to say.

Me: Well maybe I can squeeze time in during lunch tomorrow.

Collin: sounds good to me

Our text conversation dragged into the early hours of the morning. Finally, when the numbers on the microwave read 3:45, we said our goodnights. I went to sleep, my insomnia gone, and I knew that I would get to see him the next day.

In the morning I was dead tired from being up almost all night exchanging messages with Collin, and to make matters worse Galina wasn't feeling well and Ashley was out the door extra early for a swim meet, one of the many activities she was involved in.

Naturally, I had no choice but to offer to drop Nick off on my way to work and getting a teenage son off to school was certainly not my strong point. Nor was it Frank's. Not that he was around to do it anyway. I was just so used to it by then. There was absolutely nothing left intact of this unorganized family, but I couldn't blame Nick or Ashley. They were just kids and they needed their parents to pull it together.

Having a nanny around was so much easier. The last one left after Frank made one too many sexual advances toward her. And the one before that I fired because I knew she would do just about *anything* for extra money in her paycheck. By this time, I was numb to such crap. I was smart to hire Galina, who wouldn't tolerate any nonsense from him. Besides, I wouldn't put it past her to be able to beat Frank up. She was a tough one.

Driving Nick to school meant that I had to make an extra trip in the opposite direction. Great. This extra trip is really going to throw my morning off! Perhaps this is payback from a higher power, for not taking the time to be a proper parent and always relying on a nanny? Yes, payback is certainly a bitch and a half. But, for the kids, I always tried to pull myself together because someone around here needed to be the responsible parent.

While Nick was supposed to be getting ready, I found myself at my closet again. I reached for my usual professional attire then the tightly fitting teal dress caught my attention again. I looked so cute for Collin the night before. Hell, I'm not letting this outfit go to waste! Since I would be meeting with him in a few hours, I threw the same dress on and slipped into my champagne colored shoes. He'll go crazy for this, I just know it! Since I knew my son was probably still sleeping I didn't waste time putting my hair up. Instead, I left it down letting it pour over my shoulders and halfway down my back, curling slightly at the ends. Then I made my way to wake up Nick *again*.

"For the third time, Nick, please get up!" I was no longer nudging him, but shaking him roughly. When he finally got up, he stalled while eating his breakfast, stalled in the shower, and then couldn't find one of his books. Yet this brat had the nerve to blame me for us running late!

"Mom, can't you drive any faster? I'm going to be late for homeroom!"

Oh no! Not homeroom! I tried not to roll my eyes.

"I am going the speed limit Nick! We'll be there in a few minutes."

"Galina always speeds."

"She does, does she?" *Oh, boy, another thing I have to worry about.*

I continued to focus on the road in spite of Nick's moaning and groaning, and insisting that I go faster. Such a shame. I normally have a smooth peaceful *quiet* drive in the morning. One of the few things in life I can look forward to these days.

Then the drive was further compromised by the unorganized disaster the school set up during the drop off routine. Cars were pulling in and out in all directions and I was trying to find a safe place to pull over and let Nick out.

I sighed. *It's going to be a very long day!*

"Let me out," Nick demanded, pulling on the locked door handle.

"Will you at least wait until I've stopped the car?" I yelled at him.

He continued sighing, sucking his teeth, and taking deep breaths, making it so obvious to me that he was pissed.

Finally, I pulled up into a spot not too close to the school, but cars were everywhere, and he was trying my nerves with his impatience. "You're gonna have to walk a bit."

"Whatever. Just let me out here. It's fine!" *Again, with the pulling on the locked door handle.*

"Will you wait a minute? Can I 'park' the damn car before you go jumping out of a moving car?"

"Mom, you're so fu-"

"I'm so what, Nicholas?" I said cutting him off. I looked up into the rearview mirror at him, put the car in "park" and continued as I turned and looked him straight in the eye. "Go ahead Nick, finish that sentence."

"Funny," he said sarcastically giving me a sly smile. Ooh, this boy was lucky I wasn't someone else.

Not wanting to give into the temptation I felt to backhand my son I quickly flicked the buttons to unlock his door.

"Go!" I said, in an annoyed tone. He jumped out without saying "good-bye." I called behind him, "Have a nice day!" He sent me off with a lazy wave. My son was such an asshole, just like his father, but I still loved him.

Maybe I took too long during our episode, but another car peeled out hastily cutting me off on my left as I was also pulling out to the left. To avoid hitting her car I sharply turned right. Boom! I slammed into the bumper of the car to my right instead. The woman who caused the accident sped off.

I stepped out of my car to inspect the damage. A tall, refined looking man with salt and pepper hair, in an Italian suit slowly stepped out of his red Jaguar XF.

"I'm so sorry! That woman ..."

"I saw what happened," he said as we approached the back of his car and front of mine. "Are you okay?"

"Yes. You?"

He nodded. Only a scratch on mine. A small dent on his. *Whew.* I relaxed. Minimal damage and no one hurt.

"Some people must get their driver's license from a

Cracker Jack box," I said, half-jokingly in regard to that woman who hit me. Then getting nervous, I changed my tone and added, "How dare she speed around me like that. There are kids around!"

"Ma'am, it wasn't her fault, it was your fault. You dropped your kid off in a 'no standing' area." My face turned red as he continued, "See where I was parked, in the last official spot? You weren't supposed to be behind me, there are no yellow lines and there's also a 'No Stopping or Standing' sign. This accident could have been avoided. She probably wasn't used to a car being there."

I felt so embarrassed and like a failure at parenthood. However, Nick was just so anxious to get out of the car. Was I *that* miserable to be around? I felt so defeated … in life … all the way around.

"I'm an idiot," I admitted, sucking up. "I should have been more careful."

"No you're not," he said, smiling. "They should have a crossing guard. All the tuition we pay, you would think they'd do something useful with it."

"Seriously," I said agreeing. "But we still have to straighten this mess out. Let me get my insurance card."

"There's no point in going through the hassle. Don't worry about it."

I frowned at him.

"No. I have full coverage, it's fine." I insisted.

He glanced at his watch.

"I have a meeting in twenty minutes," he said, "as long as no one is hurt."

I felt terrible making him pay for the damage, but I also had no interest in starting my day with police reports and insurance phone calls. "Are you sure?"

"It's just a car right?" he said flashing me a row of perfectly white teeth.

That's "just a car"? I wasn't going to argue.

"Well, I owe you," I said handing him my business card.

He took it, glanced at it briefly then placed it in his suit pocket.

"Don't worry about it," he said very professionally, adding, "accidents happen," before getting back into his car.

I carefully backed up, checked my mirrors again, then pulled off.

It was 9:05 when I walked into the office. The day was otherwise exceptionally boring after my little excitement at Nick's school. Brooke and I greeted each other as if we were nothing more than ordinary co-workers.

At 11:30, I let Sue know that I was leaving for lunch and to run a few errands. I tried to slip out unseen, but failed.

"Heading to lunch?" Brooke asked.

"Yes," I kept my answer brief.

"Oh. Let me run to the ladies room. Then I'll join you."

"Actually, I'm going by myself."

She looked at me funny.

"Running a few errands too," I said.

"Oh," she said sounding disappointed. "Well, maybe tomorrow."

"Sure," I said and headed out, quickly, with my head down. Lying to my sister was not something I was proud of. *How was I so caught up in this charade, this fantasy, this double life?*

CHAPTER 13

When I arrived at Collin's apartment building, Ian picked up the outdated phone, announced my arrival, and buzzed me through. As I stepped out of the elevator and turned, I saw that Collin was waiting for me, this time leaning casually against the doorframe. I couldn't understand how he always looked like he belonged in a magazine ad. Today he was just as casual as the last time we met, sporting a white t-shirt and olive cargo pants, but this time he wore a loosely fitting baseball cap. *So* sexy.

I knew I looked good too, being that I wore the outfit that was picked out for him. With a warm smile on my face, I leaned forward and greeted Collin with a hug. With a warm smile on my face, I lean forward and greeted him with a hug.

"Welcome back," he said taking my hand and gently kissing my knuckles, his eyes fixed on mine.

"You look absolutely stunning!" he said as he led me inside. I beamed at him, extremely pleased with his reaction. The aroma of spices, oregano, lemon, and peppers filled the air. The delicious aromas mixed with Collin's sweet, natural scent gave me butterflies in my stomach.

There he was cooking a meal, yet his apartment was so spotless and organized – without a housekeeper! I had to admit I felt slightly intimidated because I could never keep up with things around my own house without Galina.

"Sorry that I'm not all dressed up. Between cooking, studying, and that paper, I didn't have a chance to throw something else on."

"It's fine," I said.

He pulled out a chair for me and I sat.

"Thank you," I said quietly, suddenly feeling shy. It felt like a date. *Is this a date?* This is so weird. Someone ought to make a cheater's handbook. What was I supposed to talk about? Guys don't want to hear women talk about their children all day. Can't talk about Brooke -- that would be awkward. I'm sure he wasn't interested in the trinkets and odds and ends we sold at Little Treasures. Maybe he liked Yorkies? Doubt it. I sat there, somewhat panicking on the inside, realizing I had nothing interesting to say. To make matters worse my hands were

108

clammy. Mouth was dry. Heart beating faster than usual.

"Are you okay?" he asked me as if he could read my mind.

No, I'm not. Maybe it was obvious.

"Yes," I said shifting in my seat a little. "You always ask me that."

"Well, I don't know. You're so quiet. Not like when we met," he said then disappeared into the kitchen.

"When we first met you were a lot more… um…" he yelled out from the kitchen.

"Talkative?" I asked.

"No, that's definitely not the word," he said laughing.

"But I'm just messin' with you anyway. We're just having lunch, no need to feel uneasy."

I guess it was obvious that I was nervous. *Yes, I was much more harsh and mouthy when we met. Maybe because I was indifferent to him back then? Now he's starting to grow on me. Maybe because I shouldn't be here?* I was just so confused. For all Frank's wrongs, I still had no right to cheat on him. I took vows before God.

"Would you like red or white wine?" he asked as he grabbed two wine glasses from a cabinet.

"Red, please."

Collin rinsed the goblets then dried them off with a towel and grabbed a bottle from the counter. He poured my glass, handed it to me, and then poured his. Wait. What was that rule again? Oh well, maybe I needed a little afternoon glass of red.

For once, I deserved the special treatment from someone other than our nanny. He was quickly gone again this time fixing two plates of food.

"If I didn't know any better. I'd say you're trying to get me drunk," I said when he returned with two plates.

"Me?" he asked innocently. "And why would I do that?"

"I don't know. Maybe to cloud my judgment."

"Is that right?" he asked as he placed the porcelain square plate in front of me. Then I noticed a small vase with a white rose in the center of the table. *Was this done for me or does he always have roses on his table?*

Collin bent forward, kissed me on the cheek, and then brought his lips slowly to my ear whispering, "Last time I checked I didn't need alcohol to do that."

My eyes avoided his as I tried to suppress a smile. He definitely was right about that one. Just having his lips near my ear for those few seconds sent my heart into an erratic fit. I need to distract myself quickly.

I said the first thing that came to mind. "How sweet. You went through all this trouble cooking for me?"

"No trouble at all. I love to cook. Whenever you're here I'll make you anything you want."

Why again, did Brooke let this one go? That's right, I still didn't know! I always seemed to learn something new about him. So far, there was nothing I could see to be a red flag. What was his secret? There had to be something. Well, there was one thing. His age -- 24. It sounded so young especially since I was going to be 32 in a few months.

"So, where'd you grow up?" he asked as we indulged in a combination of lemon chicken, wild rice, and steamed vegetables.

"Jersey. Westwood. That's over by River Vale, Hillsdale, Washington Township…"

He looked at me after every town I named, clueless, as if he was completely unfamiliar with that area.

"Don't worry. You're not missing much," I said. "Just trees. And fancy cars. Everything is very artificial out there."

"You're still in that area now. Right?"

"Yes. However, I'm in Alpine now. Spent my whole life in Bergen County. Literally. Never traveled. Well, *I* haven't any way."

"Never?"

"Nope. My kids have been to Italy, Paris, Florida … my husband's been everywhere, and I've never even been to Times Square."

"What? I don't believe that."

"I swear."

"How is that even possible?"

"Trust me, it is," I said and laughed. "I have a very…" I paused as I searched for the word, *"different* life." It was hard keeping details about my marriage and home life from him. It just wasn't how I wanted him to look at me. "Remember, I'm afraid of heights so that eliminates planes."

"Well, I'm taking you on a plane someday. You'll see," he said, so sure of himself.

"If you say so," I said taking another small bite of rice.

We carried on about everything while we ate. He started naming all the countries he planned to take me to. I was amused as he was very confident in the matter. Then I had to wonder where would this kid have all this money to travel the world? Or was it all talk? No, because his apartment was in an expensive area in the city, that was obvious. I couldn't ask him anyway being that it would be very rude. Before obsessing about it, I had to remind myself: *Not everything is about money anyway! Let it go, Victoria!*

The food was amazing. I offered to help him clean up, but he insisted that I sit and relax. I brought the plates to the kitchen and sat on the bar stools at the breakfast bar. I watched him from the other side and couldn't help but think, *Wait, why am I still here?* Then, I looked at his face. Beautiful. Yes, that's why, I couldn't get enough of that face. The cute creases drew against his forehead as he concentrated on the final details of some dessert he was making, drizzling chocolate syrup carefully over it. *Hmm, what I would do with that bottle.* Then he pulled out the whipped cream and topped the dessert off with it. *Whipped cream.* More naughty thoughts entered my mind. Then he looked up at me through his ever-so-sexy glare.

I blushed, then quickly fixed my eyes in another direction. Peering out the living room window, I remembered that amazing view of the city from last time.

"Here," he said and is suddenly leaning over the counter holding the red and white can upside down.

"What are you doing?" I asked, leaning away.

"What do you mean? It's whipped cream," he said, as if I were from another planet.

"Yes, I know that," I said.

He brought the can to his lips and squeezed the nozzle, a small amount of whipped cream the size of a quarter.

I shook my head.

"Eh, I'll pass," I said trying to act proper.

"You've really never done that before?" he asked, laughing at me.

"No, I'm a lady," I said smugly.

"Just try it. I promise I won't tell," he said.

"Maybe later," I said, smiling at him.

"Okay," he said, then started to inch closer to me, threatening me with the can.

"Don't you dare!" I said. "You'll mess up my dress! And I have to go back to work!"

He hid it behind his back.

"I don't know what you're talking about," He snickered

and looked sexier than ever.

I backed away from him as he got closer, then I sprinted away running in circles around the table. I managed to duck into the kitchen where I grabbed the bottle of chocolate syrup. I pointed it toward him.

"Hmm, this got real interesting, real fast," he said, not backing down.

"I think I won this one," I said holding my weapon of choice up as he did the same.

"Oh yeah? I don't think you'll do it," he said provoking me, coming closer again.

"Is that a challenge?" I asked, holding up the little Hershey's bottle with the squirt top still pointed directly at him.

"Yup," he said.

Maybe I was feeling extra silly, but just as he got close enough I decided to squeeze the bottle once and sent a straight line of chocolate syrup shooting out all over him. *Didn't think it would really work.* I got him right in the middle of his neck and the syrup started flowing down his shirt, and inside his shirt. What a mess!

"You asked for it now," he said coming after me.

I turned around and ran again. He caught me after our cat and mouse chase and wrestled me to the ground finding all my ticklish spots. I was trapped under him.

"Do you surrender?" he asked pinning both hands over my head by my wrists.

"Never," I said as I squirmed to escape.

With his finger, he took some of the dripping chocolate and dabbed it on my nose, and forehead, and cheeks, painting chocolate all over my face. Then he traced over my lips. I slowly licked it off his finger, while staring into his eyes. The mood quickly diverted from the game we started. He lowered his lips and pressed them against mine. I closed my eyes as I kissed him back able to taste a hint of whipped cream on him mixed with the chocolate from my lips. It was the sweetest moment.

I brought my hands to his face drawing him even deeper into our kiss. My feelings of want begin to unfurl within. He seemed to be into it too, but them he suddenly broke the magic and placed his hands over mine. I sighed and licked my lips as he pulled me up from the floor. *Seriously? What was that? Doesn't he know how much I want him? Or is he truly a gentleman? I really think it's the latter. I can feel it.*

112

We used damp paper towels to clean the mess. Chocolate seemed to be everywhere, on us anyway.

What time is it? I most definitely should have gone back to the office at that point. Instead, I was playing around with my little 24-year-old distraction and dessert toppings. *Oh well.* Would they really miss me anyway? His sofa was calling me and I didn't put up a fight as I got comfortable. Collin sat next to me with the little dessert plate that he prepared earlier in his hand.

"Wow. Fancy," I said.

"Mini cream puff cakes with butter pecan ice cream," he said holding a fork up to feed me. I normally would never let someone feed me. *Ever.* But with him I broke all the rules. Or they just didn't apply. I leaned forward taking a bite.

A rich scrumptious flavor of buttery cake and chocolate swam through my taste buds. The ice cream was rich, creamy, and sweet. It had to be homemade! "Did you make the ice cream too?"

"I don't want to brag, but yes."

"Unbelievable!" I said, in shock. "Well, now I have to know. Where did you learn to cook?"

He looked away, then shrugged, "I was hoping you wouldn't ask me that."

"Why?"

He sighed. "You really wanna know?"

Did I? I was a little apprehensive but intrigued at the same time.

"Only if you want to tell me."

"Fine… my ex was a culinary major."

"So, she taught you?"

He looked down and laughed. "Not exactly."

I looked at him questioningly.

"I was so busy one semester. And she was upset that we weren't spending time together. Well, she complained and complained and complained," he said and rolled his eyes as if he were annoyed at the memory. "Anyway, I took three classes with her. Cooking, baking and some patisserie class or something."

"Oh. Well, that's sweet," I said with a fake smile. The thought of him with someone else was making me cringe and I couldn't hide it well.

"Not really. I wasted half a semester. I could have been

doing something toward my major instead."

"You probably should have," I said bitterly, but it was supposed to be in my head not aloud.

"Wait…" he said realizing my tone.

"What?"

"You're not jealous, are you?" he said, sounding amused.

"Jealous? Me?" I said, my voice raising several octaves.

"Of course not! Why would I be?"

"Aw, that's so cute," he said, placing the plate aside onto the coffee table.

"Don't flatter yourself," I said, crossing my arms.

"Come here," he said, wrapping his arms around my waist, pulling me close to him. I leaned back resting my head on his chest and covered his arms with mine. Our magnetic charge began to kindle instantly.

"You shouldn't worry about it," he said running his fingers through my hair.

"About what?"

"*Her.* My ex," he said.

"Well, is she the one you were trying to avoid talking about at the office?"

"Yes. Same one. Vanessa."

"The two of you were pretty serious huh."

He looked at me questioningly as if he was wondering, how I knew.

"You have a lot of break up songs on your play list," I said to elaborate.

"Yeah, it was a pretty bad break up," he said and it was obvious that he was trying to act calm and collected about it.

"Oh." I said quietly. Did I really want to get in the middle of this?

"She's across the country," he said reassuringly.

I did a dance on the inside. Thank goodness, I didn't feel like competing with anyone. My feelings were just *so real. So fast.* He didn't exactly seem like he was over her either.

"So, if she was here, would you be with her?" I asked dragging out the issue. There go my damn insecurities.

"Why are we still talking about this?" he asked and laughed nervously.

"No," he said as he kissed me playfully, "I wouldn't be with her."

After a moment of silence, he continued, "Look. I left her

114

because I couldn't deal with her crazy psycho drama. I came here for a new start. And I found you."

"Technically, you found my sister," I teased.

"Not true. I saw you first. I swear. But you didn't even glance in my direction."

"Sorry," I said and laughed knowing that it was true.

"You're probably right. I had the wrong idea about you. That's why."

I never knew what to say to you. And I thought to myself, 'What would a beautiful, sexy, independent woman like that want with me anyway?'"

"I could think of a few things," I said turning my body around, curling both of my hands behind his head, running my fingers slowly through his soft, espresso hair that I was then so obsessed with. I brought my lips to his and waited for him to kiss me. Electric waves coursed through my body as our lips and tongues playfully touched. *Mmm, yes.* That was all I wanted. To taste and feel his lips and tongue make fireworks with mine.

We were both breathing as if we just ran a race. He pulled me closer to him at my waist as I slowly rolled my hips into him. Our thin, fit bodies fit together like a jigsaw puzzle. It was as if I was made to be in his arms.

Collin ran his hands up my back then tangled his fingers through my hair and behind my head.

"Victoria," he hummed softly.

I broke the connection for a split second, straightening up to pull my dress over my head. It landed somewhere behind me. I flipped my hair back before leaning forward to return my lips to his. Hair engulfed us again but we didn't care. He traced my body slowly with his hands and planted a line of kisses from my chin down my neck, stopping briefly before reaching my breasts and lingering his tongue around my upper chest area. I inhaled sharply closing my eyes and felt the full heat of arousal flooding my body.

He carefully maneuvered from under me, turning me to my back and was now holding himself over me, admiring me, in awe of my matching lacey white undergarments. He kissed my cleavage, stopped, and looked up at me to see my reaction. My eyes were still half-closed, but I was smiling softly. Knowing that I was pleased, he continued kissing, down to my exposed stomach. My legs were wrapped around him this entire time.

My cell phone, which was sitting on the coffee table,

began to sing its annoying melody.

"Let it ring," he said, kissing me everywhere, over and over.

"You're ... so ... beautiful ..." Collin said softly between kisses. I could get used to this. I continued to run my hands through his hair as he continued kissing my belly and my naval.

And because the universe didn't ever want to allow us to bond physically deeper than we had already, my cell phone rang and rang and rang until I finally had to reach over for it.

"Sorry," I said looking at him then glanced at the number that popped up on my phone's screen. I recognized it to be one of the kid's school numbers. It was sent to voice mail for the third time.

"Hold that thought," I kissed him again then grabbed my dress. "I'll be right back." I said quickly pulling it on before stepping into the kitchen to return the missed call.

"Yes. Hello? This is Victoria Carlisle. Did somebody just try to reach me?" I said after a man answered.

"Mrs. Carlisle? This is Mr. Peterson, the principal at Bergen Catholic High," the voice on the other end said. "I have Nicholas here in my office."

"Oh. Is he okay?"

"Yes. He is fine. However, he and another boy were in a fight during last period. He is being sent home. We need someone to come to the school and pick him up."

I sighed and had an instant headache. "I am so sorry, Mr. Peterson..."

"Mrs. Carlisle you are aware of our school's policies, aren't you? This is Nicholas' second time in my office since the beginning of the school year. We don't tolerate this kind of behavior. Next time he will be expelled."

"I am very aware, and I apologize again for his behavior. I assure you, there *won't* be a next time, I'll talk to him. I'm sending our nanny, Galina, to pick him up now."

"Very well. This evening, Mr. Washington and the parents of the other boy involved will be having a conference. Will you and Mr. Carlisle be able to attend?"

"I will be there. And again I am very sorry for the disruption, Mr. Peterson."

"We'll see you this evening. Six thirty p.m.," he said and ended one of the most embarrassing calls I ever had to endure.

I inhaled deeply. Exasperated. This kid had me exhausted.

I returned to Collin and sat next to him while I tried to reach Galina.

"What's going on?" he asked, obviously concerned.

"I think I'm completely losing control of my son."

"Why? What happened?"

"He got into a fight in school. He's already on thin ice. He gets into any trouble again, he's expelled."

"Oh. Teenager stuff," he said.

"Yes. However, at the same time he needs to get over it. We pay a lot of money for Nick's education. He doesn't appreciate what I didn't have at his age," I said before sighing and suddenly finding myself in the comfort of Collins warm hold. "I don't even know what to do anymore."

He held me a little tighter. I closed my eyes for a moment to breathe. And absorb his strong and wonderful presence. Nuzzled right into his t-shirt I slowly breathed his laundry detergent scent that I loved so much. He was like a drug to me. I paused for one more moment then looked up at him.

"I'm so sorry. I really shouldn't be complaining about this to you."

"No. It's okay. I'm here for you. In whatever way you need me to be."

"Thank you," I said as he hugged me again. *He's so sweet.* I really needed it. That's all I wanted. Someone to comfort me instead of kick me when I'm down, literally.

"And about your son," he said. "I know I don't have kids, but just my opinion, at his age they don't realize what's important yet. Teenage boys go through some crazy phases, but he'll come around. Try not to be too hard on him. That'll just push him away."

I looked at him inquisitively. "And how do you know all this? Don't tell me *you* were a trouble maker."

He laughed.

"You'd be surprised, I guess," he said as he shrugged. "We'll save that conversation for another day."

"You really are a mystery I have to unravel," I said.

"So are you," he said and then kissed my forehead.

Galina responded to my message saying that she had a fever. *That's right, I forgot!* Therefore, I figured I would have to drive to Nick's school myself.

Again, Collin and I found ourselves ending our time together, waiting for the elevator. I hate this part. Whenever I was with him, I felt so important. It seemed like everything revolved around me. However, I was also so infatuated with him that it was a wonderful combination. The complete opposite of everything else I knew before we met.

Collin and I stayed in each other's embrace until the last possible second when those elevator doors opened.

"I'll see you later," I said quietly, a little sad.

"Let me know what happens," he said as I stepped into the elevator.

"I will," I said and smiled weakly at him and the door shut, pulling me from my fantasy world and reentering the real one. The one that seemed to always be filled with drama. Why couldn't we go one day without arguments, fender benders, and suspensions? And didn't I just have a discussion with Nick a few weeks ago? Wait until I get my hands on this kid!

CHAPTER 14

I was so embarrassed sitting in that hallway while the teacher spoke with the principal. It felt like I was on trial and the jury was going to read my sentencing next.

Then it got worse. The father of the other boy that fought with Nick walked toward us – and I recognized him! It was the man I got into the fender bender with. *Can my life get any more embarrassing?* I thought to myself.

He looked up at me and I gave a quick greeting smile.

"Hello," he said extending his hand to me, and smiling. "Small world, isn't it?"

Does anything bother this gentleman? He's always so calm, cool and collected.

"John Montgomery."

"Victoria Carlisle," I said as I leaned forward, shaking his hand.

"I know," he said, still smiling. "I have your business card." Then his tone took a more serious turn as he added, "So, you're Nick's mom. Andrew told me they've been having issues."

I looked at him clueless. *Why did I not know about* issues? *Why was I the last in my family to know anything?*

"Oh, he hasn't mentioned anything to you?" John asked and I went from feeling two-inches-tall to one-inch. Sensing my embarrassment he said, "It's okay, I'm a single parent too. They're hard to keep up with sometimes."

Again, I was confused until I glanced down at my hand. *Shit, I had forgotten to put my rings back on.*

"Oh." I laughed sheepishly touching where my rings should be. "I'm not a single mom. I was cleaning my rings and forgot…"

"Understandable," he said with a warm smile, but I also sensed some disappointment in his tone. *I might as well be a single parent with Frank never around.*

"This is Andrew's last strike."

"Nicholas', too."

"Don't know what gets into these boys these days, I tell you," he said. I wondered why John was single. He wasn't a bad looking guy. At all. With a strong jaw line and piercing blue eyes, he reminded me of a formal James Bond.

I didn't have to wonder about John being single much longer as he started to share a bit of his story. "Andrew was always the hardest to handle, of my two sons, but since Susan passed away, he's really been a handful. He already sees the school psychologist. I don't know what to do next."

Before I could offer advice or say anything, John went on to say, "If you ever need to talk about the boys. Or something else. Don't hesitate to call."

I smiled and tucked his card into the side pocket of my purse.

"Thank you, I may take you up on that," I said, now feeling more at ease.

*   *   *   *

By the time I got back to my house, it was already after seven. The kids had eaten, all the dishes were done, not a spot on the counters or floor. Ashley probably handled everything. I looked out the kitchen window and could see the lights on in the guesthouse, which Galina used as an apartment. I made a mental note to go check on her and maybe bring over some soup. On another note, I dreaded the conversation I had to have with Nick. *Again*. It would start as a conversation and end in a full-blown teenage temper tantrum. If I only had it so lucky at 13. Only two years older, at 15, I was already taking care of Thomas. I wonder what Nick would do with a baby? I won't pull that card on him again. It's just old. Then when Frank gets home, there is no yelling and no tantrums. They'll just talk and then everything will be fine. Nicholas and I really didn't understand each other; my sweet blond hair brown-eyed little boy -- a perfect mix of Brooke and me, a boy who loved playing with remote control cars and water guns. Where has he gone?

I frowned at the thought as I pulled a mug from the cupboard. Tea. Yes. Tea fixes everything. Ironically, I chose the "Best Mom" mug that was a gift several Mother's Days ago. That title didn't suit me. Debra Carlisle deserved the mug, t-shirt, picture frame. Hell, I'll personally get her a gold placard with words written in diamonds. That would make her day. And for me? I deserved the keychain at best. Of course, her kids were all straight A students, sports team captains, valedictorians, meanwhile my son is in school getting into fights and I'm fooling around with some kid almost 10 years younger than me. It was so wrong. When Frank does it, then it's okay? I shrug, too exhausted to ride that emotional carousel with myself.

I place the tea pot filled with water onto the stove and waited, then chose from my endless selection of black, green, chai, and herbal teas. Ultimately, I selected a tension taming tea with chamomile, catnip leaves, and hops dropping it into the lying porcelain mug.

At last a moment to relax. A smile spread across my face remembering my afternoon with Collin.

My sweet thoughts were interrupted, too quickly for my tastes, when I heard someone come through the front door. Frank walked into the kitchen and I looked up at him.

"How'd the thing at Nick's school go?" he asked when he saw me sitting at the kitchen island with my tea. He opened the cabinet taking out a glass then went over to the refrigerator

Hmm. No kiss. No hello. Nothing. He hasn't seen me in almost a week. I sighed. What else is new?

"The conference," I corrected, "was embarrassing, but productive. You *really* need to talk to him though. He seems to listen to you."

"I'll talk to him tomorrow," he said placing the glass on the counter right *next to* the sink. *I hate it when he does that!*

"You coming to bed?" he asked.

"In a little bit," I said as he walked out of the kitchen.

I shook my head annoyed, but tried not to let him ruin my time to relax after a day of mostly uncomfortable situations. After finishing my tea and washing whatever dishes were left, I headed upstairs to the bedroom to wind down for the night. Frank looked annoyed as he summoned me over.

"Come here," he said to me standing in front of his closet.

"What's wrong?" I asked standing next to him.

"Where the hell is my black Armani suit with the gray stripes?"

Damn, I knew I forgot something.

"I'm sorry! I got thrown off with what happened with Nick today."

"You couldn't go before?"

"I forgot."

"What the hell am I supposed to do? The whole point was for it to be ready before I leave tomorrow."

Trying to be helpful, I walked into his closet and attempt to pick out something else. He did have about 100 suits.

"You can't do shit around here. I ask you one simple fucking thing!" He pushed me out of the way, so roughly that my face slammed into the wall.

I brought my hand to my lip. Just a little blood. Nothing I couldn't handle. That was my fault for completely forgetting about stopping at the dry cleaners before the conference.

"I'm sorry, it won't happen again," I said in a low voice.

"Better, not" he said.

With Frank out of the house so often, I seemed to forget how easily the littlest thing could set him off. I decided to go back downstairs for a glass of champagne and maybe a few strawberries, instead of taking any more verbal or physical abuse for the night.

Finding myself turning for comfort to the most unexpected person, I sat in my kitchen yet again getting into a late night text conversation with Collin. As usual, he asked me how I was and as usual, I lied and told him I was fine. Should I tell him? Eventually he's going to see a mark or bruise; I would have to come clean sooner or later.

Me: Can you meet me tomorrow?

Collin: Of course. Just let me know me where.

I chose my favorite park and explained to him where to find me. When I placed down my phone I imagined what would happen if Frank ever read my messages. Then, for the first time since I've had a cell phone I set a password to lock it before putting it into the night table and turning in for the evening.

CHAPTER 15

There were just too many secrets. One by one, I would have to knock them out or I would end up drowning in lies. Sitting nervously in the park reminded me of that cold winter evening when I waited for Frank. Good thing it wasn't cold this time. No, this time it was simply brisk. The air was fresh and had a clean scent. Trees were starting to turn color. Occasionally, a soft breeze would stir something undesirable in the air, like the smell of a dog in dire need of a bath, but for the most part, it was indeed a lovely day.

I knew the most private little areas of the hundreds of parks in Bergen County. Collin and I were meeting in Dunkerhook Park in Paramus. There was one spot where we could have some privacy. It was near the water, a bit of a hike from where my car was parked. Except for bird chirps, it was calm and peaceful. It was what I needed after the previous night's events, which I kept trying to block from my mind.
When Collin found me, I kept my back turned to him, my head down. *What's he going to say?*

"Hey," Collin said quietly as he approached me. I hesitated to look at him. He knew something was wrong. He cautiously touched my arm. "Victoria? What's wrong?"

I sighed then turned around slowly looking up at him.

"Oh my God, what happened?" he said taking my chin in his hand inspecting my injuries.

"I'm fine," I said turning away from his touch.

"You're not fine! Did someone do this to you?" He was angrier than I expected. Why didn't I see this reaction coming? "Who did this? Victoria, tell me!"

"Calm down," I said. I should have been flattered that he cared so much, but I was more mature than that. I *knew* he cared. I didn't need confirmation, so I continued to downplay my situation with Frank. Truly, all I cared about was my situation with Collin.

"Calm down? I can't even understand why you're so calm right now!" He got up walked and away from me.

Now where is this one going? I thought to myself. My eyes

followed him, watching him pace back and forth about five feet away from me. Then he walked back and embraced me softly. It felt so good being silent in his arms.

"Please tell me what happened," Collin said, desperately, breaking the silence.

"Okay, but promise me you won't freak out."

"Victoria," he said impatiently, then took a deep breath. "I *will* freak out! I care about you! I'm sure you know that by now!" I've never seen the look in his eyes that I did then. He looked like a hurt little boy. Was this all a mistake? No, it wasn't. He had two choices. He could run now or accept that this was my life.

"You have to promise that you won't try and get in the middle. This is *my* problem. For me to deal with."

"If someone is hurting you then that *is* my problem," he said. "Victoria, I am here for you! What part of that don't you understand?"

"No," I said shaking my head. I couldn't let this poor kid get wrapped up in my world, with all my baggage and trouble. What if he sought revenge on Frank? I can't even imagine what Frank would do to him. "Then just forget it."

"Okay. Fine. Just tell me," he said almost demanding.

"Promise?" I asked, my eyes pleading with his. I had to tell him, but I also had to know that he wouldn't try to track Frank down.

He looked away, obviously livid about what he was agreeing to.

"I promise," he said hastily.

I looked down, so embarrassed. So vulnerable. Uncovering the biggest skeleton in my closet to someone I've known for such a short time.

"This is nothing new anyway," I started. "If he gets mad, or drunk, or high ..." I looked away. I felt the lump in my throat. "It's been like this for fifteen years."

He narrowed his eyes at me.

"Are you saying ... your *husband* did this?" he asked, incredulous.

I didn't answer and he took it as an affirmation.
Collin took a deep breath, got up again, and walked five feet away from me, again pacing, with his hands locked over his head. After a minute or so of the pacing, he returned to me and asked, "Are you serious? Why do you stay with him? What is

wrong with you? You don't deserve that!"

"You wouldn't understand."

"But you're so smart. How and why would you let this go on all these years?"

"Collin, relax," I said as his voice escalated. "You're overreacting."

"You're *under* reacting!"

"Why are you yelling at me?" I asked as my eyes began to tear up. "I told you this because … well, because I want to trust you. You said I could tell you anything, but how could I if you're going to freak out whenever you don't agree with me?" I said choking back the tears.

I had never cried in front of any man before. I was too big for that. Even with all the beatings I got from Frank, I never shed a tear. All the harassment, all the degrading things I heard, I never let the bastard know he got to me. I always kept a tough interior and then let it all out when I was alone.

Now I had found a safe place in Collin. Here was someone who cared so much for me. Someone I could be vulnerable with. Someone I could honestly show myself to. Someone to whom I could expose all my worst fears. Someone I could trust. For once in my life.

I nearly collapsed into his arms and let it all out. I cried and sobbed hysterically.

Seeing how upset I was Collin's demeanor quickly changed.

"I'm so sorry baby," he said holding me, as I sobbed and sobbed and sobbed. "You're right. I didn't mean to yell at you. I'm sorry." His words were quiet as he gently caressed my head. "It's gonna be okay." He was so assuring and I believed him. I almost didn't hear his words. I felt him there and that was all that mattered to me.

My knees felt like lead and the emotions all swarmed through my body centering in my stomach. My chest felt tight, like I couldn't breathe. Dropping to my knees and with my face in my hands, the uncontrollable crying continued. Crying years, and years, and years, worth of tears and pain that I'd buried. *Oh my God, I finally let it all out.* It was the biggest burden I've kept inside. Relief was the first feeling. Then regret. Then anger. I bawled like a baby while Collin knelt beside me and held me close to his chest, soothing me. I wanted to scream. I did, a little. If he wasn't there I would have lost it. He stayed right there with me while I broke down to pieces.

I don't know how long he held me or how long I was crying, but eventually it was getting a little cooler and it seemed the sun was going down.

I finally felt the relief of getting it all out. I could only imagine how red my face was and how much make-up was smeared all over.

I looked up at Collin and he was more serious than I'd ever seen him. He was always so carefree and silly. Not that day. He was truly bothered by what I revealed to him.

"C'mon, Sweetie get up," he said. "A little walking will do you good." He extended his hand and I grabbed it, holding tightly. We walked together for a minute or two, from the grass to a full tree.

"I need to sit again," I said. We propped ourselves against a tree and sat silently until he asked me a question that no one ever asked me before.

"Do you love him?" he asked suddenly.

I shrugged. "I don't know anymore."

"You either do or you don't."

"It's not that simple. I asked him the same question the other day. He couldn't really answer it either." I said. "We have a family. A whole life together. He's not perfect. Neither am I. I guess we're doing the best we can."

"Okay. So you have kids together. And that gives him the right to …" he stopped himself, exhaling. "I promised you that I won't get involved. However, I can't promise I can sit by and watch you get hurt either. *I know I can't do that.*"

"I understand."

"How can any man ever hit a woman? I don't get it. I'll tell you one thing for sure, that'll never happen with me."

"You know, I never thought Frank was capable of half of the things he does today. The pressures of what we had to go through to get to where we are. Sometimes it's a lot of stress."

"I don't care. There is still no excuse."

"How are you so sure one day you won't come home late at night? You're tired, bills are past due. And whoever you're with at the time is nagging you at three in the morning. You might snap. Not because you're a bad guy, but because it just happens. You don't know until you're in that situation."

"Victoria, first of all it's very sick that you almost sound like you accept and excuse what your husband does to you.

126

Second of all, please don't ever compare me to him." he said and was quiet for a while as if he were contemplating telling me something.

"Do you want to know why I can sit here and say that I know it won't be me?" He finally said.

I nodded.

"Okay. I want to show you something," he said as he reached around and pulled his wallet out of his jeans pocket. He unfolded it, then pulled a picture from one of the slits and handed it to me. It was a photo of him when he was young, maybe Nick's age. His innocence in the photo made me smile. Next to him was a young girl, around Ashley's age, with soft chestnut curls and wearing a forest green prom dress. They both looked so carefree and happy.

"I've seen pictures of her in your apartment," I said. "She's beautiful. Who is she?"

"Ava. My sister."

"You guys look so sweet. You're adorable. How old were you?"

"Thirteen. And that was taken at her sweet sixteen."
Even at 13, Collin had that special something, with the same deep eyes and dark rustled hair.

"We were like two peas in a pod. Even with the age difference. We had many of the same friends. Same interests. Of course, we had our moments, all siblings do, right? I always tried to look out for her. *Always.*"

"What happened?"

"She was dating this guy. Mark. He was nineteen. I never liked him. They argued all the time. She was always crying. He had no business dating a sixteen-year-old anyway." He sighed and tried to relax after getting all worked up. He slowly continued, "After her sweet sixteen they had this huge fight. They broke up. About a week later, he came to the house. Trying to get her back."

I placed my hand on his as he struggled to collect his thoughts.

"I heard all this commotion in her room so I went to see what was going on. Can you imagine seeing the person you love the most, Brooke ... or one of your kids ... just lying there? I tried to fight him but this guy literally threw me across the room and beat the hell out of me. Fractured rib ... concussion... stitches."

"Oh no, I'm so sorry," I said, trying to hold back even more tears as I imagined all this happening to him and his sister. However, no holding back, the tears came again.

"What happened to me … it was nothing. To this day I don't care about that part of it."

"Sounded pretty serious. You could have died."

"Well, she didn't make it," he said then quickly wiped his eyes with his sleeve. "I couldn't protect her."

My stomach sank and heart hurt as he told me this.

"You know it wasn't your fault, right?" I asked and when he didn't respond I knew that he still held a lot of the responsibility for his sister's death inside. Tears, once again, fell down my face as I thought about the pain it must have caused him. Poor thing. Going through that at 13. And she was only 16?

"She was just a kid," I whispered thinking about Ashley at that moment.

"I still miss her so much," he said bowing his head against mine. Now it was my turn to comfort him. I stroked his hair and his face and felt some water. Now it was Collin's turn to cry. So sweet. So vulnerable. So unafraid to be a real man and let it all out. I was definitely falling hard for him.

Collecting my thoughts I said, "I'm sorry you and your family had to go through that." Truth be told, I was sorry my family and I had to go through it too.

This was one of the most emotional days I had in ages -- emotional in a good way. For years, I felt dead and numb to Frank's shenanigans. Today I felt renewed and refreshed.

Still holding me, Collin said, "That's why I felt terrible and really didn't want to come between you and your sister. But we ended up drawn to each other anyway." He kissed my head. "Have you talked to her about us?"

"No."

"I really think you should."

"I know. You're right," I said. In the beginning, I had no idea what was going on between Collin and me but by then it was more than obvious to me that he wasn't going anywhere and neither was I.

Now that I was starting to come back to reality, I asked Collin, "How bad do I look?"

"You're absolutely beautiful," he said.

"No, seriously."

"Your make-up is running a tiny bit."

"I don't believe you." I grabbed my purse, looked in my pocket mirror and saw mascara – all over the place. This shit was supposed to be waterproof! "This is so embarrassing. I have to wash my face. There's a public rest room nearby…"

As I stood up, he pulled me back down, into him and then grabbed my face kissing my lips softly, making me feel beautiful even if I did look like a raccoon.

What a sight the two of us must have been; both of us red-faced from crying. Me, with the added eyeliner and mascara mess.

"We must look real cute," I said, jokingly snuggling into to him.

"We sure do," he said rubbing my arms as it started to really get chilly.

It turned out that he did understand, in more ways that I wished he hadn't. We had something very unfortunate in common, that seemed to bind us closer together.

CHAPTER 16

October, along with vibrant reds, marigolds, and plums and alternating mild, chilly, and warm days, welcomed us. Collin and I continued to sneak in time for each other at least once a week. It was always my favorite day of the week. The other six were spent thinking about him or wondering if it was that day yet. Our relationship was weird; I didn't even know to call it that. Still no one knew about us. None of his friends or family, and obviously none of my friends, or family knew. Every time the opportunity presented itself to confess to Brooke, fear or distractions won. Nevertheless, the discussion that Collin and I had a few weeks prior in the park was always in the back of my mind. I was very lucky to have my sister.

Unfortunately, as my relationship with Collin grew stronger, my relationship with Brooke was slowly deteriorating. He was right. I needed to talk to her. Putting all of my anxiety about it aside, I finally went ahead and arranged a night for Brooke and me– just us.

My intentions in meeting her were not to seek approval ,but rather to confess this secret between us. I needed to come clean with her. I didn't want to dig a deeper scar between us. After all, she was my sister and she deserved the truth.

Spending an evening at Brooke's house was just what the doctor ordered for us. Because of all the previous tension it was awkward at first, but as the night went on we both found ourselves at ease and comfortable with each other. I couldn't believe how nice it felt being with my sister and enjoying her company again, after weeks of distancing ourselves from each other. In fact, we were getting along so well it almost seemed like the wrong time to tell her about my relationship with Collin. *But then again when is the right time for something like that?* I could only hope that maybe she would be happy for me? Maybe.

Just as I was thinking about Collin, I received a text message from him. I glanced over at Brooke before reading it, but she was busy cutting a strawberry cheesecake that she just finished making. Even though I was about to see him in a bit I couldn't help but respond to him. He said something silly, as he always did, making me chuckle aloud.

"Is that Frank texting you?" Brooke asked, glancing at me as she placed a slice of cake in front of me.

I laughed. "Frank? No. He would never text me." *Never*. Not to see where I was, how I was doing, if I needed anything. I wasn't *that* special.

"Oh. Well, you're such a big texter these days," she said. *She noticed? Does she suspect something? No, she couldn't, could she?*

"Am I?" I asked and laughed nervously. *I was*. Because when I wasn't with him I was texting him. And when I wasn't with or texting him I was dreaming about him.

Right now it's about Brooke, I thought as I placed my phone down and slid it to the side. Then I picked up my fork to taste the cheesecake. *Focus on the present, Victoria,* I thought to myself.

We quietly enjoyed our dessert and sipped on some fantastic white wine. Looking over at her I realized that this was one of the few times that I wasn't lying about actually being at her house, in the three months that I'd been secretly seeing Collin. Suddenly I started remembering all of the great times she and I shared growing up. Well, many of them were of Brooke, our mother and me. She was such a good mom. I really missed her. Then I couldn't help but smile at Brooke, appreciating the relationship that I'd neglected. Definitely taken for granted. And lately seemed to be falling apart.

"What?" she asked, looking at me as she took a bite of cheesecake.

With a smile now on my face I replied, "I've just missed you. That's all," as I poured both of us some more Pinot Grigio. She frowned at me questioningly. "Missed me? You see me every day."

"Yes, but that's not what I mean. We really haven't spent any quality time together. I miss that," I said handing her the glass.

She looked down with a guilty expression.

"I know," she said fixing a stray blonde strand behind her ear. "I'm sorry I've had a lot going on lately."

"Me too," I said. Brooke and I have tackled obstacles that very few sisters have. She was there for me every time I needed her and it wasn't fair to keep her in the dark any longer. I was convinced that there was nothing that could ruin our bond.

"Actually," I said. "There's something I need to tell you."

She looked up at me. "Sure. What's going on?"

I started to remember what I had recited repeatedly up until arriving at her house that day. Somehow, the words were all gone and I forgot the entire speech I had planned.

"Is everything okay?" she asked when she noticed that I wasn't saying anything. *Everyone always asks me that! How do I answer that? Nothing* has been "okay" since the day our mother was arrested in 1991. Since that moment, our worlds have been turned upside down. In the last three months, I've been happier then I have over the past 21 years. I deplored all of the sneaking around I was forced to do. It was never easy, but it was so worth it to me.

In such a short time, Collin became an important part of my life. I absolutely needed to know that Brooke didn't still have feelings for him. Taking a deep breath, I sat a little forward in my chair. Looking into her eyes, I couldn't help but wonder what she was thinking. She stared back at me as if she had suddenly become scared. I wasn't so sure of myself then. But, if I backed out I had no clue as to when I would attempt it again. So, I began.

"Brooke, I've been keeping something from you. Because, well, it may or may not harm our relationship. I really pray that this or anything else won't," I said, trying to swallow down the basketball in my throat that was expanding by the second.

"This isn't easy to say," I added.

Now sitting back in her chair Brooke looked at me and her eyes seemed to expand way beyond her normal gaze. Instantly I recognized the look. It was the same one she had when we were children and she was unsure or nervous.

"Okay, you're scaring me," she said, her blue eyes fixed on me.

"This may sound crazy," I warned as I took a deep breath dragging out what I had come to tell her.

She looked at me apprehensively and full of anticipation.

"Victoria, I promise that nothing could ruin our relationship. Don't forget what we've been through," she said, trying to assure me.

Nothing like this, I thought.

"Sometimes when I disappear, like after work or during lunch, I'm not always where I say I am."

"Oh. Okay, so where do you actually go?"

"All different places. Usually to the city though."

"I don't get it," she said. "Why?"

Okay, no more dancing around it.

"I've sort of been seeing someone else," I blurted out.

"Oh my God! Seriously?" She looked at me wide eyed in disbelief.

"I can't believe it," she said then pushed her plate to the side more seemingly now intrigued about this secret I just revealed.

"Yeah, you're telling me," I said, blowing out air that it felt like I was holding in for an eternity.

Brooke now leaned forward and said, "You're right that is crazy! Be careful though. If Frank ever found out…"*Whew, Frank was her first concern. What a relief that she was obviously clueless about Collin and me. Well not for long.*

I cut her off immediately, not wanting to hash through that part of the situation.

"I know, I know," I said in almost a whisper. "I think about it all the time. But he won't." Sitting back a little and feeling somewhat at ease now I took another sip of wine, probably to give me just a tad more confidence. Although I still felt slightly nervous. I had no clue as to how she would react once I confessed the rest. Before I could even begin, she started with the hundred questions I knew would come.

"Wait so … who is he? Do I know him? Is he cute?" Brooke was practically at the edge of her chair, partially curious and partially excited about this something scandalous in our otherwise mundane lives. It had that immediate effect on us.

My heart was racing. Can't stop now. I had to follow through. I was scared, sad and ashamed. I've betrayed my husband and my sister too. I was a terrible wife and an even shittier sister.

Brooke grabbed my hand. She searched my face for answers as we sat in silence. *Do I really have to go through with this? Who is he?* He is a complete gentleman who makes me laugh and feel safe. He gives me butterflies. I didn't think those feelings were possible any more – not for me, a woman who was married so many years and practically invisible to her husband. *Is he cute?* "Cute" isn't the word. He's simply gorgeous. Beyond reason. I love his smile. And his hair. And his eyes. And everything else about him. He was embedded so deeply into my brain that I just could not stop thinking about him.

I wished I could say all that to her. I really wished I could. I knew I couldn't. Placing my hand over hers and leaning forward to close some of the space between us I began.

"Brooke. Don't be mad at me, please don't," I warned her but wasn't sure if the disclaimer would be enough.

Now she was somewhat taken aback. Moving back in her chair a little, she looked at me and that smile that once lit up her face was gone. "Wait... why?" She crooked her head to one side, furrowing her eyebrows. "Do I ... do I know him?" she asked.

I nodded, feeling sheepish.

"You and him kind of used to date, actually," I said, and took a sip of my wine, collecting my thoughts.

"Really?" she asked, obviously confused.

"I just want you to know that I didn't plan for this to happen. And Brooke, believe me, I so wanted to tell you sooner, I just didn't know how. Besides I didn't really expect to develop feelings for him."

Now that she was no longer smiling she said, "You still didn't tell me who he is."

I didn't, did I? The butterflies were flustering about again, but these were not the good kinds.

"From the spring, this year. You two dated for a bit," I hinted, hoping she would figure it out before I had to tell her directly.

"Um. Jake?" she guessed.

"No. It was after Jake."

"Vic, I really don't know. Could you just tell me?" She sounded exasperated.

"I'm talking about Collin," I said. *There, done!* I had finally said what I had been keeping a secret from my sister, for all of these months.

"Okay. Seriously," she said. She was not amused.

"I *am* being serious."

She took in what I said for a few moments, not sure, if I was pulling her leg or not. When she began to realize I wasn't blurting out "April Fools!" anytime soon, and that it was the middle of October any way, she retracted her hand from beneath mine.

"So... *you* and Collin?" she asked looking for confirmation.

I nodded.

Then she too nodded slowly and nonchalantly pulled her plate in front of her and said nothing else. She resumed eating her cheesecake as she processed the new information. I waited forever for her to say something else.

"Brooke?"

She looked up at me.

"Can you say something? Please," I said.

"You're really telling me the truth?"

"Listen, Brooke, I'm sorry. I really am."

Nothing.

"Are you mad?" I fumbled my fingers around now somewhat surprised about feeling the guilt.

Looking at me she said, "Vic, I'm lost. Like… when? How…?" She seemed a little loss for words. "I thought you *hated* him."

"I didn't hate him."

"Alright. But, you gave me hell for weeks while I was with him. You and I even argued about it. Was all that so you could go after him?"

"No!"

"Then?" she asked, awaiting explanation.

I sighed. "It wasn't like that at all. He and I ended up in the office together during that black out in June, that's when it started."

She stared at me, her expression unreadable. *I think she's pissed.*

At my own risk I continued, "Then, you two broke up. I actually went to talk to him about what had happened. There was an attraction that was, well, very confusing to me."

"During the blackout?" she asked furrowing her eyebrows.

"How come neither of you said anything to me?"

"Brooke, I'm so sorry. I know how it sounds. I swear I didn't plan any of this…"

"You said that already," she snapped as she rolled her eyes. I was glad at that moment that she wasn't the type to lash out physically and stab me with the fork, the way she was twisting it around in her fingers and all.

"And on top of that you both have been keeping this from me for almost four months?"

"Yes. Well, really *I* have, since you two don't speak to each other anymore."

"What do you mean? Collin and I talk almost every day. Or every other day," she said. She looked at me as if I was missing something.

"Wait … what?"

"Oh! What happened? You didn't know this?" she said in

a way as if to mock me. "Well, now I don't feel so bad about being left in the dark."

I was under the impression that they hadn't spoken to each other in months. *Why would he keep that from me?*

"You're mad and I can understand," I said and sighed.

"Victoria, I'm not mad," she said. "I don't know what you want me to say." She shrugged. Then I was sure she was going to stab me with the fork. "I don't know what, like maybe, 'congratulations'?" The sarcasm in her tone made it obvious how she felt.

"Look, I needed to tell you and I did. I don't want to overstay my welcome. Do you want me to leave? We could talk about it tomorrow." Suddenly I was sorting many emotions that this conversation stirred. The tide had turned and I felt slightly betrayed. Here I had come to confess my secret only to find out that Collin actually held one back on me. This was seemingly beginning to look like all of us held too many secrets.

"Okay. I'll go now," I said under my breath when she didn't answer or even look at me. Brooke just sat there with her head down.

I went to the kitchen counter and grabbed my keys – and phone. Then I took my purse from the back of the chair and started walking toward the door.

Is she going to stop me? I looked over at her but she continued to stare at her plate.

"Brooke. I'm leaving."

Still nothing.

I didn't know what else to do. I was just as sad and confused as she was, but obviously not for the same reasons.

Now my eyes were welling up too.

I left abruptly and closed the door behind me. Then came my own tears. Flowing down my face like a roaring rapid. I couldn't fake that my tears were for my sister – or my husband. Collin brought these tears to my face. *How could he deceive me like that? He's been talking to Brooke every day? Such an important detail to eliminate. What was I missing? What was really going on?*

CHAPTER 17

I closed the door behind me. *That didn't go the way I'd hoped.* While sitting in my car I pull out my cell phone to text Collin. We had plans to meet after my evening with Brooke. I couldn't bring myself to drive off. This wasn't right.

I began typing into my phone but the excitement that was usually there when we talked was lacking on my end. Again, I wondered why he never mentioned that he and Brooke still spoke on a regular basis. It made me remember that what we were doing wasn't all fun and games. It was real and someone was going to get hurt.

Sad and confused, I started my car and drove off, careful not to speed as I had a very bad habit of letting my emotions rule my driving. I was heading toward the city to see Collin, but decided to turn around and go back. I was just too upset to drive. I didn't want to cause an accident. But where could I go? Subconsciously, I pulled back in front of Brooke's home. I sighed and just sat there with the car running, confused as to what my next move would be.

Again, my head was filled with so much noise. My life was a mess. I thought I was falling in love. I thought I found my salvation. Then I got jolted back to reality. Just as I originally thought, this whole fling was simply that – a fling, a fantasy. It wasn't real, like I wanted, like I hoped. I felt like the biggest fool on the planet.

Thinking and crying and thinking and crying. This went on a good 10 minutes or so and I tried to pull myself together. I needed to text Collin. He wanted to know what time to expect me. Now, do I really want to go there? I needed to find out the truth. Nevertheless, how do I present it to him? What do I say? How do I bring it up? How could the man who was so vulnerable and open to me, leave out the detail that he still spoke with my sister – on a daily basis? How could he forget to tell me that?

The same thoughts invaded my head — repeatedly. I wouldn't have any answers unless I came right out and asked him, would I?

I needed to contact Collin as soon as possible. I stopped crying. *Be strong, Victoria, be strong!*

Still flustered, I started to dial his number and was startled by a knock on the window. My heart skipped a beat. What the …?

I looked up to find Brooke peering at me from the other side. I pressed the button to open the window.

"Can you come back inside?" she asked.

I looked at her for a moment. Was this so we could argue some more? Because if it was, I wasn't up for it. I had enough of that in my life already.

"Please," she said. Her tone sounded sincere as she noted my hesitation. I turned the ignition off and followed Brooke into her house. I slowly returned to the table and cautiously sat down.

"We could talk," she said and seemed to be offering a peace treaty.

"Brooke, do you still have feelings for him?" I asked cutting to the chase. *Please say "no."*

"No," she said shaking her head. "Not at all. And I'm not mad. I was a bit shocked when you told me. A little betrayed. That's all.'"

"You know I would never do anything to intentionally hurt you. And he was the last person in the world …"

"I know." She paused me by putting her hand up. "Trust me I get it he's…" she thought for a moment, "someone special," she said nodding.

Oh no. She does still care about him.

She must have noticed my fear and quickly said, "But we're just friends. And I know why he didn't tell you about our friendship. Don't be mad at him."

I'm glad she understood it because I sure didn't.

"I started seeing someone too and I know I've been shutting you out a little too. And I'm sorry for that," she said. "And he knows I don't want everyone finding out yet."

"Oh," I said.

"Did he tell you why we broke up?"

"No. He told me to ask you."

"Well, I was embarrassed to tell you when it happened, but now it doesn't matter anymore," she said and kind of laughed, hesitating for a minute. "Well, do you remember the last time I told you that he and I hung out?"

I nodded. "Yes, I remember. I spent that whole weekend wondering if you two eloped or something." I laughed.

"No! Not at all. The exact opposite actually. Well, you know that now," she said. "So, he invited me to a party on that Saturday. There were like, about, forty or fifty people there. One thing I can tell you about Collin is that his friends are really cool and we were all drinking a lot, and you know I never drink." Brook began to ramble, as was her habit..

"So what happened?" I asked reeling her back in.

"We get to the party. And after Collin introduced me to everyone he leaves me for five minutes while I was talking to a group of his friends. Wow, by then I have to admit I was a little intoxicated when I ended up ..." She hid her face in her sleeves as she relived the moment.

"Oh boy, Brooke... what did you do?"

"I kissed one his friends in front of everyone," she said quickly, and peered up at me from under one arm.

"Damn. Really?" I exclaimed, sort of surprised by my sister's actions.

"I know, I know. I felt so bad about it at first. However, eventually Collin and I talked about it, and after several days, he forgave me. Everything's cool now."

"Wow."

"Besides, it did work out for the best because we're better off as friends anyway. And I like his friend a lot."

"When do I get to meet him?"

"I'm not ready yet. It's complicated. And it's all still new to me too, you know what I mean?"

"Of course. I understand," I said knowing that I could no longer lecture her. What position was I in to act all high and mighty?

"So ... you and Collin huh?" she asked with disbelief.

I nodded. "I don't even know how or when it happened. All I know is that one day I woke up and he was the first thing on my mind, as well as the last."

"Well, if he makes you happy, then I'm happy for you," she said and the look she gave me was one that said "I have my sister back" and we were about to talk as if this was not something we would hold against each other. I still sensed some tension and her words did seem a little forced. Brooke always was a bit of an actor, hard to read at times.

"So, what's going on with you two anyway? You guys just having a little fun ..." Ah, there you go, Brooke trying to downplay it. Something was up with her. She was not as *cool* as she was trying to make it appear. I immediately felt uncomfortable, but I was in no mood to downplay – this was *real*.

"It's not like that," I said quickly. My defensiveness came from a strange place with which I was unfamiliar. My feelings for Collin were stronger than I had expected and they were starting to sneak up on me.

"You sound like you like him ... a lot."

I didn't answer. *"Like" might have not been the word and "a lot" was an understatement.*

"Wow. Okay," she said looking down. Then she looked up at me strangely with question in her eyes. "Have you guys even ..."

I shook my head. "No. That's what I'm trying to tell you. Our connection is much more than just a physical one."

"That serious huh?" she asked. "Can I just tell you one little thing that bothered me? But, don't get mad. I don't want you to think I'm trying to rain on your parade. I think it's important, though."

"What is it?"

"The only thing," she said, "is that he's really hung up on his ex."

"I picked that up too. But, she's in California. Right?"

"I think so. She's always trying to get him back. I don't want you to get hurt, that's why I'm telling you."

"Thanks, but I'm not even worried about it. If you could only see how he and I are together."

She smiled at me.

"I think ..." I started to say.

"What?" She asked.

"Never mind," I said, realizing that I would sound like I was losing it if I said what I was really thinking and feeling.

"Shoot, what about Frank?" she asked me slightly turning her head sideways as if she was curious about my answer.

"I don't know, I mean what about him? I love him but he's never around when I need him. And Tommy is already gone. Ashley leaves next year. Nick doesn't say more than two words to me," I said.

"And when he does it's the wrong words I tell you," I added shaking my head and we both laughed a little. I then realized why I had been so lonely without Collin in my life. "So ,now he fills in what I've been missing, I guess."

140

"Makes sense. I'm sorry, Vic if, I haven't been around either. I didn't realize all that was going on and what you've been through lately. And sis, I'm not mad either," she said leaning over and reassuring me with a warm hug.

Suddenly, all of the misery I felt before arriving and my fear of the unknown lifted from me like a large heavy wet blanket. We finished the evening drinking a little more of our wine and indulging in more cheesecake. Our conversation was productive because I finally didn't have the burden of this secret. And after spending time with Brooke I was headed into the city for another wonderful late night of romantic surprises with Collin.

I sent Collin another text message asking if he was home yet. He wasn't, but he suggested that I meet him in downtown Manhattan, not far from where he lived. I always felt like the risk of someone seeing us was dangerous, but at the same time it was getting old staying inside his apartment all the time. I decided to take my chances. The odds of someone I knew running into us in the busy city late at night had to be one in a million.

He instructed me to go to Columbus Circle. *Great. He knows I don't know my way around!* I parked by his apartment and walked about eight blocks before getting off on the corner of 59th Street and Columbus Avenue. The air smelled like brewing rain and shish kabobs. People flooded the streets walking through each other in rows like a well-oiled machine. *Everyone is in a hurry. What could be so urgent this late at night?*

When I arrived at Columbus Circle, I searched for Collin through the throngs of people. A young couple sat by the fountain holding hands. Two students studied together on a bench. A man walked his dog while talking on his cell phone. Two young women pushed strollers that had shopping bags hanging all over them. There was so much going on all around me.

I somehow spotted Collin, who found me first, and was already walking up to me with that sexy smile planted on his animated face.

"I will be conducting a private tour of the city. Care to join?" he asked, holding his arm out to me. "We're getting some exercise, too."

"I'm okay with that," I said as my face also lit up with a smile.

I linked my arm in his and we headed toward the huge metal globe in the center of the Columbus Circle Plaza. A large coffee shop took over one entire corner. A few boutiques, Duane Reade, and apartment buildings were on the other side.

"Aren't we near where they display that gigantic Christmas tree?" I asked him as we walked. He laughed at me.

"Rockefeller Center, babe," he said correcting me shaking his head.

"Yes. *There*," I said.

We continued to walk and passed the Trump Tower on our left side. He claimed it was one of New York's most famous hotels, where many celebrities stayed when they're in the area. It was ridiculously tall and gorgeous. I was noticing a trend. Tall, large and huge structures. I guess everything in New York needed to be larger than life.

We passed the Lowes movie theatre on Broadway. The blinking lights were so bright. I looked around and felt like a child at Disney World. I've been so deprived of travel that, even though Alpine was only a few miles away, I'd still never seen most of the famous landmarks in New York. While we walked, I couldn't dispel the annoying feeling that kept nudging at me, reminding me about my discussion earlier with Brooke. I tried to find the perfect opportunity to bring it up as we waited for a bus to go further downtown.

"So, I finally talked to Brooke today," I said looking up at him as he had his arms fixed around my waist.

"Yeah? How'd that go?"

"Um. Fine I think," I said pausing. "I told her about us."

"What'd she say?"

"She was confused, and seemed hurt about the fact that I kept the secret."

"But you two talked it out? Everything's okay?" he asked.

"Yes. I'm pretty sure we're good. But I have to admit that it was a little weird for me when she told me that the two of your still talk."

"Yeah. We do."

"You never mentioned it to me."

"My bad. Is that a problem?"

"I was a little annoyed about it," I said being honest with him.

"Really? I wasn't trying to keep it from you. It just never really came up. It's not like we hang out or anything."

"It's fine. She explained it to me," I said burying my angst about the situation. I figured it would be best to drop it. There was no point in arguing. If anything, I would pay attention to any warning signs or strange behavior on either of their parts. One of the many discoveries I made about myself was a newfound jealousy that I'd developed about Collin. It sat right alongside of passion and intense desire.

We only waited at the bus stop for three or four minutes before a large blue and white bus arrived. When we boarded there was only standing room. We held onto a metal pole in the middle of the bus. Whenever it stopped, I seemed to be the only one who stumbled around idiotically every time. Collin held the bar with one hand and my waist with the other. It amazed me that when he touched me it sent a vortex of desire through me.

We were stuck together like magnets.

After about a 10-minute ride he reached up and pressed a yellow strip, which notified the bus driver to let us off at the next stop.

"Times Square," the driver said over the loud speaker.

Times Square! I lit up. Aw, he remembered.

"Wow!" I said like an amazed tourist when we stepped off.

"How have you never been here?" He shook his head at me then took my hand while I gawked at every little detail.

Lights. It was the only thing I seemed to notice. Flashing, blinking, rotating, spinning, different lights signs and banners used to advertise many different famous companies. Symbols and slogans everywhere. The biggest McDonald's ever. Everything was over the top. Huge. Extravagant. Amazing.

"It's just like in the movies," I said in admiration.

"You're so cute," he said and gave me a quick squeeze before pulling my hand, "Come on, there's a whole lot more."

Speechless, I followed him and must have looked like a deer in headlights. The city lights were blinding and the air still held the thick smell of impending precipitation. We walked into a candy store and picked out jellybeans, skittles, and chocolate covered gummy bears. He bought me a little stuffed teddy bear with an "I love NY" t-shirt. It was turning out to be just another sweet carefree night filled with laughs.

The Broadway show signs caught my attention, but not as much as a huge set of red stairs in the middle of the street. They were dazzling and distracting.

"Um what's this supposed to be?" I asked as we walked up to them.

"The ruby red stairs," he said shrugging.

"I can see that!" I laughed. "But what are they for? Are they set up for a show?"

"No."

"So then why are they there?"

"I don't know. They're always there. It's actually a ticket booth," he said showing me the side where 'TKTS' was written, also in red, across the clear siding.

"It's really random, I don't know if I like it,"

"Well, I'm random. Do I bother you?"

"Yes, you do! And I don't know if I like you either," I said throwing a handful of jellybeans at him before running up a few of the stairs. They were set up like bleachers at a football game. The top looked too high up, so I forfeited quickly, taking a seat only a few rows up. He sat next to me scooping his arms around me.

"That was a short race," he said.

"Yeah, you know. Heights," I said.

"I thought you didn't like the stairs," he teased.

"Well, at first they were random and annoying! But I think they sort of grew on me," I said smiling at him. He leaned forward to kiss me and I stopped him.

"Too many people. Maybe one day we'll have our own moment here," I said standing up.

We continued on seeing the Jumbotron, where the ball drops every year on New Year's Eve, theatres, restaurants, retail stores, and so much more. Our trip was hasty since our time together was so limited. We headed back uptown by foot.

"We should head to your place now. It's supposed to rain soon," I told him as we passed 65th and began to near 70th Street.

"Just a few more stops," he said taking me further uptown. We stopped at Gray's Papayas because they supposedly were well known and had the "best hotdogs in the city."

"So if it's a hot dog place, why's it called *Gray's Papayas*?" I asked while we stopped there.

He laughed.

"I have no idea," he said as we continued to walk side by side and strolled along Central Park West heading downtown again, where it was still busy, even at 10 p.m. The city that never

144

sleeps they say. They were right. His hand slid casually into mine and I felt that nervous feeling climbing up my spine. As if everyone was looking at us, from the hot dog vendor to the crazy elderly woman that was talking to herself.

For a moment, as we walked hand in hand, I decided to tune out everyone around us and just enjoy the city. I thought of how amazing it would be to live there. It beat the dull suburban life where every white picket fence hid a handful of lies. Fancy cars flaunted around as symbols of 60-hour workweeks spent away from families. New York? It was what it was. Trying not to be run over by speeding yellow demons, turning corners without giving your loose change away to possible junkies. They held up their life stories summed up into a sentence or two, written with a sharpie, on a piece of cardboard. It was real. It was perfect for Collin because it was just like him. Refreshingly spontaneous, with a perfect balance of mystery and beauty. It was artistic with multiple faces. It was breathtaking, like nothing I'd ever expected and everything I'd dreamed at the same time. Thanks to him, I had fallen in love with the city. And to my surprise, despite every effort I made not to, I was falling in love with him.

CHAPTER 18

My reverie floated away, leaving me behind, in the hospital accompanied by Dr. Bailey and Myra Santana who both attentively absorbed my life story as it all came back to me.

"It seemed so long ago, when I was carefree just getting to know Collin. I knew I was treading in untamed waters, but I never knew it would turn out like this. That night, when I realized I was falling in love with him, I should have just ended it. Simple," I said.

Myra handed me a tissue before I continued. Every single memory revealed itself to me. And I, in turn, told the doctors.

*   *   *   *

After seeing a smattering of what New York had to offer, with the only person I wanted by my side, we ended our walking excursion for the night knowing that rain was near. Of course, moments later it started to drizzle. The trees branching out from the park hardly able to shield us.

"I told you," I said teasingly as we picked up the pace.

"It's just a little water," he said stopping me in my tracks.

He had this way of wrapping his arms around my waist and pulling me into him playfully. I was like a young girl again, unable to control my rarely heard girly shrieks and giggles when he spun me around, and I fell into his silliness hitting him as he tickles me.

"Stop! Collin!" I yelled through uncontrolled laughter as the city spun around me. He put me down with his arms still fastened around my body.

My giggling faded as he held me close to him, our lips inches apart. As always, the playful energy evaporated as the mood thickened and breathing heightened. His face softened and eyes deepened as his arms still held my little waist.

"What's more romantic than kissing in the rain?" he asked, and it began to shower over us. He leaned forward a little and ,just as his lips brushed against mine, I pulled away, looking around, feeling a little paranoid again.

"Not here," I said taking his hand. We were a few blocks from his building when the sky seemed to open up; thick drops of water fell diagonally as we ran the whole rest of the way. My clothes clung to me as we stumbled hastily into his building, dripping our way through the lobby. Both of us still laughing, without a care in the world.

Ian looked at us, taken aback by our condition.

"Oh boy! You kids got caught out there, huh!" he said to us as we hurried past his desk.

"Yes. My tour guide forgot to bring an umbrella," I said smiling at Collin as Ian buzzed us in.

"Sorry 'bout the mess," Collin said, water trailing behind us. "I'll come back down 'n mop it up in a few."

He smiled at us, amused.

"Don't worry about it. I'll take care of it. You two better get changed before you catch a cold!" he called behind us as we hurried by.

We reached the elevators but they were both occupied on upper floors. Both of us pressed the call button repeatedly as if it would actually make it come faster.

"It's so cold!" I said and laughed huddling into him as he rubbed my arms. Finally, the elevator arrived and as soon as the metal doors opened, we scrambled inside. I looked up at him and couldn't stop giggling. He smiled at me as his hair dripped into his eyes.

"Don't even say it," he said as the elevator made its way upward knowing that I mentioned the forecast several times during our outing.

"Don't say what? That you look like my Yorkie after getting her bath?"

"Ha, you think you're so funny!"

"No sweetie *you* think I'm funny, remember?"

"Oh I remember," he said then the little 23 lit up. "Come on, we're here." He took my hand as we got off on his floor.

I could hardly be annoyed about my dripping hair or the fact that my clothes were plastered to my body; because it was those moments that made me love the experiences I had with Collin. He made me feel so young again. So daring. So spontaneous.

We moved as quickly as possible down the hall. I was shivering as he fumbled with his keys.

"Hurry, I'm freezing," I said eager to get inside and into something dry.

"I'm trying," he said. "This key doesn't work too well

sometimes." Then finally, he unlocked the door and let us in.

Collin threw his keys onto a table in the hallway and I followed behind him. He went into the bedroom, walked over to his dresser, and took out a t-shirt and sweatpants. Then he fetched a clean towel from the bathroom and handed everything to me.

"Here, just throw this on for now. I'll put your clothes in the dryer for you."

"Thank you," I said taking the clothes and towel.

"There's an extra bedroom right there," he said pointing down the hall to a door that I never noticed.

"Oh. Okay," I said.

How did I never notice that he had an extra bedroom? *Why does he have one anyway? For guests duh! Stop thinking so much!*

The room was simple and quaint and looked relatively unused. Navy blue and white bedding covered a full or maybe queen sized bed. The furnishing was vast, with one dresser and one nightstand. I stood in front of the mirror and couldn't help but smile at how ridiculous I looked, clothes glued to me, hair flat and stringy, makeup washed away. It was a relief to get out of the wet clothes. And what a nice bonus to have Collin's fresh clean t-shirt on! It fit like a dress, stopping just in the middle of my thighs. I was feeling a little naughty and decided to omit the sweatpants. I was drying my hair with the towel as I walked into the living room to find Collin standing by the balcony door, staring out into the lights of the busy city.

"Whatcha doing?" I asked from behind him.

He turned to look at me and his mouth almost dropped open to find me standing there half-naked.

"You like my new dress?" I said batting my eyes at him then spinning around.

"Love it," he said taking my hand, leading me to him.

We stood looking outside as Mother Nature drenched Manhattan.

"Wow you have such a gorgeous view," I said as he wrapped his arms around me.

"I sure do," he said looking at me. I blushed looking away.

"Oh you mean outside?" he said smiling.

"Yeah. But you can't see anything from in here," he said, unlocking the door to the balcony. He then slid the glass door open, exposing to us the terrace, cool air, and rain.

"You're right. Darn. Too bad it's raining!" I said sarcastically.

148

"What? You think that'll stop me?" he asked releasing me before stepping outside.

"You're crazy!"

"We're never gonna survive unless we get a little crazy," he said in a sing song voice quoting what he knew was one of my favorite songs.

"Yeah. Nice try. You could have Seal himself on that terrace singing and I'm still not going out there! Besides, we just ran all the way here to get out of that!"

"You have to see how it looks. Just for two seconds," he said. "You'll love it! I promise!"

"Nope," I said shaking my head. I continued to dab my hair with the towel. I was finally almost warm and dry I wasn't about to going back to square one.

"Come on, its super safe. Besides you still owe me my kiss," he said reaching inside for my hand.

I pulled away and took a few steps back. *He wasn't winning this one!*

"Sorry. You can never get me out there!" I said in a very matter of fact tone. Unfortunately, it ended up sounding like a 5-year-old who just said, "You can't make me."

"Is that right?" He squinted at me seeing it as a challenge and moved faster trying to grab me again. He stepped inside and I threw my towel at him as if *that* would actually slow him down, then I turned and sprinted in the opposite direction. We made a few circles around the sofa before I ran into the kitchen. I looked to my left and saw the stove, and to my right the counter. Cornered. Where's that Hershey bottle when I need it?

"Didn't get very far," he said teasingly, blocking me at the kitchen entrance. He effortlessly lifted me and carried me into the living room.

"No! I'm serious," I said trying to beg for my life as he brought me back to the open door stopping there, my arms wrapped around his neck.

"Okay, I wouldn't really bring you out," he said placing me down. "Unless you want to."

"Nope," I said again, shaking my head again, making my quick final decision.

"Why not? Would I let anything happen to you?"

I hesitated and had to admit that part of me wanted to. He looked at me with *that look*. That same damn look he gave me the night we first kissed. The look that kept me from being able to say "no" to him.

"Don't you trust me?" he added.

"That's so unfair," I said under my breath, frustrated that he knew how twist my arm.

"Okay," I said aloud to Collin, agreeing to face a fear I've had since adolescence. *What am I getting myself into?*

He picked up the towel I used earlier and held it over me like an umbrella. I held the two front corners to be sure I didn't get wet so that I wouldn't have to go through the hair drying process again.

I sighed before taking one very careful step outside then waited, as if the balcony would collapse under my foot. It actually seemed very safe. All cement, somewhat high, walls. Very private. *Okay I could do this.*

"Not so bad, right?" he asked, gently guiding me by my waist.

"I guess." I grimaced and reluctantly brought my other foot out. Immediately, drops of water landed on the backs my hands. The cool air took me by surprise.

When I looked down and realized that we were completely outside I panicked a little. "Oh my God, do you know how high up this is?" I was still unable to believe that I made it that far.

"I don't know. My guess would be about twenty-three floors," he said making me roll my eyes and laugh a little. "Don't worry about how high. Just look straight out."

When I could finally catch my breath, I took his advice and looked straight at the now tiny looking features of the city. The view from inside was breathtaking, but actually standing out there was magical. It didn't seem to be coming down too hard, so I lowered the towel to get a better look. A cold swift breeze made me gasp. He wrapped his arms tighter around me lightly resting his chin between my shoulder and neck. The incredible skyline of New York was unforgettable. Skyscrapers; some towering above others, lights of all different colors in every direction just like in Times Square, but multiplied. The usual city sounds were slightly muffled from the altitude and the patter of rainfall.

It didn't even faze me anymore that I was being gently showered as Collin stood behind me, his arms still wrapped around me, heart beating against my back.

I turned to face him.

"You okay?" he asked me. Water dripping from his hair

150

again, looking extremely sexy as usual.

Actually, I was. I nodded.

He slowly walked me over to the edge, holding me. He was like my own personal conservator. He made me feel safe the entire time, until we reached the wall. I knew not to look down. Instead, I turned around to face him again and folded my hands behind his neck. The stonewall of the balcony was hard against my back.

Our eyes locked in a romantic bond for a couple of heartbeats, until his lips joined with mine, solidifying everything I ever felt for him up to that point in that one kiss. It felt as if my skin was grazed with a live wire as he pressed himself more firmly against me, kissing me deeply. Rain continued to shower over us. My stomach dropped, as if I was on a speeding rollercoaster that just reached the top right before the huge plunge.

Our adrenaline and passion blended, creating a whirlwind of uncontrollable emotions and desires. Nothing seemed clearer than the fact that I wanted him at that moment, more than ever.

CHAPTER 19

On that terrace, Collin and I were lost in each other. The light drizzle suddenly increased again to a heavy rainfall. I looked up into the sky and inhaled the heavy thick rain scent that had invaded the air all night. The drops sprinkled over my face and neck. It was one of the most perfect moments I ever experienced in my life. Absolutely romantic. Absolutely sexy. I felt so unbelievably close to him. Complete comfort settled in; sending a warm, indescribable happiness coursing through my veins.

"You're so damn sexy," he said in a soft breathy tone. He embraced me, tenderly kissing my lips and chin, slowly moving over to my neck. I closed my eyes, lost in the moment. He had a gift of knowing what to say, how to kiss me, how to touch me. My heart beat a million times every second as I pulled him closer to me.

"I want you," I sighed as I gently nibbled his ear. I took his hand and ran it slowly up my thigh and to my bare bottom. He was as taken aback at my sudden impulsiveness as I was. In the heat of the moment, it felt right.

I placed both of my hands behind his head and pressed my lips against his. Heat surged through my body as his tongue slowly met with mine. His hands slid down my back and cupped my ass pulling me almost off my feet. He pressed his body into mine, and my breathing increased, heat rushed between my legs, and I could feel his erection against me. I wanted nothing more than for him to bury himself deep inside me. He continued kissing me, teasing, touching all over my wet body; enticing and prolonging my desperate desire, caressing my most intimate parts that throbbed with need.

"Baby, I want you so bad," I whimpered again, practically begging him. He stared deep into my eyes for a moment and caressed my cheek before we lost ourselves in another breathtaking kiss.

He lowered his pants slightly with one hand and lifted my leg with the other.

Collin paused a moment.

"Are you sure?" he asked, always considerate of my needs.

I bit my lip and nodded, whispering softly "Yes." But, of

course I wanted to scream, *YES!*

He finally ended my torment, entering my willing body. So slowly, so passionately, and thus began our lovemaking, our very first time. I inhaled sharply feeling the full length of him, my muscles contracting around him as I moaned softly, breaking our kiss. I buried my face into his and we moved together, perfectly connected. We both groaned and sighed as we felt our bodies truly, entirely become one.

The experience was an intense combination of pleasure and chemistry. I gripped his back and threw my head upward toward the thick perspiring clouds, moaning at every single sensation. I whispered his name between kisses and whimpers, but held back every urge to tell him what I *really* wanted to in those perfect moments, when it felt so right. And during those very moments it took every bit of strength for me not to blurt out that I loved him.

I'd always fantasized about what it would be like, but it was more amazing than I ever imagined. We were atop the 23rd floor of a high-rise building and were the only two people in the world.

"You feel amazing," he whispered into my ear moving so carefully as if his only purpose was to pleasure me. His hand planted firmly on my thigh as my leg began to tremble. And in time so did my entire body. I couldn't hold back any more and began to moan feverishly. I locked my arms under his, clenching tightly onto his shoulders. It felt like he was sending jolts of electricity through my body. Our sounds of satisfaction mirrored the long, drawn out ecstasy we shared as our bodies reached orgasm simultaneously.

We remained motionless for a minute or two, still tightly glued together, recovering. He took my face in both hands kissing me countless times.

I still felt like I couldn't move after coming back from the most paralyzing natural high ever. I sighed deeply, and for a few moments everything seemed dreamlike.

"Are you okay?" he asked and smiled, sweetly.

"Of course I am," I said running my hand against his cheek.

He kissed my forehead and said, "Let's go inside where it's more comfortable." He took my hand. Still gripping the wall I had a hard time budging, as my body filled with ecstatic euphoria.

"Yeah, I can't move," I said as my heart finally started to slow down.

His smile grew even bigger and then he laughed at me and swept me of my feet carrying me in his arms with mine wrapped around his neck.

When we eventually made our way back into the apartment, Collin brought me a big fluffy clean towel and wrapped it around me. He squeezed me tight and kissed my nose.

"Do you know how unbelievably gorgeous you are?" he said.

I felt my face flush.

"You're not so bad yourself," I said, wrapping my arms around his body squeezing him tight. *This is what it feels like to be in love!*

We were exhausted, well at least *I* was, but this kid didn't seem even the least bit tired. We found our way to the sofa cuddling for a while before I had to leave him. With my head on his chest, now wrapped up in a sage green and ivory striped super comfy towel, I closed my eyes and tried hard not to fall asleep while he played with my hair, the steady drumming of his heart lulled me. I sighed and snuggled into to him. This moment just *cannot* end, not yet.

"What are you thinking about?" he asked embracing me in his warm, strong hold.

That question. It catches everyone off guard because if one wanted the other person to know, the thoughts would have been spoken aloud.

I looked up at him knowing that we had bonded so intensely that it could only be one thing. It was scary. Knowing that I couldn't be without him, and that one day I might have to.

"Is this wrong?" I asked him.

"Why? Do you think it is?"

It didn't feel wrong, but morally it was. I felt sad to admit it, that we ignored that I was in fact married, all details aside. "There are so many reasons it is. Yet at the same time, it isn't. Does that make sense?"

"Baby, if you're happy then how can it be wrong?" he asked, brushing my hair back.

What do I say to that? I just stared at him until he kissed me again. His loving, amazing kiss that I wished was always mine. Only

154

mine. It was a wonder that this gorgeous young man had the effect on me that he did. I gave into my heavy eyelids as I rested in his arms. We could have stayed like that forever. His lips met mine again and the incredible electrical current between us made my stomach do somersaults.

When he finally released me from his spell, I decided to challenge him with his own question.

"So what are you thinking about?" I asked gazing deeply into his beautiful eyes.

He smiled again. "I would tell you, but you might run out of here, towel on and all."

I furrowed my eyebrows at him. *Wonder if he is also feeling what I'm too afraid to admit to him out loud. I think he does. But, what if he doesn't and I say it first?*

"I won't run," I said wanting so badly for him to say it.

"No. It's too soon," he said shaking his head.

Then I was convinced. Maybe it was too soon to say it. I've never felt like this, so how would I know anyway? I really had nothing to compare it to and we weren't even in a *real* relationship. We never could be, unless we made the impossible happen. Otherwise, we were just being drawn to a place that didn't have a happy ending.

He gently rolled me off to his side, still holding me, but now staring into my eyes so deeply, so intensely, that the pull made me stop breathing for a second.

"I know you feel it too," he said.

"I don't want you to get hurt," I said touching his face.

"Then don't hurt me," he said as if it were that simple.

I sighed. "And I don't want to end up getting hurt either."

"You think too much," he said as he moved stray, still damp, pieces of hair away from my face.

"Can I ask you something?" I hoped I could bring up the touchy subject.

"Ask me anything."

"Do you remember when I asked you what do you get out of this?"

"Yes."

"You said seeing me. Is that still all you want?" I asked looking up at him, staring into his eyes.

"No."

"But I'm still married. I don't know how we could ever be anything more."

"I know one day you'll realize that you're too good for him. Until then, I'm not going anywhere."

"If anything were to ever happen, well, I would love for it to be just me and you, but …"

"What?"

"The thing is I have a whole family with tons of bills. And … I'm used to living a certain way."

"Well, if you're with me none of that would have to change."

"It's really sweet that you want more for us, I do too; but I really want to be able to put Ashley and Nick through college. How am I supposed to do that if you're still in college yourself?"

"Don't worry about that, babe. I know I'll be doing big things as soon as I graduate," he said with all the confidence in the world. "I only have three semesters left after this one. That's why I take summer classes too. So maybe I'll be done in two."

I admired his determination and drive, but it just wasn't enough. He was a young kid with dreams and rich parents. I was a woman already submerged in the real world, with all the debt and responsibilities that came with it. I wouldn't dare tell him all that, though. I wasn't one to step on someone's ego. There was already enough of that done to me by my husband.

Collin must have noticed that he didn't have my full attention. I had many mixed emotions and thoughts running amok in my mind at the same time. It was quite overwhelming.

He alleviated me fears, reminding me of our cosmic chemistry, with yet another kiss that made every muscle in my stomach twist into a thousand knots. *I guess that would have to be enough for now because I'm definitely not letting him go anytime soon.*

He must have been thinking the same thing as he said,

"Stay with me tonight." He continued twisting around loose tendrils of my hair.

"I can't baby. You know that."

"Running out on me? Was it that bad?" He laughed.

"Stop. You already know why."

"I know," he said holding me tighter with hopes that it would keep me there. *I knew it – I just knew he was the cuddling type.*

I leaned forward and kissed him until both our lips were as tired as our bodies. I lay in his arms until the sound of the dryer went off in the distance and I knew that it should be my cue to leave.

I reluctantly started to sit up but he pulled me back down.

"Five more minutes," he said refusing to let me go.

"Baby, I would love to, but I really have to go now," I said pouting, knowing that five minutes would turn into five hours.

"Fine," he said seemingly dejected.

I strolled into the kitchen with the super-comfy towel, and Collin, both still wrapped snugly around me. I started to remove my clothes from the dryer and Collin poured each of us a glass of iced tea. I dropped the towel to the floor and stood naked for a moment knowing that he was watching me, before slowly returning into my dark denim jeans and maroon top.

"Wow, you *really* don't want me to let you go," he said pulling me into him.

I was thrilled with the knowledge that I was leaving him wanting more. We stood for a moment in the threshold of his apartment not wanting to end our night. Our hug was longer than usual, our kiss even longer. Finally, he closed the door behind us and walked me to the elevator.

"When do I get to see you again?" he asked me as he always did.

"I don't know. I can't wait a week to see you," I answered softly knowing we had plans for the following Thursday.

"I work tomorrow. How's Sunday?" he asked as he reached around me to push the elevator call button.

"I can't do weekends, babe," I said, since that was the only time that I might actually be able to spend with my family. That was if *they* were free.

"Monday?" he suggested.

"Monday," I said quickly running through my mental calendar. "Okay. Can you meet me after work?"

"At five?"

"Let's make it five thirty," I said then the elevator bell chimed and metal doors slid open. I looked over at it and he looked at me. It waited patiently for a few seconds before the doors closed and the elevator descended back to the lobby, empty. He pressed the call button again then wrapped his arms around me.

I rested my head on his chest.

"I'll miss you," I said holding him tightly. He tipped my chin up slowly and lowered his lips to mine wrapping us up in another incredible kiss.

A minute too soon the elevator doors slid open again and

we knew it was time for us to part.

"I'll see you Monday," I said and stepped inside. As soon as the doors closed, I missed him instantly. I felt a strange sadness as I descended through the lower floors. Tears formed in my eyes and I quickly wiped away the ones that escaped feeling silly. I didn't want to leave. *He's the one I want to be with.* After work, before work, while we slept. Always. My life was never about my happiness, or me, but it was time that changed. I knew that after the night we had together nothing would ever be the same again.

CHAPTER 20

That winter was cold, as most winters in New Jersey were. It snowed. Then it didn't snow. Then snowed some more. The holidays came and went, just as Frank always came and went. Ashley was often preoccupied with projects, midterms, homework, and sports. Of course, she made time for her friends and boyfriend in between, leaving me with the smallest slice of her free time pie.

Nick managed to not be expelled and was actually improving academically. Perhaps finding a friend in someone who was once an enemy was helping him? Lately he'd been palling around with Andrew. One day they're suspended for fighting, the next they're buddying up every day. I can't say for sure if that is a good thing or not, as Nick continued to be distant with me.

I was on my way to pick him up from the mall and realized that I was a bit early. Instead of waiting in the car, window-shopping, or maybe some actual shopping, sounded more entertaining. So, I parked my Audi in the Neiman Marcus parking lot near the mall's entrance. Frank would have had a heart attack that my car was that closely surrounded by other cars and that I hadn't gone to the valet. *Oh well. Good thing he isn't here.* I pressed the remote button twice to lock the car and walked into the mall.

On a Saturday afternoon Garden State Plaza was atrocious. Tens of thousands of people flooded through the corridors rushing around as if they hadn't had enough of it during the holiday season that just ended. Women walked with bag upon bag of things they probably didn't really need. That was me at some point. *When did that change?* I wondered to myself, walking through teenagers, and couples, and children. Lots of crying children. I ducked into Zales jewelry store, which was less hectic, and child-free.

It was also bright and full of temptations. Sparkling beauty everywhere. Two weeks shy of Valentine's Day; I was surprised that it wasn't a madhouse. The case that caught my attention held shiny white gold pieces with colored diamonds. My favorite was a necklace with a sapphire heart pendant. *Twenty-five hundred dollars, though?* Next, my attention was diverted to a case that held men's chains and rings. *Rings.* I glanced through the selection looking at the different styles, wondering which ones he would like. *Maybe someday I would be there buying him a ring. Or that we'll be buying rings together.*

"May I help you?" asked a friendly woman in a black blazer. Retail workers were usually extra friendly to me, as if they could sense that I had money. The men were usually just trying to score numbers other than their sales.

"Just looking. Thank you," I said coming back to reality. How silly was I being? Ring shopping?

I walked out of the store leaving my dreams behind and taking the worker's commission out with me.

There was nothing new or interesting in the mall. Big surprise. *Maybe I'll check out a few of my favorites while I'm already here.* Browsing around, picking out nice denim jackets and bathing suits for the upcoming warmer seasons was fun.   I cruised through Arden B, Express, Bebe, Club Monaco, and Guess. Then picked up candles at Bath and Body Works, make-up at Sephora, and a Valentine's Day present for Frank at Tag Heuer

While I stood in line at Banana Republic, a familiar voice greeted me from behind.

"Victoria?" he asked.

I turned around to be face-to-face with Mr. John Montgomery's pearly white smile. Always in a suit, even at the mall.

"Hey! How are you?" he asked excitedly.

"Good. And you? What brings you to this crazy place on a Saturday afternoon?"

"Figured I'd shop around for Valentine's Day," he said.

"Oh, of course. Shopping for a lucky lady?"

"Yes. My mother," he said and laughed.

"How nice."

"Actually, are you busy?" he asked.
He caught me off guard.

"Um, well. A little. I'm meeting my son by the theatre in…" I glanced at my watch, "about fifteen minutes."

"Andrew is there too. At the movies," he said.

"Oh, that's right! Nick did mention him being there, totally forgot."

"Apparently everything is fine now," he said.

160

"Yes. Those kids are too much!"

"Would it be too much trouble if I ask you to assist me in choosing something? I'm not good at this stuff."

"Oh, I don't know…" My words were interrupted when a small kid banged into my leg – a little too hard. *Am I glad mine are grown,* I thought. I mouthed an "ouch" and squinted my eyes to ease the little pain. John didn't seem to notice what transpired. His thoughts seemed to be elsewhere.

"Susan used to take care of the holiday and birthday shopping and what not. I'm torn between two pieces of jewelry at Zales, it'll only take a minute," he said convincingly.

Cheap! He used his late wife as leverage. This guy was good.

"I just came from there," I said. "Sure, I guess it won't be a problem. It's near the theatre anyway." I gave in.

We were silent as we moved together toward the front of the line. Not that we could say much more, as the person in front of me started gabbing on her cell – very loudly. I looked at John and rolled my eyes. He smiled softly, knowingly.

I finally paid for my clothes and we walked out together. He held the door for me and relieved me of some of my shopping bags. *What a gentleman. Why was the universe suddenly throwing nice, handsome, single men in my path? Maybe it was a sign to let me know what else was out there.*

We went back to Zales where he showed me two different gold bracelets for his mother. I made a brief comment about the necklace that caught my attention earlier. He agreed that it was gorgeous, but said she already owned too many necklaces. We ultimately decided on a pair of dangling diamond earrings with a matching white gold and diamond bracelet.

As we walked to the theatre together, we got to know each other a bit more.

"I've actually been considering closing the office," I said to him after he asked me what I do for a living.

"Your business isn't doing well?"

"No. It's not that. We're doing fine. But, Michelle is moving on, Sue is retiring. I have no interest in hiring new people, especially when I can run things from home. My daughter is leaving in a few months, as well as our au pair, so I'll have the time and space for it," I said in a low voice.

"You don't sound too excited about it."

"I'll just miss them. Ashley and Galina. That's all." And I

wasn't thrilled about the idea of being inside that house all day, but of course I didn't feel comfortable enough to say that yet.

"I'm sure the boys will want to walk around without their parents chaperoning behind them. Would you like to stop for some coffee?"

"Oh. I really can't," I said glancing at the time.

"Okay. But you *do* still owe me," he said somewhat jokingly, reminding me of the awkward way we met.

"I'll take a rain check."

He pulled a business card from the inside pocket of his suit then tucked it into the outside pocket of my purse.

"Here you go," he said.

"I already have your card."

"Figured you lost it. Since you've never called."

"I didn't lose it!" I reassured.

"Next time for sure. Coffee," I said. Then I wondered if I should quickly remind him that I was married. I didn't have a chance as the people walking out of the theatre created confusion, and John and I began to look for our sons.

At the entrance of the Lowes, in the upstairs of Garden State Plaza, on cue as a movie must have just ended, dozens of people started to stroll out. Moments later the boys also came out of the theatre. Nick spotted me and immediately looked annoyed at my presence.

"Mom! Why are you here?" His tone was short as he focused solely on me, totally ignoring John and Andrew, who seemed to be having their issues anyway. Andrew seemed equally as frustrated that his dad didn't wait in the car for him either. *Kids!*

"Uh. Were you planning to walk home?" I asked, challenging him.

"You should'a just waited in the car!"

"I did a little shopping first. Anyway it's almost dinner time; I was thinking we could grab a bite to eat."

"Me and you?"

"Yes."

"No, I'm good," he said shaking his head." Could we please just go home?"

"May we interrupt a second?" asked Mr. John Montgomery, smooth as ever, as he just glided in with his son, Andrew, who exchanged a friendly nod with Nick. The mystery behind boys and testosterone and fighting over a girl, then

162

becoming friends baffled me.

John looked directly at Nick and asked, "Could I have a word with you?"

Nick gave him an "are-you-serious" look, which John ignored as he pulled him gently aside.

I tried to overhear them, but there was way too much mall ruckus. Nick looked at the ground then up at me. After their little private conversation, they both walked back over to me.

"I'm sorry mom. We could go eat. If you want," Nick said. *What the...? Did he just switch my son for some other kid?*

After recovering from shock, I agreed and instructed him to go ahead and find us seats in the food court, which was directly below us.

"Wow! What did you say to him?"

"Nothing much. I didn't like his tone with you so I put things into perspective a bit."

"But seriously. What did you say? Because it worked."

"I was honest with the kid. I told him to appreciate you because you won't always be there. Andrew lost his mom suddenly two years ago, so he has no mom to go eat, or shop, or even argue with."

"Wow, you are *good*," I said, still in shock. "But thank you."

The four of us enjoyed a quick bite. It was pleasant and innocent. I enjoyed John's company a lot and Nick seemed to like him, too. It was nice to have a friend. I double-checked my purse to make sure I didn't lose his card. Maybe I will call him after all.

CHAPTER 21

I woke up on Valentine's Day morning in the wrong bed with the wrong man. Somehow, I was never spared the disappointment, time and time again. I made my way downstairs and began making breakfast when Frank came down. If he only knew how much I wished that someone else would be sharing this day with me — this *life* with me. A smile formed on my face thinking about Collin.

"You're happy this morning," Frank said to me as he sat at the table.

I quickly thought of a cover-up.

"I'm just thinking about something funny Brooke said."

I sat down with him and had to admit to myself that it was nice when he wasn't being a monster, which for the most part was after he drank, which unfortunately was all the time. At least we had this left; these rare moments.

"These last few weeks have been so busy! On Friday afternoon Brooke and I had to leave orders to fill today," I said, proceeding with our matter-of-fact work related small talk. If we ever talked, it was like that of a business meeting the majority of the time.

"Before I forget, were you in New York last Thursday?" he asked and I almost choked on my orange juice. How did he know? More importantly, *what* did he know? Did someone see me? Did he see me? A million thoughts raced through my mind and I wanted to panic, but I had to open my mouth and say something. Fast.

"I wasn't," I said with a confused expression. Really? That was the best I could do? The 'it wasn't me' line.

"The EZ-pass statement came in and showed a toll charge at the Lincoln Tunnel last Thursday."

Damn EZ-pass! I could have sworn I took it off every time I went to see Collin. The stupid thing *still* reads even when it's shoved deep in the glove compartment buried under millions of papers.

"Oh! Last Thursday!" I said as if I had just recovered from a short case of amnesia. "Yes, Brooke needed to run into the city and I gave her my tag."

"For what?"

"I can't remember. I told you, it's been so hectic, with these last minute orders that we've been trying to accommodate," I said and waited to see if he would buy it.

"Oh," he said, seeming disinterested in what I had to say anyway.

"You would think people would plan better. As if this holiday didn't come on the same exact date every single year," I said.

"Holiday?"

"Yes, today. Speaking of, what are we doing tonight?" I asked Frank as I started to clear the table.

"Tonight?" he asked obviously clueless.

"Tonight. Do you want to go to dinner? Or maybe a movie?"

He looked at me as if I had 10 heads then I felt like I did.

Maybe we weren't the couple of the year, but at least we usually spent our holidays, birthdays and anniversaries together. Was one of the few things we had left for us going out the window too?

"Today's Monday. I have to work all night."

After a few moments and my blank stare, I turned around and began to silently place the dishes into the sink. Once pots and pans were clanked together a little harder than usual, he suddenly realized that I was mad.

"Oh. Is today Valentine's Day?"

I turned around looked at him shocked. Hurt even.

"You know I can't keep track of this stuff. You should have said something days ago."

"I never needed to before."

"But I work more now than I used to. If you wanted to do something you really should have told me."

"You're right Frank. It's entirely my fault," I said still scrubbing extra hard on each dish.

Don't even worry about it, Victoria, you have someone better to enjoy the evening with! Although I did feel a little guilty, as if he was my back up plan. How was I supposed to know that Frank was going to leave me hanging?

Frank continued drinking his coffee and gathering his things for the day while I stood there and finished washing all the dishes to give Galina a break from it for once.

"Heading out?" I asked as he grabbed his keys from the

key hook.

"Yes," he replied dryly.

"Are you actually coming home tonight?" *Oops, there goes my mouth again.*

"I'll be home tonight, but don't wait up," he added as he walked out.

Don't worry I won't.

I finished washing the plates from Nick and Ashley's breakfast and grabbed Frank's coffee cup that he left on the counter *again*. Was it that hard to step the extra three feet to place it in the sink? Collin never did that! In fact, *he did my* dishes for me. *Sigh.*

I left the kitchen spotless for Galina and pulled out a card that I bought for her. I scribbled a quick message of appreciation and mentioned to take the morning off. I placed a $100 gift card to the spa inside it, a box of chocolates next to it, and left everything on the kitchen counter. Then I picked up my phone, typing into it, sending Collin a text message.

Me: Happy Valentine's Day!

Collin: You too babe!

Me: Valentine's dinner tonight? ☺

At least I knew that *he'd* be happy to spend the romantic day with me. And knowing that it was short notice I didn't even mind if we just ordered a pizza, something simple. It would be perfect, as long as we were together. We already had plans to celebrate the following day too, so we could do something special then. My phone chimed and I picked it up, excited to read what sweet thing he had to say.

Collin: Tonight? I would love to but I can't.

No? Was that a 'no'? Seriously, was I just turned down twice?

Me: What?

166

Collin: I have plans. I thought you did too. I'm sorry.

I was getting tired of his many friends who took up so much of his free time. *He's young.* I had to remind myself constantly. But Valentine's Day? It was highly unlikely that he was having beers with the guys. Without thinking it fully over, I typed and sent the first thing that came to mind.

Me: Is it a date?

Maybe I was out of line asking him that. I was supposed to be spending the time with my husband and wanted him to just sit around by himself? *Yes.* No matter how unfair it was to ask it of him. Before he wrote back, I sent another message.

Me: Sorry. You don't have to answer that.

Collin: No, Victoria I'm not going on a date! Not at all.

Is he annoyed at me? Probably. The one thing that turned him off about me was my insecurities.

Collin: We can still do something tomorrow

Me: Okay.

Am I really going to be doing nothing on Valentine's Day? How was that even possible? I had not one but two men in my life and *I* was spending the night alone? Sitting around sulking for a bit, I decided not to let it get to me. *Fine then.* Maybe I'll just have dinner with one of *my* friends.

I searched through my purse and found the business

card that was still in the outside pocket. I dialed the numbers and waited.

"Hello?"

"Hi. John? This is Victoria, Nick's mom."

"Hey! How are you?"

"I'm great. Hey, listen, I know this might be very last minute but I was wondering if you're available tonight. I know its Valentine's Day and you're probably busy but…"

"Tonight would be great," he said cutting me off.

"Oh, okay, great."

"What did you have in mind?"

"Honestly, something simple," I said.

*   *   *   *

A boat ride in Jersey City at the Newport Yacht Club wasn't my idea of simple, but at least going out for a bit would get my mind off of this complicated life of mine.

I wanted to leave right from work, so I'd get home at a reasonable hour. It was only Monday and I had a long week ahead of me. Plus, I wanted to be well rested for my date with Collin on Tuesday. Not that I'd rest – how could I, I was always so wound up thinking about him.

Since this little 'date' was just with John, I dressed casually — a red top for Valentine's Day and casual black slacks with sensible shoes since we were going on a boat. And, of course, a heavy jacket, as it was still winter in New Jersey.

After work, I went to the bathroom to pull my long hair back in a ponytail and tucked it under my winter hat. My face looked a little stressed, but that was okay. It wasn't a real date. My heart obviously belonged to someone else.

The idea of this 'date' was to take my mind off him, and Frank, and the difficulties with my son; but sitting in traffic for two hours wasn't very fun. Maybe this wasn't a good idea, but it was too late to back out now.

It was hard finding a parking spot near the marina and it took a long time to walk to the boat. By then I was freezing. I also worked up an appetite, but I didn't dare tell John that — he might suggest dinner and I didn't want him to get the wrong idea.

And there he was, walking toward me with a huge

168

smile on his face. He looked anxious, a little goofy – and *old*. Not nearly as debonair as the first few times I saw him. Maybe it was his yacht club clothes. Who wears white pants in February? *Be nice, Victoria,* I reminded myself. *Be nice!*

John's eyes lit up as I approached him. "Happy Valentine's Day, Beautiful!" Oops, maybe he does have the wrong idea.

"Thank you! And a Happy Valentine's Day to you too, *Buddy!*" I said, emphasizing "Buddy" trying to create a more casual tone, quickly walking ahead of him onto the boat, ignoring his hand that was held out to help me get onboard.

This is going to be a very long night.

"So you're a boat person?" I asked.

"Yes, you can say that I'm a boat enthusiast."

"It's really gorgeous," I said, pretending to be interested. Truth be told, we could have been on a rowboat or the Queen Mary and I'd be equally unimpressed. Frank's friends had boats, so this wasn't anything new to me. Boats just weren't my thing. Regardless, I tried to enjoy the experience.

Even though the air was raw, the view of Manhattan was breath-taking. I stared into the city, knowing that Collin was out there somewhere and I wished he were here in my arms instead.

"A penny for your thoughts?" John asked.

"Oh," I said. His voice broke my dream-like trance. Thinking fast, I lied. "I was just worrying about the kids."

"I know. The boys are a handful."

"Boys? As in … plural?"

"Oh, didn't I mention I had an older son, Jacob."

"No, I didn't know."

"He's already in college and that's a whole new set of problems. In fact, that's the only time I hear from him … when he has a problem … which is probably why I failed to mention him before. Out of sight, out of mind."

"That's terrible!" I said. Although I couldn't help but laugh, as that's how I've been feeling about my husband lately.

"But believe me, I can relate in other ways."

"I'm sorry to hear that," he said and took this as an opportunity to put his arm around me.

Whoa! This was so not in the plan. Pulling away, I looked directly at him in shock. "Uh, John, did you forget I'm a married woman?"

"I know … I know," he said, "but you don't seem happy."

"I'm not," I admitted. "But I took vows, I'm committed.

I'm not the runaround type." Of course, this wasn't the main reason that I rebuffed John's advances. However, he didn't need to know about all of the skeletons in my closet, either.

"Neither am I," said John. "I never cheated on Susan. She was my heart and soul."

He put his head down and said, "I'm sorry, Victoria." He lifted his head and looked me in the eyes again, adding, "I'm just so lonely. She's been gone five years … five *long* years … and you're the first person I felt a little bit of …" He paused as he searched for the right words, then added, "A bit of life … Victoria, you brought some life back into me. I feel alive around you. And I thought you may have felt something for me too, but I guess I was mistaken."

I felt so bad for John. He had everything going for him. He was handsome, wealthy, and very kind. Another woman would snatch him up in a heartbeat.

"John, I'm sorry if I led you on in any way," I said. Then added another white lie, "If circumstances were different, then maybe …"

"Of course," he said, disappointedly. "Ain't that always the way."

He walked me back to my car, both of us silent. There was nothing more to say. We weren't going to be friends, I figured. We did have our boys as common ground, but that was about it. Who knew? Maybe if he lightened up a bit there'd be a chance of a friendship. He was just too serious … and too intent on having me as more than a friend. I just couldn't take any more drama in my life, and nothing is more dramatic than someone who wants to be more than friends when you're absolutely not interested. I may have been young when I met Frank, but I certainly wasn't naïve anymore.

I clicked open the locks of my car door. John walked ahead to get the door for me. Once I got in, he kissed my cheek and said, "Be safe."

I was at a loss for words, so I just waved and faked a smile. I put on my seat belt, turned on the ignition and drove away. Looking in my rear view mirror to see John standing there dumbfounded. *You're a heartbreaker, Victoria.*

I felt bad, but honestly, I didn't do a damn thing to lead him on. It was safe to say he was slightly delusional. *Sigh.* What a disappointment my Valentine's Day turned out to be. I wondered if I should text Collin. No, I'll leave him be with

170

whatever it was that he was doing.

When Frank walked in that night, I was lying in bed thinking about everything. Why did I stay in this unhappy marriage? Why can't I just be honest with myself and follow my dream of being with Collin? And why *did* I lead John on? Why do I always need attention from men? Why don't I have more girlfriends?

Frank thought I was asleep when he disappeared into the bathroom leaving his rings, watch, and phone behind on the night table. I could hear him singing in the shower, so I knew he'd be awhile. That man was definitely worse than a woman when it came to grooming. He always took longer than I did to get ready. And, ooh, that off-key singing, it was one of his many bad habits I could never stomach.

Lying in my own bed no longer felt warm and cozy. It was cold and uncomfortable. I guess finally feeling affection will open one's eyes. Looking around in the dark, I couldn't help being overcome with a feeling of floating in an empty abyss. *Nothing left for me here.* How I could still lay there was a mystery to me after everything I'd been through.

I had to ask myself repeatedly: Was there really anything left between Frank and me? Anything other than our children and home? What was I holding onto? Was my staying there purely fueled by fear? *Maybe I really need to move on. What could he do to me that he hasn't already done? I could get a restraining order if I needed to. Couldn't I? Please! Like that would do anything.*

Better plan. One day Frank would go to work, come home and all of our stuff would be gone. I would have each of the kids pack a bag and leave everything else behind, including the bad memories. I would never step foot through that front door, climb the elegant spiral staircase, or scrub my blood from marble tiles again. Yeah, I'd miss that staircase and everything else that comes with it – my weekly facials and massages, the fancy car, and the clothes … all the clothes, the designer labels … all of perks. But none of that defined me. Did it?

Yes, but I can leave all that behind. I'd still be me. A cheaper version of me. A happier version. I could spend the rest of my life in a beach house in Tahiti with an amazing view of clear water, bungalows on the water-literally, and white sandy beaches. Ashley would love the year-round tropical weather. Nick would enjoy surfing huge waves. Kiwi could run around and bark at seagulls. I would lounge in a bikini while I worked on my tan and watching Collin, his abs glistening in the sun while he flipped steaks on our patio and smiles his amazing smile at me. *Then* my life would be perfect.

Just before I fell asleep, with my fantasy to come alive in my dreams, I was jolted back to reality by the buzz of Frank's phone. He'd left it on the night table, which was rare. Very rare. I ignored the wailing of its cry for attention. Frank was still in the shower. Again, the phone buzzed and its brazen blue light now illuminated the corner of my room. My dark abyss was shattered when the light caught my attention. It was probably one of his friends trying to get in touch with him. Or not.

Curiosity won. I leaned over to see who it was that had invaded my privacy at 1:15 a.m. Two text messages had come though, both from unsaved phone numbers.

It was bad enough that the first text read, "I miss you already." However, when the second one read, "Thank you for the beautiful flowers! See you next weekend." I wanted to be perturbed, angry, or have some emotional response to what I had just read. I was dry from it all, burnt out because it wasn't a surprise, in fact was just … *old.*

It did make me wonder exactly what my purpose was in this marriage. I wanted to think that there was more to my being here than for this man to have something to take out all of his anger out on. His ideal wife had passed on long before our first real fight over his cheating on me. Or was I supposed to serve as nothing more than a trophy? Someone to show off at social functions, hanging onto his arm, while he got off looking like husband of the year. How cliché.

Rolling back over onto my side I sighed, wishing my fantasy could be my reality. It didn't have to be in Tahiti, or on an island at all. I would be happier living in a cardboard box in the ghettos of Newark with Collin. *Wouldn't I? It always haunted me a little. Daydreaming about it was amazing, but could I ever really take that step? Make such a tremendous change in my life? In myself? He was so young; did he really know what he wanted? And, in all reality, what would become of my family? Would we all move into his two-bedroom apartment in Manhattan? Of course not. Then again, anything had to be better than slowly dying, being suffocated by this marriage.*

Adjusting myself in the bed again, I found comfort in one thought. At least I wasn't unknowingly being cheated on and sitting by like a door mat. Then again, a part of me always wondered if Frank had treated me with love and respect would

172

I still be with Collin? I wanted to believe that one relationship had nothing to do with the other, as I loved them both in very different ways. But, when I was honest with myself, it came down to just that. Which one? And one day I would have to choose.

My thoughts were disturbed when I heard the bathroom door open and Frank's heavy footsteps walking back to our bedroom. Quickly, I resumed pretending deep slumber. There was no sense in addressing any of the text messages. I knew exactly what would happen if I did and it sure as hell wasn't worth it. Unable to fall asleep for a while, I tried desperately to sort through my emotions and come up with the answer to that one challenging question.

CHAPTER 22

In the morning, Frank was still in bed when I closed the door on my way out. It felt like I hadn't slept at all. Insomnia was becoming a normal part of my life. Nothing should have been shocking or hurtful at that point, but it seemed impossible to turn myself into a complete robot as Frank had.

I left early because I was to meet Collin at his apartment before work. It was 6:30 am when I trotted out to the car. While driving, that text message crept into my mind again. *How could Frank spend Valentine's Day with another woman? I wasn't even going to do that! Does that make me the other woman?* I had no idea what to think any more. Ultimately, I wasn't sure how much more of his crap I could take. Collin was definitely the best choice for me, emotionally at least.

I got into New York just before 7 a.m. Not bad timing, although I knew that this was pre-rush-hour traffic. Parking in a local garage seemed to be the only option, as most cars hadn't left their parking spots for the morning yet. Before leaving my car, I checked my face in my visor mirror. Now, not only did I feel tired, I looked it!

It was surprising to be able to hear my black Dolce and Gabana heels clicking against the sidewalk. This early version of the non-chaotic New York streets made it much easier to enjoy the big city. Yet even at 7 a.m., it never ceased to amaze me the sights you see in New York City. A punk rocker, with a green Mohawk at 7 a.m.? *Really?*

But yes, even frazzled and exhausted as I was, I enjoyed this early morning alone time, just walking the streets and taking it all in. New York made me come alive. So,by the time I reached Collin's apartment, I felt better.

Walking into the lobby, I couldn't help but smile slightly at Ian. Nodding back with a large smile attached to his round face he said, "Good morning, Miss Carlisle." Reaching over, he buzzed me into the building. His actions made me secretly glow a little inside. *I'm considered a regular guest here.* And it is always quite entertaining that he calls me "Miss." I snickered to myself wondering if he thought I was some college girl that Collin picked up. Then again, it was sometimes as if I lived there, and that felt strange. The elevator started to climb and the floor numbers grew into the teens. I kept thinking about how often I'd been there often enough that several neighbors would recognize me and engage in friendly small talk. On occasion, I'd picked up groceries for Collin's apartment, helped him clean, and even rearranged some furniture. *This really is a double life, isn't it?* It was the weirdest idea flickering through my mind, and in that same instant I looked up to find myself on the 23rd floor.

Since Collin was expecting me, he left his door unlocked and I let myself in. Closing the door and walking straight down the hall I was overtaken by the rich smells coming from the kitchen. The air filled with a salty-sweet aroma of bacon and pancakes. Smiling now I found Collin slightly bent over while he put the final touches on the table setting. He looked up at me and smiled instantly. That same captivating smile he has given me since we met.

"Good morning, babe."

"Good morning, sexy," I said walking over to him wrapping my arms around his neck. "You have no idea how much I missed you." I finally felt at home in his hold again.

"Sorry about yesterday. You're not mad at me are you?"

"Remember what you said to me once? Well, how could I be mad at you?" I said before kissing him. "Collin, this is so sweet!" I took my seat unable to help but smile back at every effort he always made for me, even eight months into our relationship. The table looked as if it was set for breakfast in a restaurant. Two settings were placed, mirroring each other. On the table, pancakes were piled high. Scrambled eggs, strips of bacon, hash browns and toast all sat on serving plates. He even had already set out coffee with all the little extras. There were two glass carafes one filled with milk and the other held what seemed to be freshly squeezed orange juice. Alongside of them, and placed in the middle of our table, was a skinny vase with one red rose in it; which over time I discovered was in fact only there for me.

Looking across the table at me with that smile he said, "I missed you too."

As if I was a little girl looking at her first doll, a smile swept across my face. Collin made me so happy that I forgot everything that weighed on my mind, as usual. It was because of things like this that made me sigh and continue to imagine that there was still hope for romance beyond what life had shown me.

Of course, a silly question popped into my head, as if I was comparing Frank to Collin; or the comparison of that life to what this one may hold for me. How did I go from one extreme to the other? Shaking my head, placing a napkin onto my lap, and once again finding myself smiling at Collin, we began enjoying our shared breakfast.

Just then, Collin's phone rang and he glanced first at me then at the phone sort of hesitating to answer it. This morning was too beautiful to be interrupted by a phone call. However, after glancing at the caller ID he obviously didn't agree as he looked back up at me he said, "Um. Give me a minute?" He asked. But it wasn't really a question, because before I could respond he was already gone from the table. Of course, after the previous night's ordeal I was done with phone calls and text messages going off. And because it was only 7:40 in the morning I then had to wonder who could be calling him so early. *Maybe it's his job? Or his mom? No, it's 3 a.m. where his family lives.* Not wanting to become paranoid, I exhaled and tried to sit back and relax. I did however find myself occasionally leaning in to see if I could overhear any of the conversation. Once again my inner self screamed, *Stop being so paranoid! Get a grip!*

But, after sitting in the chair and finding myself eating a breakfast alone, I was getting a little annoyed. After another three minutes, Collin returned to the table and placed his phone next to his plate.

"Sorry about that," he said as he grabbed our coffee mugs and headed to the kitchen to refill them. Now, my fingers most assuredly began to itch wanting to grab his phone. I was once again becoming uneasy. *And why not?* I thought. But this was Collin -- I didn't have anything to worry about. Did I? Ah … paranoia was taking over and who was I kidding? Of course Collin was kind, but he was also young and gorgeous; and by the books, single. Why wouldn't I have some competition? I definitely did if he was with someone else less than 24 hours ago. Is that who called him? *Oh no.*

Sudden jealously rumbled in my stomach and then I

just *had* to know. Just then, Collin returned to the table, sat down, and placed my cup of coffee down in front of me while smiling with the great smile that made me weak in the knees. How could I not trust him?

"Thank you, baby," I said and leaned across the table to kiss him, I "accidentally" knocked over a glass of orange juice, spilling it all over him. Of course, he jumped up surprised. Hell, I wanted to laugh a little but held it back.

"I'm so sorry!" I gasped.

"It's okay. Uh, I'll be right back, again," he said heading to his room.

So, our post Valentine's breakfast wasn't going as smoothly as planned. I felt a little guilty and knew how ridiculous my actions were, but I couldn't resist and needed to reassure myself. It was no secret that I had trust issues, anyway. Quickly, I grabbed his phone to see his last call. The name on the recent call log read 'Britney' and she had called five minutes ago. As well as calling earlier in the morning. Last night, and yesterday afternoon … I scrolled quickly and noticed that they talked late into the night for over an hour.

I now noticed that there were several calls. It seemed that Collin talked to *many* people. Okay this wasn't news, but most of them were females. *Who are Jasmine, Melissa, Eliza, and Britney? And Blondie?* Although, if I could calmly recall through the anger that was starting to build, maybe he might have mentioned the first two or three names. Two of them from school and I'm sure one was his cousin? But in the last eight months we have been together he never mentioned a Britney. Ugh, not this again! Whoever she was they spoke often. Yet he told me about the others? Not to mention I was curious as to whom the hell "Blondie" was. Maybe Brooke? *Was he playing me harder than my husband was?* Wow, what a disturbing thought!

Collin returned wearing a light gray sweater and dark denim jeans with rips in them. Stopping before the table, he ran his fingers through his hair, with a distant look in his eyes, and for that millisecond, he looked like he was modeling. Geez, how easy it was for me to forget why I was mad. That quickly dissipated as I remembered. Probably because I still had his phone in my hand. At that point, I didn't even bother trying to hide it. I knew that I'd been taking time away from my family and priorities for this kid and I needed to make sure we were on the same page. I really didn't have time for games. Looking right at him I sat back in my chair and said, abruptly, "I have a question. Who the hell is Britney?"

This seemed to shake his facade a little. For once, he looked taken aback by my direct question. Looking back at me and not smiling he said, "You went through my phone?" He looked surprised and somewhat disappointed.

I was battling my conflicting emotions. Was anger going to settle in, or was I going to be the shy girl who was caught with her hands in the cookie jar? So I said, "I wasn't really going through it…" *Well, yes I was.* "I just wanted to know who was calling you this early and who you felt was important enough that you needed to interrupt *our* time and walk away to answer it."

Collin's face dropped. He looked upset.

"Victoria, give me my phone," he said, and desperately tried reaching for it.

I backed away from him and stuck it in the rear pocket of my jeans. I wasn't stupid enough to give it back so he could erase any undiscovered evidence. *Been there done that.*

"Now would be the time for you to be honest with me," I said.

"Really? Are you this insecure?" he asked, exasperated.

He was actually mad. I don't think I'd ever seen him mad, at me anyway. His face grew red. But he wasn't the only one. And using one of Frank's famous words – insecure -- wasn't helping him either.

I wanted to be sorry for snooping, but my jealousy wouldn't let me; and I was also starting to get alarmed by his defensiveness. *He must be hiding something.*

"Do you know what I go through to be with you? Sneaking around, being away from my family…" I must have sounded so stern and angry, but I was also fighting back tears.

"Of course I do. What's your point? I thought we were past this." Now he looked like he was fighting back tears as well, but I was so pissed off I totally ignored his emotions and just worried about mine. At that moment, I just couldn't be loving and caring. Not even if I tried. My female hormones were raging. I just had to let it all out. I held in so much for so long. It was like an unknown force took over me; and I just spilled it all out.

"So did I, but not if you're spending hours entertaining other girls — and from the looks of what's on your

178

cell, there are *many* -- while I risk everything I have for you. So who are all these tramps anyway?"

"The little time we have together and you want to spend it arguing?"

"I'm not arguing with you, I just want to know who you're spending all this time talking to. And spending Valentine's Day with," I said sounding so bratty and defensive, but deep down my heart felt like someone took a knife and stabbed it.

"Is that what this is about?" he asked in a sincere tone, slightly calming down. He put his hand on my shoulder and lowered his face toward mine. He said softly, "Babe, you do realize that I'll be working in the film industry someday, right? Do you know how many people I'll be interacting with on a daily basis? You're going to have to learn to trust me. This whole episode – it's just not cool."

I sat there pouting because it sounded so much like when Frank would tell me why he had women calling all the time. Because they were his employees and co-workers at the club. And at one point I was stupid enough to actually believe him.

Finally, shaking my head, I said, "I don't know what to think any more."

"I do have friends you know." He started to sound annoyed again. He took his hand off my shoulder and backed off, started to pace around the room.

"Friends? Yeah *friends*, yet I've never heard of half of them or met any."

"Do you really want me to sit here and go through my entire phone book? Give you a whole back story to each and every single person?" His voice was almost sarcastic, but I guess it was his way to let me know how irrational I was being. He sounded so convincing and I wanted to believe him, but I wasn't ready to back down yet.

Even though it was a rhetorical question, I decided to answer it anyway.

"Yes. I do," I said knowing that I was going too far. He let out an exaggerated sigh and said more to himself, "You're starting to sound like Vanessa, I swear."

He really knew how to get under my skin! He knew that comparing me to his ex-girlfriend always made my confidence recoil. This was not the time to bring her up. "You hate when I compare you to my husband and now you're doing the same thing to me?"

"Sorry, but you do. This jealousy thing is getting old."

"Okay. At least just tell me who Britney is and I'll drop it."

"That's not how it works, babe."

Is this kid trying to school me on relationships? Now a bit more annoyed I said, "You really can't stop dancing around it and just answer my question? What are you hiding? Is she your girlfriend or something?"

He ignored my inquisitions and asked, "What have I ever done for you to not trust me?"

"Well, for starters, you're supposed to be spending time with me today and you have some other girl calling you."

"I can't control who calls me!"

"You know what... I know what this is. I lived this already. If you're screwing other girls the least you could do is be honest with me," I said getting up and gathering my belongings.

"What's your problem?" he asked grabbing my arm.

"*You are*," I said pulling my arm free. "Because you're playing games with me. I don't have time for this shit."

"Yeah, *I'm* playing games. You're married, but I'm the messed up one. Okay." He threw his hands up in the air and sighed in exasperation.

"No. Don't even try to go there! When you met me, with your smooth-operator-lines in my office, you knew exactly what you were getting into!"

Once again, he grabbed my arm. When he spoke, his voice got soft and serious again. He had such patience and it seemed it was hard for him to stay completely mad at me. He seemed to be trying so hard. "Look, I would introduce you to Britney and all my other friends personally if you weren't so damn jealous all the time."

I didn't fall for it. Again, I pulled my arm away. "Sweetie, don't get it twisted. I personally couldn't care less about you, or Britney, or whatever you want to do, or whoever you want to do!" I made my way to the door feeling as if a bomb was ticking on the inside. I had my back to him and despite the anger, I also felt remorse. *We don't argue.* It was all too familiar. Standing there for a moment feeling those damn tears that always formed, I hoped that he would stop me from walking out.

"Victoria…" he said quietly from behind me as my hand is on the door knob.

Yay! I knew he cared. Should I make him sweat just a little longer? I just stood there, for a second.

"Victoria," he said again.

With my guard down and ready to apologize, I slowly turn around feeling sheepish. "Yes?"

"I need my phone back," he said, nonchalantly.

Then the bomb went off. His phone? That's what he stopped me for? With all the arguing, I had forgotten that I still had it in my back pocket. His damn phone. With all those bitches' numbers in it. I was fuming! He wants his phone; I'll give it to him!

I reached around and pulled it out.

"Of course, how could I forget? Here, you could call all your precious girlfriends," I shouted and threw the thing at him. It hit him in the chest and smashed to the floor sending it into pieces. He stood there with his mouth open – speechless.

I stormed out and slammed the door behind me feeling every single emotion rise inside me all at once. I started to regret letting myself immersed into yet another gulf of lies and heartache.

CHAPTER 23

I was furious as I continued to the elevator. *How could he? All men are jerks, regardless of their age. None of them can be trusted!* The whole ride down the elevator I cursed him in my mind. *What a waste of my time. Wow. How quickly he turned into an asshole ... just like that!*

Then it dawned on me, I was comparing him to Frank. *Again.* Seriously? If Collin was many things, he certainly wasn't the asshole Frank was. Collin was sweet and caring, and sometimes immature and all over the place. But if there was anyone he was nothing like, it was Frank.

No one was at the front desk so I quickly took a seat in the lobby to collect my thoughts. When our breakfast date started, I sat there admiring Collin and how far we've come. Was I mad at *him* or was I taking the anger I had for Frank out on him?

Every minute that I sat there, guilt began to settle in. Collin didn't actually do anything wrong. Even if he was talking to another woman, as much as I wouldn't like it, even if it made me want to break every window in his car, I had no say in what he could and couldn't do. The sad fact was that Collin and I were not exclusive.

I sat there for a while wondering if I should go back upstairs and apologize. I wasn't sure if he would want to see me after I threw such a tantrum. I also felt terrible about running out after all the effort he had put into our date.

"Trouble in paradise?" Ian's words interrupted my thoughts.

"Oh, Ian, I didn't see you."

"Just stepped out for a smoke ... I wish I could quit once and for all," he said. Then added, "So, what's going on, sweetie? I can tell something's wrong. I've never seen you so unhappy."

He's obviously never seen me at my house. Was I always happy when I was there visiting Collin? "Well ..." *Should I or shouldn't I?* It was hard to decide if I should get Ian involved, but then I just went for it ... blurted it all out. "Well, Ian ... I'm just not sure where I stand with Collin. It's just that he's so young, so good looking and just so good period! He's nearly perfect!"

Ian smiled then said, "He's really a good kid and I know he's crazy about you. Absolutely smitten."

I smiled.

"If anything ... well, I really shouldn't say this," said Ian, "but, if anything, it's *you* he's concerned with."

"M-m-me?" I stuttered, obviously confused.

"Yes, *you*, dear lady! You're the ..." he paused, came closer to me so no one would hear, "the married woman."

I was shocked. So Ian *did* know! Collin really talked about me that much? Collin must have also been just as confused as I was. We were so wrapped up in each other ... all the fun, all the magic, all the passion ... we never explored the reality of it all.

"Oh my God, Ian, you're right!" I sighed replaying the entire argument. "Please buzz me in; I have to talk to him."

"Of course," he said walking over to his desk to press the release button.

Feeling completely foolish, I reluctantly made my way back up to Collin's apartment. Rather than letting myself in this time, I rang the bell and waited. And waited a bit more. And when he finally opened the door I stood there with an apologetic expression on my face. He had the phone to his ear and looked like he was resisting rolling his eyes at me. Then he sighed, tookmy hand, and lead me back into his apartment.

I looked at him and tried to telepathically let him know that I wanted him to hang up so that we could talk. He understood my unspoken message and body language, but made sure to let me know that he's still going to do what he wanted.

"Brit, I'm gonna have to call you back," he said to her, eyes fixed on me.

Really? Was he just dying for me to leave so he could call her! Jeez. And he had to throw it in my face! I took a deep breath but kept my game face on.

"Glad to see your phone's not broken," I said sort of lying.

"Yeah, don't worry this stupid thing randomly breaks into pieces almost every day," he said jokingly, trying to ease the mood.

"Sorry. It was really immature of me," I said as I sat on the sofa.

He sat next to me, turned to face me, and said, "Victoria you know what we have... it's already complicated enough as it is, but if we're not on the same team then this will never work out."

"I know. I know. You're right. And I shouldn't have attacked you like that."

He took me into his arms and I considered it as his way to accept my apology.

"You really think I have time for another girl? I can barely handle you as it is!" he said squeezing me tighter.

For a moment I was happy again in his comforting embrace. Then I remembered what started the argument in the first place. He wanted me to trust him and that was understandable. But at the same time he *was* spending time with someone else, and that still worried me.

I freed myself from his hold and looked up at him.

"Well, you found time yesterday," I said frowning.

He sighed then laughed a little.

"That really bothered you?" he asked caressing my face.

I nodded nuzzling into him again. "I want you all to myself. I know it's selfish."

"Baby, last night I was at my school, messing around with cameras and sound equipment. They have a tech room with tons of stuff for students to practice and get some hands on experience. But the only nights I don't have class it's usually packed. Since yesterday was Valentine's Day I guess most people had other plans, so I was finally able to get in."

Wow, so he wasn't with someone else last night! But I was. Oops, I wished I had known that. Then I wouldn't have spent my evening listening to John ramble on about boats.

"Oh," I said feeling guilty. This kid really is focused on bigger things, like school and his future. I needed to start thinking about the same thing. My future.

"You know... If you would have just asked me I would have told you that, silly woman," he said taking my face in his hands then lowered his lips to mine.

"I'm sorry. I promise I'll work on my jealousy," I said then kissed him back.

"But can you blame me? You're... so... irresistible," I whispered to him intermittently between kisses. He tasted amazing and as usual, I wanted him instantly. I leaned back on the sofa and pulled him forward with me. My heart raced and breathing increased as he moved from my mouth to my jaw-line and neck, planting a line of seductive kisses.

I wrapped my legs around him so tight, as if to trap and claim him. He kissed me slowly, deeply, gently parting my lips and teasing my tongue with his, knowing all the while how much I wanted him. He slowly pulled away from me, leaving me hanging there.

"Where are you going?" I whined, pulling him back onto me.

"Shh!" He put his finger over my lips. "Don't move. I have an idea." He walked to the hallway.

"Um, really?" I exhaled, then slumped back into the arm of the sofa.

"It'll be fun," he called from the hallway as he fished something from the closet.

I sighed again impatiently.

"Yeah? I bet I also know something that'd be fun," I said suggestively.

When he returned he was holding a modern and expensive looking camera.

"Nice camera," I said.

"*Nice?* This is a Nikon D300," he said very matter of factly, as if I was supposed to know what that meant. Boys and their toys!

"So…?" I asked.

Then he removed the lens cap and focused it on me.

"*So*, it's a seventeen hundred dollar camera. Borrowed it yesterday and I'd like to try it out," he said looking at me through the viewfinder. He twisted the lens a few times to adjust it before he began clicking away.

"Babe, stop!" I covered my face with my arm. "I look terrible!" It was too early in the morning and last few times I checked I looked tired and stressed. "Are you seriously trying to take pictures of me right now?"

"Yup," he said. I kept my arm up, hiding my face.

"Come on, stop hiding!" he said as he lowered my arm.
I sighed, exasperated. Did he forget that I'm still in heat over here? "Can't this wait?"

"Nope," he said, amused at how frustrated I was. *What a tease.*

"Because?"

"Because I think you look pretty damned sexy right now," he said, *he always knew what to say*. I could feel my face flush a little. *Do not jump off this couch and rip his clothes off*, I have to recite to myself repeatedly.

"Well when you put it that way…" I sighed and gave in. "But delete these after!"

"Okay, whatever you say."

"I'm serious!" I said shooting him a look before feeding into his little game. The last thing we needed were pictures floating around.

Laying back, I put my hands over my head and posed; then switched after every few clicks. I let him have his fun because I knew I would soon have mine too. I smiled a little just thinking about it.

"That's perfect. God, you're so pretty," he said enthusiastically. He snapped a few more as he entertained me.

He then placed the camera on the coffee table and came closer to me again. He kissed me even more intensely, then knelt next to me and… ugh, again with the camera. I continued to play along with him, giving him the most sexy seductive poses and expressions I could create. Then taking it up a notch I slowly pulled my shirt over my head and threw it at him, revealing my black and red lacy bra. His reaction was exactly what I hoped for, but I was surprised that he didn't toss the Nikon to the side. Next to go were my jeans, which made their way to the floor as well. I had wild desire in my eyes, and my body - which was covered only by my matching lingerie set - screamed with want.

"This game isn't fair," I said crossing my arms. He smiled at me, then gently tugged my hand pulling me to him. I also knelt on the floor in front of him and ran my hands from his belly button slowly up his chest. I took a deep breath and exhaled slowly. It's taking everything inside me to keep my composure. He turned me into this crazy sex fiend every time I even thought about him…let alone touched him. I pulled his shirt over his head and dropped it next to us.

"My turn," I said reaching for the camera. Even though I had no idea what I'm doing I tried to figure out the high tech gadget. He showed me what to do and I had fun taking close ups of his six-pack and beautiful smile. We were having fun again, as we always did, in the most playful and sexy ways. He turned the camera around and kissed me, taking a few self-portraits of us together.

"Okay, enough of this thing," I said taking it from him and setting it down on the coffee table. Collin stared deep into my eyes. He said nothing, but pulled me close to him and just like that, we switched from this cute giddy couple playing sexy photo shoot to I-just-want-you-now.

He picked me up, with my legs wrapped around him, and carried me into his bedroom.

With my hands in his hair and his arms around my body, our mouths pressed together, we fell onto the bed tangled in one another wrapping up in the sheets. I ran my hands all over his half-naked body and he did the same to mine.

He disappeared under the azure sheet kissing my naval and continued planting kisses, traveling up that tiny faint line of hairs along my abdomen. A shaky nervous breath escaped me as his hands followed the outline of my body, gently caressing every single part of me. He came back up kissing me again, then stared deep into my eyes touching my face as if it were made of porcelain. The way he looked at me gave me butterflies.

"You're so perfect," he said, lost in his own words, "why couldn't I have met you first?"

I stared back at his beautiful face smiling at him, feeling serene and still playful at the same time. This day was meant for us. To be silly and seductive and feel wanted. Not to argue and fight.

"Well. Because you were like six. And that would have been creepy," I said, teasingly.

We both laughed, but only for a second then his focus was all on me again. Intense, and not wanting to ruin the mood, he slowly pulled the sheet from my body admiring it in the glow of the sunlit room. Slowly enticing me, his kisses trailed lower, disappearing between my legs and pleasuring me in a way I had never have been before. It sent me to my own personal, blissful cloud of pleasure and romance. I enjoyed every second of being the star of his fantasy. The tingling feeling started to blossom, my moans harder to suppress. Rising from deep within my belly, heat pooling between my legs. My fingers clenched tightly into the sheets as I lost control of everything.

I panted heavily, coming back to my senses. He crawled over me kissing my belly, then my breasts, slowly circling my nipples with his tongue. Never giving me a moment to catch my breath. My fingers entangled themselves into his hair. He held himself on his elbows, hovering over me. I tugged him by the hair until his lips met mine again. Tasting a mix of him and myself on his tongue.

"Are you getting rough with me," he asked trying to act tough as he loosened my hands' grip and pinned both of them over my head.

"Maybe," I said. I tried to break free, but he had a tight grip with one hand around both of my wrists.

"Mmm, you're so strong," I said enticingly.

His chest muscles rested against my breasts as he held himself up with one arm and reached down with the other. He shook off his boxers like a magic trick and I lifted my leg wrapping it around him. I squirmed and groaned as he ran his nails lightly along my inner thigh sending tickling wanting feelings that all zoned to my most intimate parts. With my hands still over my head, I couldn't even touch him. He kissed me deeply and intimately and I whimpered under him at the torturous teasing. Wallowing in the moment we stared into each other's eyes, mine pleading desperately.

"Baby...please..." I said imploringly, softly under my breath.

He smiled his captivating half smile at me, enjoying watching me writhe beneath him. "You really want me don't you?"

"Just give it to me already," I sighed.

He finally complied, lowering his body to mold itself against mine. He sank himself slowly inside me and we moaned simultaneously as our bodies united carefully, sensually, and perfectly in every way possible. My insides quivered feeling the incredible fullness. Our delightful rhythm, not too fast not too slow, sent me instantly back to my rapturous island. I clenched his back and tipped my head up as those mind blowing feelings of ecstasy overcame me. My legs started to stiffen; my pelvis arched into him, so anxious to feel ecstasy again. I begged him not to stop as I fervently screamed out all kinds of incoherent gibberish. My senses were brought to a majestic state. Then it felt like the butterflies from earlier exploded into a billion tiny butterflies that were now wonderfully fluttering from my neck to my toes and everywhere in between. Every part of me, except my heart, relaxed again.

Our pace slowed down while I recovered, breathlessly beaming at him as he touched my face. Then we continued again for I don't know how long. We were world where time stood still. Nothing existed, just that same magical place for the two of us and the pleasures we bestowed on each other. He gently rolled me onto him, never breaking our connection.

I knelt over him and we sat facing each other moving in perfect unison. Stomach muscles that were once relaxed began to clench and churn again preceding that delicious familiar sensation. I couldn't believe it. *Three times?* It swept through me once more as we clung to each other, both erupting together in gratified bliss.

I exhaled slowly, melting back into the sweet cotton candy dream beneath my body. Every organ and vein still pulsed and tingled as my shudders gradually subsided. Nestled right up against me, I could feel Collin's heart pounding too. He tickled my face with the stubble on his chin and sweetened my lips with his. His hair was now drenched and fell across his forehead, curling into his eyes in the sexiest way.

"You work so hard for me," I said brushing the dampened mess back with my hand, as we lay together so close, face to face, our noses touching.

"It isn't work at all, my love," he said in a low voice, with that half smile. Kissing my lips again. Caressing the side of my face, he possessed me with his brown almond shaped orbs of promise.

My feelings were something I'd never experienced. My heart felt so full I was afraid it would burst. They swooped into my consciousness, making me completely aware of what was happening. I had fallen in love with the most amazing person in the world and the love was equally requited. I knew it and I felt it. I wanted to say it.

"I need you," I whispered instead. "Please don't break my heart."

"I'm right here, baby," he said kissing my forehead.
With Collin and his warmth swaddled around me, I felt so comfortable and peaceful. I snuggled my head deeper into his pillow and my body closer to him, closing my eyes. He kissed me and ran his fingers gently across my side again.

"Please, baby let me sleep. I'm so tired," I said, my eyes still closed.

"Okay," he said resting his forehead next to mine.

"Wake me up in twenty minutes," I said, again closing my eyes.

He continued to stroke my face and brush my hair back. I felt safe as I drifted away. Just before I fell asleep he whispered, "I love you," sending me into a sweet dream world.

Suddenly I was far away, but Collin was right there with me. I wore a long white dress that was tight on top and hugged my body, flowed around my ankles in a magnificent white fan. My hair was fastened neatly in a side bun with silver flower pins holding it into place. It was a still warm day, unlike the one I left behind. We were on an exotic tropical beach where the air smelled like sun, salt, and sea. Palm trees swayed gently in the breeze. Collin stood, also wearing all white, next to a man who wore black and white. They stood under a lacy white arch with white orchids and pink snapdragons entwined in it. Birds sung for us as I glided slowly to him. I couldn't hide the smile that spread across my face as I reached him. The feeling radiated through my body. He reached for my hand as I took my place by his side. We faced each other both smiling. Placing my hands into his, we linked our fingers together. The man with us began to speak...

I opened my eyes feeling a soft touch against my cheek. Back here again, in the world where we can't really be together.

"You woke me up too soon," I said closing my eyes again, desperately trying to return to where I was.

"I didn't want to. You were having a good dream," he said. "You were smiling."

"It was amazing," was all I said feeling a little funny about sharing it with him. Then, another thing popped into my mind. *Did he tell me that he loved me?* Or was that part of the dream? No, it was definitely real.

"Say it again," I whispered looking into his eyes hoping it wasn't only my imagination.

"Say what again?" he asked innocently.

"You know," I said smiling faintly.

He smiled at me and kissed my forehead lightly, before gazing at me with new eyes, a look I've never seen as they twinkled into a deep mesmerizing stare.

"I love you, Victoria," he said sincerely and just for that second my world stopped. I wanted to hear the words for the longest.

Feeling like my heart was wearing a sweater I smiled at him and finally was able to utter the same words that I held inside since first feeling it months ago.

"I love you too," I said then placed a soft kiss against his lips.

"I have something for you," he said reaching across the

bed to the night table, pulling open a drawer. He grabbed a small white box and handed it to me.

Oh my God please don't be what I think it is. No. That would be impossible. Yes, maybe I had been looking at rings and having dreams but please don't let this be a ring. I continued to stare at the closed box not knowing what to say. Okay, it's a little bigger than a ring box, I told myself, trying to stop freaking out internally.

"So you gonna open it or…" he said as he waited patiently.

I sighed then reluctantly opened the box. Phew. It wasn't a ring. It was a white gold chain with an iridescent bluish pearl colored stone pendant.

"It's so beautiful. I love it!" I gasped then carefully removed the dazzling piece of jewelry from the box.

"I spent weeks choosing the perfect gift for you and I picked this one for a reason. The gem is a moonstone. It's kind of my way of telling you how I feel. And it's supposed to keep you protected," he said as he fastened it around my neck.

My eyes quickly welled up. "Thank you, baby. I'll never take it off," I said noticing that I always wanted to cry when I was with him, but in a good way. I took his face softly into my hands.

"I really do love you so much. You're so good to me," I said before kissing him passionately.

Our chemistry was triggered again as we let ourselves get caught up in the moment. Before I knew it, we were at it again. Hands all over each other, one electrifying kiss after another. Connecting with our transcendent bond again. Thriving on pleasuring one other until we were both completely spent. Afterwards we just cuddled for a while, still making believe that time didn't exist. Maybe I had to get to work and maybe I would eventually have to step out of my zone and reenter the life I always ran away from, but not yet. Just for a few moments longer, in his arms, because the day really was meant for us.

CHAPTER 24

By the time, I walked into the office it was just after lunchtime. I made every attempt to return my hair and make up to their state before Collin got a hold of me. Casually strolling up to the reception desk, I greeted Brooke.

She looked up at me.

"Where were *you*?" she asked with a hinting undertone.

"Oh. Nowhere. With no one. *Not* celebrating Valentine's day," I said holding back a huge smile.

"I knew it! You're lucky you have the best sister in the world. I kept everything under control over here," she said, jokingly.

"Okay good," I said. "Wouldn't want Sue going girls gone wild, dancing on the desk and stuff." What a relief that everything was back to normal with Brooke and me ... joking around again, no tension, just being sisters.

She laughed then turned to the printer grabbing a small pile of papers. "These all came in today, most of them you could look over and ship out on Friday. Oh and a shipment came in this morning and I was able to send out everything else that was on backorder."

"Cool. Thank you so much," I said taking the papers from her.

"And Brooke," I lowered my voice, "all joking aside I really do appreciate you covering for me."

"It's no problem," she said and smiled.

"So how was your night yesterday?" I asked her.

"Oh. It was fun. Nothing special, though. I told you it's not a very serious relationship yet."

"This guy has had your attention for ten months now and it's not serious?"

"No. But that's fine. We hung out with a group of friends, went to Friday's."

"So when do I get to meet the mysterious bachelor?

192

What's his name again? You *never* talk about him."

"Taylor," she said, "And I'm afraid to introduce you two. Not yet."

"Why? Do you think I'm going to steal him from you? Because I promise that was a one-time thing," I said teasingly.

She laughed. "No, I don't want you to judge me."

"Really? Me? Wow, I'm actually a little hurt."

"Yeah, well, I wouldn't blame you. The situation is a bit... different."

"Oh. I think I know."

"You do?" she asked, sounding alarmed. Wow, what was the big secret that she practically was having a heart attack over?

"It's some married guy, isn't it?

"Vicky..." she said giving me a look.
I couldn't help it. "Or he has kids? Super young? Super old?"

"I promise I'll tell you when I'm ready. Last time I got all excited, then messed it up and embarrassed myself. I want to be sure this time that it's real before I introduce you. You know how it is, plus I don't want to jinx it."

"I guess that makes sense," I said and sighed, defeated.

She redirected the focus to me and said, "Should I even ask you how your date was? Not that I can't tell."

"What? What do you mean?"

"You're blushing," she said, "and I won't mention your hair!"

"Oh my God! Really?" I felt my face burn. I pulled out a compact from my purse and tried to quickly get rid of the evidence of my passionate morning. *I thought I did that already!* Brooke saved me by pulling a little bottle of hair spray from her purse and she handed it to me.

"It's not that bad," she said amused. "So... details?"

"Well... Notice anything new?" I said lifting my head up a bit so she could see my new favorite piece of jewelry.

"How could I not! It's beautiful. Wait; please tell me Frank didn't get you that."

"No, Collin did. Why?"

"You know what that is, right?" she asked.

"Yes a moonstone," I said, confidently, but then realized that I didn't know much more than that.

"You have no clue what it means do you?" she asked completely amused at me.

"No." I admitted. "Well I think it's for love and protection. Why? Do you know?"

"Yes. Because it was on 'Vampire Diaries' and you know me and that show! I just had to look it up," she said. Then she began rambling on and on about the latest episode getting off track as usual.

"So… about my necklace…" I said my words trailing off.

"Oh yeah, sorry. The moonstone is usually given from one lover to another as a token to show their eternal love."

I was a bit shocked when she said this. So was Collin trying to tell me something else? Something more? It may as well have been an engagement ring then. My feelings for him were strong, but I questioned if they were strong enough to live up to his expectations. Or maybe I was over thinking things again. He probably didn't even know its whole meaning. No, I'm sure he did if he spent that much time selecting it. Maybe? I shook my head to clear my thoughts.

"What else could it mean?" I asked.

Brooke slid her chair closer to her computer and opened the search engine to do some research. She clicked at the mouse and typed "moonstone definition" into the search box. A few results popped up. She scrolled down then selected one of them.

"Okay I found it," she said then began reading, "the moonstone gem meaning is -- passionate love that will fly you to the moon."

"So… maybe he's just trying to say that the sex is good?" I said jokingly trying to downplay it.

"But, listen to this, it is said if you give your lover a moonstone necklace that you will love them forever. See!" she said giving me her I told you so look.

"Let me see that," I said scooting over next to her. I took over the mouse as I scrolled through the rest reading the webpage.

The powers of the moonstone are deeply linked to the moon itself focusing on love, fertility, fortune, and extra protection during dark times. I continued to read on then understood why it was the "perfect gift."

The website read:

The Moonstone:
- Opens the heart to nurturing qualities as well as assisting in the acceptance of love.
- Assists in completion of one's own destiny.
- Is known as the gemstone of wish fulfillment.
- Tends to work on things needed versus things wanted.

With both of our feelings so strong, what was I supposed to do about the fact that I was still married to Frank? Was this going to eventually drive my relationship with Collin into the ground? I wanted to trust my heart, which told me that everything would be okay if I left Frank for Collin; but my fears were of what Frank would do if he found out, and of winding up penniless. It just needed to remain an affair for just a while longer.

Brooke's words broke me out of my trancelike state as she said, "So, what if Frank notices your necklace?"

"He won't," I said shaking my head. "And if he does I'll tell him you gave it to me."

I continued to gab to Brooke about my eventful morning, careful to leave out anything that I wanted to keep between Collin and me. Besides the personal things, I told her a little about the argument, the pictures, and our exciting first – of expressing our love to each other. She seemed genuinely happy for us. I, too, was happy for us, but could only hope that the happiness would last.

CHAPTER 25

Every gas station, fast food restaurant, and auto body shop seemed to fly by; the car couldn't move fast enough. It was a hot May evening, two weeks had passed since the last time Collin, and I spent time together because of schedule conflicts. I was busy helping Ashley with her graduation rehearsals and prom. We threw a huge going away party for Galina since she was going back to Russia at the end of June. Collin spent most of his time preparing for finals and finishing end of the year projects.

I sighed, unimpressed by New Jersey's landscape and traffic. I cannot imagine that we really need 30 gas stations before the tunnel. Finally -- 'Last exit in NJ' the sign read and my internal child was dancing.

The usual congestion at the tollbooth seemed extra annoying today as cars squeezed by to be first. Another lane opened suddenly and it was a rat race to get there as a red Honda almost hit a silver Nissan. The man in the Nissan blared his horn. I decided to avoid that lane altogether.

It was time to dodge potholes and try not to get side swiped by speeding black and yellow demons. The streets of New York were 80 percent taxi, 10 percent bus, nine percent pedestrian, and me. Red light. Green light. Red light. Red light again. This routine continued every block, for several blocks. I exhaled exasperatedly. This was always such a tedious commute. But in the end it would be worth it, I reminded myself. Finally, I pulled over by Collin's building. Perfect! A spot right in front. That was rare. Once my Audi was parked, I pulled my phone out to send him a text message.

Collin and I planned to go dancing at a nightclub called Greenhouse. The weather was warming up and we wanted to do something fun. I came to the conclusion, after almost a year of sneaking around, that there were many places Collin and I could get away with going to in public and remain unseen, and this was definitely one of them.

He wrote back that he thought we were meeting there. *What was he thinking! He knows I would never drive down to the village!*

Well, I'm not losing this spot for anything. Guess I'll have to catch a cab.

I stood on Central Park West Avenue and stuck my hand out to hail a cab. *I'm such a professional now*, I thought pleased with myself at how quickly one pulled over. Or maybe it had something to do with my outfit. I smiled at the thought knowing that I looked extra stunning that night, but it was for my "someone special." I quickly scrambled into the cab and told him, "Greenhouse in the village please."

The driver was talking and talking and talking the whole way there, and driving as fast as he was talking. Twice I went flying off my seat when he slammed on the brakes.

"Easy there!" I called anxiously from the back seat.

"Oh, I'm sorry, Miss," he said, as he once again glanced at me through the rearview mirror.

Conspiring a way to get to my destination in one piece, I offered him a $10 tip if he would slow down.

This time he didn't look in the rearview mirror, he actually turned around and smiled. "Eyes on the road ... please!"

I sent Collin a quick text message to let him know that I was almost there. *And another cab ride from hell was almost over!* He waited for me on the corner and I had the driver pull over.

Collin stepped up to the passenger window to pay the driver for me, but I quickly handed the cab driver the money myself and included the $10 tip I'd promised. Collin had to stop trying to impress me with money. I really didn't want him to think of me that way. It was bad enough that I couldn't convince him to pick a low key venue. He was determined to show me that he could live up to what he thought were my standards.

I knew he didn't really have it to spend. Although he thought he did, since his mom set up his trust fund with more than I would ever leave for any of my kids. And his dad made sure to pay off his credit cards every month. Yes, we've had little arguments about these things over the last few months, but tonight I wasn't getting into that with him.

Collin sighed, but said nothing about it as he opened my door for me. I placed my hand into his and stepped out of the cab. The air was refreshing since the cab driver was blasting the air conditioner. The May night sky was a thick dark sheet with tiny diamonds twinkling from afar. It was a beautiful night.

"You look amazing," he said admiring me.

"Thank you. And you'll have me fighting off the vultures

in there," I said. He looked super sexy, sporting a black pinstriped button down and dark washed jeans. He was due for a haircut, as usual, so his unkempt hair looked extremely sensual – and when I got closer to him the scent of his freshly washed hair and light cologne had me wanting to skip this dance club and go directly to his place.

"I'm not looking," he said wrapping his arm around my waist as we walked.

"You smell amazing!" he said to me. I was wearing Amber Romance by Victoria's Secret. But I didn't say anything, I just smiled.

My brand new tight red Marc Jacobs dress seemed to draw a lot of attention. My favorite nude pumps made my legs look long and slender, and I felt super sexy. My hair was in a loose up do and looked like it was about to come undone any moment. Together, we were the cutest couple in the city.

We approached Greenhouse, where a tall, built man stood to check our IDs. We both pulled out our driver's licenses and handed them to the bouncer. He scrutinized mine for a second, and then Collin's, reading the information with a flashlight shining on each one then looked up at each of us. He said nothing the entire time before handing them back to us. We walked into a small room between the front doors and the club entrance where a woman at a small podium collected $30 from each of us.

Collin held my hand and led the way walking through a set of glass double doors. The music blew us back as we entered the dim room. The nightlife was in full force. Dazzling hanging colored lights surrounded the entire venue. Glitter beads dangled from the ceiling bouncing the laser light reflections around the room creating a kaleidoscopic effect. The room, otherwise, was dark except for the bluish purple glow. Little lilac colored sofas lined the walls of the VIP area and had white leather pillows thrown about. We made our way to the bar through a crowd of already drunken dancers.

"We're too old for this," I said. I laughed as I looked around. Of course, this was *his* idea. I would have chosen something ordinary and boring like a movie or a Broadway show. But it was his turn to choose our date and this was what he picked.

"Don't start," he said smiling at me.

There appeared to be two floors to the club. The main

floor, where we were, had several different bars. We waited for our drinks at the smallest one.

"I shouldn't be drinking," I yelled to him over the music.

"Just tell me what you want," he said, pulling me close.

"You mean besides you?" I whispered in his ear then gave him a flirty smile. I thought for a moment.

"Fine, Apple Martini!" I said feeling brave.

The model looking, longhaired, young woman at the bar leaned forward to take our order from him. Her breasts were practically falling out of her top. He told her our order and brought his attention back to me, completely unfazed by Carmen Electra's twin.

"Did I tell you how beautiful you look?" he said kissing my cheek.

"Yes, but you could tell me again," I said with a smile.

The bartender scooped ice into a metal shaker, poured several different liquors over it flipping each bottle over, showing off her quick impressive technique, before placing the metal top on. She shook it up, mixing the ingredients, and then poured the neon green result into a martini glass finishing with a maraschino cherry. Then she grabbed another small glass, filled it half way with a light brownish amber colored cognac, and handed us our drinks. Collin handed her a card and told her to open a tab. *I'll let him have this one.*

We hung out by the bar for a while, absorbed in each other's presence, enjoying our time together as the '80s and '90s classic songs blared through the speakers. The smile that was on my face when the night began stayed in place throughout the evening. We engaged in private jokes about everything around us, from ridiculous outfits and hairstyles to people who thought they could dance. I never stopped laughing when I was with him.

Modern day radio music played for a few minutes then suddenly a techno song took over, then Spanish music. We danced a little by the bar and continued to order drinks. Sometime between my second martini and first Long Island iced tea, the alcohol started to hit me. I almost regretted letting him order me some blue drink that he handed to me with a pineapple piece and cherry on a little umbrella toothpick.

"Always trying to get me drunk," I said taking the cold glass from him.

"You're on to me," he said kissing me again then took my

hand moving us away from the bar.

Blue, green, and red laser lights blinded me as we took the dance floor. A little mirrored disco ball spun slowly above us. A potpourri of people; men both young and old, women classy and trampy, young couples, groups of drunken college kids, men dressed as woman, women dressed as men, surrounded us and of course there were the little half naked dancers that gyrated on a platform next to us. It was all a little overwhelming and unfamiliar. I squeezed Collin's hand tighter and pulled him closer to me as I noticed that every prowling female wanted to steal him from me. But, no matter how good any of them looked, it was me who had his undivided attention. The thrill of knowing he was all mine sent a wonderful feeling through me.

The liquor had begun to take over, and I found myself thinking I knew how to dance while exaggeratedly singing the words to Usher's "DJ Got Us Falling in Love," to Collin. He laughed with me as he placed his hands in mine, which were somewhere in the air. The DJ switched genres again this time playing "Hold You" by Gyptian. This slowed us down a bit as the beat echoed through our bodies. I was tipsy and pressed up against the one person with the most amazing scent in the whole world. That celestial chemistry began to simmer. He wrapped my hands behind his neck as we moved in harmony with each other. Everyone around us was insignificant, the music and lights surreal and distant. The alcohol made me bold. Still glued together, I kissed him, a real deep passionate exchange between the two of us.

I brought my lips to his ear.

"I want you," I whispered to him running my hands slowly through his hair. Biting my bottom lip, I folded my hand behind his neck and said, "Come on, baby, let's get out of here."

"You read my mind," he said taking my hand.

We began to make our way through the crowd. So many bodies. The club was packed, hundreds of people flooded the dance floor, everyone drunk and bouncing around in disharmony, passing through was a challenge. We walked together toward the exit, but I spontaneously decided to pull him in the opposite direction.

He curled his arms around my waist. "You're going the wrong way, babe..."

"No, I'm not," I said with a hinting secretive smile. I

200

urged him again to follow me. We turned the corner where the club's restrooms were located. I started to walk into the ladies room then stopped in front of the door and turned to face him. "You coming?"

"Seriously?" he asked realizing my martini-fueled plan.

I nodded biting his bottom lip.

"You're crazy, you know that?"

I shrugged feeling bold. "I guess I am," then I brought myself close to him then whispered, "Never gonna survive unless we get a little crazy... right?"

He smiled at me then quickly checked behind us while I peeked inside to make sure the coast was clear before we both ducked into the rest room.

No one was in the ladies room to witness me and Collin in our sudden wild, passionate display, hands all over each other, lips uniting, breathing frantically as we stumbled together into the nearest stall. I shut the door and turned the latch to lock it behind us.

I shoved him into the wall and pressed my body into his, kissing him greedily. His other hand tangled in my hair, messing up my hair-do, so what the hell, I pulled out the clip letting the strands flow free. I flipped my hair around knowing that he went wild for my long wavy tresses.

I just had to have him right there. I ran my hands under his shirt along his firm chest, pressing so hard a button popped off.

"Hey, easy, girl!" He laughed so hard and kept going ... he ran his hands slowly up my thigh and under my dress.

"Ooh, naughty girl," he said when he realized I wasn't wearing any panties.

"Do you ever wear any?" he said jokingly then pulled my hair tipping back my head and pressing his lips against mine. I looked up at the round lights that seem to move across the ceiling on their own while he kissed my exposed neck.

"When I'm with you... what's the point?" I breathed into his ear, then pulled on it gently with my teeth and ran my hands along his strong abdominal muscles, then let my fingers trail further downward. I unbuttoned his pants voraciously, as if some other force was taking over my actions.

I worked his pants off then lowered my body, balancing against the tilting world around us. My lips traced a line down his stomach as I enclosed my hands around him. I tugged further down on his boxers freeing him from them. Without hesitation, I began to devour him, taking as much as I could in my mouth, delicately moving my tongue around in a steady motion. I loved the satisfied groaning and breathing sounds he made that I knew I caused.

"That feels so good..." he said lost in his own words. His hands tangled again loosely through my hair.

I quickened my pace, getting high off his reaction. Sliding my lips further and further, taking in a little more than half while bobbing my head in a perfect rhythm. Glancing up at him, our eyes locked for a moment as I gazed at him erotically for a moment before he closed his eyes and I could feel him slightly twitch.

"Okay... baby... stop..." he could barely get the words out. He gently tried to raise me up, but I was still in control. I knew he was almost there and enjoyed his short, jagged breathing for a few seconds longer, until he abruptly pulled me up. He lifted me to my feet, picked me up, and then pressed me hard against the wall while I wrapped both legs around him.

"You're so fucking sexy," he whispered to me, firmly pinning me between him and the stall, his erection hard between my legs. With my arms around his neck, I held onto him and pushed my body more toward him wanting so badly to feel our magic. With a quick motion, he entered me effortlessly as I was so ready for him. I nearly screamed once he was fully inside me. Our pace wasn't our usual slow, and sensual love making. It was hard and fast, but with the same sensual intensity.

I moved my body to meet with each thrust and couldn't control my exclamations as they came from a place of exaggerated bliss. Trying to suppress my moans was just as impossible.

"Shh..." he said while nibbling on my ear but I just kept getting louder and louder. It was so good. And wild. And dangerous.

He knew I was right there as it was beyond obvious. He took my face into his hands, kissing me deeply, muffling my screams as I exploded into a million pieces, amazed that I was still holding on to him. After me, he buried his face against my neck and groaned, as it was his turn to release.

Then bringing his lips back to mine, we kissed again until I lifted my head again panting heavily.

"Oh my God you're amazing," I whispered breathlessly, smiling as I slowly lowered my feet to the ground.

We could hear as two women walked into the bathroom into the stalls next to us. I tried to stay still and quiet and was happy that each wall reached the floor so they wouldn't be able to see the extra set of feet in there with me. I didn't know how much longer I could stand, my legs felt like butter. But I remained still, and silent, holding Collin tight.

We listened to the women gossip for a minute or two while they washed their hands and as I looked at Collin, I wanted to laugh feeling so giddy and drunk. We could hear the door swing open, letting in the sounds of the blaring music then their voices faded away.

I started giggling uncontrollably and he looked at me and started laughing.

"This is so gross," I said. It was as if we both came out of trance, realizing that we were in a public restroom.

"Hey. Wasn't my idea," he said, teasingly.

"Who cares… it was hot."

"*You're* hot," he said with his forehead against mine. He placed his hand against the small of my back pulling my body close against him ready for round two.

"Later," I breathed before kissing him deeply with my fingers entwined in his hair. I pushed him away playfully, then quickly fixed my dress as he buttoned his pants. I shook off toilet paper from the bottom of my heel then we quickly snuck out of the bathroom, back into the craziness of the nightclub before finding our way to the exit.

The night air was mild and still. I remained in Collin's hold as we challenged the city together. We got onto a city bus, but I wanted to get off when we were still 10 blocks away from his place. The rocking motion was making me queasy. I hoped I wouldn't get sick in front of him. *I knew we drank too much.*

We hopped off the bus and the air felt so much better. We walked the remainder of the way along Central Park West. That street usually scared me because of the wall that stood precariously between the park and the sidewalk. That particular street wasn't well lit and was usually very deserted at night, with exception of the occasional sleeping hobo. While walked, it started to feel like someone was following us. I glanced around, but knew it was my constant paranoia. *Don't feed into it.*

I stopped Collin in his tracks stepping in front of him,

throwing my arms around him.

"I love you," I said as he hugged me tight. Everything was perfect for that moment as complete happiness overtook us.

We were almost to where my car was parked. I could see it. We were almost across the street from his building. I stopped again. But this time I really had a funny feeling. *Something just isn't right. Call it woman's intuition, call it anything you want, but something wasn't right.*

"What's wrong?" he asked, sensing my discomfort.

Again, I looked over my shoulder, but there was no one there. I was dying to get upstairs to the apartment. Not only was I scared about whatever it was I was sensing, but my shoes were finally starting to hurt my feet. I couldn't wait to get them off.

"I don't know I keep feeling like there's someone…"

"You always say that," he said whisking me in his arms again. "Relax, baby, relax. We're almost home." Then changing the tone, he whispered, "I can't wait to get you out of that dress."

For the first time in our relationship, I ignored his advances. There was definitely something wrong and unfortunately, this time I was right!

Paranoia was warranted when someone in a dark hoodie proved to be lurking nearby. His face was concealed by the shadows. I had such a bad feeling and goose bumps flooded my arms.

Collin suddenly went into protective mode shielding me with his body.

"Just keep walking," he whispered, getting me to walk a little faster, which was so hard at this point. I was drunk, my feet hurt, I wasn't holding up very well.

Then the stranger became vocal and totally startled me.

"Whoa … whoa! It's okay," he said. "I'm a family friend. Right, Victoria?" He looked right at me with an ominous smile. Collin held me even tighter.

Now I was more scared than ever. *Damn! It's someone who knows me and saw me with Collin.* I started shaking. *I am so screwed!* I squinted, trying so hard to figure out who this was, but still couldn't recognize him in the dark especially since I was so intoxicated, the entire city was spinning.

"Who's there?" I asked again and contemplated if we should run or not instead of waiting for his reply.

CHAPTER 26

Too shaken to move, I stood there as the stranger lowered his hood and the revelation had me in shock. My luck couldn't get worse than that. "Juan Carlos? What are you doing here?" I shot him an icy glare. Then I knew it wasn't bad luck that brought him there. It's as if he was waiting for me.

Before he could say anything Collin, who knew every detail about this horrible excuse of a man, spoke first, "Wait... *you're* Juan Carlos?" I could feel the muscles tighten in his arms as he kept me behind him. I could sense that Collin wanted to beat the hell out of him.

"Yeah. That's funny you know about me and I have never heard of you," he said. Cocky as ever, Juan Carlos was mistakenly assuming that I talked *good* about him.

"Don't worry about who I am. Why are you here?" Collin asked.

Juan Carlos looked at me, looking me up and down. "Victoria, I hope I'm not interrupting anything. I didn't know you were babysitting. And don't you look very sexy, by the way."

"Don't be an asshole," I said through clenched teeth.

Unsure if it was because of drinking earlier in the night, or because of the threatening situation, Collin seemed to be in fight mode. I was now standing in front of him trying to figure out what to do with the completely touchy situation.

"So you're not going to introduce me to your little friend?" Juan Carlos continued to instigate.

"Why don't you come out from behind those bushes and I'll show you how little I am." Collin was brave. Did he really think that he could take on Juan Carlos? This was not good.

"Collin ... no!" I whispered in a begging tone.

"Oh is that right?" *Shit! He heard him.*

"Yeah, that's right, you heard me," Collin said too wrapped up to pay attention to my pleading. *Great. He's just asking for trouble.*

I placed my arm in front of him to bring him back to earth for a second. "Collin, please. Let's just go upstairs. I'm so exhausted. This can wait."

"Do something then," Juan Carlos continued to egg him

on.

I kept myself as the only thing standing between a drunken fistfight. Collin had no idea what he was getting himself into. He was trying to protect me, but I wasn't sure that he actually could. This drama was sobering me up fast.

"Stop! Both of you!" I said and felt like I was stepping in between two teenagers.

"What is that gonna do? It's not helping!" I said to Collin before turning to Juan Carlos. "What the hell do you want?"

"I don't know what all this hostility is about," he said trying to sound like the victim. "I see my boy's wife with some… *kid*. And, well, now I'm in this awkward position."

"What? Suddenly Frank's your best friend now?" I said scoffing at him.

"I'll be his when I tell him what his wife has been up to."

"Do whatever you want," I said rolling my eyes. "I don't have time for this shit. It's your word against mine."

"I love how he believed you last time."

Shit. He was right. Okay plan B.

"He won't care anyway," I said.

"Okay, then why don't I send these pictures to Frank and we'll see what he says?" He held up his phone scrolling over several pictures he took of Collin and me together. *What a creeper.*

All right, I get the point. What do you want?"

"Me? I just want to talk."

"Then, talk." Collin chimed in hostilely.

"Babe, stop," I warned to him in a low voice knowing he was only making things worse.

"To her," Juan Carlos said eyeballing me. "Alone."

"No," Collin said stepping in, guarding me again. "Figure something else out, 'cause that's not happening."

Juan Carlos ignored Collin and looked at me. "It's your decision. I'm not interested in talking with pretty boy over there. This doesn't concern him."

Damn. What do I do? I dreaded that something like this was going to happen one day or another, but *really?* Why did it have to be him that caught us? It was bad enough that he knew, I didn't need Frank knowing too. Juan Carlos always had a thing for me. I could use that against him. Use my charm. Make him some empty promises maybe.

I took Collin a few steps further away then turned to him

and quietly said, "Frank can't see those pictures."

"So, what do you want to do?"

I sighed. "What choice do I have? I have to talk to him."

"Are you crazy? That's not even an option."

"Babe, its fine. I'll get him to erase those pictures."

"No. You're out of your mind if you think I'm letting you go anywhere with him. You'd better find another solution."

I was taken aback for a second. "Letting? I'm not asking for your permission. This is my problem and I'm going to handle it."

Our conversation was interrupted by Juan Carlos.

"Ahem!" he said clearing his throat to let us know he was still there, "I don't have all night."

Collin looked at me and exhaled impatiently. "Victoria, I swear if he doesn't shut up…"

"Give me a minute," I shouted to Juan Carlos; then turned back to Collin.

"Please be smart about it and let me go with you."

"You heard what he said. Just me. Anyway, I'm a big girl. I can take care of myself," I said crossing my arms. I was getting a little pissed with Collin, thinking I couldn't handle myself.

"You're making a mistake, I don't agree with you," he said shaking his head.

"You don't have to agree. This isn't your decision to make. Don't worry, nothing is going to happen."

"I don't trust him," he said still unconvinced.

"Okay, Collin. I know you're trying to protect me, but you're starting to piss me off." I knew my tone was harsh, but I needed to take care of this on my own. I didn't want Collin to get involved. I didn't really want to be alone with Juan Carlos, but at the same time I didn't need a body guard either.

Finally, Collin realized he wasn't winning this one.

"You have ten minutes," he said to Juan Carlos in the most threatening way possible.

"Relájete, *backstreet boy*," Juan Carlos said putting his hands up as if he were surrendering. I actually understood that he was saying, "Relax."

"I'm just looking out for everyone's best interests," Juan Carlos said again trying to play the good guy.

"Si te duele su te mataré!" Collin warned in the same threatening tone. I didn't know what he said, but I guessedit wasn't something friendly.

He paced around for a few seconds while I walked away. Then he turned around and punched a sign, probably wishing it were Juan Carlos, before sitting down on a bench to wait for me, defeated. I watched him for as long as I could, my head over my shoulder as I walked away with Juan Carlos. Collin didn't sit very long. Within seconds he was up and pacing again.

Our eyes locked one last time before Juan Carlos led me into what was probably the most dangerous place in the entire city that late at night. My mind worked a mile a minute trying desperately to devise the ultimate plan because, at this point, our lives depended on it.

I walked as slowly as possible, so that we wouldn't get too deep into Central Park as Juan Carlos quietly led me further and further away from Collin. To slow him down I used my feet hurting as an excuse.

"So where the hell did you pick this kid up?" he asked as we walked.

"Look, if you want to talk, that's fine, but I'm not interested in talking about him with you. It's none of your business."

"Whatever you want, sweetie," he said.

When nothing was accomplished aside from being so far into the park that we were now walking down a small set of stairs, I finally decided to call him out. "Why did you follow me?"

"I don't know what you're talking about. I was just minding my business..."

"Juan Carlos, cut the shit! I know you followed me, you were right by my car."

"Maybe I did."

"So, did Frank send you?" I softened my tone, as being riled up wasn't going to help the situation any. It was very late, yet sporadically people were still walking their dogs. Couples were even jogging together under the lamplights. I didn't want to make a scene with Juan Carlos. As if him finding me with Collin wasn't embarrassing enough. And I was comforted by the fact that people were around. Otherwise, it would be very scary, especially since we stood close to a tunneled area.

"Frank?" Juan Carlos asked, breaking my thoughts. "You know he's too much of a fuckin' drunk to notice this shit. I've got to hand it to you though, he's completely clueless." These words may have been the only good news that would be coming from this man's mouth.

Juan Carlos continued, "Not me. The minute I seen you all dolled up that night, red lipstick, sexy green dress, I knew something was up. I wanted to see for myself and followed you. Guess I was right."

"So… are you gonna tell Frank?" I asked, my voice small and worried.

"No. I'm sure we could come to an agreement. You give me what I want and you're secret's safe with me."

"What do you want? Money?"
He laughed cynically. "Money? What the hell would I need *your* money for?"

"Then what? Why do all this?"

"You already know what I want," he said grabbing my arm, pulling me into a tunnel that was completely pitch black.

I'm supposed to be handling this. This isn't going as planned.

"Stop!" I said snatching my arm from him. I wanted to try desperately to keep a passive demeanor but with this jerk, it was impossible. "Could we please just figure something out?"

"You know I'm a little offended that you let that little corny mother fucker get a piece of that ass when you could be with a *real* man," he said reaching again to grab my arm pulling me into him.

"Don't do this. We've known each other for twenty years," I said trying to be rational, "We're like family right?" As I said this in the fakest, most convincing tone ever I thought my Apple Martini would come up any minute.

"Look, all I want is one night and I'll erase the pictures, and pretend I saw nothing. No one will be the wiser. Not Frank. Not your kids. And not even your little friend." Condescending as ever, he was really annoying the hell out of me. All types of emotions overtook me. I was sad, angry, and terrified. *Think fast, Victoria, think fast!*

"You just said you don't care about what I do. Now you're trying to blackmail me."

"Blackmail is such an ugly word. This is just a deal between friends. Everyone wins."

I thought hard about what he said. Not that I trusted him, but all I had to do was give in and my secret would be safe? It sounded so easy. But it wasn't. What did he think I was?

Furious with myself for even considering it for a second, my eyes narrowed as I squinted at him. I would rather take my chances and let him tell Frank.

"So, how about our deal?" he said.

Thinking fast, I said, in a seductive tone, "Well Juan Carlos, I always did think you were a sexy man, I just didn't want Frank to know."

A big smile came over his face, as well as a look of surprise. He just stood there, dumbfounded.

"Well, big boy, come over here." I encouraged him to get close to me. He slowly put his big arm around me and drew me closer.

I brought my lips to his ear and whispered, "I'd rather die before I ever let you touch me," then I lifted my knee into him, kicking him in the nuts and he doubled over. Shocked at my strength, I stood there stunned for a second; then attempted to turn around and run but he tripped me grabbing my ankle.

Losing my balance, I fell straight to the ground. I tore my dress and scraped up my hands and knees. But who was I kidding? Even if I did get away, I wouldn't get far in those shoes or barefoot. *I was doomed.*

He dragged me across the rubble bringing me back to him. Blood was running down my hands and legs. I was such a mess, yet I still tried to crawl away.

"Well, maybe you'll get your wish you little slut," he said then punched me in the face. It stung, but was nothing new to me. I turned my head away and shook it off. I don't cry for my husband I'm sure as hell not going to cry for him.

"That's all you got?" I said spiting blood in his face.

"I always told Frank he gives you too much fuckin' freedom. And look... His nice little virgin girl turned into a whore."

"Do whatever you're gonna do," I said. "You know he'll be here any second…"

"Frank ain't comin' here for you."

"Not him."

"You talkin' 'bout your lil backstreet boyfriend?" he asked and then laughed vindictively. "Is that supposed to scare me? It's okay baby, I won't let him ruin our fun." He then opened his sweater a little revealing the black handle of a gun. "Heh. You know what he said to me back there?" Juan Carlos was holding me by the hair. I was so helpless and so unsure of what to do next.

He continued. "He said if I hurt you that he'll kill me. You wanna take bets? Who do you think will get to it first?"

"No! Please leave him out of this. This has nothing to do with him."

"Aw. Aren't you two just the sweetest fuckin' things? Fuckin' Romeo and Juliet over here," he said. And laughed again.

"Why are you doing this?"

"I told you. I want you. All this could go away if you would just co-operate."

"Okay," I said nodding. Then continued, pleading, "Really. I swear. I won't fight you. I'll do whatever you want. Please just don't hurt him."

For a moment, he looked shocked. "Good. You're finally coming to your senses," he said but he grabbed me so hard, pinning me face first onto the concrete. I squirmed a little, but as I promised, I wasn't going to try and fight back. Tears run down my face, he ran his hands up my leg and under my dress.

"I see that you're all ready for me," he said when he noticed that I had nothing on underneath. I heard the sound of his zipper open and closed my eyes, hoping for him to get it over with.

With impeccable timing, Collin appeared from nowhere and charged at Juan Carlos knocking him off me and an immediate fistfight broke out.

For a short moment, there is space between them.

"Kid, you sure you wanna do this?" Juan Carlos challenged as they circled around fists up. "Come on hero…" his shit talking was interrupted by Collin punching him directly in the mouth. Juan Carlos tried to shake it off, but before he could react he was hit with a second punch. He ducked the third punch and suddenly had the upper hand.

They slammed into the wall a few times and it was too dark for me to really see what's going on. It all happened so fast. Very confusing. Everything happening in flurries. One minute the battle seemed even as they went back and forth swinging at each other while I cried, screaming at them to stop and fearing the worst.

They wrestled around, rolling on the ground and I was unsure of who was winning the fight. Collin got in a few blows, relieving me for a moment. But it was a very short lived moment, because suddenly Juan Carlos was on top of Collin again. This time, hitting him over and over, not letting up his merciless thrashing. I couldn't just lay there and watch Collin become a bloody pulp. I grimaced and pushed my body up from the concrete, my head whirling. Quickly, desperately, I looked around for anything I could use to help. A large rock? A stick? But there was nothing...so impulsively I threw myself right into the middle of the melee and grabbed Juan Carlos in a chokehold.

"Get off him!" I screamed, holding on like a starving animal protecting its last scrap of food.

But my strength suddenly gave out. In what seemed like no time at all, Juan Carlos escaped my grasp, twisted his body around violently, and threw me like a rag doll. My head hit the ground and I groaned in excruciating pain, frozen in shock. My eyes met Collin's; in that moment, I was ready to share our bitter defeat with him.

CHAPTER 27

I lay on the ground with tears blurring my vision, but I could still see Collin's face. Instead of giving in, however, his mouth stiffened and his eyes narrowed, as if someone had ignited a raging fire in his heart. With a sudden burst of energy, he twisted out from under his adversary, and whirled to his feet again. He stumbled slightly, but his determined face showed no sign of any pain as adrenaline took over. Collin's fists flew as though shot from a machine gun. Juan Carlos launched his own barrage, but it paled in comparison as he took blow after savage blow to his face, not returning one hit himself. Then, in the blink of an eye, Juan Carlos hit the pavement, motionless, his face covered in cuts and bruises. *Wait, what just happened?*

Collin stopped to reach into Juan Carlos' pocket and pulled out his phone where those pictures were saved. Yanking the memory card from its back, he smashed the phone to the ground. He made his way to my side and knelt beside me for a second placing the card into my hand. Then quickly, as if flipping a switch, he turned off his hostility and looked into my eyes.

"Are you okay, baby?" he asked as he cradled the back of my head with his hand lightly pressing his forehead into mine.
Still in shock from everything, I nodded then glanced over at Juan Carlos. He was still on the ground and cunningly reaching into his hoodie.

"He has a gun," I quickly warned Collin, who just as quickly left my side. Completely undaunted by what I told him, he walked up to Juan Carlos and stepped on his wrist before yanking the gun away from him.

Then in those moments, I barely recognized Collin. It was as if he let his anger cloud his judgment. He must have been rationalizing his actions in the heat of the moment when he pointed the 9mm straight at Juan Carlos at close range.

"No! Wait! What are you doing?" I found my voice, as I'm jolted into reality.

"Ending this. This asshole doesn't deserve to breathe."
Initially Juan Carlos looked at him in shock, but that quickly was

replaced with doubt.

"Hey now. Why don't you put that down before you hurt yourself," Juan Carlos said, jeering.

"Oh don't worry, I won't," Collin said cocking the gun.
I completely understood what he felt, but I knew I couldn't let him go through with it.

"Baby, look at me," I said trying to get his attention. "Please don't do it!"

For a second Collin contemplated my words. Juan Carlos didn't think he would shoot, but I didn't doubt him. My sweet Collin was gone, as our situation brought something out in him that scared me. I didn't put anything past him at that moment.

"Don't be like *him*. We're better than that," I said looking into his eyes, trying to bring him back to me. Gradually he started to snap out of the dark trance that possessed him, slowly lowering the gun.

But like the asshole that he was Juan Carlos jeered on, going one step too far, "That's right... listen to the whore."

Like a spontaneous reaction without even seeming to aim Collin lift his hand again and shot.

"NO!" I screamed at the top of my lungs, the loud explosion deafened me. I closed my eyes, buried my face in my hands, and started weeping hysterically. A million thoughts went through my head ... but the one that overruled them all was the fact that Collin would go to jail for first-degree murder.

But I was quickly distracted. Juan Carlos was still alive. Instant wailing told me that. A puddle of blood formed under his leg as he held it, groaning desperately. I always thought I would enjoy seeing the day that he got his, but I didn't. Not even a little. The way he lay there, curled up, defeated and in so much pain. Juan Carlos was a real bastard, but he was still a ... a human being.

Collin still aimed the gun at him, but looked at me. "If we let him go he's just going to run and tell your husband everything."

"No please..." Juan Carlos completely changed his demeanor and was for once at our mercy.

"Was I fuckin' talking to you?" Collin whipped the gun across his face, knocking his head back to the ground. Then he turned back to me, looking for an answer. *It's up to me if he lives or not?* I wanted to look at Collin like my hero, but I had never seen that side of him and didn't know what to make of it. My

214

expression should have told him what I wanted, but he didn't agree with me.

He argued with himself, walking a few feet away from both Juan Carlos and me, before finally lowering the gun completely turning to me again.

"Do you know where this asshole lives?" he asked.

I nodded, sobbing, "Yes."

Collin brought the gun back up to Juan Carlos' face.

"Listen, you good for nothing piece of shit. You do not look at, touch, talk to, or breathe near Victoria, or her kids, ever again. If I hear anything, I will find you and next time it will not be your leg. Do you understand?"

Juan Carlos nodded.

"Good," Collin said. Then he really went a bit too far, kicking him repeatedly in the stomach, body, and face.

"That's enough!" I screamed holding my head, which throbbed painfully. Juan Carlos lay limp, curled up, coughing and bleeding.

"Please," I mouthed.

Collin approached me gently, completely transforming again in a split second. "Come on; let's get you out of here." He knelt to help me up. I instinctively backed away from him, terrified.

"Babe? Come ..." he said again trying to reach to me.

"Don't ..." I said with my hands placed firmly into the ground. "I can do it." I used all my strength to ignore the pounding in my head and pushed myself up.

"You sure you're fine?" he asked placing his hand on my arm. I jumped back again pulling away.

"I just want to go home." With my dress torn, arms and legs dirty, feet throbbing and face still wet from tears I hobbled away from the scene. I glanced behind me and Juan Carlos was still lying on the ground, motionless. Collin walked close behind me as we escaped the park. He looked completely done in -- finished. Like he'd been through a war. Like he'd aged, terribly.

He seemed like a very different person. The two of us wobbled, trying to get our bearings, but we knew that was not going to happen for a long time. We've been through it all together. If we survived this, our relationship would survive anything.

"You know we can't just leave him like that," I mumbled as we got to the street.

"Are you kidding?"

"He has no phone; he's bleeding a lot and could die."

He looked at me unmoved and shrugged slightly, "And?"

"Collin..."

He rolled his eyes, but dialed 911 leaving an anonymous tip. After he hung up, he continued to trail behind me. I couldn't look at him and wanted nothing more than to get to my car and go home.

"Victoria, talk to me," he said catching up and walking along side of me.

"What?" I snapped. I stopped next to my car and opened my clutch to fish out my car key.

"You said you're fine, but you're not acting like you are," Collin said, sounding so concerned. Then he looked at me questioningly. "He didn't …"

"No," I said cutting him off. "But, you really didn't need to do all that. I told you I would handle it."

"Well, it didn't look like you had it under control."

"Neither did you," I said in a low voice.

"Why are you mad at me right now?"

"You went too far. I feel like I don't even know you."

"Why? Because I know how to fight? Jeez, babe... I'm not the bad guy here."

I looked around as if to make sure no one would hear me.

"You were really going to kill him?" I asked, whispering.

"And do you know what he was gonna do to you?" Collin was outraged. "The only reason I didn't is because you stopped me."

"You would be able to live with that?"

"Knowing that there's one less scumbag to worry about? Yes."

We approached my car and I pressed the button on the remote to unlock it. Before I could pull the handle open, Collin leaned in front of my door blocking the key hole.

"What are you doing?" he asked.

"I'm going home."

"I don't want you driving like this."

"I'm fine."

"You're not fine. Come up for a few minutes. Please."

"Collin, I'm drained, and I need to get home..." I cut myself off when, out of habit, I grazed my hand over my neck then realized that my necklace was missing. *Oh my God it must have broken during the struggle.*

I panicked a little and checked to see if it was anywhere on me.

"Damn it…" I said aloud, but mostly to myself.

"What's wrong?"

"My necklace… It's gone! I have to go back…" I said alarmed.

Collin grabbed my arm. "No, you can't go back there. Just let it go."

My eyes watered up. *Let it go?* He had no idea that it was my most prized possession. When I wore it, while we were apart, it still felt in a way as if he was always with me. I looked away feeling my heartbreak a little.

He noticed how upset I was and quickly said, "Sweetie, I'll get you another one."

It was a nice gesture, but it wouldn't be the same to me. He didn't realize that I saw that simple piece of jewelry as a constant reminder of our love. Now, not wanting to drive, I sighed and followed him into his building.

When we were inside, I did everything to hide my face from Ian. Collin and I both looked like we had gotten into a fight in a dirty field.

"You kids okay?" Ian asked, quickly standing up.

I nodded.

"Rough night," Collin mumbled. We walked to the elevator with our heads down.

Inside the elevator, I avoided Collin's eyes. I felt detached from him. Guilt overwhelmed me for dragging him into my mess of a life. At the same time, I didn't know how innocent he was anymore either. Was he not the soft gentle man he'd been portraying to me the entire time? I couldn't deal with yet another violent man.

Collin let us into his apartment. I took my shoes off and left them by the front door as I did at home. He went to the bathroom sink and washed the blood off his hands and face, then disappeared into the bedroom. I went in next, using soap and water to try to bring my appearance back to some semblance of normal. I sat quietly and uncomfortably on the sofa. A minute later, he came out in a fresh t-shirt and navy blue sweatpants. The clean, docile young man I fell in love with was back.

He went into the kitchen for a moment, then sat next to

me and handed me a glass of water with ice and slowly placed a cold washcloth against my swelling cheek. I shuddered a little at his touch, a habit of trauma.

He gently pulled me to him stroking my hair. "You know I would never hurt *you*. Right?"

I exhaled slowly, letting myself relax in his hold.

"Look at me," he said tipping my chin up. "I don't know who these people are that you let into your life, but I'm not one of them. And I know I scared you before, but I could never let someone hurt anyone I care about." He paused and added, "Not again."

Of course, he was thinking about Ava. For a moment, while all the drama was happening, I had forgotten what he'd been through in the past.

I curled up in his lap while he held me.

"Do you have any idea how much I love you?"

My eyes filled with tears that rose from many different emotions. My heart jumped and suddenly I was mute.

"You're sure you're not hurt?" he asked me again.

"I'll be fine," I said. "Sorry if I was acting weird with you before. I've never seen that side of you."

"I'm sorry, too. I would have never let you see me like that, but he left me no choice." He said, then took a moment to collect his thoughts. "I was in a very dark place for a whileafter what happened to my sister. I had so much unresolved anger that I started getting into fights in school. But I was starting them with kids who I knew I couldn't beat."

"Why?"

"Because I was stupid and young — and determined to prove something. Maybe to myself, I don't know..." he said trailing off, lost in his thoughts for a moment. "Anyway, I ended up mixing in with a few of the juniors and seniors who ran something like a fight club. I was the youngest one in there."

Wow. I never imagined him having a dark side. But then again, so did I. And it was hard to conceive what kind of trauma he went through, especially having been so young.

Collin continued his story and said, "But that wasn't getting me very far. A lot of my friends and family tried to talk sense into me. I almost was kicked out of school. I would have lost everything, but there was really only one person who could get through to me. Then I started to change for the better."

"Oh." I said realizing what he was implying. "It's okay, I understand. And I know you wouldn't hurt me. I just was a little shaken. It was as if you transformed in the blink of an eye. Something I've seen twice before."

"Twice?"

"Yes, my husband does that. But my father was like that, too.," I said, surprised at myself that I had brought him up. "I know he wasn't always an asshole. But it doesn't matter because any pictures or anything else I had of him I burned long time ago. He was an alcoholic. I spent about six years of my life watching and listening to my mother get abused. When Brooke was four he tried to molest her, which caused my mom to snap. She shot and killed him. My mother got a twenty-five year sentence for protecting her daughter."

Collin looked at me stunned. Obviously saddened by what I had revealed. "Victoria… how come you never told me that before?"

I shrugged.

"Because, well, look at your parents. Happily married. They seem like a picture-perfect couple. And you. So good. And sweet. And driven…," I said while I softly caressed his face. "I didn't want one more thing hanging over my head that magnifies my imperfections. I just don't want to feel any more damaged than I already do. Especially not when I'm with you."

"I wish you could see how you look through my eyes," he said. "I don't see damaged, or whatever other delusions you have about yourself." He shook his head, never releasing my eyes from his gripping stare. "What you do to me… no word in the universe exists yet that could even come close to describing it."

He always knew exactly what to say. But he wasn't just saying it. I knew that he truly meant it. Even through the most turbulent storm, together, we were still stronger than ever.

CHAPTER 28

Obviously, I was on edge for weeks on end after the incident in the park. My daily routine was tainted with extra paranoia as I practically tiptoed around Frank, wondering everyday if he knew anything. Luckily, I hadn't heard anything from or about Juan Carlos and he seemed to have gotten the message to back off, at least for now. But I didn't doubt for one minute that I had seen the last of him.

With everything that was happening around me, I decided to do something for myself, for my peace of mind. I found a shooting range in upstate New York where I went to practice alone a few times. The timing seemed like it was right to finally learn how to use that intimidating thing inside my nightstand. Just in case.

Sitting on my bed, staring at my shiny, silver weapon, I was in a fog, with many different thoughts swarming through my head. My mind began to wander and, as usual, I missed Collin so much. The last time we hung out it was in the second week of June and the only reason it happened was that I pushed the matter. He was very busy writing a script for his cinematography class' final project. I promised to stay out of the way if he let me come over. Just being in his presence was comforting, especially after our world was so recently shaken.

We sat in his living room quietly with 'Everything' by Lifehouse playing softly in the background. I read a magazine as he wrote in his notebook. I peered up at him while he diligently jotted something down. His gorgeous hair fell delicately across his forehead. He's really handsome, I remember thinking as I stared at him in awe, his eyes following the text on the paper. He stopped then, his soft, dark eyes glowed as they met with mine.

"What's up, baby?" he asked me as I continued to stare.
I sighed happily then shook my head as if to silently say "nothing," not wanting to be a distraction. But I couldn't help it. I leaned over and rested my arms around him, my head on his shoulder. He turned to face me and his lips brushed against mine.

"Who am I kidding? I can't work with you here." He closed the notebook and tossed it onto the end table then leaned back pulling me with him. We were lying down, face to face, as he caressed my cheek and I brushed his hair back, combing through it with my fingers.

I know for a fact that he got no work done that night. Well, at least on his script, that is. After that I backed off a little, knowing how important that project was to him.

I was startled out of my reveries when a loud cacophony of men's voices downstairs echoed through the house. *Oh yeah, it's poker night.* That means technically I'm hosting, being the 'good wife' that I was, or made myself out to be. I quickly wrapped my weapon in a white handkerchief and replaced it into the night table drawer.

I went downstairs to make sure that everyone was comfortable. Every hand should always have a beer or highball glass, and the hors d'oeuvres tray and chip bowls should never be empty. These were the silly things that mattered, but I actually enjoyed it because it made me feel, even if only for a night, as if my life was normal. Most of Frank's friends who came over worked at the club with him and were the stereotypical bunch. All of them except for Paul Carlisle.

Paul hardly ever came over, but that one particular night he did. I loved Paul. He was so good with the kids just like Debra. So down to earth. After finishing in the kitchen, I sat next to him and played a quick hand with him while the others were outside smoking.

"I hope he's not giving you too much trouble," I said about Nick who was staying with them for a few nights.
"Nick? Never, he's a good kid," Paul said glancing up at me from his hand of cards.

I laughed and said, "Twenty-one" as I laid down my cards to show I won the hand, and then added, jokingly, "Are we talking about the same Nick?" But of course we were, because he probably was such a good kid when he was with them. He only really gave me trouble, which seemed all too familiar.

The buzzer in the kitchen went off interrupting our conversation and I excused myself so that I could pull everything out of the oven. Today I put down a plate of wings, a tray of deviled eggs, mozzarella sticks, a bowl of chips and dip, and potato skins.

"Thanks Vic," Paul said as I handed him a cold beer and sat again. "You're welcome. How's Debra?"

"She's good. She always asks about you. You should give her a call."

"Oops sorry," I said when I realized that the beer wasn't a twist off. I went back into the kitchen again to grab the bottle opener. As I passed through the hallway, the guys were returning with a trail of smoke following them. I looked in all the drawers until I finally found the opener. I quickly sprayed a can of air freshener in the hallway then went back to finish my chat with Paul.

And when I returned Frank was sitting in my spot next to Paul. I reached over him and handed Paul the opener then stood around for a moment unsure if I should bother trying to find my way in. It was already packed, the guys were carrying on, and I felt out of place.

Paul noticed me standing there and offered me his seat.

"No, no, it's fine," I said wishing Frank would have been the one to offer instead.

"I don't mind. I'll scoot over," he said, insistently.
Before I could answer, my husband laughed. "Don't be ridiculous. I'm sure she was just seeing her way out."

"Actually, I wouldn't mind hanging out for a bit," I said.
Then Paul chimed in, "She could sit for a few games. She's really good!"

"Yeah, women playing poker. That's just what we need," Frank scoffed.

"Don't you have some dishes to wash or something?" His mocking comment was followed by him slapping my ass.

I exhaled under my breath and rolled my eyes. *What a stupid chauvinistic comment to make.* He knew I could play, and probably beat him at it too. But of course with the other guys around he *would* act like that.

Despite Frank's distasteful behavior I continued to cater to the guys until they were all settled in. Then, when I started to feel like an annoying waiter, I finally disappeared upstairs for a while to let them have their 'guy time'. I felt like I had nothing better to do. The kids were all out with their friends and there was no cleaning that needed to be done, thanks to Galina. I found myself bored on a Friday night. This sure wasn't how I pictured myself spending my Friday nights when I was younger.

I wasn't old and already had children who were too cool to hang out with their mother. *I need another baby around.*

Wait… did I just think that? I shook my head wondering if the thought crossed my mind because I knew I was getting older. It was a pointless thought that needed to be quickly dismissed since I knew it wasn't even a possibility anymore anyway.

I plopped onto my bed and looked around my room for a moment. It was so elegantly decorated, of course not by me, and looked like it came out of a magazine. I never dreamed my house would look like this. *Have I come a long way or not?* It was so hard to tell.

As I stared at the speckled sheet of tar through the skylight my mind couldn't help wandering again. Succumbing to my boredom, I decide to log into my Facebook account. My homepage showed all of the fabulous things people were doing with their Friday nights. Michelle was already at a happy hour in Ridgewood. Brooke was in New York. I couldn't see what Collin was doing because we weren't friends on Facebook, understandably to hide what was going on between us. I decided to be nosey anyway. His profile picture was so sexy. It looked like it was taken at his school as he looked off to the side with his messy hair and beautiful half smile that I loved.

I sent him a text message. He didn't respond. *I would love to be with him tonight.* Who was I kidding? I would love to be with him *every* night. What could I do to keep busy? The mini bar in our bedroom caught my eye. An unopened bottle of Grey Goose vodka. *Why not?* I thought as I proceeded to open it and poured myself a small glass over ice. Then I added a splash of cranberry juice. I continued to drink by myself for a while until I noticed the room started to tilt. I had no water bottles in the mini bar so I decided to go downstairs to get a glass.

From the bottom of the stairs I could overhear the guys talking, all of them unable able to hide that they've been drinking as their volumes rose and jokes were made. The conversation sounded raunchy. I normally would never have eavesdropped but it was impossible, as loud as they were being.

"What about that new one, Desiree?" It was Frank's voice, louder than everyone else's. "She's a real piece of ass, that one!" More laughter. And one, I couldn't make out the voice, started singing, "Desiree … sweet Desiree …" sounding like a drunken sailor.

It all sickened me. It was like a train wreck, I didn't want to look but curiosity got the best of me

Frank continued, bragging, "Yeah, I banged the shit out of that fresh, eighteen-year-old sweet ass just last week!"

"No!" they all said in unison, in mocking disbelief.

Okay, this was it! I couldn't – and wouldn't – take anymore. I ran downstairs and yelled at him, in front of all his friends.

"You're such an asshole! Is this what you do all day? Fuck around with girls Ashley's age… You're so pathetic."

The guys looked at me stunned and didn't know what to say. The years that I was with Frank I always had a very particular way of carrying myself in front of his friends. Quiet, elegant. I would never raise my voice or use profanity. And I would never disrespect Frank. But I was too mad and maybe a little drunk to care. Nonetheless, I still expected Frank to look surprised or maybe apologize but instead he started to yell.

"You really have nothing better to fuckin' do? Sitting around listening to our conversation? *And* you're drinking? You're an embarrassment! Get your ugly fat ass back upstairs."

"I can't fucking stand you," I muttered shaking my head and heading back upstairs.

Back to the room, drowning myself in straight Vodka again. Everything around me was moving, or maybe I was moving. Completely unsure I sat on the edge of the bed. It felt a little like I was on a merry go round, in slow motion.

Suddenly a dark presence thickened the air. Glancing up from my whirlwind mind state my eyes met with Frank's. *Shit, when did he get in here?* He looked pissed.

"How many times do I have to tell you about the way you behave? Especially in front of the guys."

"What the hell do you expect? When you're there laughing about sleeping with other women while I'm in the other room?"

"Watch your tone," he warned.

"Why don't you watch yours? Actually, how about I start respecting you when you respect me? That's how it should be."

I wanted to hold back, but I couldn't. What was I thinking? All of a sudden, I was bold. My mouth was big sometimes but in the end, physically I couldn't back it up.

"What?" He was enraged and pushed me, almost knocking me over.

No, not again. Not another one manhandling me. It was just too much. Too much for my heart, too much for my soul and I was

224

just too physically exhausted to engage in yet another fight knowing that I had a way out if I made it downstairs.

Frank stood there staring me down, but I jumped off of the bed and desperately made a run for the door. Naturally, Frank came after me. I ran as fast as I could and lost my balance on the curve at the bottom of the stairs. My ankle twisted a little and I stumbled down the remaining three stairs, falling smack down in front of my brother-in-law.

"Shit, Victoria; are you all right?" Paul asked helping me up.

"I need to get out of here," I mumbled, continuing down the hallway, using the wall for support.

"Is everything cool? Heard a lot of commotion," Paul continued, following me.

Frank, the high and mighty, entered his room of minions. Everyone stopped talking and stared at Paul, Frank and me.

"Victoria, get back upstairs."

"No, I'm leaving!"

"I'm not asking you, I am telling you! Right now!" he said trying to scare me.

"For what? So you can beat the shit out of me?" I asked as I tried to stand tall. "Why don't you go ahead and hit me in front of all your friends." I knew I was embarrassing him in front of everyone. And I knew when they all left that I was in trouble. But none of that rationalization made its way past the alcohol as I challenged him. I had reached my emotional limit. Enough was enough. All the shame, humiliation, sadness and regret … it all came out at that moment. There was no holding back. Not anymore.

Paul stepped between us.

"All right why don't we all calm down," he said looking at me then at Frank.

I grabbed my keys. I wanted to say more, but stormed out and sat in my car for a minute, instead. Watching the door. Waiting to see if he would come after me. He wasn't coming. *Big surprise.* I wiped my eyes and tried to focus as I put the car into reverse. *I shouldn't be driving.* But I also couldn't go back in there. Taking a deep breath and trying to focus on the road, I drove off. Unsure of where I was going … but it was just one of those situations … I don't know where I should be, but it's not *here.*

Then, as usual, fear changed my thoughts. *Good job Victoria…I'll be paying for that one tomorrow.* That's for sure… My thoughts continued to race in my head as I drove erratically down the highway. The liquor started to kick in harder. *Fuck that. I don't care. It's done anyway. Screw him. I'll show him! When I have the courage, he'll be sorry.*

Maybe I should have gone to Brooke's. Any other fight with Frank would have sent me straight to Brooke's house in the past. But the only person I was thinking about was Collin. Even when I wasn't thinking. And I couldn't believe that I somehow made it to his apartment. *Thank God, I wasn't pulled over.* I sat in the car for a minute contemplating going inside. The chances of him being home seemed slim. It was a Friday night and it was after midnight. Then again, he had been wrapped up in schoolwork.

I wasn't even wearing shoes when I ran out of my house. Reluctantly, I made my way barefoot into Collin's apartment building. Stumbling into the lobby in disarray was one of the most disgraceful things I could have done. Thankfully, Ian wasn't there or he might have been really concerned. I had a spare key that Collin gave me months ago, so I quickly rushed past the unfamiliar concierge as she eyeballed me. I didn't doubt that my makeup was running and pupils dilated as I hobbled to the elevator, my ankle still tender. Once inside the elevator I tried to fix my hair a little.

It was almost 1 a.m. Would he be mad at me for just showing up? He always told me to come by no matter what time. *But he didn't write back to my text.* I tried to rationalize with myself. He might be sleeping and I could crawl into bed next to him. Finding comfort in the idea of being able to cuddle with Collin I quietly opened the door and let myself into his apartment.

CHAPTER 29

Although I heard voices chattering, I continued to walk into Collin's apartment anyway. When I was in the living room, I found myself in the room with two young women, one guy, and Collin. They were all sitting around the coffee table with tons of papers everywhere. Suddenly everyone stopped talking and looked up at me as if they'd seen a ghost. I stood speechless for a moment then scampered away, escaping to the bathroom. Collin came after me.

"Hey… Victoria? What's going on? I didn't know you were coming here," he said as he shut the bathroom door behind us.

I sat on the edge of the tub. "I'm sorry I sent you a text. I didn't know you had people over. This is so embarrassing. Look at me, you must hate me…"

"Relax. It's fine. Did something happen? Are you hurt?" he asked sitting beside me.

"No. Just my ankle. But I'm okay. I just really needed you."

He hugged me and slowly made everything better. "You know I'm always here, sweetheart."

"Thank you. I know you are," I said holding him a minute longer. "You can get back to your friends though. I'm fine."

"I would ask them to leave, but we're finishing up that script I've been working on. It's due on Monday. We're almost done. You could join us too you know, you don't have to hide back here."

I hesitated for a moment still feeling embarrassed. "Maybe. Let me just wash up."

"Okay," he said then kissed my forehead before heading back to the living room.

I never met any of his friends and now I'm going to? Of all times! Washing my face and brushing my hair, then looking at my reflection, I had second thoughts. I still looked terrible from all the recent extra stress, especially with no makeup.

Reluctantly, I reentered the living room. And his friends

looked up at me. Collin was doing something in the kitchen so they introduced themselves.

"Hi! I'm Jasmine," said the dark skinned girl with long black hair, dressed simply in a blue summer dress. "And this is Melissa ..." The skinny redhead with a big Julia Roberts smile got up and shook my hand.

"And this is David …" Jasmine continued.

"Hi, how are you?" said the cute Irish kid with long, light brown hair, wearing a My Chemical Romance t-shirt.

I remembered Brooke did tell me that his friends were nice. I suddenly felt a little at ease.

"Hi, nice to meet you," I said. "All of you!" I smiled, shaking all their hands. Jasmine went a step further giving me a genuine hug.

"So are you his wife?" Jasmine asked me unexpectedly.

Shit, my ring is still on! Why did I always have it off when it was supposed to be on and on when it should be off! Damn what do I say? Collin walked into the room and I turned to him for help. He smiled at me and nonchalantly played it off, wrapping his arm around my waist.

"Yes, this is my absolutely beautiful wife, Victoria."

"It's so nice to meet you," Melissa said. None of them gave it a second thought.

"So how did you guys meet?" Jasmine asked.

I smiled and looked up at Collin. I guess it would be okay for him to tell the truth about meeting me in my office, but before I could say anything, he spit out, "It's actually a really funny story; we were in the middle of Times Square…"

His friends leaned in, their eyes lit up and they were all ears.

Where was he going with this? Okay I could play along.

"Yes. It was right on those ruby red stairs!" I added then smiled at him.

"I was taking a picture and lost my balance, and then my heel broke," I said then quickly shut up before the story became too far-fetched. But *nothing* was too far-fetched for Collin and his wild imagination.

"I guess I was in the right place at the right time because when she tripped I caught her. And there I was, with this angel who literally fell into my arms and I decided I could never let her go," he said looking at me. *Yes, there he goes again.* I guess we only could wish and pretend that our life was a happily ever after fairy-tale. Until then these stories and fantasies of us being together forever were nothing more than that; stories and fantasies. Or what I liked to refer to as our moonstone dreams.

"Aww!" the two girls said in unison, completely getting sucked in.

"Instant chemistry!" David said. *Him too?* I wanted to laugh, but I held it in.

"Of course! Could you blame me," Collin replied.

"I mean look at her," he said making me blush.

"You're gorgeous," said David to me, agreeing.

The girls nodded, also adding their own compliments. I suddenly felt a little coy. Then Collin hugged me and gave me the sweetest kiss in front of everyone.

"Okay, okay enough about me," I said, my face turning scarlet.

The mood of the room was so warm and welcoming. So unlike what I was used to at home – if you could call it home – with Frank. I just wanted to move in and stay here forever. I felt so safe. So loved. And of course, so very happy.

Collin turned the conversation back to business, which of course excluded me for the most part, but I never felt left out. Throughout the evening Collin either had his hand on my leg, or he'd give me a tight squeeze and a kiss on the head. The girls always looked at me and smiled, never ignoring my presence. And David always asked if I needed anything, each time he got up to use the bathroom.

It was just all so surreal. No matter what the situation, life with Collin really was like living a dream.

They finished their script; then everyone headed out leaving us alone.

As soon as Collin and said goodnight to his friends/colleagues, he softly shut the door behind him, and suddenly turned to me and was all over me like bees to honey.

"I adore you!" he said, grabbing my face and kissing me intensely. Even though we were living a lie, I was very much in his world.

Collin reclined on the sofa and held his arms out to me.

"Come here," he said. I was drawn into him like a moth to a flame.

"Okay, *husband*," I teased, laying my head on his chest. "Your friends are so nice. How did they not know that you're not really married?"

"Cause they're from my school. We don't talk about things like that," he laughed.

"Well, I'll be your wife for the night," I said wrapping my arms around him as he combed his hands through my hair.

"Just tonight? You sure?"

"What are you trying to say?" I asked looking up at him smiling. Then my smile quickly faded. "You wouldn't want to marry me," I said shaking my head.

"You're crazy. If I could, I would marry you in a heartbeat," he said melting me with his words and delicate touch.

"Why do you always know the perfect thing to say?" I whispered.

My happiness only added to the passion, making this one of the happiness nights of my relationship with him – oh, hell, make that the happiest night of my *life!*

After getting all wrapped up in each other as usual, Collin paused, took my hand and led me to the bedroom. I sat on the bed, leaned back and looked up at him, seductively, as he stood over me, enjoying the view. Then he knelt over me, slowly peeling his shirt off before his body covered mine like a blanket, warming me instantly as he lowered his lips to kiss me repeatedly.

We never stopped kissing while we undressed each other. We held each other tight and began to make love. Together we were always taken somewhere universally perfect. My hips rolled slowly into him, following his steady tempo. Our perfect rhythm was never disturbed while he artfully moved with me, even as I twisted and turned under him. This time, the third round of orgasms, he climaxed first and I followed shortly afterward, catapulting to my little cloud. Then, I collapsed in ecstasy, and lay sprawled out on the bed, wearing a satisfied smile.

I closed my eyes turning my head to the side, sighing audibly. Happily. Running my hands through his hair, as I so loved to do. I was completely content and satisfied, and could have stayed there with him like that forever.

Lightly running the back of his hand across my face he lowered his lips to my ear nibbling my earlobe and said, "Don't rest yet, I'm not done with you."

My eyes blinked open to meet with his. *Is he serious?* We had already been at it for hours. Well, it wasn't like I could ever

230

get enough of him anyway. "I hope not," I whispered and returned a passion fueled kiss of our building want and desire. Every nerve in my body was completely stimulated and tingling wonderfully. I finally got the strength and pulled Collin back toward me.

We held each other tight as we both panted heavily, both lethargic and covered in each other's sweat from hours of lovemaking. We stared at each other like two teenagers, in love for the first time.

Lost in his eyes only wonderful thoughts possessed me. *Beautiful. Delicate. Passionate. Please don't let this end.* I thought silently while mumbling words of love, expressing everything I felt for him in that moment and always. He whispered passionate words back to me.

I continued to gaze into his eyes. He smiled at me and kissed me deeply while our bodies moved in an intense yet tranquil tempo. I kissed him back taking his face in my hands.

"Tell me you love me," I sighed, just wanting and needing to hear it as much as I felt it.

"I love you," he whispered, for the 100th time, then planted kisses in a slow steady pattern from my ear to the side of my neck. Then we started round four. This time I just lay back and let Collin do most of the work and quickly we were both ready to release together again. We knew each other's pleasure points so well, we could practically dictate with our bodies whether we wanted it to be quick or linger throughout the night. We usually made love twice a night, the first being slow and the second being quick – or vice versa. But this was the first time we ever managed four rounds. It was the one night I truly let myself go, not worrying about work, or *anything* for that matter … just let myself be the beautiful woman Collin made me feel like I was.

I closed my eyes as my senses were scattered to the stars. I couldn't hold back anymore; and clenching his back, screaming out his name, we both found our sensational release together.

My body trembled under him long after my ecstasy passed. My lungs worked double time as I gasped for air. I finally knew and understood the feeling that all those love songs were describing. I was breathless and infatuated by him. Suddenly tears that I couldn't control or explain suddenly streamed down my face.

Collin gently traced my cheekbone with his fingers.

"What's wrong?"

"Nothing, my love. You just make me so happy," I said weakly and closed my eyes.

"I hope someday you'll let me make you happy every single day," he said as I turned to my side, his arm draped securely across my body and our legs entwined. I entangled my hands with his, curling my body closer against him. Physically exhausted and emotionally elated, we cuddled together.

"Someday," was the last thing I uttered before fatigue took over and stole me away from him.

CHAPTER 30

The next morning I woke still snuggled close to Collin while he was fast asleep. I turned my body to face him and watched him for a while. *He's so beautiful*, I thought as I gently touched his hair. He looked so peaceful and I wondered if, and hoped that, he was dreaming about me. Careful not to wake him up I kissed him softly and climbed out of bed, then disappeared into the bathroom.

This was the first night I ever actually stayed the entire night. There wasn't anything here that said 'Victoria'. Not even a toothbrush. So, of course, none of my toiletries either. After all of my stress and aggravation with Frank, I cried all the make-up right off my face. I really looked a mess. Collin's crappy Ivory soap would have to do the trick for a quick face wash. Ah, I felt too good today to think of all that shit. The cold water felt great splashed on my face. I felt refreshed and alive. What is it about New York City water that's vastly superior to New Jersey's?

After drying my face, I glanced down and noticed that his hamper was full. I grabbed an empty laundry basket and filled it along with anything else I saw lying around. Bringing everything into the kitchen, I sorted out two loads then filled the washing machine and started the first one.

While I was in domestic mode, I stood around thinking what next? *Hmm I should make him breakfast?* He always beat me to the kitchen, making me wonderful dinners or having me come to his place early in the morning for breakfast. This time it was my turn. I pulled out eggs, butter, and milk from the refrigerator; then rummaged through the cabinets for cinnamon and bread. With French toast in mind, I quietly pull a pan from a lower cabinet and begin cooking.

While reaching across the counter I unintentionally knocked over a pile of papers. The large gold and maroon letterhead was hard to ignore and I noticed the words "Congratulations" written in bold. *Okay I will not read* it I tell myself ignoring the papers remembering what happened when I went through his phone. I wouldn't be nosey. I glanced over at the French toast and noticed I needed to flip it, which I did, before quickly returning the papers back into the neat pile they originally were.

I returned to the stove and flipped the French toast. Then set the table, not as nicely as he usually did, but I tried. I glanced at the clock, 8:15. One more thing. I transferred the wet clothes to the dryer before I snuggled back in place next to Collin.

"Good morning my love," I said as I kissed him.

"Mmm. I love waking up next to you," he said as he hugged me tight. "What time is it?"

"Eight-fifteen."

"Why are you up? It's Saturday," he said in a lazy tone. He yawned loudly as he stretched his arms; then closed his eyes again.

"No, I don't think so," I said as I shook him playfully. "Get up sleepy head I have a surprise for you."

"Okay," he said, and then sighed, stretched again and slowly scrambled out of bed.

Good Lord, did this boy look hot! In nothing but boxer shorts, those tight abs were a sight to be held! They were calling me. And that wasn't the only thing. *Calm down, girl!* I told myself. One more go around and I wouldn't be able to walk!

I went into the kitchen and squared away the dirty dishes while Collin was in the bathroom. When he came out and walked into the dining area, I was so excited to, for once, be able to impress him with my kitchen skills. He hugged me and then lifted me off the ground.

"I knew I picked the perfect wife," he said squeezing me tight then kissing me before putting me down.

"C'mon, let's eat before it gets cold," I said. We sat at the table and Collin insisted on serving me, cutting my French toast and even pouring the syrup for me. Always the gentleman and so sweet!

"This is so good!" Collin said, talking with his mouth full. "Mmm ... perfect!"

"I'm glad you're enjoying it!" I smiled at him. Then I remembered the papers I stumbled across. I didn't want to appear obsessed over them, so I decided to casually bring it up.

"Babe, you told me I could talk to you about anything right?"

"Of course." He put down his fork and stopped eating. He leaned close to me and said, "What's up?" He looked so concerned.

"Please don't be mad." I paused, trying to find the right words. Then continued, "I swear I wasn't snooping, but when I was cooking I saw some papers you had from the University of Southern California."

"Oh. You did?"

"Yes. I didn't read them nor anything but… well can you understand my concern?"

"Yes. I'm sorry. I was planning on telling you about that."

"When?"

"I was going to. I just wasn't sure what I wanted to do yet." Collin's mood turned more serious as he spoke. It seems he, too, was trying to find the right words. "Sean got me a connection from where he works and I considered using it. I applied to the school so, just in case the opportunity arose, I could finish my semester there."

"Oh," I said quietly.

"Don't worry I'm not going." *What? He's not going? This was an A-1 opportunity. Why wasn't he going? Because of me? I secretly hoped not.*

Not wanting to come across as the unsupportive *wife,* I figured I'd play this one out and act encouraging. "Collin, I looked the school up. It's number two in the world for what you want to do. *And you got accepted.* Why would you turn something like that down?"

"Are you really asking me that?" He smiled again.

"Please don't stay because of me. This sounds like such a great opportunity for you."

"It is. But I can't go. Not unless … well … uh …"

"Not unless *what,* Collin?" I asked. "Spit it out."

"Well … would you ever consider…"

"What? Tell me!" I said, demandingly.

"Never mind."

But he didn't have to say a thing … I got it. "I would love nothing more than to be far away from here with you, but you know I can't."

"Well, then there's nothing else to discuss," he said quietly. I could feel that he was disappointed, but it's not like I was asking him to stay either.

"By the way, before I forget, while we're talking about

Cali… I have some friends coming for a few weeks, so if you don't hear from me a lot it's because I'm busy with them."

"Okay," I said somewhat listening to him but still feeling out of sorts about the previous topic.

"Because I know how silly you can be sometimes, if we don't talk," he added.

I smiled at him and continued to eat. *Why does life always have to be so difficult? Can't things just ever be easy and nice? Now, time to break up this little fantasy once again, as I have to go back to my sad, unfulfilling life, feeling unloved, unwanted and worse of all, disrespected. And dealing with yet another aftermath of an argument with Frank.*

Later that afternoon I hid out at Brooke's house because I wouldn't dare go home. I knew Frank was going away again on Monday morning, so I just had to avoid him until then. When Brooke came home from the mall to find me vacuuming her living room, I didn't have to say anything else. She already knew the routine. I would be staying there in the spare bedroom, which may as well have been my other room, since I already had clothes, make up, and shoes in the closet. My extra toothbrush was in the holder in her bathroom. I would just need to let Galina know that I would be home by Tuesday and see if she were interested in the overtime. At this point, it would just be a matter of checking in on Ashley and taking care of the Monday morning routine. If she were unavailable then Ashley would just have to stay with me too. Then that reminded me that I also needed to call Debra to confirm when to drop Nick off.

Just as I finished sending Galina a text, my phone rang.

"Hey Deb! I was just going to call you and let you know that any time after five today should be fine to bring Nick. We're at my sister's house."

"Actually I wanted to talk to you about that," she said in a serious tone.

"Oh…? Okay." *Uh-oh, what happened now?* I shut the vacuum cleaner off so I could hear her better.

"Paul and I were talking this morning. We were thinking maybe it would be best if Nick stays here a little while longer."

"Longer? Like another week?" I was confused. What was going on?

"No, Victoria, not a week. Maybe a few months or so. This will give you time to get your life together…"

"Excuse me? Get my life together? What exactly is that supposed to mean?" I decided to put the vacuum cleaner away.

236

I wrapped up the wire and walked it over to the closet. I needed to sit down. Maybe even a drink. I sat on the sofa a second to catch my breath.

So, did Paul rat me out? Tell Miss 'Perfect Mom' about my fight with Frank last night? How dare he; especially after all his hearty laughing concerning the strip club dancers. He certainly wasn't a saint either!

"Come on Vic. We don't mean it like *that*. This is what family if for. To help during hard times. We can take Nick off your hands for a bit so you and Frank could maybe go to counseling?"

Whoa, this was so out of line. I got up again. "Look, Debra, if you don't bring my son home I will come over and pick him up myself!" I was furious, walking quickly to the bar in the living room as I spoke. I got a tumbler from the cabinet and reached for the Skye Vodka. I was ready to hit 'end call' until her next words interrupted my action.

"He doesn't want to go home. He told us. That's why we thought to give you this time to provide a..." she stopped to search carefully for her words, "more stable... environment for him, and yourself."

No, this can't be happening! I knew I wasn't going to win a Mom of the Year award, but I wasn't *that* bad! I poured the vodka. "So, let me get this right... you and Paul decide to keep my fifteen-year-old son from me because you think he's old enough to make this kind of decision? You know I shouldn't be wasting my time talking to you. I could call the police, this is considered kidnapping!"

"Don't be like this. We are trying to help you."

"I didn't ask for your help."

"Well, if you want to get the authorities involved go ahead. I didn't want it to have to come to that. I would highly recommend that you reconsider. You would lose custody. Is that what you want?"

"I can take care of Nicholas, just like I took care of Thomas and Ashley."

"Really? Let me in on how you plan to do this. You and your husband are always drinking..."

"I am NOT always drinking..." I paused, realizing I had a glass of pure vodka right in front of me. Yeah, actually lately I may have been over doing it. And I couldn't speak for Frank, he had a drinking problem. Everyone knew this. I guess the not so secret skeletons in our closet were becoming obvious even to others now. I was starting to feel defeated.

"You have arguments that escalate to a very unsafe level. It's not healthy for the children. It's not healthy for you!"

Defeated again. It wasn't Paul who ratted me out … it was Frank … and myself. Our actions spoke louder than words.

"Like I said … We are not trying to steal your son away. He loves you very much, but, honestly, he has been so happy here the last two weeks. Maybe now isn't a good time to talk about it but I also wanted to bring him to a friend of mine, she's a therapist."

"So let me see if I am getting this right. Apparently Frank and I are terrible drunken, angry parents that fight all the time, and now my son needs therapy?" I blurted out sarcastically. Then I listened to what I'd just said, and it was frighteningly true. I can't fight her. I probably would lose a battle in court. Did we need to subject our children to even more calamities than they've already endured? Maybe we did scar our children, Nick receiving the worst of it. I should have been stronger and left Frank a long time ago. Now I am losing everything because him.

"Don't say it like that. I don't know how to give him the guidance that he needs to deal with some of his feelings. I think it would be very helpful."

I was done arguing. "Please just let me meet her, and talk to him before you commit to anything. Please, Debra he's my son."

"I wouldn't do it without your permission."

I sighed. I felt like I was signing away my life. This was my son. One of the few things that kept me whole, no matter what he said or did, in the end of the day he was my baby. But I had to stop being selfish and do what might actually be best for Nick, for once. Finally after a long silence on my end I swallowed the lump in my throat, not wanting Debra to know that I was about to cry. "So, how does this work?"

"Whenever you can, bring him some clothes, shoes, any of his things that he'll need. And don't worry! He has Chuck and Matt to hang out with. We're going to the water park tomorrow, and camping next weekend. Trust me Vic; he's going to be so happy." Good for you Debra Carlisle, you had a perfect TV sitcom happy family. Lucky me, I had to choose the messed up Carlisle brother. I brushed aside my feelings of envy momentarily so I could finish the humiliating conversation.

"So you want him to stay there just for the summer?"

"However long you need." It went back to being for *my* benefit. That's reverse psychology for you.

"And when school starts?"

"It's only the beginning of the summer. We can all sit together in a few weeks and figure something out."

"I'll bring his things today. I want to see him. Let me gather everything I'll be there in a bit." *No more hiding from Frank. My son is involved now and this is serious. He could do whatever he wants to me, he's not going to win. Let him try to humiliate me, let him try to beat me to a pulp, I don't care, he's not going to come between me and my kid! I think I proved last night that he's not going to win this game and that I won't be staying around to put up with his shit. I do have other places to go.*

"Okay. See you then."

I hung up. I didn't feel like saying *bye*. I was offended, embarrassed, sad, and angry. I knew that Debra meant well, but she didn't have any idea how much this would be one of the hardest things I would ever do.

*   *   *   *

I drove back to the house. My mood switched from that of pity to supreme anger at Frank. The bastard destroyed my life. He took everything I ever had – my dignity, my sense of worth, even my good looks as I always appeared so worn out and tired, old before my time. Now my kid! I was completely *spent*.

I was fuming. I didn't even realize I was going 15 miles over the speed limit and slammed on my brakes when I got to the red light in town. Then my damn cell phone rang and it was a blocked number!

"What!" I screamed, answering like a raving lunatic.

"Whoa! Uh… Are you, okay, babe?" It was Collin. Oh yeah, I told him to block his number whenever he called. Through all the red I was seeing I had forgotten.

"Yeah, yeah, everything is just fine. What's up?"

"Um. Is this a bad time?" He asked.

"No, no, it's all good. Some asshole cut me off, that's all." I lied and softened my tone. I was too riled up to deal with his goodness. He was just too good and I didn't need him to protect me. I love that man with all my heart, but now was just not the time to share my frustrations and complaining about my life was getting old.

"Oh, okay, cool," he said, going back to his chipper self. "I was thinking … you know how we never get to spend time together on Sunday? Maybe tomorrow can you please make an exception? My friends absolutely loved you and David got extra tickets for us…"

Collin kept talking, excitedly, about something, but I wasn't paying attention. I just kept saying, "Yes, yes, sounds good to me … yeah, sure … of course …"

"Awesome, can't wait! You're gonna love it! I'll see you tomorrow at noon! Love you babe," He blew me a kiss and hung up the phone.

Did I just commit to something? Ah, not the time to worry about it. I have bigger fish to fry right now.

When I reached my home … or, make that my mansion, because it never felt like a *home* … I parked the car in front of the garage, not inside. Frank hates that and I did it for spite. I walked in and slammed the door behind me in a huff, threw my bag on the coffee table and headed upstairs.

I went into Nick's bedroom and pulled a suitcase from his closet. While packing his clothes, the my anger subsided and was replaced with a sense of relief. I remembered what Nick witnessed as a baby and child. He wouldn't have to be subjected to anything like that anymore. If he stayed here, he would be all alone once Ashley and Galina were gone. Debra was a great mom, even if I didn't want to admit it to her. I knew that he was safe.

I sat in Nick's room on the edge of the bed with yet another drink in my hand. Screw it; what else did I have to lose? Looking around his room and imagining it empty, my heart clenched as tears formed.

Just the previous night I'd cried tears of joy and now there I was crying in defeat. I realized that it didn't matter if I was ever happy because Frank was going to rip up and stomp on anything I ever had.

After two suitcases were filled, I wheeled them downstairs and put them by the front door. Then I walked through my empty house, like a zombie, feeling a bit dead inside. Everyone was out of the house. On the saddest days of my life, I've thought about the only way out. To free myself from Frank, I would have to get rid of him. I was sick and tired of him, his shit, and the charade that we put on.

My emotionless state of mind was the exact what I needed to motivate me to go through with my plan. I was tired of feeling trapped. I walked over to the nightstand and pulled out my handgun. It was wrapped in a handkerchief, which I carefully unraveled. I held the silver pistol tight around the grip.

I paced around my room for an hour or two, my heart beating out of my chest. I knew I couldn't live like this anymore and I finally needed to take control. It wasn't a crime to defend myself. I had been to the shooting range enough times to know exactly how to use my gun. I knew that I had enough witnesses and previous police reports that backed up my case. Any jury would side with me. *Self-defense,* I continued to tell myself.

After some time passed, I positioned myself in a chair that was adjacent to the bedroom door.

As I sat there and waited, I realized that I was scared. And I wasn't scared to shoot my husband; I was scared of the person that was sitting in that chair. The person he turned me into was heartless. No second thoughts. No remorse. No sorrow about what I was about to do. I was almost eager for him to walk through the door so I could end the nightmare that I had been living. I wanted him, for once, to feel intense pain and know that I caused it. His life finally would end, letting mine begin.

Hours passed and I continued to think. I decided that I wasn't going to aim to kill, at first. I wanted to disable him first, let him suffer while I explain to him why I was doing it. I needed the closure because I was not a murderer, but I was a woman scorned and was passed my breaking point.

The hardest part of the entire plan would be to force myself to shed a tear at the funeral, to not look compassionless and guilty.

I thought about my mom and realized I was following in her footsteps. Her breaking point was when our father tried to molest Brooke. We could handle a lot of shit, but once the children were involved it was a completely different ballgame.

Even if I ended up in jail, it was a sacrifice I was willing to take. Being in jail and knowing that Frank was gone forever would have been better than the hell that I was living in. I clutched at the grip realizing how sad that was. *Jail* seemed better than my life. If it weren't for images of my children, sister, and Collin in my mind I wouldn't have had the strength to push me that far, and finally realize that I deserved more.

The sound of the front door shutting downstairs broke

my train of thought. I rose to my feet and planted them firmly positioned the way I would at the shooting range. I raised my hands with my finger on the trigger. My hands were steady as could be, and I knew I was ready.

Once the footsteps stopped all I could think about was the many times I pleaded for him to stop; stop insulting me, stop beating me, stop raping me, and never once did he ever show any mercy. My aim was high and perfect and as the doorknob turned and it slowly opened, I was more than ready to shoot.

CHAPTER 31

"Mom?"

Her words broke my sinister trance.

I blinked and snapped out of my hypnotic rage realizing that it was my daughter who stood there while I pointed a gun at her. I quickly turned around and shoved it onto the top shelf of my closet then turned back to face her. She was looking at me as if I had 10 heads.

"Mom?" She said again, "What are you doing?"

"Ashley! You scared me! I knew nobody was home then suddenly heard footsteps. I called down to see who was there but you didn't respond." I added the lie, so it would be more believable.

"Oh, I didn't hear you. Sorry. I'm going out with Morgan after work I just wanted to borrow your white shoes. Mine are all dirty," she said still standing in the threshold, hesitating to enter my room.

"Sure," I said trying to force a happy tone then quickly hurried to grab the shoes from the closet. I handed her two different pairs of strappy white sandals.

"Thanks," she said leaning forward to take them from me. "Are you sure you're okay?" she asked looking at me strangely.

"I'm fine. Go ahead, have fun and please be careful," I said as she was leaving.

Once the door shut behind her, I collapsed onto the bed and lost my composure. What if I had pulled the trigger? Just thinking about it had me frantic and I no longer felt as confident as I had earlier about my plan. Maybe my anger was getting the best of me. There had to be another way. I decided that I would have just one tiny glass of wine to help me de-stress. That's all. I still wanted to wait for Frank. We should talk and find a happy middle in this dysfunctional marriage. If he was so unhappy, couldn't he just let me go? These thoughts raced through my mind as I poured myself a glass of White Zinfandel.

I sat back down in the same chair again, but this time

feeling more frazzled and tired than before, I waited patiently all the while trying to come up with an answer.

The slamming of the bedroom door startled me, jolting me out of a light slumber. *What? When did I fall asleep? How long was I sleeping?* The sky was completely dark and I was still in the chair in my bedroom with an empty glass halfway in my grip. Without enough time to think I quickly rose to my feet to confront my opponent.

"Hey. Just getting in from work?" I asked casually, acting as if I didn't know the altercation that was brewing. He had no idea what I had up my sleeve if he tried anything. Which he would. Of course, he would.

He ignored my question as well as my calm demeanor. "Where the fuck were you all night?"

"Calm down. Where else would I go?" I said as I pulled the hair tie off my wrist and quickly pulled my hair up into a tight bun.

"Don't think I forgot about what happened," he said … his tone harsh and firm like a drill sergeant.

"Frank, I know it was wrong of me to make a scene. But you don't think you owe me an apology? For once can't you admit that you were wrong, too?" Yes. I was now definitely too different of a person to accept anything else. I had grown, changed … and this was going to end one of two ways. Either he would need to change or it would be over.

"You seem to forget how this works," he said as he proceeded to take his belt off. "Get on your knees."

"No," I said standing my ground … not even shuddering an ounce. "Things are going to change around here Frank. You never worry that you'll come home one day and I'll be gone because of the way you treat me."

He scoffed. "Real cute, Victoria. No, I don't. Ever. Because I know you know better than that. Where the hell would you go, anyway?"

I looked at him my eyes piercing, but I said nothing. Little did he know.

"Exactly. And you've been pissing me off lately. I don't know what the fuck has gotten into you but you better shape up real fast and stop acting like you're fucking irreplaceable. Now I'll give you five seconds to get on the floor like the dog that you are before I come over there and grab you myself!"

Maybe a few years ago I would have kept quiet but how

244

could I not respond to that? I knew what it was like to be treated like a queen. I was too good for Frank. Even if it got me killed, I couldn't hold my tongue any more. Why did it take me so long to realize?

So he wasn't going to change. Big surprise. At this point, all I needed was to get him mad enough to get one hit in. And that would be the last time he ever did.

"You know what Frank. I wasn't at Brooke's last night," I said smugly.

"And? You act like I give a shit where the fuck you were."

"Maybe you will when you know that while you were here with your asshole friends I had my legs wrapped around someone else screaming out his name over and over. *All night long!*"

His reaction was instantaneous as he raised his hand then swept it across my face. The blow threw me violently to the ground. Losing this battle wasn't an option, I reminded myself through the stinging of my cheek, trying to ignore it. For the first time all I could think about was my future and myself. Now I just needed to get to the night table and this could all be over.

With all my determination, I erased him from the room along with every degrading thing that poured out of his mouth with one goal in mind. Turning my body to a half crawl half run position I make my dash toward the nightstand, only a few feet away. Frank tried to grab me but remembering how it disabled Juan Carlos I turn around and attempt to kick him where it hurt the most, but because of our positioning, I was only able to land a blow to his stomach. This still slowed him down for a moment; and knowing that my life depended on it, I reached desperately at the night table drawer yanking it all the way out. Everything came crashing out. Books, some coins, spare keys. Shit! It's not in there!

Temporarily my doom seemed clear to me, as Frank was already recomposed and lunged at me again. The next closest thing, I grabbed was the table lamp. The plug's sudden yank from the outlet caused sparks to fly. He grabbed my ankle and I smashed the base into his hand. He screamed and it seemed as though I had control. I was much faster than Frank. Still virtually unharmed, I attempted to pull myself up so I could make a run for the closet. It's right there on the top shelf! I'm so close. So damned, close. I reached up. I felt around for the metal grip…*I got it!* Failing to look behind me, I was yanked suddenly down to the floor. My whole body hit the tiles, hard.

The gun fell from my hand and slid away from me.

Frank reached behind him and grabbed the lamp that I used as a weapon and picked it up to use it on me. I shielded my face and head, but was not giving up. *I will gain the upper hand. I have to!* I tell myself repeatedly, staying strong, and waiting for him to make one mistake, my one chance to grab the gun.

My spirit was crushed when I heard the bone in my forearm break from the force of the lamp smashing into it. I cried out in pain and instinctively tried to protect my new injury. I cradled it close to my body, which left my head exposed. Then he hit me again, hard enough that I saw stars. My vision was blurred and I was immobilized in shock and pain.

"You asked for this," Frank said twirling the cord of the lamp around my neck. I tried to pull it away, but my efforts were futile. I saw no way out of this. I could feel my energy fade and I grew weaker. Hopeless. My lungs burned as I desperately gasped for any ounce of air that could sneak past the securely ever tightening garrote. I felt lightheaded. I closed my eyes and knew that this was how I was going to die…

*   *   *   *

When I woke up, I grimaced and attempted to bat my eyelashes several times before I could fully open only one eye, the other one was swollen shut. Finding myself in a hospital room and in excruciating pain would have been much more traumatizing if I hadn't seen Brooke sitting at my feet. She was looking down at her phone and didn't notice that I was awake.

I tried to take in everything all at once. I was in so much pain, and was shocked to be alive. I looked over to my side and saw my oldest son Thomas sitting there.

"Tommy?" I could barely whisper because my throat was so sore.

"Mom," he said realizing I was up. "Thank God…" He hugged me gently being wary of my injuries.

What a sight. Thomas. He was my absolute pride and joy.

It was a wonder that he was the offspring of someone so dark and evil because he wasn't even an ounce of either. I missed him so much and felt like it's been a lifetime since he was last home.

"When did you get here?" I asked knowing that he was

246

last on base in Texas. I was so confused.

"I'm in town for Ashley's graduation next week. Remember?"

No, I didn't remember. Damn, I was a mess. Realizing I didn't remember, Thomas just rubbed my arm gently and kissed my forehead. "You'll be okay, Mom. Stay strong."

"Tom, give me and your mother a minute please," Brooke interrupted firmly, sending him out of the room.

"God, my head hurts," I said lifting my hand to it only to see a fresh cast wrapped around my arm. The memory flashed back into my mind and I had to close my eyes tight and try to ignore it.

"How did I… How did you…" I stuttered unable to gather my thoughts.

Brooke explained everything to me. It turned out that Tommy was planning to meet up with Ashley after leaving the airport, but he decided to drop his bags off at home first. When he got inside he heard all the commotion. He broke it up. My heart ached knowing that he had to go through that. *He saved my life.*

"I was so scared. I almost lost you today," Brooke said as she choked back tears.

I wanted to respond to her, but I couldn't stop coughing every time I tried to talk. Brooke reached over to grab a small blue pitcher from the end table and poured a cup of water, then handed it to me.

"Thank you," I said after taking a sip. "Don't worry, I'm not going anywhere." The battle continued to replay in my mind. It was the first time I ever fought back. If it wasn't for the fact that I'd been drinking I probably would have been alert enough to remember where the gun was.

"Damn, I really thought I had that," I muttered annoyed at myself.

"Had what?" Brooke asked as she looked up at me.

"Nothing," I said. I shook my head, not wanting to let her know what I had planned. If she knew that I could have avoided that fight, she would be furious.

"Where is Frank now?" I asked, then took another sip of water still feeling like someone torched my vocal cords.

Her eyes grew dark at the mention of his name. She looked off to the side. "He's in a holding cell at the police department. They're waiting for you to complete the police report, then you can press or drop charges." She inched closer and looked up at me. When she spoke again, her tone more serious than ever. "He could be charged with domestic violence or probably attempted murder. You could put him in jail for a long time."

I pressed my head back into my pillow. It was too much to process. I knew what she wanted to hear, but I felt like we'd already had that conversation time and time before.

"I think the police are waiting to talk to you. Should I tell them that you're awake?"

I nodded, even though I didn't feel like seeing anyone. I rather wanted to get Brooke out of the room. She left, only to return with a nurse hot on her heels. She was young, heavyset and very glamorous for a nurse. She was nice too.

"Just checking your vitals, honey," she said, sweetly, as she did her job. Then a doctor walked in. He wasn't as friendly, more serious and professional. He was old, with Benjamin Franklin glasses and a little moustache. He started explaining all my injuries to me and showing me x-rays, while the nurse tried to start an IV. It was obvious she was being careful, but it still hurt.

I was still in shock from waking up in a hospital in a cast and wrapped in bandages. Hearing my actual injuries described to was a harsh reality check.

Suddenly two police officers, one man and one woman, came inside and asked me for details of the incident. I gave them descriptions of the fight while they jotted notes.

Listening to the story as well, Brooke looked like she was going to be sick. Then the young male officer asked me if I wanted to press charges. I was officially overwhelmed.

"Yes." Brooke answered for me. I shot her a look and she backed down a bit.

"Miss, please don't move your arm," the nurse said. It was the first time she wasn't so sweet and she was starting to annoy me. She kept missing my vein and instructing me to stay still, which I found impossible. Questions were coming at me from everywhere.

"Ma'am, we need to know if you want to press charges against your husband." The male officer said again.

Again, Brooke answered for me and said, "Yes." Then she knelt down next to me and whispered, "Do you want me to call Collin for you? He doesn't know anything." I didn't want him to know … not yet.

"Should I call Collin?" she asked again.

"Um," I said trying to gather my thoughts.

Not even giving me a second. As the police repeated, "Ma'am? We need to know."

And while the nurse kept telling me, "We need to get your vein."

"Carolyn, hold on just a moment," the doctor said to the nurse. "I need to explain one more x-ray to the patient."

It was all too much. Too crazy. I just couldn't take it anymore. I desperately needed to be alone.

I put my hands over my eyes trying to tune everyone out for a moment to think. "Can everyone get out of my room?"

No one seemed to listen. Everyone continued to speak at once so I needed to get loud. "Everybody get out! GET OUT! PLEASE! PLEASE! JUST LEAVE ME ALONE! CAN I JUST HAVE A FEW MOMENTS OF PEACE FOR ONCE IN MY LIFE?"

Everyone in the room froze in their places.

Brooke turned to the police officers and then the nurse and doctor, "You should probably all give her a few minutes," she said.

"You too," I said quietly to her.

Brooke looked at me in disbelief and her eyes began to tear up. She was going to say something, but instead turned around and walked out ahead of the officers, nurse and doctor.

I finally had the room to myself. It was a bittersweet victory as different thoughts invaded my mind. *What to do about Frank. What do I say to Collin? Will Debra and Paul file for full custody of my son now? Does Ashley know anything? What will she think?*

I exhaled, uncomfortable on a bed that could pass for a cement slab. *I need to get my mind off everything.* Looking around that room wasn't helping either. The room was dull. *The walls are white. The floor is white. The blankets are just off-white enough to be annoying.* Faded yellow curtains hung down from white hardware. Surely, the person who decorated the rooms was either blind or just cruel.

The only window in my room was to the right side of my bed. It stretched across the entire wall and showed a dark, desolate street, the silhouette of swaying trees, and the solid deep ebony sky. Everything, including the faint voices in the halls, indicated to me that it must be around three in the morning.

I pressed the little red button that was attached to my bed to summon the nurse. This time a different one walked in, and I recognized her from another time I was there. She smiled at me, but it was more of a pitying smile than anything else. She asked me what I needed, then was on her way again leaving me alone again to do even more thinking.

CHAPTER 32

I discovered more cuts and bruises as the night wore on. I hadn't really slept yet as the room slowly started to illuminate with daylight.

I figured I could try to sleep for an hour or so before the annoying beeping tripled, the volume of voices elevated, and random nurses and doctors traversed in and out of my room to assess me. I figured wrong.

A social worker came in to ask me a million questions. Followed by Dr. Benjamin Franklin, Carolyn-the nurse, and other workers taking my lunch and dinner order, just in case I ended up staying there another the night. I sure hoped not! This went on all morning, and the afternoon dragged on with a continuous parade of different people trafficking through my room. I couldn't wait to leave. The discharge process was being held up by the large amount of paperwork and follow-up appointments because of my situation.

Brooke returned to my room a few minutes after my lunch was brought in.

"Did you get any sleep?" she asked.

"Not really."

She lifted the cover of the plate of food to see untouched chicken and potatoes. "You haven't eaten, either. How do you expect to get any better?"

"Brooke, I just want to go home, take a shower, and get a full eight, or more, hours of sleep. Then, I promise, I'll eat too."

"I know sweetie, I asked them for you. Another hour or two, okay? Hang in there."

It wasn't like I had a choice in the matter. "All right." I sighed exasperatedly.

Brooke received a text message. She glanced down at her phone reading it then looked up at me. She was hesitating ... I wondered if she wanted to tell me something.

"What is it?" I asked.

"Are you up to having a visitor?"

"Uh ... what do you think?"

"I didn't think so. But ... well ... I doubt he's going to take 'no' for an answer."

"Who? Please don't tell me you're talking to Collin? Great ... you told him already? I told you that I wasn't ready..."

"I know I know. I tried to give him the run around. But when you didn't show up today he knew something was up. He asked me a million questions. I didn't want to lie."

"That's right. I totally forgot about that. So, is he on his way here?"

"Yes. But, if you don't want to see him..."

"No. It's okay. I do. But look at me."

"I got you," she said reaching for her purse. She pulled out a little make up bag and started with a ton of concealer.

"Ooh, be careful. My face feels tender ... go gently."
Brooke was more careful as she continued with the concealer, then foundation, a touch of eye shadow, and lip-gloss.

She handed me a compact mirror. *Wow, I still looked hideous.*

"I can't believe I'm going to let him see me like this."

"Stop, he doesn't care about that. He wants to talk to you."

She got another text. "I'll go downstairs and sit in the lobby. You want me to send him up?"

I shrugged. "I guess."

After Brooke walked out, I started to feel nervous, and self-conscious. I parted my hair with my fingers letting it fall diagonally across my face, covering one eye. My heart started to beat faster and faster. Then it practically stopped when Collin slowly entered my room. He shut the door behind him and made his way over to me. I made another pointless attempt to look down and away but Collin sat next to me and there was nowhere to hide. I knew my eyes still looked puffy and bruised even under my makeup. He didn't say anything about my appearance, but I could see dismay in his eyes. He reached over and touched my hand as if I was a cracked piece of glass.

"Hey," I said in a low voice with a weak smile.
He didn't know what to say. I shifted over and he sat on the bed next to me. He took my hand in his, kissing it softly, staring into my eyes. There was more pain in his eyes than I felt, and it wasn't long before he wiped tears from his and then mine.

He rested his head lightly against my chest and I stroked his hair. We spent the next few minutes sharing each other's pain in silent agony. Regardless of the pain I felt, both

252

emotional and physical, having him there with me always lifted my spirits the amount I needed to stay strong.

"I can't believe he did this to you," he said as he suddenly looked up at me. "I shouldn't have let you go home yet."

"Babe, don't. I already told you that you can't always be there to protect me."

"Well, I *can* take you away from here. Please come with me to California. He can't hurt you there. We can get away from all this craziness." All I got from what he said was that he still wanted to leave.

"I thought we talked about this already."

"I know but… that was before."

"Collin, nothing's changed."

"How can you say that?"

"This might be new to you, but it isn't to me."

"You know how much it bothers me that I want to be with you, while you want to be with him."

"That's not fair. You know that's not true."

"Then what is it?" he asked.

I was so over the same conversations. The one I always had with Brooke about leaving Frank, the one I always had with Nick about his behavior, and now this one — all the times Collin wanted to know where we were going and why I couldn't just pick up and leave my husband to be with him. Too exhausted, I shook my head, "Don't do this. Not here."

"I'm starting to think it's *you* who doesn't want to make us happen."

"Me? You're the one who sounds so unsure about where you want to be. Do *you* even know what you want?"

"Of course I do. I want more for us. I want what we had the other night; but instead of making up a story, I want it to be real. I want you with me every morning and to know that you're safe. I already told you that I can't sit around and watch you get hurt."

"And you know I want those same things."

"But you also tell me all the time that you would be with me if there was a way… and this happens. And I have an amazing opportunity offered to me. *To us.* Maybe it's all the universe's weird way to give us our chance to be together."

"Okay, Collin. Then what? We're going to ride off into the night in a fucking white horse and carriage too."

He blinked at me stunned.

Then I caught myself.

"Damn. I'm sorry, I didn't mean that. I just ..." I sighed as the overwhelming feelings took over again. "This is why I didn't want to see you yet." Closing my eyes, I took a few seconds to collect myself. It wasn't his fault that I was there and he didn't deserve for me to take out my anger on him.

"Babe," I continued, lightening my tone, "don't get wrapped up in the fantasy that we created. I'm not saying it wasn't amazing. But all this isn't about me and you. All I'm trying to say is that this isn't some fairy tale where we get to run away together and live happily ever after."

"The only reason why it can't be is because of you."

"Me?"

"You're the one who keeps it from happening. I know that you think I can't take care of you."

"I don't need anyone to take care of me. And what do you expect me to think? You don't really know what it's like to be living in the real world paying bills."

"Are you really going there with me again?" he asked, frustrated, running his hand through his hair.

"Come on, I don't mean it like that. But you told me yourself that your parents still help you pay for everything..."

"That's only because I'm in school and you know that."

"So, if I went to California with you where are we supposed to stay? In their basement?"

"Obviously, I would get us a place."

"I don't know. I'm just not really sure what to do about anything anymore."

"While you're figuring it out, what am I supposed to do?"
I couldn't say anything. I knew exactly what he *should* do, but did I really want to admit it? Would I be okay without him for a while?

"Baby, I'm asking you, because I don't know," he said again, when I didn't respond. I had no choice.

"Well... then... maybe it's best if you focused on yourself for a while," I said struggling over the words.

I was almost unable to handle another disappointed look after getting one from everyone else I cared about, but there it was again. It obviously wasn't what Collin wanted to hear or expected, but I could only be honest with him at that point.

Defeated again. It felt like I was losing everything.

He wasn't settling for that as an answer.

254

"I'm so sick of this," he said then rose from the bed. I thought he was going to leave, but I was surprised when he took a seat in one of the guest chairs, not looking at me.

"What are you doing?" I asked him.

"Waiting."

"Collin, just give me more time to think."

"Oh, take all the time you need. That's not what I'm waiting for," he said in a serious tone.

"So, then… what?"

"If you're not going to do anything then I will."

"Well, then you'll be there a really long time because Frank is still locked up," I said knowing that it wasn't true.

Unfortunately, so did Collin.

"No, he's not," he said calling my bluff. "Because you dropped the charges."

"How do you know?"

"I just do."

Brooke! And I knew why she did it too. She thought that if I wouldn't listen to her then maybe I would listen to Collin. They could try to talk sense into me all they wanted, but Frank being in jail wasn't what I had in mind. He would get a few years at best then when he got out, when my life was finally perfect, he would find me and ruin it all over again. That wasn't an option.

"Please don't do this here," I said.

Collin stood up walking over to my side again. "I can handle it. You know I can."

"I told you I don't need you trying to fix all of my problems. And this isn't a test of who's stronger."

His phone received a message and he pulled it out of his pocked and glanced down at it.

"Well, I guess we're about to find out," he said after reading a text message.

"I swear, even if nothing seems to make sense now, it will soon. I do have a plan. I can't explain it to you now, but this isn't the answer. Causing a scene in a hospital? Then what?"

"Then you won't be the only one with a broken arm," he said in a grim tone. "And then it'll almost be even."

"This isn't the time or place for this," I said, but nothing was working and I hated to resort to this, but I had no choice. If Collin got his hands on Frank, it wouldn't end well. Then we could really forget about our "moonstone dreams."

"If you don't leave right now I'm going to call security," I threatened.

"On me?" he asked, looking at me in disbelief.

"Yes."

"I don't care. Do it."

But it was too late because I recognized the loud footsteps in the hallway getting closer and closer to the door. The doorknob turned slowly before it opened and Frank entered the room. There was nothing more for me to say or do. I had to face the inevitable. The tension in the air was thick as I sat silently and waited for something to happen.

CHAPTER 33

Should I say something? I wondered to myself. Even if I wanted to, I was frozen. For the first time my entire love triangle was in the same room at the same time.

Collin took a few steps away from me toward Frank.

"You must be Victoria's husband," he said so casually.

"Yes. Frank Carlisle," he said extending out his hand.

Collin ignored Frank's gesture and practically rolled his eyes at him.

"Yeah. I know who you are. I'm an intern here, just doing routine checks on all my patients," Collin said convincing as ever.

"Oh. Okay," Frank said, *so clueless.* But Frank already looked a little uncomfortable and nervous about talking to me in general. He was used to receiving the cold shoulder from anyone who worked in the hospital when they knew he was at fault for my injuries. Frank's eyes focused on the floor. The Queen of England could have been in the room and he wouldn't have noticed.

Collin wasn't even the least bit shaken by Frank's presence. He was very slick. He strolled over to me put his hand on mine then said, "If there is anything you need..." For a moment, our eyes locked. I knew exactly what he meant.

I nodded.

"Thank you so much for all your help," I said smiling slightly at him.

Then Collin walked up to Frank again and because he wasn't the type who could just walk out without leaving a message, regardless to whether Frank understood it or not.

"Don't worry about your wife. She's in really good hands," Collin said.

"All right. Thanks," Frank said before Collin walked out of the room.

Wow. Collin and I definitely fed off each other when it came to improvisation. I was grateful that he didn't pick a fight with Frank. He only did it for me, and I was sure he wasn't happy about it. But I would definitely have to deal with him later.

"Can I sit?" Frank asked, interrupting my thoughts, once we were alone. Now that my real love left the room, I suddenly felt icy. My expression was hard and unwelcoming.

"I'd rather you didn't," I said, my tone punitive.

"Okay," he said, looking down, then he took a few more steps toward me.

"That's close enough!" I said, sternly, putting my hand up.

"Victoria, I'll get to the point. Last night, in the holding cell I couldn't stop thinking about you. And about *us*. I couldn't sleep ..."

"I hope you couldn't sleep. Jesus, Frank, you tried to kill me!"

"No, you know I would never... I was only trying to scare you. What you said ... that shit really pissed me off. Then the more I thought about it. I knew you just made all that shit up to get me mad. I know there's no one else. You just wanted me to feel how you do all the time. Right? I get it now."

This man is delusional if he believed he could say anything to make this better. The only reason I agreed to letting him come talk to me was that there were so many authorities and witnesses on site. He seemed sincere, although his apologies always did. "Whatever," I said, staring out the window.

"I also thought about how you said you think we need to change. I think we should too."

We? No, you need to change asshole! My chest tightened, as I desperately wanted to launch at him and claw his eyes out. I drew in a slow breath trying to slow my heart rate down.

"That promise I made to you years ago in the park — I haven't really lived up to my end, have I?" He went on, his tone mopey and apologetic.

I still didn't say anything. I was just so angry and in shock at the same time. Also still a little shaken from the close call just a few minutes prior. Honestly, nothing he was saying touched me even a little. Actually resisting the urge to roll my eyes was challenging.

"They said you could leave in an hour or so. I'll take you home," he said.

"Look, Frank, I respect you coming here to tell me this. But right now I don't think I can. I need time. I'm staying at my sister's for now." *Good job Victoria. You didn't say what you're really feeling. Let him think everything is fine. Let him think that he'll eventually*

258

be forgiven.

"I'll take you there then," he said desperately.

"No. Brooke will take me."

"Well, if you need anything, anything at all, I can it bring to her house for you. Just let me know."

"Uh huh."

"I'll go now," he said turning to leave. He waited for a few seconds expecting me to tell him to stay. That sure as hell wasn't happening.

After Frank left I felt like I could exhale. Luckily, it was only a few more minutes later that I was finally released, but not before dozens of phone numbers, prescriptions, and appointments were thrown at me. Brooke brought me to her house, but she made it obvious that she was upset with me the whole ride there. I was so confused because I felt so adamant about leaving Frank, but a part of my heart ached at the thought of really ending our marriage. It didn't make sense. I should have hated Frank so much, for everything, but I just couldn't. No matter what he did to me, I would always be that scared, hopeful 14-year-old girl holding on to the promise of the perfect family. *And this might have been the biggest problem of all.*

*   *   *   *

Another Monday morning rolled around, but it didn't feel like it. Michelle was training at her new job. Sue called out sick. Brooke and I were surrounded by boxes, as half of the office was packed up. We were both on our second cups of coffee and it wasn't even 10 a.m. yet.

Trying to pack with one good hand was pointless. It was exactly three weeks after my release from the hospital. Everything was taking twice as long. We planned to be moved out by Aug. 1st, which gave us less than three weeks to sell, throw away or store the large furniture, and pack and move the small supplies. I had no idea how we could finish without extra help. I sat in the chair and scrolled through my phone while Brooke taped up a box.

She looked up at me noticing that my mind was somewhere else.

"I think this is the right thing to do," she said reassuringly as she scribbled "storage" across the box with a red sharpie marker.

"Metoo. That's not what I'm upset about," I said

shrugging.

She looked at me again for a moment then looked down and quietly said, "I know."

"I will miss spending my day with you guys, but I need a break to sort everything out."

She sat by me and put her hand on my knee. "You should stop worrying. It's a good idea to try to cut off anything forcing you to stay here."

"That's not what I'm doing," I said as I stood to refill my coffee cup, and then turning to glance over at her I added, "You act like I'm going to flee the country."

"Maybe not the country. What about the state?" she asked suggestively.

"Yeah?" I grabbed the coffee pot by the handle and filled the mug halfway then added two packets of sugar and creamer.

"And go where?" I asked then brought the mug carefully to my lips for a taste.

"California?"

Her unexpected revelation made my hand jerk and I spilled coffee everywhere. "Collin told you about that?" Jeez, those two told each other everything. I was starting to wonder whose side they were both on.

"Not directly. No," she said.

"So, how do you know?"

"We all went out last night ... a few friends he grew up with are in town."

"Yeah. I know," I said in a low voice.

"Everyone thinks he's making a mistake, turning down that job offer he has over there."

"I never told him to. In fact I encouraged him to go." *Sort of.*

"I know. But you and I both know why he's staying."

"Yeah. Because of me," I said quietly. "And we're slipping away with all the drama surrounding us. If he stays here, and throws everything else away, he's eventually going to resent me down the line."

"Then I think you need to do something before you lose him."

I looked down at my phone and wished he would call or text me. I wasn't sure why he was avoiding me. Besides one text message that read 'I love you, sorry I've been so busy,' I haven't heard from him. Either he was still mad at me for not pressing

260

charges on Frank or he was too busy with his friends who were staying for the month. One thing I did know was that all these time gaps between us lately were killing me.

"Did he ask about me?" I asked looking up at her.

"Of course he did. He's so worried about you. And the sad thing is that I never know what to tell him."

I frowned. "I miss him. I don't even know where we stand. We've never gone this long..." I had to pause as my heart sank at the thought that I hadn't seen Collin in three weeks.

"Victoria, you know he still cares about you. But you guys need to get away from here. Seriously."

How could I leave? I had to finish packing up the office and I couldn't just leave Ashley yet. And was I really truly ready to end my marriage? I already knew that the answer to that question was 'no.' But maybe I needed to try to think things through.

As if she read my mind, Brooke answered my unspoken concerns. "I already told you that I'll take care of anything you need me to. Ashley could stay with me until she leaves for college. You don't think Frank will give me a hard time do you?"

"He won't bother you," I said knowing that I was the only one he ever bullied. And after being arrested and put on probation he couldn't even look at me the wrong way without worrying about going to jail. In fact, Frank was doing his best to appear the perfect husband by sending me flowers to Brooke's house every few days. He picked up groceries for us and brought my car to be serviced. He was doing everything I wished for throughout our entire marriage. I wondered if his behavior would stay that way if I went back home. Then again, it never had in the past, so what would make this time so special?

A year ago, I would have never guessed how much my life would have changed. I also never could have imagined falling so deeply in love with Collin. He was someone I underestimated when I met him. I wasn't completely ready to fully commit to him yet, but I felt like he wasn't going to wait for me on the sidelines forever either. Picturing my life without him was impossible, and the reality of it was unsettlingly close. Brooke was right. If we didn't do this I would probably lose him forever.

"Okay," I nodded. "Maybe we both need this. Maybe *I* need this. I'll talk to him. As crazy as this sounds I guess I'm going to California." I made my decision and for the first time in a while, I actually felt some of the anguish crumble away.

Brooke beamed at me, pleased with my decision.

"I'm happy for you," she said throwing her arms around me. "You deserve a break any way. This will be the first time you're doing something for yourself. Don't worry about us."

"Sure you're okay without me?"

"Victoria, I will handle everything. You took care of me growing up, now it's my turn."

"I can't wait to tell him," I said excitedly. "But … won't it be a little weird? We haven't seen each other or spoken at all."

"I don't think so." She glanced at the clock and suddenly lit up. "Hey! You know what? I think he mentioned that he'd be in Montclair today studying. You know… that really cute place that the two of you go sometimes."

"Oh. The teahouse in Montclair? Insanitea?"

"Yup. That's the one!"

I shrugged again. Why not? It seemed a bit stalker-like, but I really wanted to see him. I could surprise him and break the good news. Insanitea was a peaceful, quiet place where Collin and I escaped to a few times during the winter. It was very cozy and the staff was super welcoming. Spending the rest of the afternoon at one of my favorite venues, cuddled up with Collin and a mug of the best Island Coconut tea in New Jersey, sounded much better than one handed packing and stressing out.

Since we drove to work together in my car that morning Brooke and I headed to Montclair in an attempt to run into Collin. She drove because she was treating me as if I was handicapped for the last three weeks.

Montclair was a good 40 minutes from where the office was located. It felt like a long drive, but I knew we were close because I recognized the large beige building with the burgundy roof when we passed by Montclair State University on our right side. The school's digital clock displayed 12:25 followed by '80 degrees.' I glanced around and the thought to uniting with Collin launched me into my fantasy world. When we finally had our chance, just the two of us, this would be a great town to live.

All the little boutiques, restaurants, coffee shops, and delis, gave the town its quaint appeal. Montclair, where city meets suburb, was known for its diversity and many various activities and sites to see. It was so clean and much more genuine than where I lived with Frank. Collin and I could buy a beautiful house, something small and simple with six bedrooms, a pool, and a fireplace. I would bring Kiwi and we could get another dog. Probably a Labrador, since I knew they were his favorite.

And I would never get tired of the scenery. White, pink, and yellow trees stood brilliantly in front of us as we emerged from an underpass. Red and golden tulips lined a small park. In the center, a lake with a fountain sparkled in the sun, capturing the full beauty of Montclair. Yes, this exquisite town would be perfect for us.

When we turned from Valley Road onto Bloomfield Avenue, my heart raced a little knowing that we were near. I exhaled audibly and Brooke looked over at me.

"Nervous?" she asked.

"A little," I said. It was so weird. I wasn't sure if I was nervous because I was anxious to see him because I was making such a huge decision, or if I thought I might have been a bit hasty in making that decision.

The teahouse was on our right side and I tried to see if I could spot Collin, but a truck passed by at the same time, blocking my view. There was no parking on Bloomfield Avenue, so Brooke turned right onto Fullerton then pulled into an empty space. We were a few blocks away, but I didn't mind. *I could use the fresh air and a few extra moments to think.*

Brooke and I strolled down the block reveling in the warmth and gentle warm breeze as we turned onto Church Street.

"Hey look, Red Mango," I said as we passed the storefront. "I heard they have great frozen yogurt!" I was so excited. It was as if Brooke and I were there on a day trip.

She looked at me questioningly. "Um…did you forget what we came here for?"

"No."

"Are you stalling?"

"A little," I said, then sighed. "I'm just thinking before I see Collin. Of what to say. We only briefly spoke about the California thing once. I don't even know if that job offer is still on the table. And if it is, and he's still considering it, I need to make sure that it's really what I want. Before getting his hopes up, I want to be certain." I spoke as we continued to walk, passing by 'Cupcakes', 'Ruby Boutique', and several jewelry stores.

"But if you stay...would it be because of Frank?" she asked looking at me. "Please don't tell me you're falling for his 'mister nice-guy' bullshit again." She sounded annoyed. I didn't answer her because it would have been a waste of air. "You seem to forget that he does this every single time, Victoria! And each time you get sucked right back in..."

As she continued her lecture, I tuned her out and was taken aback by a store called 'Spring Showers'. I stopped to admire the storefront, where the ferns, irises, lilies, and hanging flower baskets, accented the hot pink painted entrance that drew me in. I fell in love and had to check it out.

"Are you even listening to me?" Brooke asked annoyed.

"Not really, sorry," I admitted since the conversation was very old at that point.

She exhaled and followed me into 'Spring Showers'. Its interior was breathtaking, like a rainfall of flowers and trinkets. A phantasmagoria of colors. Everything wonderfully set up for summer. Each table, ornately decorated with each respective color, displayed dozens of different items. Some with flowers and cards. Others with soaps and candles. Soft contemporary music lulled through the speakers. Around every corner of the store, which carried a wonderful peony and gardenia fragrance, were glass curios with even more knick-knacks and souvenirs. And in the back yet more brilliant displays with silky tablecloths that draped to the floor. It was exactly what I imagined Little Treasures might have looked like if I had sold our merchandise from a store instead of online.

I stopped to look at the chocolate covered pretzels that called to me from behind a glass display. Brooke pulled my arm.

"Come on," she said, "We didn't drive all the way here for candy."

We turned again on South Park Street and I decided not to feed into my temptation to shop. It was a bad habit I developed to relieve stress. Urban Outfitters and the super cute boutique next door to it, where I would have gotten a ton of things for Ashley, would have to wait.

Turning one more time to find ourselves on Bloomfield Avenue again, feelings of anxiety rose within me. But they were accompanied by excitement to finally see my love again.

I looked at the ground as I half listened to Brooke while we strolled.

"I can't wait to get there," she said.

"Have you ever had their mango tea? It's to die for. Wait… You like black tea. So then, you have to try the Angel's Dream tea. It's a mix of blackberry and…" she cut herself off mid-sentence and I looked up at her.

"Oh no…" she said in a monotone voice and gripped my arm as if she'd just seen a ghost.

Clearly, through the large glass window of Insanitea there Collin was sitting with a beautiful young brunette. *Very beautiful.* Her hair was styled in soft curls, cascading her shoulders. Her smile was big and bright – perfectly straight teeth. She looked tan and healthy.

They were all into each other laughing and looked like a happy couple. I stood there for a minute absorbing the image and felt sick. He was looking at her the way he looked at me.

My heart seized and my stomach cramped. I couldn't move. All I could do was stand there and stare, until my eyes started to sting, and felt cloudy.

"I'm so sorry…" Brooke said. "I thought he'd be here alone."

Watching him with someone else set something off deep within me. I wanted to walk away. I really did. But when the girl reach over and brushed Collin's hair aside and kissed him on the cheek my composure, whatever was left of it, shattered instantly. I started toward the door and Brooke grabbed my hand stopping me.

"Victoria. Not a good idea," she said disapprovingly.

"I just need to talk to him." I didn't even believe myself as I said it. And didn't expect her to either.

She shook her head.

"Not now," she said trying her best to soothe me. "Let's just go to the house. You could talk to him later. Look at you. You're shaking."

The shock and hurt roared through my body like thunder unfurling within.

"I can't," I said shaking my head. I pulled open the door as I saw nothing but red as I walked inside, eyes blazing with wrath. I couldn't think or see straight and I went inside to confront them.

CHAPTER 34

Any chance of being calm or rational was long gone. I stormed up to the bistro table where Collin and the brown-haired woman were cute and cozy, quickly bulldozing their little utopia for two. Brooke was close behind me.

"Victoria?" Collin looked at me surprised and quickly stood up. "Uh ... what are you doing here?"

"I should ask you the same thing."

Before he could say anything the young, pretty girl, he was with also stood up, linking her arm into his as if to claim him.

"Who the hell is she?" she asked him looking me over from head to toe.

Brooke pulled my arm.

"Come on, let's go. You guys are making a scene," she said to me, her eyes pleading. She was right. The energy in there was serene and whimsical. A young couple glanced over at us noticing the commotion.

"You know what. You're right," I said to Brooke lowering my voice, not wanting to draw any more attention than we already had. "This is ridiculous. Let's go."

Brooke turned around and led the way quickly pulling me toward the door.

"Wait. Victoria, can we talk outside?" Collin asked, following behind me.

"There's nothing to talk about," I said walking briskly, as I narrated to myself that I wouldn't cry.

"Wait..." he said calling after me. " Babe it's not what you think."

I turned to him, a quick impulse to get a few words in the matter.

"Don't even..." I said putting my hand up. "How stupid do you think I am?"

I was interrupted by Collin's pretty sidekick who stepped outside, looked me up and down, and then looked at him.

"Baby, what the hell is going on? Who's the chick?"

He tried to be cool even in the touchiest of situations.

"Gimme a minute," he said to her.

For a second she turned around and seemed as if she was going to cooperate, but no... That would have been too easy. Instead, she changed her mind spinning around then looked at me.

"You good? You better not be comin' here to start no drama," she said suddenly sounding like she needed a grammar lesson.

"Everything's fine," Collin said to her again.

"Hm. Okay," she said giving me a dirty look. "As long as this bitch ain't starting with you." She wrapped her arms around his neck leaning forward to kiss him.

"Chill out," he said leaning away from her. "And don't call her that," he added and seemed a bit annoyed as he freed himself from her hold. She didn't look pleased.

With her hands on her hips, she looked at him and narrowed her big brown eyes. "Wait a minute. *Who is she Collin?*" Her tone was now more demanding. "Well?"

"His wife!" I said, confidently and so sure, that Collin was going to put this bitch in her place.

Her eyes widened and her mouth dropped open. And Collin looked shocked. She turned to him to elaborate.

"Um…" He was caught off guard and stammered unable to answer. My confidence level took a quick nosedive. I thought it hurt seeing him with someone else but this was as if someone was literally stabbing at my heart.

Now I was the one with a confusing mix of emotions.

When he looked completely stressed out and remained speechless I realized that I wasn't the only one who was being unfaithful. "Are you kidding me?" was the only thing that could out of my mouth before the lump took over.

At that point, the mission was to get out of there without creating any more of a scene than we already had. Unfortunately, when making that decision I underestimated my emotions. I felt Collin grab my arm as he tried to stop me from walking away.

"Baby, please," he pleaded with me, trying to explain his way out of the messy situation. I turned to look at him and only one thing crossed my mind. *You've been spending time with someone else while I'm here suffering, and crying, and missing you!* The feelings traveled through my body and I suddenly slapped him so hard that my hand stung. He looked at me with an expression as shocked as I felt. *I can't believe I just did that.*

Neither of us had a chance to react because there she was again, his little girlfriend, so quickly in my face screaming at me in Spanish. She started to take her earrings off.

I chuckled at her sardonically.

"What? Are you gonna fight me?" I yelled at her then turned and looked at Brooke. "This fuckin' girl is ridiculous."
Collin looked so frustrated with the brown-haired woman.

"You're acting so immature, go back inside!" he said firmly to her.

"But Collin…" she argued.

"Vanessa! You don't listen. You're always trying to start problems!" he said walking away from her and toward me again.

A firework set off inside me when he said *that name*. The explosion deafening. *Vanessa? As in his ex-girlfriend?* Suddenly my head filled with noise.

"Wait, hold on, this just gets better and better," I said, acting like I was amused. "This *bitch* is your ex?" I asked challenging her. With no hesitation, she was at it again.

"What the fuck did she just call me?" She tried to attack me as he literally held her back. She began muttering something to him under her breath. They went back and forth and I couldn't understand them at all. I didn't even know whose side Collin was on. He sounded mad at her even though I was out of line too. *I need a Spanish dictionary!*

"You're lucky he's holding me back!" she screamed over Collin' shoulder. I didn't entertain her. She was a kid, just like him.

"Real classy girl, Collin," I said to him rolling my eyes. "You two deserve each other."

I'm not fighting over a guy. This is crazy.

"Let's go," I said to Brooke. We turned around and started to walk away. I could hear her still yapping behind me. I wasn't paying her any mind, nor was I planning to, then I felt something hard hit the back of my head. "Ow! What the hell?" I turned around and on the ground beside me was a yellow-wedged sandal.

"I know she didn't just…" I grumbled. *That's it! I tried to be mature.*

Without hesitation, I rushed up to her and shoved her hard. I put every ounce of anger I felt into it and she went flying back landing in a sitting position.

Collin who apparently missed half of the action turned around and looked at me then threw his hands up. "Victoria, what the hell?"

My mouth dropped. *Me? Is he serious?* I just was assaulted with footwear, yet I was being yelled at? I stood there shocked for a moment, but Vanessa jumped quickly back to her feet and started to swing at me, missing. So, like most women, she grabbed hold of my hair. I did the same and we spun around a few times, hair balled in fists, free arms swinging at each other.

The claws came out. She got in a few blows to my head as I wrapped around her body. I freed myself from her animalistic grip. Even though they were standing right next to us Brooke and Collin's screams came from a faraway place. They tried to break it up, but she and I were locked in a wrestler-like hold until we both ended up on the ground.

This poor girl was in the wrong place at the wrong time and had no idea what she just threw herself into. She became the victim of a deep rage that had been brewing for years, fueled mostly by a dangerous combination of pain, love, and betrayal. And it was unleashed in that moment. Blood rushed to my head as I swung with both my good and broken arms. She didn't even have time to react as my right fist followed the left smashing into her cheek and upper lip.

I assaulted her as if some angry force took over my body. She was pinned under me. I hit her repeatedly, in the grip of an irrational heated fury with which I was unacquainted. I couldn't stop if I wanted to. My consciousness hovered over my possessed body, trying unsuccessfully to rationalize with it. She completely forfeited covering her face with both arms. The one sided fight was broken up when someone finally pulled me off her.

My mental state had become a remote, dark, dangerous place. Nothing made sense. An ounce of guilt came across me, as that image of her on the ground was all too familiar to me. As Brooke dragged me away, it felt surreal. Slow motion. What did I just do? A young woman came out of the teahouse, threatening to call the police. I suddenly had tunnel vision and all I could see was Collin who wasn't even looking at me. He wasn't the least bit concerned with me. He was by Vanessa's side, helping *her* up.

My head was still spinning. I just wanted to go home.

"I'm so done with this..." I grumbled to Brooke as my

heart drummed against my chest. I was so sad, yet no tears formed. Pressing the button to the SUV, the doors unlocked. Brooke quickly took the keys from me.

"I'll drive," she said and I climbed into the passenger seat.

I let out a long exhausted breath. Brooke opened the driver side door and slowly slid into the driver's seat and a thick tension grew.

She didn't look at me as she started the car and pulled out of the parking space. "You okay?"

I didn't answer. My head was pressed against the car window as my eyes fixed on the white line on the road.

"I'm so sorry," she said. "I had no idea."

"Just drive," I ordered.

There was nothing she could say to me and I had nothing else to say. We didn't talk the entire ride home. When we pulled into the driveway, I still was at a loss for words. It didn't feel like I had a hand anymore the thing was so numb. My cast was stained with blood.

I couldn't even try to speak. I knew that the second I opened my mouth it would trigger a waterfall instead. And I couldn't help but wonder if Brooke knew what was going on and this was her way of telling me? After all, she was hanging out with Collin just the night before. *She must have known something.*

I glanced at my phone as it went to voicemail again. The five phone calls and four text messages from Collin that were ignored would have to remain that way for a while.

There was no way sitting inside Brooke's house would be healthy for me, or us either. The hurt I felt was almost screaming for revenge, I didn't want to be that way with him. It was spiteful and after the scene outside the teahouse, maybe we were even. Regardless, I couldn't bring myself to be the bigger person. I pulled out my phone and sent a text message to John then from inside the car I hopped over to driver's seat when Brooke stepped out.

"What are you doing?" She asked.

"I just need to take a drive."

"You should come inside," she said.

"I'm fine."

"So, you're just going to act like nothing happened?"

I closed my eyes and inhaled slowly, then patiently exhaled. Sometimes Brooke chose the wrong times to want to talk. Why couldn't she talk the entire 40 minutes that we spent inside the car?

"Hun, I know you're hurting. I mean it was kind of obvious," she said. "Please just come relax, take a quick shower, and if you still want to get some air I'll come out with you."

"Brooke, I don't need your sympathy."

She hesitated for a moment before continuing. "Sympathy? I'm your sister. Look, I didn't want to say it but what you did back there... well that wasn't cool. You're so angry and..."

I sighed interrupting her, completely uninterested in a lecture. Did she think I didn't know that I was out of line? The last few weeks of my life have been circled by violence and Collin and my relationship was at the center of it all.

"Just forget it!" She threw my key and stormed off.

I opened the door and stepped one foot out.

"What?" I yelled to Brooke not wanting her angry with me too.

"You don't even realize it," she said with tears in her eyes.

I shrugged, exhausted. All argued out.

She looked at the ground then hesitated before walking back over to me. She picked up my key and handed it to me.

"You're turning exactly into the person you hate the most," she said quietly then shut the driver door before walking into her house without looking back.

That shook me to my core. *Was I turning into Frank?* Maybe. Maybe I was. It was the last thought I had before I found myself driving to John's house

CHAPTER 35

The sky took on a luminescent, yellow-streaked, pinkish hue just before the sun began to rise. This beautiful July morning already started the wrong way, and it was only going to get worse. The clock in my car read 6:15. It was still early enough for me to get back to the house and hopefully Brooke hadn't noticed that I spent the entire night out.

It was embarrassing, showing up to see John Montgomery the always crisp always clean lawyer, in the condition that I was in the previous afternoon, but I didn't really care. Luckily, his late wife was a nurse and his house was full of medical supplies.

My new blood-free cast looked much better even though my hand still felt like hell. I fished through my purse and found the prescription bottle with the blue pills that I got from the hospital. Before even having breakfast, I took a few of them with a water bottle that was in the car.

John lived on the other side of Alpine, which was only eight minutes from Brooke's house. My car radio wasn't on yet and it was the first quiet moment I had since the previous day. Inevitably, Collin crept into my thoughts. In fact, he never left. Thinking of him made me uneasy. Knowing that he could give his attention to someone else brought on so many confusing emotions. Was he that unhappy with me? *Yes.* I sent him right into the arms of the only other person he's ever been in love with. *Or was he with her the entire time?* Imagining anyone that wasn't me holding, or kissing, or comforting him made me nauseous. Well, maybe it was my pre-meal pain meds that I'd ingested minutes earlier.

The sad reality, the thing Collin and I had avoided for a year, finally stood right in front of our faces. It was never going to work out between us. It was obvious that he didn't know what he wanted. And maybe subconsciously this whole time neither did I. What a complicated thing we were involved in.

Neither of us was emotionally available to begin with. Did

272

we entrap ourselves in the fantasy that we created to avoid what we didn't want to face in the real world, or was our love real? I knew one thing for sure - I needed to talk to him.

Tuesday morning? He had a summer class at 10 a.m. I could get back to Brooke's, shower, get dressed and be in the city before he left. Not wanting to show up unannounced, I sent him a text before heading over there. What would I say to him? So many questions and I didn't know where to start. *How could he still have any feelings for that thing he was with yesterday? Did she spend the night with him? Was he rekindling their relationship during the time he'd spent away from me? Was she the real reason he applied to the University of Southern California?* There wasn't enough time to think anymore as I found myself parking near his building.

The butterflies in my stomach were awoken and the weaker side of me was screaming at me to turn back. I stood in front of his building for a few minutes feeling light headed, wanting desperately to stall the conversation that needed to happen.

Taking a few deep breaths, I gave myself a quick pep talk. I walked into the lobby and Ian's warm smile greeted me initially, but quickly faded and was replace by a somber expression. My makeup-less, tired, anxious face said everything.

He knew something was wrong and he buzzed me in without engaging in his usual friendly small talk. I nodded as if to say thank you and moved on. The slow ride up to floor 23 was torture as well, and what felt like an even longer walk to his door.

My shaky finger pressed the little black doorbell. Scenarios flashed through my mind as I waited nervously. What if that trashy witch is there with him? What if I see him and can't go through with it? What if … The last thought was interrupted when Collin opened the door.

Our usual passionate energy was absent and our greeting awkward as we stood, cold and quiet, in each other's presence. He looked as tired and drained as I was.

"Hi," I said, in a nervous, little girl voice. "Can I come in?" I asked awkwardly.

He stepped aside, letting me in, and closed the door behind me. The air between us was stiff. *He was so mad at me.* My stomach knotted. I was already a mess inside and I wanted nothing more than to be in his arms, him holding me, me kissing him. Instead, we were acting as if we meant nothing to each other.

Collin stood by the breakfast bar and I stood by the sofa. I felt too uncomfortable to sit. He wouldn't even look at me. His eyes wandered from the floor to the wall.

"So. You wanted to talk. Right?" He sounded cold.

Oh. Okay. *Just get it over with!*"Listen, about yesterday," I started.

"I...I don't know what came over me." My voice wavered. "I acted childish..."

"Childish? You were a complete psychopath..."

"I know. I know. I swear I wasn't there to argue..."

"You could have fooled me."

"Baby, you know me." I tried desperately to defend myself. "I just wanted to talk to you. I wasn't interested in starting drama with her ... she came at me."

"She was just talking shit," he said trying to be diplomatic.

"Wait. Are you serious? Were you not there? Why are you defending her?" I asked unable to hide the outrage in my tone as I narrowed my eyes at him.

He looked down and brushed his hair around with his hands exhaling exasperated. "Victoria, how old are you? You're supposed to be better than that. You could have ignored her. You know how much I hate this drama shit."

"Ignored her? She threw a fucking shoe at me!"

"I didn't see that. Are you sure?"

"No, I imagined a big yellow wedge hitting me in the head!" I said then blew out air out of my mouth, in a huff, as I plopped down on the sofa. I'd not eaten since the incident and was becoming lightheaded. I paused for a moment, closing my eyes. When the dizzy spell passed I tried to continue where I left off, but was sidetracked. "I still can't believe *that's* the girl that first stole your heart."

He sighed and sat next to me. "I'm sorry. I didn't see all that. I guess that makes you both crazy."

"Fine," I said, shrugging, somewhat agreeing. "But if you're gonna talk to someone else you deserve so much better..."

"I've known Vanessa for a very long time," he said cutting me off. "She's got a temper, yeah, but she's a good person... when you get to know her..." He stopped when he glanced at me and caught my disinterested glare.

"She's disgusting," I muttered.

"Anyway …" He tried ignoring me.

"I expected better from you…"

"Are you done?" he asked rolling his eyes. I sat quietly. "Is that why you're here? To talk about my ex?" He was visibly annoyed.

"Maybe I'm the one who should be angry. How could you not tell me that she was coming here? Don't you think that was an important piece of information that you decided to leave out?"

"She came along on the trip with her brother, Edwin, – who is one of my friends. It wasn't a definite thing until the last minute. I didn't say anything to you because look how worked up you get."

"Can you blame me?" I asked looking down at my hands. "Look. Yesterday, when I saw you with *her*, you looked so ..." I paused fighting through a lump that was building to the size of an orange. Every muscle inside me cringed and twitched in dread, the vision of him with her haunted me. "Happy," I finally admitted. "And I guess maybe that's why I lost it."

"I'm sorry. What you saw… me and her..." he said unable to find the right words. "The thing is…I can't really push her away. I've tried. Then it's always this damn circle. Why do you think I'm here?" he asked frustrated. "Part of why I came all the way to New York was because I needed to be away from her. And to move on."

"Well… did you?" I asked.

Again, he couldn't answer me. Then it was clear that the only reason I had him to myself this entire time was because of the distance between them. What if I did pick up my life and left Frank and everything else behind and go to California with him, only to find him in the arms of Vanessa again? Where would that leave me? I then had the answer to the thing that scared me the most.

"So then… she's the reason why you haven't called me in three weeks?"

"No. Well, yes and no. Maybe I was a little wrapped up in spending time with her. I'm sorry. But that's only because I wasn't sure where we stood after I left the hospital. Me and you. No matter what you tell me, I know that you're always going to go back to him."

"Do you love her?" I asked him trying to fight back tears.

"There will always be a part of me that has love for her."

"You know what I mean. *Are you in love with her?*"

"I… I don't know," he said with a guilty expression.

My efforts were no match for the river that was building behind my lids. A single tear ran down my cheek, followed by another.

Collin's mood immediately changed -my crying always did something to him. He slid a little closer and angled his body toward me. "I'm sorry. I didn't mean to hurt you." He gently touched the side of my face, drying my cheek. His voice softened more as he brushed a few hairs behind my ear and said, "You already know how I feel about you, though."

"I don't want to compete with her," I said, rubbing my forehead with a shaky hand as I tried to collect my nerves.

"Well, that's what I've been doing since the day I met you," he said. "But, you have nothing to worry about because she's leaving on Friday anyway."

The knots tightened. I wanted to turn and kiss him and for us to be okay again. *This is so hard.*

"Look, Collin," I said, not falling into it with him, keeping my intentions in mind. "I've been thinking a lot these last few weeks."

He looked at me, waiting for me to continue as I paused for I don't know how long.

"When I ran into you yesterday it wasn't an accident. Brooke told me that you would be there. And I went because I had something to tell you."

"Oh, okay. So, what is it?"

I proceeded, quietly. "I wanted to tell you that I decided to go with you … to California."

"Really?" he asked with a hint of disbelief.

"I thought about it. And at first, yes, it sounded like the right thing to do. It felt right," I said placing my hands in my lap as my nerves swam.

"But after some thought," I continued, shaking my head, "just because it *feels right*, doesn't mean that it *is*. Does that make sense?"

"Not really," he said disagreeing. He must have known the direction the conversation was going.

"Our relationship isn't healthy. Maybe it brings out the worst in us. Look at how I acted yesterday…and you…that night in the park."

"Wait. Those are two completely different situations. It's

276

not even fair to make a comparison."

"Okay…fine. But you know what I mean. Babe, please don't make this harder than it already is."

"Make what harder?"

By staying with him, I was being selfish. Giving him false hopes of a future that didn't exist. *Come on, you can do this. If you really love him, you'll do the right thing.* I decided to just say it. "I don't think we should do this anymore."

"Do *this*? What…you mean *us*?" he asked.

"Yes. Us. Whatever this is. One day we're lovers, the next we're pretending to be married, and now…we're just desperately holding on to something that should have ended a long time ago."

"I know you don't mean that."

I sighed.

"I really do love you so much," I whispered then ran my fingers through his hair knowing it would be the last time I would ever feel the softness brush against my palms.

He pulled away from me defensively.

"So that's it? You came all the way here just to break up with me?" he asked trying to act indifferently; fighting back his real feelings.

"No. I came here to be with you, but now I realize that I have to let you go. You don't need this. Look at all the bad things that have happened to us. And you said it yourself that you need more and, well, I just don't have more to give."

"Then forget what I said. We'll leave things the way they are. I can deal with that for now."

"And then what? We keep sneaking around? Seeing each other once a week, constantly looking over our shoulders to make sure no one sees us?" I shook my head. "No. You were right. You do need more… and so do I."

"I don't get it. You said that you decided to go with me to Cali. And now you're just giving up?" he asked trying to reason with me.

He was going to make it so hard for me to go. If I told him that I was thinking about working things out with Frank then he would try even harder to win me over. And if what he really wanted was to leave, then I would be keeping him from that. I knew that Collin felt like he needed to protect me. The only way he would know that I was serious was if I brought up my security issues again. That was the one argument where he was always defeated.

"Collin." I said pausing again. "I decided to leave my husband. I know I should have done it a long time ago. You've helped me realize that."

"Wait. So, then why are you breaking up with me?"

"I already told you. We need to let go."

"That doesn't make sense either. Is this some kind of test? Because if it is I thought we'd be past that by now."

"Collin, I don't want to hurt you." I sighed and put my hand on his.

He pushed my hand away and stood up abruptly.

"Stop treating me like a kid Victoria! Look, if you have something to say just say it."

"You know how much it scares me to end up broke. I've been there before. No food, no electricity, I can never be that way again. Yesterday, after...the whole...incident. I..." Looking at him was impossibly difficult. I choked on my words as each sentence spilled out with a new bout of tears. I didn't want to, but I knew that I had to break his heart for him to let me go. It was the only way he would. So that he could move on and have a real life.

"Babe, look, I get it," he said. "I think we've both been very confused, and drained. A lot has been going on, but you know we'll get through this too."

I looked at him as tears continued to flow down my cheeks. I sat, silently building the courage that I just didn't have. I really wished it were true that I was leaving Frank, but that tiny bit of me couldn't accept a failed marriage either. All I ever wanted was the perfect family life that I never had growing up, and that my mother never had. Not to sneak around having an affair forever. And not to run away with this kid expecting everything to just magically fall into place, especially when he wasn't fully committed to me.

He sighed as he walked over to me. Bending forward, he lowered his eyes to meet with mine. As he took my hand in his, he said, "We're both really exhausted. It's too early for this. We haven't spent any time together in weeks. Let's turn off our phones and just lay in bed all day; if you still want to we could talk more about it later." Then he pulled me gently to my feet. I fit right into his arms like a puzzle piece. For a second, as his lips touched mine, I trembled inside and out, dissolving instantly.

"I missed you so much, baby," he said kissing me again. Then he took my hand and started to lead me to the bedroom. As usual, he tried to use his charismatic charm to change the subject and draw me into his trap. I knew that once we were in that bedroom and our chemistry ignited I would forget all about the issues that still existed outside of our little paradise. *No. Not this time. No more pretending.*

I stopped in my tracks and withdrew my hand from his quickly. This caught his attention.

He frowned at me. "Victoria…"

I closed my eyes, blinking out more tears, and just stood there. I held my breath for a moment— and then remembered the guilty feeling that overcame me on my way to John's house the night before. I knew that the only reason I went there was out of spite after seeing Collin with Vanessa. If he knew, it would crush him. Not knowing what else to say I suddenly blurted out, "I slept with someone else."

He froze. Then he furrowed his eyebrows at me, speechless. He backed away from me before finding his voice.

"Wait... what?" His expression grew dark under a shadow of disbelief.

"No, you didn't," he concluded after considering it for a moment. "I know you're just trying to push me away…"

"I'm sorry," I interrupted him then waited for him to say something else. "I know how it sounds but...he has a good job. He already did the kids thing. He's older and financially stable..."

"What the hell are you talking about?" His voice was becoming increasingly louder.. "Since when is there somebody else?" He threw his hands in the air and began to walk away from me.

"I'm so stupid. Falling for this shit again," he said to himself.

"I'm sorry. But I thought you would understand."

"Understand what?"

"That if I leave Frank…" I said. I paused and tried to stay strong. I continued, "… it would have to be for someone like John." I knew it was one of the meanest possible things I could have said to him and, in that moment, I hated myself.

"So you're telling me I wasted a whole year with you...playing these games...after everything I've done for you?"

"I know you're mad, but..." I stopped speaking, as he

seemed to tune me out.

"Just shut up. Seriously, stop talking. I swear, you're worse than Vanessa. At least she's not materialistic," he walked briskly to the door and yanked it open. "You need to leave! I can't even look at you. You had me though. I'll give you that. I actually thought you cared about me. Good job. You deserve a fucking Emmy."

"Don't say that. You know it was real. I never said anything that I didn't mean."

"It doesn't matter. Just go."

"Babe, I'm sorry…"

"Victoria, get the fuck out of my apartment."

And that was my cue. So, with a heavy heart, I slowly walked out and as I passed him the icy exchange between us made me want to crumble.

I had never gone through a break up before. As I walked to the elevator my feet dragged, my legs felt like Jell-O. I felt like every part of my body weighed a ton, even though I had probably lost so much weight during the recent stressful week.

The numbers lit one by one very slowly as I held back tears while in the elevator. I slowly filled my lungs with air then exhaled, steadily. The lump in my throat tripled in size from an orange to a watermelon while I processed everything. This is it. We're not coming back from this are we? *I had to do it. I had to let him go.* I repeated this mantra hoping to eventually believe it. Hoping to find comfort in the words where my heart couldn't in the situation.

I felt queasy and like someone stabbed me; but getting past my own selfish feelings, all I could think about was how much Collin deserved a real relationship. Someone he could have lunch in public with. He should be on the phone all night and first thing in the morning. He should fall in love. I couldn't be responsible for keeping that from him anymore. Even if I was going to hurt every single day after I walked out of there.

I darted to my car collapsing inside; shaking all over. This kind of heartache was so unfamiliar. I wanted to run inside to Collin and have him take me away from the pain of reality, but there was nothing I could do about it, no one else to turn to, except I found myself desperately reaching into my purse for the only thing that could numb me a little.

I sat in my car and sobbed uncontrollably. I was so emotional, and once I drove off I would return to the life and everything else I knew before Collin. Eventually I would feel normal again...wouldn't I? When I finally regained my composure, I accepted it. With a hole in my heart that might never be filled, I left New York City behind, leaving a piece of me behind.

CHAPTER 36

After leaving Collin's apartment, I never made it into work that day. Or the next day. Or even the rest of the week. My new home was Brooke's house, in the spare bedroom where I spent more time crying and sleeping in one week than I *ever* did in my own house. The lights were always off, the door was always locked, and a collection of teacups, wine glasses, and little orange bottles began to pile on the nightstand.

Unsure of what day it was I grabbed my phone to check. Tuesday already? Again? Boy, was I lucky to have loved ones around me. Brooke and the women at the office took care of the remnants of packing. I did absolutely nothing. Every day I promised myself things would be different and every day they weren't.

Sometime in the afternoon, I peeled myself out of bed to have a cup of tea. Afterwards I curled right back into the same spot where I had spent the majority of the last few days.

It was then that I understood what Collin meant by a bad break up. I thought that time healed all wounds, but this one was like losing a vital organ. I simply couldn't survive without him. It seemed impossible. *I'm so stupid. Should have left with him when I had the chance!* What I wouldn't do to feel his lips pressed against mine, taste his sweetness, and feel his every muscle against my body. I missed his smile, and laugh, and the way we used to play around. His wonderful clean scent. And of course his beautiful, soft, hair.

The day's sun began to descend; and evening peered through the summer sky. I tried to clear my thoughts as they put me emotionally further and further from where I wanted to be.

Wondering how Collin was doing was no longer an option. Every thought of him came with an ache that stabbed at my heart. I would stand in the torch of the statue of liberty, bungee jump off the George Washington Bridge, and swim in a pool of tarantulas, anything so we could be together again. The pain was worse than feeling my own arm break, looking down at my cast the memory so fresh. *Even that was healing.*

I heard a knock at the bedroom door and responded that it was open, assuming that it was Brooke. *Who else would it be?*

"Hey," she said standing in the doorway. "Can I come in?"

I nodded then quickly flipped my pillow over to the dry side. Although there was no point in trying to hide it since my eyes were an easy give away.

"Are you ..." she started, sitting next to me, "are you okay?"

There it was. The question of my life. I shrugged. She brushed the hair away from my forehead, the same way I once did to her when she was young.

"Did you eat today?" she asked.

"I had some tea."

She frowned at me.

"You can't keep doing this," she said, "I'm worried about you."

"I know."

"Do you want to talk?"

"No."

"Victoria, you haven't talked to me in a week. Please."

"What do you want me to talk about?"

"I don't know. You never told me what happened."

I didn't. I walked into her house that afternoon, walked right passed her and straight into the guest bedroom. She went ahead and took care of everything for me without me ever needing to ask her. And until that very moment we had hardly exchanged two words.

"Brooke, I'm sorry I'm not in the mood for gossiping or girl talk."

"That's not why I'm asking. I just thought you might want to talk about it."

"Not really. But I have a huge migraine," I said reaching across the night table. She quickly swiped away the bottle of painkillers from me.

"Come on. What's your problem? My head is killing me I need those!" I protested.

"Maybe you have a headache because you haven't eaten. Come downstairs, I'm about to make dinner."

"I'm not hungry. Please give them back."

"Vicky, I wasn't going to say anything, but you have to

ease up on the meds. You haven't even been taking the ones you're supposed to take and you've been over doing it with these things, drugging yourself up for a while now."

"I'm not in the mood for a lecture, Brooke."

"Look, I'll help you with whatever you need me to. But you also have to do your part and take care of yourself. Otherwise, it's not fair to me, Michelle, Sue, or anyone else who's been helping you out. They think you have a stomach virus or something."

"If it's such an inconvenience then I'll take care of my own stuff," I said as I began to sit up. "If that's what you wanted you should have just said something."

"Don't be like that. You know that's not what I meant."

"Okay. I'll try to eat. But if I still have a headache…"

"Then I'll give them back to you," she said and sighed.

We went downstairs and on her counter, there was a large flower arrangement. My heart jumped a little. Especially since I haven't received one message or phone call from Collin since I left his apartment.

"What is this?" I asked casually.

"Oh," she said as she started to pull chicken and vegetables from the refrigerator. "That came a few minutes after I got home."

I grabbed the card that was attached.

I'm really sorry about the way things have been.
Please come home. –Frank.

I tossed the card across the counter. Disappointment wasn't the word. Brooke looked at my expression then picked up the card glancing at it. She exhaled and rolled her eyes also tossing it back where it was.

I sighed and she looked up at me. "I hope you're not seriously falling for this shit again."

I didn't say anything.

"Victoria. It's such a vicious cycle. You end up in the hospital. He's sorry. He'll change. You go home then it starts again."

"Brooke you know nothing about what it means to be in a committed relationship. Have you ever listened to marriage vows? For better or worse…"

"You sound so stupid," she said rolling her eyes. "Just like mom…"

This enraged me so much that I found myself suddenly lunging at her, grabbing her arm hard.

"Don't you ever talk about your mother like that — she was protecting you!"

Brooke pushed my hand off.

"If she wasn't with that asshole there would have been nothing to protect me from," she said glaring at me.

"You just don't understand," I said. "But you wouldn't. You've never been in a committed relationship long enough to get it."

"Yeah," she said. "And with the wonderful role models I had, it figures. As far as I'm concerned you're *both* weak and stupid."

It must have been obvious how furious I was. My jaw tightened up as my muscles clenched. She had no right to ever speak about our mother that way. Brooke hardly even remembered the incident that put our mother behind bars. As I so closely related to our mom, understanding her fear of leaving our father.

Brooke looked at me and noticed that both of my hands were in tight balls.

"Are you going to beat the shit out of me too?" she asked, which almost instantly relaxed all of my muscles. I said nothing to her and stormed off.

*   *   *   *

Brooke only tolerated another week of my depression and state before she started trying to motivate me in other ways. But nothing worked. I found myself sitting on the porch when she approached me, taking a seat in the patio chair next to me.

"So, I need to talk to you," she said.

I had another migraine. This seemed to be a daily thing. It was a cool evening and the refreshing breeze was easing my tension. Talking, and discussing, and hashing through painful memories wasn't my idea of how I wanted to spend the rest of the night.

"It can't wait?" I asked feeling exasperated.

"No," Brooke said as she shook her head. "I have

something to tell you."

"Okay. What's up?"

"Well, first, I know you don't want to hear this but I'm really concerned about you."

"Oh?"

"I know you've been upset about your break up which is understandable..."

"I don't want to get into this right now," I said as I stood up. It was the first time all day that I had a few minutes that I wasn't drying my eyes with a tissue. While making my way toward the door her words stopped me in my tracks.

"I talked to Collin," she said.

Of course she did. It always seemed at the most convenient times while he and I were having problems, or in this case, broken up. There she was to save the day.

"So?" I asked over my shoulder.

"Look, I'm sorry for getting in the middle...but is it true? That after the fight, you went to see that lawyer guy?"

"Is that really any of your business?" I snapped feeling defensive. Yes, I did go see John because he was the only neutral person in the situation who I felt like I could turn to at the time. We spent the whole night talking over cups of Earl Gray tea. Maybe there was a bit of chemistry, maybe I was confused, but I didn't actually act on it. It might have been a stretch to lie to Collin about it, but in the end, it was all to protect him.

"He already was the other guy, Victoria. I mean every time you went home to Frank it hurt him. Why the hell did you need to add John into this?"

"You wouldn't understand. Why do you care anyway? If you feel so sorry for him, why don't you hook up with him then? Or has that been the plan all along?"

"What the hell is that supposed to mean?"

"You finally got what you want. I've been thinking a lot and I figured it out. I know you don't want me and Collin to be together. You never did."

"How could you say that?"

"Oh come on the gig is up. You could wipe that doe eyed look off your face."

"Do you hear yourself? Where is this coming from?"

"It was your idea to go to Montclair when he was there with Vanessa. I know you knew it and wanted me to catch

286

them. At the hospital, did you even attempt to stall Frank from coming up to my room? And you were the only other person who knew that Collin and I were meeting in New York the day Juan Carlos caught us. You've supposedly been dating someone, why haven't I met him?"

"Do you really believe everything you just said? While you've been sulking, sleeping all day, and drinking away your problems I've been taking care of your daughter, your bills, the office; seriously? What would I get out of sabotaging your relationship with Collin?"

"I don't know … either to get him back or simply just because you couldn't stand to see how happy we were."

"That's right. Everyone is out to get you. Do you know how ridiculous you sound? You always do this, you know. Don't you dare try to turn this around on me and play the victim! You never could own up to your mistakes, could you?"

"For the first time I think I did the right thing."

"I hate to tell you this but you *didn't*. And I'm hurt and offended that you have the nerve to accuse me of everything that went wrong in your relationship. *You* were the problem. You're irrational, condescending, and insecure. Your jealousy is extremely annoying. And you let your trust issues with Frank destroy every relationship around you. You let him define who you are; and until you figure *that* out don't bother trying to get close to anyone."

And with that Brooke would never again have to tell me she wasn't a child any more. Even if I didn't like what she had to say I still heard every bit of it, and respected her for saying what had obviously been on her mind for a long time.

"I'm glad I know how you really feel now," I said feeling two-inches tall. "Maybe it's best if I didn't stay here anymore."

"Victoria, don't be like that. I'm sorry if I was a bit harsh but you were out of line too."

"It's not that… look…uh, I think I owe it to my marriage – to myself – to try to make it work."

"Hon, I love you, I really do. Even if we argue, I'm always here for you, but if you go back to Frank then… I'm sorry, but I can't help you anymore. I don't have anything left in me to see you end up in another hospital bed…to have to stay strong and find a way to explain it to Tom, Ashley, and Nick. I just can't."

"I think it'll be different."

"Why?"

"You've seen it yourself. He's been sending me flowers, and calling to check on me. He's even been texting me every night. All I ever wanted was to be with one person who will treat me like a queen. It's been eighteen years. I don't know if I want to throw that away if I could have everything with the person I am already married to."

"Here we go again," she said rolling her eyes. "Well, before you do that can I please tell you what I came out here to say right before you started to jump down my throat ... if you'll let me talk?"

I put my hand out as if to tell her to continue.

"So, Collin wanted me to find out, from you, if you are really starting something with this other guy, John. And obviously you're not. Right? So he really wants to talk to you. Tonight at ten o'clock, he'll be at the red stairs in Times Square. I don't know why he picked there. He said you should know where it is…"

I nodded at her and smiled on the inside at the thought of reuniting with him there. The random red stairs. In the heart of the city.

Brooke continued and said, "He's not ready to let you go. But if you don't go there tonight…"

"I get it," I interrupted her then glanced at my watch. 9:15.

"Whatever you decide to do, I hope you think it through first," she said then went back inside the house.

I slumped into the patio chair again. Oh, my sweet, amazing, Collin. He couldn't just forget about me and move on? Why does he still want to be with me? I was too much of a mess for him. Why didn't he understand that? Realistically I could never get Frank out of the picture. My rage passed and I entered the emotional grey area where I'd been stuck for a while. I knew what it felt like to be without Collin. Could I really live without him and endure that void forever? I had 45 minutes to make the most important decision of my life.

CHAPTER 37

While driving I wasn't even paying attention to the streets or signs, or which direction I was going. Instinct brought me to my destination because I was so familiar with the route. Before leaving Brooke's I spent a little time washing my face and, for the first time in weeks, followed my whole make up routine. Tonight I chose red lipstick, for that rare occasion. I sprayed a little Marc Jacobs "Daisy" on because I knew he loved it. Finishing off with a fuchsia dress and black suede pumps, I was ready.

During the drive, I pictured Collin - the romantic, always having fresh roses for me. He sure was persistent. Every time I imagined him while we weren't together it seemed like a dream, always a fantasy where everything was perfect. It was almost too good to be true. Were we really in love with each other or with the idea of being together? How was I supposed to know the difference? All I had ever know were other peoples' idea of what love is supposed to be. With nothing else to go by, that night I decided to do what's best.

After parking, I glanced at the clock. 9:55. I sighed, feeling only a little nervous. The hum of the car motor faded softly as it turned off. I shut the door behind me and stepped outside. My body shuddered and little goosebumps formed since the temperature dropped. It smelled as if it was going to rain. I took another deep breath and, with a mountain of confidence, approached the front door of my house.

Entering my home for the first time in weeks felt strange. Adding my shoes to only one other pair by the front door was even stranger. Then I changed my mind, slipping them back on, wanting to sport the entire outfit. Nick was still with Debra, Ashley already went off to college, and Galina was back home in Russia. Not even Kiwi was there to greet me because I let Ashley take her to keep her company in her new apartment by her school. It was just Frank and me.

Maybe, if this were any other time, I would have chosen Collin over my husband. But I had already spent so much time trying to get over him that I didn't want to go backwards, especially if Collin and I were only living in a fantasy.

Upon receiving that last text message from Frank saying that he really wanted to talk to me tonight, and that it was important, it felt right honoring his request. I felt a bit guilty for being so hard on him. The last few messages I sent him said that I hated him and wanted a divorce. Our marriage got uglier as time passed, and I wanted to make amends and possibly suggest couples therapy.

Before all the stresses that life threw at Frank and me, we were a devout couple — the absolute envy of our circle of friends. There just had to be some of *that* couple still there, somewhere buried inside both of us. I couldn't give up the house where I raised my kids. I couldn't give up my luxurious Audi that Frank bought me for my birthday. He promised that he would stop drinking and was already 20 days sober. I couldn't say the same for myself, but that wouldn't be a problem.

The house was so quiet. The clicking of my heels against the marbled stairs echoed through the hallway. The rooms were dimly lit and seemed abandoned. I entered my bedroom to find Frank packing a bag. *Another business trip?*

"Hey," I said walking into the room.

His eyes lit up as he looked up at me. "Victoria. Wow, you look really nice."

"Thank you," I said smiling.

Then he glanced at my cast. "Um, how's your arm?" He looked down as he sheepishly scratched the back of his head.

"Oh. Better…could come off next week, actually."

"Listen, I'm really sorry…about that…about everything. The way I've been to you…" He paused, collecting his thoughts. "I haven't had a drink in three weeks, and I start anger management next week."

I knew it. The man I've known since we were high school sweethearts still existed.

"I know. I'm so proud of you. Is that what you wanted to talk about? I got your text."

"No…not exactly." He walked to his dresser and removed a few papers then handed them to me.

"These are for the club. The realtor listed it last week and we have a few offers already. Your name appears on the lease so I need you to sign these papers."

"Oh. I had no idea you were selling."

"I would have told you sooner. Things have been really hectic lately."

"Are you sure that's what you want to do?"

"Yes."

"Isn't this kind of out of the blue?"

"Well, yes, all of it is but, it is what it is, right?" he asked as he shrugged nonchalantly.

"Wait. I'm a little confused Frank. I'm not sure if we're on the same page."

"I'm talking about the divorce."

"What?"

"You told me that you wanted a divorce. You haven't been home in almost a month. What did you expect me to think?"

It annoyed me how Frank was really trying to talk about our marriage as if he knew all the facts. He was never there. I wasn't absent for a month, we both were for almost 15 years!

"Frank, I was just angry when I said that…actually the reason I'm here is…"

"Vic, maybe you were right. We have no more obligations to this family." He couldn't look me in the eye. Was he really asking me for a divorce? After everything he put me through he didn't feel any 'obligation' to make it work?

"This shit ended a long time ago. We've been dragging it out for a while," he added.

This shit… Was he referring to our marriage?

I was so confused. I knew the conversation. I should have had a response, but as usual I was thinking too much and no words came out. What was I supposed to say? That it was okay?

"So, you don't think we could ever go back to the way we used to be?"

"I don't think so."

I guess I couldn't argue with him or try to convince him that our marriage was just fine, so I just nodded in silent agreement. Imagining my life different than it had been was bizarre for me. Since I was 15 I knew nothing but being a mother, having responsibilities, and being a wife. Regardless of our difficulties, we struggled to get to where we were and I didn't know what to do from there.

"What would we do with the house? And our stuff?" I asked.

"I don't care about the house. You can stay here." Even when Frank thought he was trying to be nice he was still arrogant. He didn't care if it hurt me for him to so casually say that he didn't care about the house where we spent all those years raising our family. He seemed so eager to end our marriage.

"I don't want to live here by myself. We can sell the house."

"Fine."

We continued to have a very civilized conversation, as if we were making a business transaction. I felt a little numb to it all.

I've been trying to figure out how to release myself from this jail of a marriage, and he made it so easy for himself when he decided that he was done. He had found many ways to infuriate me, but this was by far the worst. I should have felt relieved and free, but instead, to my surprise, I was emotionally wounded.

Yeah, of course I was emotionally wounded after our casual conversation about ending our 15-year marriage. For the first time in my life, I'd be living all alone in this big house until we sold. But that was minimal compared to what was really troubling me.

Frank smiled softly at me as he zipped up his suitcase.

"We'll talk," he said and left me alone.

"Take care," I said, getting a little choked up, but not because Frank was leaving. No, that wasn't it *at all*. The truth was I couldn't stop thinking about Collin. Now that I was very free – and guilt free – I realized, yes, I really do love him. This whole affair between us, certainly wasn't just an affair, nor was it infatuation or a fantasy - it was *real. The real thing.*

I made a huge mistake and I couldn't take it back. *Now what? Where is my life going now? What is my purpose in life? Not too long ago I had choices, save my marriage or go with my heart. Now there were no choices. My life finally reached a stop – no, more than a stop, a dead end.*

I ended up spending the first three nights in that vacant mansion, completely alone, while Frank stayed at some hotel.

On the third night I slept in Ashley's room, because being in that huge bed by myself was just too much. I wasn't totally alone. No, Brooke called once or twice to check up on me, but the energy between us wasn't quite the same after our argument.

And my sweet Tommy called too. Ashley called from college. She sounded good, which made me feel some sense of worth, that I was a good mother to her, at least. Haven't heard from Nick in some time, but that was expected. I was surprised to hear from John who called my cell and invited me to lunch, which I declined. I had to laugh, that man never gave up.

No matter who or what distracted me, my thoughts always returned to Collin, but sad to say it was definitely too late for us.

I am such an idiot! If I hadn't gone back and forth with him in the first place, we'd be together right now. Knowing that we really could have had our chance to be together was killing me. Especially the way it all panned out. I guess timing is everything. Frank is now no longer an issue. It would no longer be an affair. What Collin and I wanted the entire time is now a possibility, and the cruel irony was that it had all been taken away by my uncertainties. Brooke was right; maybe I should go back into therapy.

I pondered these thoughts repeatedly in my head. I went to make myself some tea. I was so depressed and disheartened that I just needed to sit down. I ended up drifting off into outer space when I heard the teakettle whistle, snapping me out of my trance.

I got up to pour the hot water into my cup and spaced out as I watched the hot steam rise. I took a deep breath and was ready to think again…or more like thinking was ready for me again…the 'what if' voices invaded my brain…I couldn't silence them. I was going crazy thinking about Collin constantly; more so now than ever before.

The worst part of it all was that I just couldn't bring myself to tell him how I really felt. How could I? After all this, he'd think I was playing games. He probably wouldn't want to get back together anyway. *Or would he?*

I sat there for hours staring into space. Before I knew it, my tea was cold. I dumped it in the sink, rinsed out the mug then filled it with a semi-dry Chardonnay instead before going to bed. Laying there, flat on my back thinking, wondering, regretting, for hours as I stared at the ceiling. The nights were so long now, and by the time I finally fell asleep it was almost daylight. This was my new routine. Falling asleep around 5 a.m. and then getting up around 3 p.m. – sleeping a good 10 hours every day. Not wanting to get up, not wanting to move. I never left the house. All my time was consumed by heavy thoughts of

Collin. I was so scared of the intense connection that he and I shared that I destroyed it. It's now so clear to me that I was unaware of what was going on while it was happening.

Somewhere deep down inside I knew that we were still meant to be together. I wanted to believe that I left him because I thought it was what was best for both of us. A whole month later, with him completely out of my life, the flame was still burning strong as ever. For me anyway. And here I was sitting in this mansion, beyond depressed, and not doing anything about it because pride kept me away. I didn't want to admit that I was wrong.

But wait a minute – isn't that silly? True love has no room for pride. I had to take the leap. Put everything aside, my fear of rejection, failure, heartache, all of it. After all, there was once a time when he had faith in us and believed that we could overcome any obstacle. Now it was my turn. *Come on, Victoria, straighten up and get your act together. You know what you must do!*

But, yeah, easier said than done. With my days and nights all mixed up, I knew I had to first get my act together, physically, in order to do this right. I decided I would go to bed at a decent hour. I brewed some water and made myself some Sleepy Time tea in order to relax instead of the wine for once. It was time to move forward. To be a real woman. No more games. No more insecurity. I was finally going to give 100 percent to Collin – it was what he deserved, the best Victoria I could be, and not just visually – but in mind and spirit as well as in body.

So I found myself, that summer evening, walking into the very building where I thought I would never step foot inside again. A neighbor who recognized me held the elevator door for me as it closed.

"Hey. How are you? It's been a while!" he said as he pressed the number eight button. Then he pressed 23 for me without my needing to say anything.

"Great. How about you?" I asked trying to force a smile.

"Are you sure you're 'great'?" he asked, being concerned. "You sure lost a lot of weight … and you didn't need to."

"Oh," I said. "No, I'm okay, really, just some work stuff … that's all." I forgot I lost about 15 pounds. Yikes! I went from a perfect size 4 to a one. I did look a little drawn in the face and my clothes were loose and sloppy. But I wasn't worried about it. I knew that once everything was back to normal I would start feeling and looking myself again. And I wanted to focus on being a better person.

So I continued to engage in pleasant small talk with Collin's neighbor, staying focused and positive, until he exited on the eighth floor. The rest of the way up I continued to fantasize about throwing myself into Collin's arms as soon as the door opened, but realistically that wasn't happening. First, I needed to figure out where he stood. I had to respect it if he wanted to have nothing to do with me ever again. But I hoped, so much, that his feelings for me were as strong as mine were for him. *I know he still loves me.*

The ding of the elevator snapped me out of my daydreams and I began to approach apartment J. I could feel my heart racing despite my promise to myself to keep cool. I stood there and waited after I rang the bell. After waiting longer than usual, I concluded that he wasn't home. Disappointed, I turned around to walk away then heard the door open behind me. That was when my hands clammed up, heart in my throat, somewhat excited and somewhat nervous I turned around again.

Nervousness left as shock took its place. Standing in front me was a pretty, tall, blonde female wearing Collin's boxers and t-shirt.

CHAPTER 38

This was the one scenario that I didn't prepare for. I hesitated for a minute to ask for Collin because I didn't know who she was. Maybe it was a little obvious and I was in denial. *She's wearing his clothes. Jeez, he moves on fast. What do I say?* Apparently, I was taking too long and she spoke first.

"Um … yes? Can I help you?" she asked as if I had just walked into a department store where she worked. She had a friendly smile and was warm and welcoming. She was very at ease and it was the strangest thing but I suddenly felt like I was going to burst into tears.

"Uh …" I tried to find my words. *What do I say?* I think to myself again.

I wanted to believe that I didn't know what Collin saw in this girl, but it was beyond obvious. She looked like something out of a music video. Her long blond hair was braided off to the side. She had a clear complexion and was flawlessly pretty even with no makeup. She made even me feel like a plain Jane.

"N- never mind … sorry to bother you," I said, the words coming out in waves as I suppressed the shock.

I turned around again but when I didn't hear the door close I stopped and looked over my shoulder. She was standing there looking at me funny.

"Everything okay?" I asked.

"Um … don't I know you?" she asked as she scratched her head.

Before I could answer, she chimed in again. "Yeah! You're…Victoria…right?" she asked excitedly.

I tried to figure out if I knew her. No. Definitely would have remembered her face. Not wanting to tell her that I had no clue who she was I played along.

"Yup … that's me," I said with a forced smile.

"Oh my God! Please, please come in!" She practically begged me. She motioned me into Collin's apartment. I

296

reluctantly followed behind her.

His place looked a little different. There was something about it, but hard to spot right away. The furniture was rearranged and some of the décor was new. Otherwise, most of it was the same.

"Wow. I finally get to meet you! I've been hearing all about *you* for over a year!" she said as she went into the kitchen and came back with a glass of water for me.

I wish I could say the same. I gave up, deciding to confess.

"I'm sorry. I really have no idea who you are," I said sheepishly.

"Really?" she asked, shocked.

"It's okay. Collin's such an idiot sometimes," she said rolling her eyes. "He tries to avoid drama, that's probably why he didn't tell you about me. He gets weird like that. Anyway why am I telling you this like you don't know?" This college aged girl just rambled on and on and on yet I still didn't know who she was.

"I could kind of see why he didn't," I said.

She looked at me confused. "Why would you say that?"

At a quick glance, it wasn't that hard to guess who she was at that point. At least that she was spending a lot of time there. A few of her things were randomly strewn about. A hairbrush on the barstool, make-up on the coffee table, high heels by the sofa. To make matters worse there was no sign that anyone else was home either. *Okay, this is awkward. Why did I agree to come inside again?*

"Obviously you and he have a thing … and I really didn't come here to start an argument so …" I said putting my hands up. I already beat up his last girlfriend so picking a fight with the new one was out of the question, no matter how jealous I was of the super model Barbie and the fact that she was very cozy in his apartment. She was too nice for me to be mean to her anyway.

"Wait. You think me and Collin?" she interrupted herself with laughter.

"Don't be silly," she said playfully pushing my arm. *Okay this girl is excessively happy.* Then a part of me felt a small sense of relief.

"Well…what was I supposed to think?" I asked nodding to her outfit.

She looked down at her attire and realized how it appeared.

"Oh my God! Duh! It's not what it looks like. See last night I realized that I totally didn't have any clean jammies, so I kind of had to steal his clothes."

Then I cringed a little. *She slept over? This is so confusing.*

"I'm sorry but, was that supposed to make me feel better?" I asked.

Now she looked like I just asked her an SAT question.

"I don't know, I guess."

"So how do you know Collin?" I asked trying to find the underlying cause of the situation.

"We're BFFs," she said cheerfully.

Did she really just say BFF?

"As in best friends?" I asked. *What are we 12?* I looked at her skeptically. I think I would need to take a nap after having a conversation with this overly perky girl.

"Jeez, did he tell you anything about me? We're, like, super close and he never mentioned me? So not cool!"

"Maybe he did. I'm not sure. I still didn't get your name."

"I'm Britney!" she said and smiled.

Britney. I suddenly had a Vanessa flashback and recoiled a little.

"Oh, yes. You did come up once or twice," I said. "I believe you were the start of one of our biggest fights."

"When you threw his phone at him?" she said and frowned. Yeah, great, she knew everything too.

"Yes," I said quietly, feeling embarrassed.

"I'm so sorry. I felt so bad about that when he told me. I was so used to being able to call him whenever when he was single I didn't think twice about it."

"Yes, I was very upset when I saw that."

"I wasn't trying to cause problems," she said.

I then felt a little guilty. "It's okay. At the same time I shouldn't have been snooping either," I reassured her, acknowledging my faults as well.

"You laughed when I suggested that you and he are an item. So has it always been platonic?" I asked trying to act casual.

"You have nothing to worry about," she said now reassuring me. "Let's just say that he's not my type."

Not *her* type? Collin was every woman's type. God, he

was gorgeous, and funny, and sweet, and well...*perfect*. And being there was making me miss him so much more. We've been talking for a few minutes, there were so many missing pieces of information, and I just wanted to see him already.

"I don't mean to sound rude but ... so ... why are you here?" I asked. Oops, it sounded rude anyway.

"Oh. Um ... I live here," she said.

Not knowing how I felt about that I decided to say nothing instead.

She continued. "I've only been here for a few weeks. I'm saving for an apartment. My girlfriend and I had a huge fight and she kicked me out."

"Your friend?"

"No my actual girlfriend," she corrected.

"Oh," I suddenly felt a little like a jerk.

She pulled out her phone and moved next to me.

"See. That's us last Memorial weekend," she said showing me pictures from a BBQ. They were of her with a tomboyish looking young woman with auburn hair and green eyes. I didn't see that coming. I really needed to learn to stop jumping to conclusions.

"I'm sorry. I didn't know what to think when you opened the door," I said laughing sheepishly, suddenly feeling a bit more comfortable.

"I'm so mad that we never met sooner. I've always wanted to meet the girl that drove my best friend crazy. He talked about you all the time," Britney said. She was very easy to talk to and I quickly understood why she would be Collin's closest friend. I guess if I hadn't been so jealous during my entire relationship with him he probably would have introduced us sooner.

I stayed and talked to Britney for a while. It turned out that she traveled a lot so there were many times she was out of the country for weeks at a time. She and Collin went to middle school together. She moved to New York a year before he did. I always knew that he was a little reserved but he really did keep so much from me.

"It was one of the hardest things for me to watch him go through," she said about our breakup. "He was completely lost. You have no idea."

"That's why I'm here. I made the biggest mistake ever, letting him go. I have to tell him that myself. Do you know what time he'll be home?"

She started at me despondently. "Uh…"

"What?"

"Damn. Um … I didn't want to be the one to tell you this."

"Tell me what?"

"Well … That Collin isn't here," she said.

"I know that …"

"No. I mean. He's not in New York. He's in California," she said reluctantly. "You didn't know?"

Suddenly it felt like the wind was knocked out of me and I didn't hear anything else she said to me.

She continued to talk but all I heard was a drawn out noise inside my head.

"Victoria?" she asked, bringing me back to earth as I sat there speechless.

"Sorry, I didn't hear the last thing you just said."

"I said that he had one more day to choose between you and the Production Coordinator position. He chose you.

But you never showed up. So that night he packed up his stuff and literally left on the next flight out."

There it was again. More information that he left out. He didn't tell me about the position either, he completely downplayed it, and yet he still chose me. *And I chose my marriage and money over love? Maybe I didn't deserve him.*

"Are you okay?" she asked compassionately.

"Of course. I'm fine," I said, my voice squeaking slightly.

"Why wouldn't I be?" I tried to shrug off the fact that water was pooling in my eyes. I turned my head to quickly whisk them away with my sleeve. Then I stood up. "Well, I don't want to waste any more of your time…"

"It's okay if you're upset," she said cutting me off. "I understand what you're going through."

"No. It's nothing. It's been over a month. I don't know why I thought… any way… I'd better go."

"Look, I know you don't know me but, well, I feel like I know you. And Collin would hate it if I know that you're not okay and let you go anyway. You look so pale, and skinny. Could I at least make you something to eat?"

"No, I'm fine. Thanks," I said, but then I began to wonder how she knew that I wasn't always this skinny and how she recognized me when she first opened the door.

"Wait… how do you know that I lost weight?"

"Oh … because I've seen the pictures."

"Pictures? Collin doesn't have any pictures of me."

"Yes, he does."

There were pictures of us? Really? It might be the only memento that existed of our relationship. I had nothing else, except for my one little I Love NY teddy bear that was buried in my dresser with the shirt from the night of the black out.

"Do you know where they are?" I asked.

She nodded then disappeared down the hall and walked into his room then came back with two photographs in her hand. She handed them to me. My hand trembled a little. They were from our Valentine's Day date. He never told me that he printed any of them. Seeing his face again. Seeing us together. We looked so happy. So in love. I couldn't hold back. It absolutely broke me. I wanted to run out of the apartment and cry by myself but instead there I was, sobbing hysterically in front of Collin's best friend. So embarrassed.

She sat next to me and put her hand on my shoulder.

"Aw. Don't be upset."

"I can't help it. And I only have myself to blame."

"He loves you. He just needed space. Give him some time," she said reassuringly.

That's what he does when he wants to get over someone. He ran away from Vanessa, now he was doing the same to me. *To get over me.* And for all I knew he'd probably end up with her. I shook my head and collected what was left of myself. "I have to go."

"Here, I put my number in for you," she said as she handed me my phone back from when I was showing her pictures of my kids. "Feel free to call me if you want to talk. Or for anything."

"Thank you. And Britney … please don't tell him about this. I don't want to mess up whatever he has going on over there. I know you guys are close, but just do me that one favor."

She nodded hesitantly. "Okay. And I'm serious about what I said. If you need anything…"

"Thank you," I said again then realized that the photos were still in my hand. I handed one to her and held the other one. "Can I keep this?"

"I won't say anything," she said smiling sympathetically at me.

I said goodbye to her then exited the apartment. Stepping into the elevator, I could almost feel when Collin kissed me after our first time meeting at his place. The same way I did that night, I leaned back against the wall feeling winded, but this time not in a good way. *So he went off to pursue his dream. Well, good for him. I guess.*

As I reentered the lobby the flashbacks continued -- us running hand in hand soaking wet, and the time I sat there talking to Ian and wondering if Collin was all that he seemed. The image of us walking in dirty and bloody couldn't help but to haunt me a little too. Now this. Walking out of his building wondering if I would ever see him again.

I sat in my car, frozen. I couldn't cry any more. Staring at the picture of that happy couple one last time, an extreme sadness came over me. I carefully put the photo into the glove compartment tucking it in between several papers and the driver's manual.

I started the car and headed back to New Jersey. *Now what? Victoria, you really blew it this time.*

CHAPTER 39

And there I was with nothing left. Nothing, except for a large empty house, an expensive car, our stuff, and loneliness.

For days, I found comfort drowning in the same inhibiting substances that Frank had over the last few years. There I was again lying in bed, hair hadn't been done in days, probably lost 10 more pounds and asking myself the same question over and over -- now what am I supposed to do?

All of the sudden, I woke up to someone lightly shaking me. Confused I looked around, groggily "What … what time is it?" I grumbled.

"Eight thirty." The sound of Frank's voice instantly disappointed me.

I rolled to my back and stared at my ceiling. "Ugh. What do you want?"

"Jeez. How much did you drink today?"

How much did I drink today? Who knows?

"Just answer the fucking question, Frank. Why are you here? You don't live here anymore, remember?"

"I came to get some more of my stuff. Victoria, you don't look too good," he added as he walked over to the closet.

"Well, thank you, you always know the sweetest thing to say."

"Look, I didn't mean it like that. You just seem, out of sorts. Have you been taking your meds?"

I let out an exaggerated groan … so sick and tired of everyone treating me that way.

"I'm just sayin'; cause every time you stop taking them you get like this. And if you still are taking them, you shouldn't be drinking like you've been."

"I'm not fucking crazy, Frank. You are. Fuck off... I hate you..." I muttered incoherently as everything in my body took over.

"Vic... your doctor told you a million times that if you skip the mood stabilizers it could really..."

"All right! Just shut up already." I reached across the bed to my night table and grabbed the first random pill bottle I could get hold of. *Who cares... they all do the same damn thing anyway.*

"Where's your phone?"

"In my car. Why?" I purposely left it in there because I was so sick and tired of people bothering me all day ... asking me if I was okay.

"I'm calling your sister before I go. I don't want you to stay here by yourself."

"Wow, *now* you give shit," I said then stretched onto the bed defeated. "Do whatever you want. I don't care."

Frank turned the light on inside his closet and pulled out a large suitcase. Half of his things were gone already and watching that closet quickly become a hollow space, I felt like I could relate to it. And he was taking all his things where? Surely not to a hotel. That was obvious.

"So what's wrong Frank? I wasn't pretty enough for you?"

"Victoria, don't do this. It was both of us."

"Oh. It's not you it's me? Okay," I said rolling my eyes. "So who is she?"

He looked at me a bit surprised but at the same time wasn't going to play completely stupid either. Instead, he sighed and continued to pack a few of his things into a suitcase.

"Fine. Just ignore me. Whatever," I said.

Again, he said nothing, which only served to further infuriate me. I reached over to the minibar and grabbed a crystal whiskey tumbler. Not even realizing I had it in me, I heaved it across the room, just missing Frank's head and it smashed into the wall. He looked over at it, startled, and then looked back at me. "What the hell, Victoria?"

"It slipped," I said shrugging. Then I stood up. My steps were jagged as I quavered toward him. The anger I felt was immense, as he started removing his shirts from the hangers one by one, calmly placing each one into the suitcase. Leaving that poor closet empty. With nothing. No purpose. He just used the damn thing until he was done with it.

"Here let me help you," I said grabbing viciously at each garment pulling them down off the rod making a huge pile onto the floor. Frank grabbed me by the arms and sat me down,

304

trying to subdue me.

"I get it, you're pissed. But you have to understand that I was going to try to make it work with you. But then things got… complicated."

"Go to hell Frank!" I said then started sobbing.

"Where are your keys?" he asked.

"In the same spot I always put them," I answered him without thinking.

"I'll be right back. I'm going to get your phone so you could call Brooke. I don't want to leave you here like this," he said then quickly left the room.

What an asshole. He has no idea how to try to comfort me. I'm not even crying for him. I hate him so much!

I sat there on the ground for a minute or two crying tears of anger trying to think of how I could get back at this jerk. He's not just going to walk out on me that easily! As those last thoughts crossed my mind, Frank stood in the doorway with my cell phone in one hand and a photo in the other.

*   *   *   *

"Do I really have to talk about the rest?" I asked Dr. Bailey and Myra feeling so exhausted from reliving the last year of my life. Suddenly all the memories came back to me. I guess they never really left.

"It would be helpful if you did," Dr. Bailey said.

"What's the point? You already know the rest," I said bitterly.

"Do you?" Myra asked.

"Of course," I said nodding. I looked down at my right arm, which had so many cuts. Everything from my shoulders to my hands stung. And it felt like my lungs were going to collapse.

"A few nights ago, when you arrived, you tried to tell us what happened. But your story didn't match your injuries."

Just like my most recent hospitalization, I started to feel irritable. They were prying and I wasn't ready to travel down that road yet. Being there all alone, without anyone familiar by my side this time, hurt. I closed my eyes, exhausted, tilting my head up into the pillow. "How long have I been here?"

"Three days."

Really? I opened my eyes, looking at the ceiling.

"Does anyone know…" I paused nervously,"why my sister isn't here?" My eyes looked from Dr. Bailey to Myra, waiting for an answer.

Myra looked down, her expression woeful before she looked up at me and said in a regrettable tone, "Victoria..."

The sudden change in her demeanor didn't make sense.

"You have to tell us that," Dr. Bailey said.

"Frank found the picture in my car. Just like last time… he tried to kill me. I fought back. He set the room on fire with me in it. The firemen saved me," I said in a very matter of fact tone. "What does that have anything to do with Brooke? What are you keeping from me?"

Dr. Bailey crossed one leg over the other and leaned back. He and Myra exchanged looks but they said nothing to me.

"What? What is wrong with everyone in this place?" I asked starting to feel my blood boil.

"Please don't get all worked up again," Myra warned. "We don't want to sedate or restrain you again."

"Why am I being treated like this?"

"Victoria, only you could tell us what really happened. *The truth*," Dr. Bailey said giving me a stern look. "If you're not ready today then we can resume tomorrow." And with that he stood up. Another night laying here then rehashing this session again? Maybe I needed to come to terms with it. With everything.

"Okay." I nodded and cleared my throat. I closed my eyes ready to finally face what happened that night. I continued from where I left off.

*   *   *   *

I looked up at Frank as he slowly walked over to me. He handed me my phone.

"I already called, she's on her way," he said then gave me the picture that he was holding.

"I was never good at talking. You know that. I figured maybe if I show you, you'd understand," he said.

It was a photo I was too familiar with. I'd seen it personally four other times before. It was a sonogram of an unborn baby.

"What is this?" I asked.

306

"Like I said I wanted to make it work with you. The first week of AA meeting that was my goal. That's all I talked about.

Then she, her name is Savannah, told me that she's pregnant. Don't you understand? It was like a sign. I have to do the right thing and be there for her, the way I was there for you."

"Why the hell would you show me this? You think this would help?" I asked, and then threw the photo on the ground. I felt completely sick. This had to be the sickest marriage in history and this man had the balls to tell me this. This was a 17-year fever. That was all it was. That's all my whole life has been. A disease. No — a poison. It destroyed everything that it touched. Then something was born; something darker than during our last fight. Something deeper than the pain I'd been feeling.

I looked at Frank and was certain he would melt under my burning gaze. While I stared at him every single voice of reason yelled at me, waving red flags trying to stop me from reacting viciously. *Don't engage in a physical battle. Remember what happened last time. You'll lose! You'll die!* But for the first time, they were silenced. I couldn't bury this one. All the agony and pain I endured burst out all at once. Being beaten, raped, disrespected, humiliated, and taken for granted; and worse than everything— else losing my real one true love. For him? For nothing. And *he* was leaving me?

I quietly stood up and retreated to the bathroom, emptying the bottle of Percocet, one pill after another, using an open bottle of vodka that was on the sink to swallow them.

"Are you trying to kill yourself?" he asked trying to "save" me like an idiot, not even realizing that I was just trying to make myself numb enough to prepare for the battle.

"What the hell are you thinking?" he asked snatching them away.

"My fucking head hurts looking at you," I said yanking the bottle from him. "Why the hell does everyone keep doing this?"

We struggled back and forth in the bathroom over the bottle, until I began to push him and get more physical, screaming at him and hitting him while he tried to hold me back. We both slammed into the mirror, cracking it, sending pieces of glass showering over us. My next thought was cloudy, but I knew I needed to get something, something so that I couldn't possibly lose.

I quickly made my way downstairs but Frank didn't come

after me. I can't remember how I got to the kitchen so fast. Everything was in flashes.

Then I was back up in the bedroom holding the first thing in sight. A shiny butcher knife. Standing in front of the doorway hoping to finally know what it's like to feel the tables turn. *He's not leaving me that easily. I'm not ending up alone. No. I don't deserve to be alone.* Still standing there, only 5'4" tall, but the most dangerous thing in that room at that moment. The blade reflected against the lights. With his suitcase all zipped up in his hand he looked over at me.

"What are you doing?" he asked.

"I hate to tell you this, but you're not going anywhere."

He laughed nervously.

"You think I'm kidding?"

"What are you gonna do?" he challenged scoffing at me.

Suddenly I broke down in sobs. "Why are you doing this to me? I hate you. I hate you. I fucking hate you so much. I don't deserve this!" The words tumbled from my mouth in a roaring river, flowing beyond my control. I was screaming, but couldn't even hear myself. At one point in time I was on my knees, bawling, with the knife still clutched in my grip. I realized that my pain wasn't for him. It was the culmination of my married life ending and the loss of my soul-mate because of the asshole who stood right in front of me. Suddenly I raised my head, slowly, and me this gaze; I felt my glare pierce him.

Frank looked at me and had no idea what to do. *He's actually scared. Of me.* The rush was phenomenal.

Frank walked slowly toward me, somehow managing approach me slowly and steadily, his voice seemingly calm. "Victoria. Just… give… me… the knife."

"Wouldn't you like that?"

He inched closer and closer to me. I extended my hand and held it up so that the sharpest edge and tip was pointed directly at the center of his chest.

"You're not leaving. Not that easily. So I can end up looking stupid. And everyone will pity me? For some other stupid fucking bitch? No!"

He lunged quickly to grab the weapon, but I swung fiercely, as if I was swinging at multiple versions of him standing before me. The knife cut his hand.

"What the… You're crazy!" he said as blood dripped from the gash.

I turned it around on myself.

"If you think that's crazy you're gonna love this," I said pressing the blade against my inner forearm.

"Victoria, don't do this…" he pleaded.

I ignored him, lost in my own madness.

"Look what you did!" I scolded. Now blood ran down my arm.

"Why would you do that? That's not going to help anything," he said. Barely even hearing him, I sliced my arm yet again. And I couldn't even feel it.

"Think about it. If I'm dead… and you're the only one in the room … with your history, I believe that puts you in jail for a very long time," I said and it seemed like the only logic that could get though my grim mental state at that moment.

"Victoria, you need help." He gingerly moved toward me, cautious of my every move.

"Well you're the one pissing me off! Maybe you need help."

"Listen, your sister is on her way. Just give me the knife. Please. Everything will be fine," he said as if he was talking to an unstable child.

I threw the knife at him and ran to the mini bar, grabbing the vodka and whiskey bottles and throwing them with all my strength, not caring where, what, or *who* they hit. Some hit the wall, some hit him. All shattered on impact, exploding in shower after shower of glass.

Reach. Throw. Reach. Throw. This became the process for a while. I hadn't a clue as to what was crashing to the floor, and I couldn't care less. As a vase shattered sending glass in every direction, I willed Frank's face to shatter just as easily.

It appeared as if I was suddenly able to see the world revolving on its axis. It spun and spun and spun. Then I could see Frank again, standing perfectly still and staring at my hand. I looked down at it. There was a lighter in my hand. *Not sure when that happened.*

I stared for a moment at the pile of clothes before as every hanger in his closet dangled empty. The entire wardrobe of expensive jackets, suits, shoes … everything, right there. It was too tempting not to.

I didn't have to think twice. This is what I had wanted to do for 18 hellish years. The lighter left my fingers and as quickly as it left my hand flames devoured the clothes. The fiery maelstrom spread across the floor, eating up the carpet. Finally, even the curtains and walls began to disappear.

And for one split second I felt peace as silence filled the room inside my head.

I should have run. I should have followed Frank.

"Come on," he said pulling at me as the flames engulfed the room. I nodded and began to walk slowly behind him.

Then it hit me. I could be free. Free from this crazy life of pain. Free from crying every single day. The second Frank stepped out of the bedroom I slammed and locked the door. I leaned my back into my dresser and pushed it in front of the door to keep it closed.

I need to be alone, for once in my life.

The fire spread quickly. Smoke consumed the room and I began to cough, the heat unbearable.

I found myself back in the bathroom, where the cold floor tiles were soothing. Tired, I laid down. Looking in the broken mirror. One last time. This pathetic thing. Beautiful? Nothing beautiful about a swollen, purple, eye socket. This woman… nobody wants anymore. I have… nothing… left. My thoughts were as scattered. My breathing slowed and I began to lose consciousness. It felt, and looked, like half of my blood volume now stained the rooms' floors.

Seems like this should hurt. But it doesn't. *I'm so numb. This isn't real. This isn't real. This can't be real… Am I dead? None of this is happening. Is it? It feels like I'm falling asleep…*

But I realized that I was very much alive when a desperate banging began on the other side of the bedroom door.

"Victoria! We need to talk. Please, I'm so sorry! Let's talk. Can you open the door?" I can hear Brooke frantically pleading with me. "Vicky? Can you hear me! Open the door!" She banged and banged, but the sounds eluded me as I stared into the flames.

The dizziness that began to consume me was just too much to fight off. I said a quick prayer. I was sorry that I messed up in this life. But my life line had expired. I couldn't keep letting everyone rescue me. *Please just let it end. I give up. I just want to be with you, where they can't hurt me anymore.* My eyes began to shut out the world.

And somewhere…

Distantly…

Bang. Bang. Bang.

310

Then...a stampede.

But I no longer cared about what' went on in my bedroom, or to fight the heavy weight of my eyelids. Instead, I started to follow that distant, welcoming, warm, bright light that gently pulled me in. What a wonderful floating sensation. No more pain. Just a soft fuzzy angelic feeling. I reached out. Wanting nothing but to feel that sweet embrace. And to … let go.

CHAPTER 40

My head lifted up and I returned from my reverie, the faces of Dr. Bailey and a teary Myra Santana greeted me again. They followed me through my long, reminiscent, sad journey, which brought me right back into that hospital room.

"So ... that's what really happened," I said quietly, almost to myself. The truth being as much a discovery for me as it was a revelation. "And here we are."

"You've been through so much." Myra matched my tone in disbelief.

I nodded solemnly and wiped away tears.

"It was a huge step that you came to terms with that. Don't worry, Mrs. Carlisle. You're safe now. And we're doing everything we can to help you get to a place where you feel that you could move forward again," Dr. Bailey said.

"You're on the road to a healthy recovery," Myra added trying to stay positive.

Brooke was there when this happened. The fire! Did something happen to her? Waking up in a hospital wasn't new for me, but not having my sister there was a first.

"Wait ... so Brooke ... is okay, right?" I asked, my voice enveloped with fear.

"Yes, she's fine," Myra assured unconvincingly.

"Oh. Why is she not here?" I mumbled to myself.

"We spoke to her," Dr. Bailey chimed in. "When you arrived, unable to remember anything. She was right by your side. When the doctors confirmed that your injuries looked self-inflicted she was very upset, angry, and confused."

"She probably hates me."

"From what you've told us it sounds like she cares about you more than anything. But, I would give her some time," Myra said patting my hand and standing up. "Get some rest. You've had a long night."

"When can I leave?" I asked remembering how much I hated the overnights in the hospital.

"You've made huge progress today," Dr. Bailey said. "We will need to keep you here for a few more days for evaluation and testing. As soon as we feel that you are stable enough, then you could be on your way."

Hmm. On my way? Back into the real world after something like this. How does that work? Everyone will look at me like a fragile thread of glass that may shatter at any moment? Or they'll be afraid. As if I didn't already have enough on my plate. I turn my head to the side and try to fall asleep despite the discomfort and ugly memories. *Maybe it was better when I couldn't remember anything.*

Waking up after a few hours of intermittent sleep, a headache blossomed at my temples, and rubbing my eyes didn't eliminate it. *I've been sleeping on and off for three days straight, stuck in this damn bed! How can I still be so tired?*

I spent another week and a half in Bergen Valley talking to psychiatrists, therapists, social workers, doctors, nurses, and everyone else with a clipboard, until I was all talked out. I had to fill out personality tests and surveys. Throughout the sessions I talked about Frank and tried to forgive him for some of what he had put me through. I had the hardest time talking about Collin. My heart began to hurt more and more as I thought about what I'd been through with him. It would be such a long road to recovery, but getting over him would be by far the biggest obstacle. But, moving forward, I would need to be a stronger person so that nothing like this would ever happen again.

I woke up again no longer knowing what day it was any more. Shortly after the sun rose, Myra walked into the room. *She's always here. How many hours does this girl work?*

"How are you feeling this morning?" she asked. There was something so comforting about Myra, but I think it was also that I just really missed Brooke.

"Not sure how to answer that," I said.

She held a clipboard as usual.

"Well, hopefully this will make you feel better," she said as she held the clipboard up for me to see.

"What's that?"

"Your discharge papers; you can go home today."

I returned the news with a half-smile. *Home?* I have no idea where that is anymore. The empty house with the burned bedroom? I wonder if any of it was repaired. No. Who would go there to fix it? When I got home the first person I'd need to call is Brooke. I also had to make sure I hadn't traumatized my kids. I doubted they knew the details of why I ended up in the hospital this time. Next, I would have to find a good contractor. Finally, I would need to search for a good divorce lawyer. Yes, back to the real world.

Myra peeked into my room, but seemed to be in a hurry.

"Victoria, someone is in the waiting room for you to take you home," she said hastily. My eyebrows furrowed in confusion, but before I could ask, she quickly disappeared back into the hallway. *What? Someone actually came to pick me up? But who? Maybe she meant a hospital employee.*

Dr. Bailey came in to give me one last speech about not missing my medications and coming back for a check-up in two weeks. My mind wandered a little while he talked, wondering who was in the waiting room and what I was going to wear to leave.

"And please, you have our direct numbers for emergencies as well as the twenty-four hour help line. Do not hesitate to use them." Dr. Bailey was still going on.

"Thank you," I said. "Um ... what clothes ..."

"I'll have the nurse bring something your size from the Salvation Army clothes," he said before bidding me a friendly farewell. After a few minutes, some random nurse brought in the plastic bag which held my belongings. There wasn't much left, my wedding band, diamond stud earrings, a pair of socks. I signed for them and left the hospital gown in the laundry hamper.

I caught one last glance in the mirror and saw the same tired, makeup free, knotted haired woman that has been on the other side for far too long now. I promised myself a long hot shower as soon as I got home.

While walking through the hallway every nurse wished me luck, except I didn't have a chance to say good-bye to Myra, who was the most sincere person I encountered during my stay there. Shifting my weight nervously from one foot to the other, I felt self-conscious about seeing anyone, so I stood on the other side of the waiting room door for a moment. Fixing my hair one last time, and eager to get out of that white linen, white walled jail, I strolled in curiously, nervously wondering who awaited me on the other side. I stopped in my tracks with genuine surprise at the person who stood before me. I needed a moment to process it before a smile spread slowly across my face. My heart triumphed as tears welled in my eyes at the feeling that someone really did care for me.

"Hi. Wow, I didn't expect to see you here," I managed to say over a lump in my throat.

"You ready to get out of here?"

I nodded.

"Yes. Please," I said, readily taking the extended hand as we walked out together to greet a bright, beautiful September morning.

I entered the hospital two weeks ago on the most hopeless, dark day of my life. I died and came back, not knowing why I was given a second chance. My second chance at life. This one won't be tarnished. I madethat promise, leaving that hospital behind me and locking away every bad memory inside it. I moved forward with an open mind to a new beginning.

Diamond Love

Moonstone Dreams Series Part II

CHAPTER 1

It was a very dark, weak and confusing time in my life to be alone. Regardless of how nice Dr. Bailey and Myra Santana were to me at the hospital, when I walked out on Aug. 18, 2012, I would have been happy to see anyone – ecstatic to see any familiar face.

But I wasn't exactly expecting John to be standing there in the waiting room, nor did I expect to find so much comfort in his company. I was determined to not fall back into my pre hospital routine or bad habits. And even though I was feeling incredibly heartbroken -- and broken in general -- the determination to be a stronger person kept me moving forward. *Well, most days.*

John drove me home that day but it was difficult to find comfort in my own house again. There were too many traumatizing memories. The empty house reminded me that I truly was all alone. I couldn't sleep there. From all the times that I've ever spent with John it was obvious that he was lonely so it wasn't a huge surprise when he asked me if I needed a place to stay. Not wanting him to get the wrong idea, my initial instinct was to decline his offer. But also being in a position where I didn't want to be alone either, I second guessed myself.

Thankfully, John informed me that he was newly involved with a woman from his firm named Judy. My focus was towards anything to keep from getting into a dark place again. So there I slept, every night in a guest bedroom in John's house. Somewhat missing my old life and grateful that a new one was slowly, or eventually, beginning.

I still managed to have my good days and my bad

ones, but didn't everyone? Even though I didn't hear from Frank once since the night of the fire, it wasn't wise to pretend that he disappeared forever. One of these days he would pop back into my life, and it would probably be at the worst time, but I would be ready. That was a promise I made to myself. My children were the only good that came from my relationship with Frank. I didn't want that man anywhere near me, ruining my progress, messing with my head.

I hadn't seen Brooke who randomly decided to go upstate New York to finish the classes she needed to complete her bachelor's degree. She and I agreed, through email, to split the work from "Little Treasures," which she had been running by herself from home while I was in the hospital. I made sure to bring my desktop to John's house and this kept me actively working and busy for at least some of the days.

My other days consisted of tea, talks, and dinner with John. The nights were very different from the composed person I pretended to be during the day. Late night crying sessions when I was by myself were something that just didn't stop. Of course I missed Collin the most when I was all alone with nothing but the distant lull of the night to keep me company. Even when several more weeks had past and I thought time would erase the memory of us.

It was one night early October and as I lay in my bed the emptiness set deep in my belly as my throat tightened and eyes tinged with the familiar sting, but I couldn't cry. I was all cried out. And exhausted as my endless turning and position switching began early that particular night.

I closed my eyes tight and there it was. His arm draped across my body, as each other's warmth comforted both of us. His face nestled into my hair as he breathed steadily against my neck and all I felt was serenity. But of course it wasn't real. I was at a stand-still of the interaction of past, present, and future. Too immobilized to walk in either direction. But I knew that the haunting sheet of emotions that enveloped me daily wasn't going to disappear on its own.

The next morning I felt different. As if I knew what I needed to do. I contemplated all day but wasn't sure if I was making the right decision. When John was home I sat in my favorite spot in his kitchen -- on the barstool where I had a great view of the aquarium in the dining room.

He had the most elegant salt water fish with green,

pink, teal, and purple rocks and plants strewn about. Canary yellow, fire orange, electric blue, and multicolored striped beauties graced through the water. I usually really enjoyed watching them but my mind was somewhere else.

There I was sitting with my phone in my hand and all I could think about is what he's doing. *What is Collin doing?* I could picture him, so cute, so responsible, taking charge on some movie set, just like he did when he and his friends were working on their project. *What exactly is a production coordinator?* I wondered. Whatever it was it sounded important and despite Collin's carefree ways he knew when to put all nonsense aside and get serious. He's was so amicable. *I really can't stop thinking about him! And it's been so bad these last few days especially.* Would it be selfish if I disrupted his life, just for a moment? Would it be wrong of me since I was there with John? No. That wasn't an issue. We're just friends anyway.

My biggest setback was that I didn't know what to say. And it would crush me if I didn't get the response I was looking for. I glanced over at John who was making some boring fish platter. Even if John was available he was too boring for me. The truth was that I wanted to be with Collin and *only* Collin. I would never think twice about it again. If he wanted me in California, well then that was where I would be. Because it was all I wanted…

Diamond Love is now available on Amazon.com

Acknowledgements

I would like to show extreme gratitude to every friend and family member that supported me through my journey lifting my spirits and encouraging me along the way. And thank you so much to all my fans and those who have read the book and plan to read the series!

Thank you for understanding when I was in ghost mode for a while. I appreciate every single one of you and just to name a few: Pat, Caroll, Monique, JP, Andrea, Miguel, Cindy, Cheryl, Sherri, Michael, Jill, Laura, Robin, DeShawn, Michelle, Evelyn W, Jasmine, Frank, Michele, Legna, Millie, Evelyn F, Raissa, Ellina, Amanda, Miriam, Johana, Hugo, Heather, Diana, Mike, Kenrisha, Bilynda, Aja, Latisha and Rachel.

Robert - None of this would have been possible without you by my side. I love you so much! Thank you for answering all my many random weird questions never giving it a second thought.

Mom - Thank you for everything! For my whole life, you've always pushed me to follow my dream and encouraged me with my writing!

Papi- You've never doubted me. Thank you for supporting me with whatever I get into.

David- Thanks for always being there for all of us!

Cerica- You are an absolutely inspirational person. You have driven me in ways I don't think you even know.

Andrew- Thanks for being a great friend and for taking time away from your project to help me with mine!

Darrius- You've put up with me for 11 long years but more than ever during this 2 year journey, and it wouldn't have been the same without the long in depth discussions, insomniac text messaging, and all your changes and suggestions.

Nikki- Every single time you looked at me I was on my computer! Thanks for sticking by me, with not only this, but through all of ~~my~~ our many endeavors!

Ingrid Sauer- Thank you for letting me do a cover of your amazing venue Insanitea where I spent so much time writing this novel, cozying up in there with a cup of your delicious Angel's Dream tea!

Hannibal- Thanks for your support and helping me with events at GainVille in Rutherford!

Michael Andrisano- You're writing has definitely motivated me to put my all into my work.

John Adamus- I learned so much that I didn't know about writing from you. I thank you for your patience with me when this was just a mess on paper and a few ideas. You're a great writer and at everything you do!

Mary Anne Mistretta- I saved the best for last! I am truly blessed to have found you and I cannot wait for our future ventures. You're the only other person who I can say has a connection to these characters in ways that nobody else besides me does. You envision everything the way I mean for it be and help me bring it to life. You're inspirational and a pleasure to work with. You add sprinkles to the ice cream and I don't care if that's corny! Thank you times a million!

Like S.C. Miotto @ www.facebook.com/scmiotto - for updates on latest projects, to ask questions, or leave comments.

Email S.C. Miotto: smiotto23@gmail.com

34993116R00192

Made in the USA
Middletown, DE
14 September 2016